With a Golden Sword

DFZ Changeling Book 2

Rachel Aaron

Series Information

By a Silver Thread

With a Golden Sword

To the Bloody End

Other Series set in this World

The Heartstrikers, starting with Nice Dragons Finish Last

The DFZ, starting with Minimum Wage Magic

See the back for more details!

Copyright and Publishing Info
With a Golden Sword

Aaron Bach
"Writing to Entertain and Inform."
Copyright © 2023 Rachel Aaron

ISBN Paperback: 978-1-952367-22-9

Cover Illustration by Luisa Preissler
Cover Design by Rachel Aaron
Editing provided by Red Adept Editing

Chapter 1

"Lola Daniels!"

The lady at the vet counter bellowed the name over the din. The office had only just reopened after the Fenrir disaster, and the temporary waiting room was packed with people frantically demanding their pets. Their shouts echoed chaotically off the makeshift metal walls, but all that noise stopped when the woman stepped forward.

She looked like a doll come to life. Her waist-length blond hair was huge, thick, and shiny as glass. It fell in bold ringlets down her back, a stark contrast to her white lace dress, which looked as soft and delicate as a freshly fallen snowflake. Her rounded cheeks were as pink as peonies, and her blue eyes were so sparkly they literally shone in her heart-shaped face. She walked to the vet counter as regally as a princess, flashing a heartbreaking smile at the awestruck assistant holding the cat carrier.

"Is that my sweet kitten?"

The woman nodded, her freckled face red as a tomato as she handed over the meowing crate. She was flusteredly attempting to prepare the release paperwork when the dazzling beauty strode out the door, leaving the entire office gaping in her wake.

Like most DFZ businesses these days, the vet was operating out of a temporary trailer on the campus of Algonquin Tech, the largest of the DFZ's three magical universities and one of the only places Fenrir hadn't stepped on. The rest of the city was still under frantic reconstruction, the elevated highways writhing like a nest of snakes as the Spirit of the DFZ raced to put herself back together.

Since the near-total destruction of a city spirit was a once-in-a-lifetime event, magical researchers had come from all over the world to watch. They took turns observing the rising buildings from a spindly construction platform at the edge of the safe zone. The beautiful girl strolled right beneath them, swinging the furiously meowing cat carrier like a picnic basket as she made her way toward a gap in the fence that was supposed to keep civilians out of the reconstruction area. She was only a few feet away when a ghostly blue light lit up the shadows beneath the academics' observation deck.

The unspeakably beautiful girl turned around with a sigh, placing a perfectly manicured hand on her delicate hip. "You're stalking cats now?" she asked in Tristan's mocking voice. "That's a new low."

The blue light flickered as the man got off his silent all-black motorcycle, the mirrored visor of his helmet reflecting the beautiful girl's scowl back at her as he held up a small spiral-bound notebook.

I knew she wouldn't abandon Buster.

"Yes, well, that's not your business anymore, is it?" Tristan said, tucking the meowing carrier under the princess body's slender arm. This freed his hand for the sword that appeared a second later, its blade shining like silver lightning in the dark.

The Rider scrambled when he saw it, writing furiously on the pad with his nubbin of golf pencil.

I'm not here to fight!

"I find that highly doubtful," the fairy replied, lifting his sword until the point was level with the Rider's mirrored visor. "You've already shown where your loyalties lie. Not that there was any doubt, but even so…" The sword flicked down to the Rider's leather collar. "The blood mage was a fool to send you to face me without your head."

Victor doesn't know I'm here, the Rider wrote. *I came by myself.*

Tristan rolled the girl's jewel-like eyes. "Oh, *please.* You're a dog on his leash. You can't go anywhere without his knowledge."

He's busy right now, the Rider insisted, his handwriting growing desperate. *I'm not here to cause more trouble. I just wanted to tell her I was sorry.*

"What does that matter?" Tristan asked in a cold voice. "I warned you the day I taught you the knighthood oaths that you'd regret swearing yourself to that man. You made this bed knowing full well what it was. You don't get to be sorry now that it's time to lie in it."

I can trade, the Rider promised. *I wrote a letter. If you could just pass it on to her for me, I'll tell you what Victor is doing.*

Tristan's pink lips curled in a sneer. "Such a terrible knight, spilling his master's secrets. But while I appreciate your willingness to betray the blood mage, you have nothing to offer. Everyone already knows what Victor is doing."

He vanished his sword to point a slender finger over the Rider's shoulder, and the helmeted knight turned sullenly to face the billboard that loomed over the evacuation camp like a cliff. It was impossible to miss: a dazzling, twenty-foot-tall AR-enhanced advertisement depicting Victor the Hero pointing his golden sword directly at the viewer, daring them to "Avenge your city! Join the Hero's Army today!"

"I'm afraid your master's already given away the goods," Tristan said, moving Buster's crate back to the girl's delicate hand. "But don't worry. I won't tell Lola I saw you."

The Rider's shoulders slumped as the lovely girl blew him a kiss and ducked through the hole in the fence, vanishing down the road that only fairies could see.

<center>~~~</center>

Back in the guest room at Tristan's barrow, the real Lola was where she always was these days: sitting at her sister's bedside with a worried look on her face.

It had been three weeks since they'd escaped Fenrir's vessel at the bottom of the Sea of Magic, and her sister still hadn't woken up. Tristan and Morgan kept telling her it would happen in its own time, but they were fairies who'd been alive for who knew how long. "In its own time" could mean centuries to them, by which point her mortal sister would be dust.

"Come on," Lola whispered encouragingly, brushing the dark hair away from the sleeping girl's forehead. "Just open your eyes. You can do it."

She reached out with her magic as she spoke, probing for the dream that would take her into her sister's mind. The connection had happened so easily back in the Sea of Magic, but all she got now was a big fat nothing.

Lola pulled her hand back with a sigh. Aside from that first hand squeeze right after she'd brought her into Tristan's barrow, her sister hadn't moved since she'd arrived. She didn't twitch, didn't blink, didn't react to stimuli. She didn't eat, either, or pee or get bedsores or any of the other things you'd expect from someone in a coma. If her chest hadn't been rising and falling with her breaths, Lola wouldn't have said she was alive at all.

It was more like caring for a statue than a person. She got so frustrated at one point that she'd asked Tristan point-blank if he'd trapped her sister in an enchanted sleep of his own, but the fairy had sworn up and down that he hadn't done a thing. There was no magic preventing Lola's sister from waking up. She simply wasn't doing it.

"You know," Lola said, reaching down to touch the silver thread that wrapped around her sister's wrist, "when I said I'd wait as long as it took, that wasn't a challenge. I'm still going to do it, but would it kill you to give me a sign? I'd settle for a nightmare at this point. Just give me *something* to show you're still in there."

She held her breath as she finished. As ever, though, her sister did nothing, and eventually, Lola flopped back in her chair with a huff.

"I'm not giving up," she said stubbornly as she rose to her feet. "But I am going to find some dinner. Would you like to join me? I've got a whole list of places that are absolutely worth getting out of bed for."

She wiggled her eyebrows enticingly, but her sister remained as still as ever. Shaking her head in frustration, Lola shifted her gossamer, switching out the comfy sweats she wore for sister-watching for a more presentable chunky-sweater-and-jeans combo. She was just tweaking the colors to match the darker complexion of her sister's face—which had replaced the yogurt lady as Lola's default form—when she heard Tristan's musical voice.

"I'm back!"

Lola turned her head just in time to see the guestroom door burst open to reveal the most ridiculously pretty person she'd ever seen.

"What in the world are you wearing?"

"Something fun," Tristan replied, prancing into the bedroom with a toss of the sparkly-eyed princess's golden curls. "Also practical."

Lola glanced pointedly at the tiers of lacy ruffles threatening to crowd her into the corner. "In what universe does *that* count as practical?"

"Oh ye of little faith," the knight replied with a dazzling smile. "You are looking at a carefully honed strategy. Alberich's antics have got everyone thinking fairies are hideous monsters, so, naturally, I went for the opposite."

"You definitely don't look like you belong with the Wild Hunt," Lola admitted, shielding her eyes against the glare of his blindingly white teeth. "But what about what you went out to do? I don't see—"

The fairy flicked the girl's delicate hand, pulling a plastic cat carrier out of his gossamer like a rabbit out of a hat.

"*Buster!*" Lola cried, grabbing the meowing box and hugging it to her chest. "Thank you, Tristan!"

"Thanks *are* in order," the fairy said, finally shedding the dazzling girl for his usual—though no less elaborate—appearance of a handsome modern knight, complete with a fencing saber sheathed at his hip, a heavily tailored military-style jacket worn over his shoulders like a cape, a poofy silk shirt, and pants so tight they looked painted on, all in spotless, snowy white.

"You wouldn't believe the line I had to wait in to retrieve that overfed creature," he huffed as Lola opened Buster's carrier. "If we weren't so deep in your debt already, you'd be feeding me dreams for a month."

Lola nodded thoughtlessly, too busy petting her cat to pay attention to his grousing. She'd been so worried Buster would run from her again, but his eagerness to get away from the vet must have wiped the whole owner-turning-into-a-monster incident from his mind. He shoved his head aggressively into Lola's palm, giving her his anxious meow in the loudest voice possible.

"My poor baby," she cooed. "They gave you a bath, didn't they?"

The cat meowed again as Lola cradled him in her arms.

"Thank you for going out to get him for me, Tristan, and for letting him stay here. It really does mean the world to me."

"I know," the fairy said as he pulled another treasure out from behind his back. "But just to gild my lily a little further, I also happened to pick up some takeout from your favorite Thai place."

He waved the paper bag temptingly in front of her, and Lola's eyes grew huge. "I could kiss you right now."

"Please do," he purred, but she'd already snatched the takeout bag from his grasp. Food in one hand and cat cradled safely with the other, Lola barreled past Tristan into the living room, where the fairy queen was sitting on the sofa.

"I don't understand how you can eat that... *material*," Morgan said as Lola started laying out a grid of paper cartons on Tristan's glass coffee table. "It's not even magic."

"I beg to differ," Lola said, placing Buster on the sofa so she could eat. "Carbs are the greatest magic, and they're a lot easier to come by than love."

"Nonsense," Morgan said, using her newly regrown hand to change the channels on the wall of TVs Tristan had installed to keep her entertained. "There's no emotion humans offer up more eagerly than love. If Alberich's stupidity hadn't turned the whole world against us, I'd be back to my full power after one night of clubbing."

"I don't think that's love," Lola said, pulling out a plastic cup filled with bright-orange Thai iced tea.

"It's the best sort of love," the queen insisted. "Hot, intense, electric." She turned to give Lola a predatory smile. "Trust me, changeling. You haven't lived until you've had an entire ballroom writhing at your feet."

Lola supposed a queen would feel that way. Unlike her terrifying, fear-eating husband, Morgan existed exclusively off human desire. She was even pickier about her food than Tristan, accepting only the freshest, most intense feelings of infatuation.

That wouldn't have been a problem if she'd been able to go out and hunt for herself. The fairy queen was so beautiful that even Lola sighed sometimes when she looked at her. A face like hers would have no trouble finding willing victims, but the rest of Morgan still hadn't recovered from her imprisonment inside Victor's soul.

Thanks to Lola's help, she'd managed to regrow all of her limbs and digits, but even changeling dreams weren't enough to rebuild an entire fairy monarch by themselves. Despite three weeks of nonstop eating, the queen's body was still as delicate as a spring crocus. She spent most of her time lying on Tristan's couch, watching the news to catch up on the decades she'd missed. At least, that was what she was supposed to be doing. In practice, she mostly just seemed to be making herself angry.

"Look at this nonsense!" Morgan snarled, pointing a pencil-thin bandaged finger at the screen showing footage of nightmarish riders galloping through the skies above Berlin. "Is that fool *trying* to play right into the blood mage's hands?"

Lola took a nervous sip of her painfully sweet orange tea. Alberich's Wild Hunt had been raging across Europe and Central Asia every night for the past three weeks. Those news channels that weren't showing shaky-cam footage of the Hunt destroying buildings and trampling people with their horses were running constant coverage of the European Union's decision to reverse their fifty-year ban on blood magic so that the Hero and his army could be brought in to "eliminate the fairy menace."

"'Eliminate' indeed," Morgan said, glaring at the screens. "Humanity used to write ballads of our splendor. Now, they talk about us as if we were vermin, and it's all Alberich's fault!"

"He always was a hunter," Tristan said, taking a seat beside his queen.

Morgan snorted. "Try 'selfish idiot.' Between his circus and Victor Conrath's propaganda, they've got the whole world believing that blood magic is their only salvation from the evil fairy menace, which is utterly ridiculous. Fairies don't even *have* blood. It's a strictly human form of magic, but thanks to that moron giving Victor his bogeyman, the 'Hero' has the whole world convinced he's the solution to all their problems."

As the queen spoke, one of the news channels began playing a clip showing a knot of humans dressed in the signature red coats of the Hero's Army taking down a troll in the Paris suburbs. It was impossible to feel their magic through the screen, but Lola knew those gestures. That was Victor's magic, and it was cutting through the monster like chainsaws through a rotten tree.

"You see? You see?" Morgan cried. "That troll should have clubbed them into paste! But now that Victor's got his 'Hero' on TV every night convincing the whole world that his teachings are the only weapon capable of stopping the fairy invasion *he* unleashed, blood magic has become deadlier to us than iron."

"Is iron deadly to you?" Lola asked, reaching for a carton of sticky mango rice. "I thought that was just a story."

"It *was* just a story back when everyone had forgotten about us. Now, thanks to my idiot husband, all the old banes are back again."

"My queen is right," Tristan said with a troubled frown. "I used to be able to go anywhere in the modern world without care. Now, I feel menace radiating from every wrought-iron embellishment. Crucifixes, too, not to mention churchyards, lines of salt, holy water, and don't even get me started on the blood magic charms Victor's got his people selling in every supermarket." He shook his head. "It's made going about our usual business highly inconvenient."

"Try 'impossible,'" Morgan spat, glaring at the screen. "At this rate, every mage in the world will be stained with blood magic by New Year's, and we won't even be able to leave our barrows!"

Lola chewed her sticky rice with a sigh. She didn't fault the fairies for being more concerned with themselves than for the people Alberich was terrifying and murdering every night, because she wasn't any different. Even with the grisly horrors splattered all over the twenty-four-hour news channels, all she could look at was the text crawl at the bottom of the screen reporting on the thousands of mages who'd flocked to the DFZ to join the Hero's Army.

She might have kept Victor from becoming a god when she walked Fenrir away from him that night, but he seemed to have gotten everything else on his wish list. Just as he'd predicted, anti-blood-magic laws were being struck down all over the world, and mages were arriving in droves to learn his secrets. Losing to Fenrir didn't seem to have set him back at all. Everywhere she looked, he was worshiped and beloved, the Hero who was still saving the world with every fairy monster his followers struck down.

But while Lola hated every second of Victor's success on principle, her biggest concern was Simon and Valente. She'd sworn she'd save them, but as Victor's influence got bigger, her options, which had never been many, had dwindled to nearly nothing. Things wouldn't have been so dire if she'd still had Fenrir, but her once-powerful connection to the giant wolf had dried up within hours of the monster's defeat. She couldn't even go outside of Tristan's barrow without Victor's Black Rider following the dream she'd fed him straight back to her.

The way Lola saw it, her only hope at this point was the fairy queen. Morgan might look like a cancer patient at the moment, but twenty years ago and for centuries before that, she'd been an even greater monarch than Alberich. If there was anyone left who could free Simon and Valente from Victor's clutches, it was her, which was why Lola had been cramming dreams down her throat as fast as she could eat them.

Unfortunately, feeding up a fairy monarch was taking a lot longer than she'd anticipated. At this rate, Victor would have the whole world worshiping at his feet before Morgan got strong enough to leave the couch. She was wondering if there was any way to speed things up—trick herself into falling in love with the queen so Morgan could get the rush of infatuation she needed to put herself back in fighting form—when she heard a crash from the other room.

The sound sent her leaping off the couch, spilling freezing-cold sugar tea all over herself as she whirled toward the guest room door. Tristan and the queen also jumped, but their glares were pointed at her, which was about the time Lola realized that her cat was no longer sitting next to her.

"Oh no," she said, eyes flicking between the empty couch cushion and the open door to the guest bedroom. "If that was Buster eating one of your low creatures, I am *so* sorry."

"It wasn't one of mine," Tristan said, placing a hand on his sword. "Can you go look?"

Lola didn't see why Tristan couldn't go himself. He was the one with the weapon, and it was his barrow. She was still worried about Buster, though, so she cleaned the spilled tea off her gossamer and crept around the couch. The noise had stopped by the time she reached the guest room, but when Lola poked her head inside, she saw her sister's body heaving on the bed.

Lola ran to her with a shout. Her sister had curled into a ball by the time she got there. She was clearly still unconscious, but her hands were clenching over her middle like there was a horrible pain in her stomach. Lola was frantically trying to straighten her out to see what was wrong when she felt a stabbing pain in her own middle.

Her gossamer had been behaving so well since Victor's blood drained out, it took Lola a ridiculously long time to recognize the sensation as the same one she'd felt in Alva's court. She was opening her mouth to shout a warning when her magic turned over on itself, opening a tunnel for a small, golden, madly grinning figure to step through her into the room.

Chapter 2

Lola shouldn't have been surprised. No matter how well it was behaving now, her gossamer hadn't actually changed. It was still the same magic she'd always been made from, and how many times had Alberich told her she was part of his kingdom?

But knowing she should have expected this didn't stop the shock as the Underground King strolled out of her. He paused when his feet hit the guestroom's carpet, shaking out his scarlet-and-gold hunting jerkin as if he'd just come in from the rain. He looked over his shoulder next, peering around Lola at the girl who'd finally stopped convulsing on the bed.

"My treasure!" he cried, throwing out his arms. "You look so well! I *knew* my changeling would keep you safe."

He smiled at Lola, but she was still frozen solid. Rolling his golden eyes, Alberich released her with a snap of his fingers, sending her lurching to the floor as all her pent-up struggles were released at once. She scrambled back to her feet a second later, grabbing the bed for support as she yelled at the king, "I do *not* claim you as my guest!"

"Ah, yes," Alberich said, flashing her a sharp-toothed grin. "That was the boon I asked for last time, but such trivialities are no longer required. I'm here as a conqueror today, not a visitor, and because I wanted to see my… *Wife!*"

His voice rose in delight as Lola turned to see Tristan and Morgan standing in the doorway. It was the first time Lola had seen the queen on her feet since this started, or ever. But while she was obviously depending entirely upon her knight to keep her that way, Morgan still managed to meet Alberich's gaze with an imperious scowl, lifting her chin so that her golden hair flowed over her emaciated body like a cape, though not enough to hide it.

"You look horrid," Alberich observed, turning accusingly to Tristan. "Why haven't you healed her yet? And you call yourself her knight."

Before Tristan could answer, Morgan grabbed the doorframe to haul herself into the room. "It's your fault I'm so weak, you selfish fool! Your reckless Hunt has brought back all the old banes and added new ones on top of them. How am I supposed to feast when the only food around is the bitter hatred you've taught humanity to throw at our kind?"

"Simple," Alberich replied. "Be less picky. You've always looked down your nose at fear, but you're the one who's starving while I have more magic than I can use." He flashed the queen a preening grin. "One hour with my Hunt and you'd be your old self again, though still not as powerful as me."

"You mean bloated," Morgan said with a sneer. "You're riding high right now, but we all know what humans do to the things they fear. They've already turned to the blood mage for weapons to fight the panic *you* kicked off. Your greed is going to get us all killed!"

The king flopped onto the foot of the guest bed with a sigh. "Don't be so dramatic. It'll take Victor years to spread the knowledge of his tacky magic wide enough to impact our numbers, and meanwhile, my court is growing off the scale."

"For how long?" Morgan demanded, straightening to her full height, which wasn't much in her current state but still put her taller than her childish husband. "Do you even comprehend how quickly ideas travel these days? Victor Conrath is flooding the global media with images of fairies being destroyed by blood magic. He doesn't have to teach them his ideology. He just has to make the world believe his magic can kill us, and then *we* will be the ones who are hunted."

Alberich rolled his golden eyes. "Do you enjoy being so negative?"

"Not in the slightest," Morgan said. "But you—"

"Have given thought to all these issues," Alberich finished for her. "And I already have a solution. That's the other reason I stopped by, besides seeing your lovely face."

The queen arched a sharp golden eyebrow as Alberich flopped onto the bed, lounging beside Lola's comatose sister like a decadent emperor. "The blood mage and I have concluded our agreement. So, naturally, it's time for me to kill him."

Morgan's scowl slipped a fraction. "You're going to fight Victor?"

"It won't be much of a fight," the king assured her. "Especially since he failed to become a god."

He leaned over to give Lola a wink, and she clenched her fists.

"He's done a good job on the pivot," Alberich went on. "I thought he was done for after that humiliating display with Fenrir, but his ability to command the media's attention and how quickly he's collecting blood mages have proven more irksome than expected. So, like the mighty lion pestered by the buzzing fly, I'm coming to crush him. I've already steered my huntsmen toward the DFZ. Minus a few stops for good slaughter along the way, we should arrive to dispatch the blood mage within the week." He flashed Morgan a blinding smile. "Still want me to stop?"

"I'm surprised you're bothering to ask," the fairy queen replied with a flip of her golden hair. "You're going to do whatever you want no matter what I say. Just don't expect me to help. I've had enough of that man's blood to last an immortal's lifetime."

"I'll present you with his head on a platter as soon as it's off," Alberich promised, his eyes shining with glee. "How wonderful it will be to have you in *my* debt for once, pretty wife."

"I'll believe it when it happens, foolish husband," Morgan replied, but she wasn't scowling anymore. "I wish you good hunting."

Alberich hopped off the bed to give her a sweeping bow. Lola took her chance as soon as he moved, rushing in to cover her sister's body with her own.

The king gave her a flat look. "What are you doing?"

"Protecting her," Lola said, clutching the sleeping girl. "I won't let you hurt her ever again!"

The king burst out laughing at this, which only made Lola angrier.

"This isn't funny! You stole my only family!"

"But that's what makes it so hilarious," Alberich cackled, wiping his eyes. "I'm not sure what's the better joke: the fact that you honestly think that girl's your sister, or that you actually believe you can stop me. I mean, just *look* at you."

He snapped his fingers, and Lola's gossamer jumped in reply, springing her off the bed and spinning her around on her toes like a music box ballerina.

"*Now* do you see why it's funny?" the king asked, spinning Lola a dozen more times before dropping her in a dizzy heap on the floor. "I'm your king. You are made from *my* gossamer. You can't fight me any more than you can fight your own magic, which is why I'm leaving my treasure in your care."

Lola, who was already crawling back toward her sister, stopped with a blink. "What?"

"I don't need her anymore," Alberich explained. "Don't get me wrong, her exquisite fear kept my entire court alive for decades. That potency is a treasure, but I'm no longer imprisoned, which means prison food is no longer required. I've got a whole screaming world to feast on! Who'd go back to the same-old-same-old after that? But just because I've got options now doesn't mean I'm done with her. How could I be? She's a treasure! *My* treasure, and I never let go of what is mine."

Lola had heard that line before. But before she could shout any of the blistering things she so sorely wanted to say, Alberich froze her in place again so he could reach up and pinch her cheeks.

"Don't look so fearsome," he cooed, stretching out the gossamer of her cheeks like he was pulling taffy. "This is what's best for both of us. Just think! My most precious possession, jealously guarded by one who would die to keep her safe. I couldn't create a better vault if I'd stored her in my own barrow. Why, you're practically a member of my court already!"

"I'm not loyal to you," Lola snarled, pushing her stretched-out checks back into place as the Nightmare King let her go. "And I'll never let you near her again!"

That was supposed to be a threat, but Alberich just laughed, turning to blow a final kiss at his scowling wife before he stepped into Lola's shadow, flitting down the tunnel he'd made through her magic back to wherever he'd come from.

Lola shivered as his presence faded. She was still working on getting a grip when Morgan clapped her bandaged hands together.

"Well, that went better than expected."

"We were due a good turn," Tristan agreed, finally releasing the death grip on his sword. "I just hope the fool can keep his attention focused on one thing long enough to actually get the job done."

The queen had a good laugh at that, but Lola was staring at both of them in horror.

"How can you be so calm about this?" she asked. "Did you not hear what he said?"

"Did you?" Morgan asked, tilting her head. "Alberich's rampage is obnoxious, but Victor's the one actually causing our problems. If Alberich's Hunt kills him in his own city, all of this

Hero nonsense will be over. Why should we complain?"

"Because if Alberich loses, Victor will be stronger than ever!" Lola cried. "You weren't with me when I was inside Fenrir. You didn't feel how close he got."

She pointed over the queen's shoulder at the Wild Hunt coverage that was still playing on the living room's wall of TVs. "Alberich is the whole world's bogeyman right now. If his Hunt comes to the DFZ, he'll be playing right into Victor's hands. Once he's got his monster, all the Hero needs is to march out there and do exactly what he's been teaching everyone his magic does—kill fairies—and he *wins.*"

"You're giving the blood mage too much credit," Morgan scolded. "Conrath is impressive for a mortal, but the only reason he was able to touch Fenrir is because he was controlling the beast through your girl." She tilted her head at Lola's sleeping sister. "Alberich might be an idiot, but he's still a fairy king, and Victor is only human."

Lola narrowed her eyes. "The human who took your head."

"With treachery!" the queen cried. "This is a completely different situation! Victor pulled a clever move by turning his magic into one of our banes, but Alberich's Hunt has been terrorizing an entire continent for weeks. He's bloated on fear, and that makes him strong. Possibly even stronger than I was at my height, and this is precisely the sort of fight he's best at."

She smiled over her shoulder at a TV screen showing an interview with the red-coated blood mages who'd hacked down the troll. "I think Victor already knows he's doomed. That's why he's been sending his stooges to fight the Hunt instead of going to Europe himself. He's scared."

Lola shook her head. "Never assume you know Victor's plan. That's how he tricks you into letting your guard down."

"Oh please," the queen said. "I know the blood mage spent a lot of time teaching you to fear him, but my husband's words weren't idle boasting. If Alberich brings his Hunt to the DFZ, it *won't* be much of a fight. Victor and the fools who follow him will be slaughtered. The only question I have is how are we going to turn this to our advantage?"

"It does present a unique opportunity," Tristan said, drumming his fingers on his sword hilt. "No matter how decisively they win, battling the blood mage's army will still weaken Alberich's forces. If we strike while he's wounded—"

"We can get him back in hand," the queen finished with a grin.

"Assuming we can rebuild our own power before he arrives," her knight cautioned. "You're nowhere close to your full strength, and our court still numbers only two. If Alberich is already heading this way, we have a lot of ground to cover in a very short amount of time."

"Then we must work quickly," Morgan said, striding back into the living room with more vigor than Lola had ever seen her put out. "Come, knight! Let us plan our attack before we both end up groveling to that boy-faced twit."

Tristan bowed at her command, but he didn't follow immediately. Instead, he turned to Lola. "I know you have your doubts," he said quietly. "But my queen knows Alberich better than any living being. If she says he'll win, he'll win, but it will go more smoothly if you don't give the blood mage any more weapons."

Lola jerked back. "I would *never* help Victor."

"Not intentionally," Tristan said, giving her a wise smile. "But I know that look, Lola-lion. Your head is ever full of heroic intentions, but if you set foot outside this barrow, the Black Rider will snatch you up and take you back to his master, and I might not be fast enough to leap to your rescue again." He placed a heavy hand on her shoulder. "I want you to stay here."

It wasn't an unreasonable request, but Lola ducked out of his grasp. "You don't give me orders."

"Then do it as a favor," Tristan said, stepping back to the doorway. "If not for me, do it for your sister. After everything you suffered to set her free, it'd be a shame if she were left unguarded because you went and got yourself captured."

Lola was ready to bite his head off for using her sister against her, but that was just the anger talking. It actually warmed her heart to see Tristan looking out for her, though she suspected it had more to do with protecting their strategic situation than any actual concern for her well-being. It was still a lot of caring from a fairy, though, and Lola decided to accept it as such.

"I won't do anything stupid."

Tristan arched an eyebrow at the non-answer, but he let it slide, turning on his heel to march after his queen. Lola followed him into the living room under the pretense of grabbing the rest of the dinner she'd abandoned on the coffee table. But the moment Tristan vanished through the door that led to the part of the barrow where the fairies went to do their secret fairy things, she rushed back into the guest bedroom and shut the door.

She'd wanted to wait until her sister woke up before doing anything rash, but after Alberich's announcement, Lola was suddenly facing a hard deadline. Even if Morgan was right, and the Wild Hunt *could* crush Victor utterly, Simon and Valente were both still under the blood mage's boot. As his knight, the Rider would die for sure. Simon's fate was less certain, but Lola was positive Victor wouldn't let him escape. They'd both definitely be in the blast radius when Alberich's Hunt landed.

Unless she got to them first.

It was a heady, dangerous thought. Lola had been scheming up rescue plans for the past three weeks. There wasn't much else to do when you were staring at someone who never moved. But while she'd come up with all sorts of out-of-the-box solutions, she hadn't thought of anything yet that stood a chance of actually working. Everything she'd gotten Tristan to tell her about the knighthood oaths made them sound utterly unbreakable, and she didn't even know where Simon *was.*

If this was still the normal DFZ, Lola could have just hired another mage to cast a tracking spell, but the destruction of the city had thrown everything into chaos. Even if she could find someone to take the job, Simon's house had been crushed by Fenrir. That didn't mean there wasn't still a usable material link buried under the wreckage, but with Valente able to track her anywhere thanks to the dream she'd fed him—a decision Lola refused to regret, but was definitely working against her at the moment—she couldn't even step outside to find it without getting snatched.

It was so *frustrating.* She'd gotten free of Victor's pills, but his hand still blocked her at every turn. She was getting herself good and worked up over the unfairness of it all when she spotted a scrap of paper stuck to the bottom of Buster's cat carrier.

Lola grabbed the plastic box with a huff. Even if everything else was on fire, her fur baby deserved a clean crate, especially since she was probably going to have to shut him inside it to keep him from eating Tristan's servants. But when she peeled the paper off the textured plastic to toss it in the trash, Lola saw it wasn't a receipt from the vet as she'd assumed.

It was a note.

The piece of blue-lined memo paper was cheap and soft with a jagged edge across the top from where it had been torn off the spiral binding. Lola recognized what it was the moment she touched it, but that didn't stop her eyes from going wide when she turned the paper over to reveal two lines written in the Rider's blocky hand.

St. Claire's Hospital, Rm 5020
Simon

She crushed the note in her fist, burying the evidence deep inside her gossamer even though there was no one here to see it except her sleeping sister. You couldn't be too careful in a barrow, and Lola already knew that Tristan wouldn't like this. She wasn't sure *she* liked it, because slipping her a note with the one thing that could convince her to leave the safety of Tristan's magic sure looked like bait.

The thought had barely crossed her mind before Lola tossed it back out. What had happened under the arena that night wasn't Valente's fault. Victor had ordered him to kill her, and she knew from Tristan just how impossible it was for a knight to say no. She was also pretty sure this wasn't one of her former master's plans. Victor had never cared enough about her non-work life to realize she had a cat, but Valente knew exactly how much her furry chonk meant to her. If he was sending messages via Buster, it had to be because he wanted to help.

Or because he was still following Victor's kill order and had gotten tired of waiting.

Scowling, Lola pulled out Simon's phone—which she still had—and typed the hospital's name into the search bar. As expected, St. Claire's turned out to be a classic Skyways for-profit institution on the north side of town, the sort of place celebrities went to get their secret plastic surgery done. It was also outside of Fenrir's arc of destruction, making it the perfect location for Victor to stash someone he didn't want the rest of the world knowing about.

Also the perfect place for an ambush. Not that the Rider *needed* to ambush her, but the rest of Victor's forces were another story. Maybe her old master had decided Valente had failed long enough, and this note was just the bait he'd been ordered to lay for a new trap.

Lola's mind was leaping through all the ways this could go wrong when she made herself stop. Trap or no trap, this was the first lead she'd had in weeks, which meant she had to take it. Quickly. She wasn't sure how fast the Wild Hunt could ride across the sea, but it didn't sound like Alberich was planning to take his time. If she was going to save anyone before the hammer came down, it had to be *now.*

"So much for not being stupid," she whispered, glancing at her sleeping sister. "Ready to do something rash and ill-advised?"

As ever, her sister said nothing, but the question hadn't been for her. Lola had to know if *she* was ready. She'd been working on how not to get Rider-snatched the moment she stepped outside the barrow for weeks now, and while she did have a plan in mind, it was going to be rough, assuming it even worked.

There was no way to know until she tried, so Lola retrieved Buster from the floor and moved him to the chair behind her.

"This is going to look pretty weird," she warned. "Don't freak out on me."

Buster gave her an annoyed meow and hopped onto the windowsill overlooking the snowy mountains, ignoring Lola completely as she began working her gossamer like clay.

<div align="center">~~~</div>

Thirty minutes later, she'd created a perfect replica of herself. It wasn't just in looks, either. The fake Lola could talk and answer questions with the same knowledge as the real one, provided no one asked her anything too complicated. It was the sort of creation real fairies made all the time, but it was Lola's greatest work of gossamer ever. She'd never attempted anything close to this complex before, but she'd had a lot of time to practice during the long, dull days waiting for her sister to wake up, and the results showed.

"What's your name?" she asked the gossamer double sitting in her chair.

"Lola," the copy answered without looking up from the crime drama she was watching on Simon's phone.

"What's your favorite food?"

"Christmas sugar cookies that are at least half icing but only if they have the hard icing because the soft kind is gross. They should crack when you bite into them and be covered in sprinkles but not the silver ball kind because eating metal is weird."

That was *exactly* Lola's opinion. The TMI answer would never pass, though, so she made some adjustments. When her double was finally able to answer simple questions normally, Lola plucked the phone out of her hands.

"Hey!" the other Lola cried.

"I'll give it right back," the original promised, struggling to operate the large phone with her now much-smaller-than-usual hands.

Making such a complex creation had taken nearly all of Lola's gossamer, leaving her with barely enough magic to form the child body she was currently inhabiting. This was by design. She hadn't forgotten what Tristan had said when she'd found him waiting by her car the morning after the Paladins arrested her. He'd gone to where the *majority* of her gossamer was, which meant the compass fairies got when they ate her dreams wasn't foolproof. They were drawn to the largest piece, so if Lola left the bigger percentage of herself inside the barrow, Valente should think she was still here.

As would Tristan, which was very convenient. She'd meant it when she said he didn't give her orders, but pissing off the only person protecting you from certain death was generally considered a bad idea. He was busy with his queen at the moment, though, and so long as no one pried too hard, the double made a perfectly passable Lola. If she played her cards right, Tristan wouldn't even know she'd slipped out until she came back with Simon.

Smiling at her cleverness, Lola turned her attention back to the cell phone. Just like the doppelganger, copying advanced electronics was a trick she never could have pulled off back when she'd been on Victor's pills. Cars and other devices whose purpose could be summed up in a few words were one thing, but something like a cell phone that had to interact with a network of real signals and security checks to function was a whole other ballgame.

The closest she'd been able to get before was a radio that picked up actual radio waves, but Lola was a different changeling now. Five minutes after she'd taken the phone from her grumpy double, she had a working copy of her very own.

She held the cell phone up like a trophy when it was finished. She wasn't sure if the leap in her abilities was because Victor's blood was gone or if not being terrified all the time had finally allowed her to harness her true potential. Whatever the reason, Lola loved it. Her magic was solid as a rock these days without a single pill, giving her the confidence to try things she'd never dared before, like squeezing her entire consciousness into the body of a gossamer ten-year-old.

It still wasn't easy. Lola made things that were bigger than her all the time, but going smaller was a lot trickier, especially *this* small. She'd whittled her current body down to the barest essentials to make sure as much of her magic as possible remained with her decoy. The result was a terrifyingly thin waif of a girl made of barely enough magic to keep Lola functional.

Forget making cars or disguises. She was running on so little, Lola wasn't sure she'd be able to jump her mind back to the rest of her gossamer if the Rider did catch her. She justified the risk by telling herself she'd be no more dead than if she'd gone out with more magic and gotten caught like that. There was just no safe way to do something this dangerous, so Lola sucked it up, sliding her shiny new phone into the pocket of the little girl's poofy purple coat.

"Here," she said, returning Simon's original cell phone to her double. "I'll be home in a few hours. Don't gain sentience."

"'Kay," the other Lola said, her eyes already glued back to her TV show.

When Lola was sure she'd stay that way, she grabbed Buster off the windowsill and wrestled him back into his crate.

"I'm sorry," she said at his angry meowing. "But I've seen what you do to spiders. If you disembowel one of Tristan's pixies while I'm out, the whole jig is up. Just sit tight. I promise I'll bring you back something nice."

She gave him her best smile, but the cat just lashed his tail resentfully. Resigning herself to being hated for a while, Lola walked over to her sister.

"I'm going to rescue our brother," she whispered, squeezing the sleeping girl's warm hand. "Don't move until I get back."

It was the same joke she always made. But while her sister didn't move or twitch or do anything that could possibly be interpreted as a response, Lola swore she felt the silver thread pull a little.

That was probably just wishful thinking, but it made her feel like her sister was with her as she crept through the empty living room toward the hallway where Tristan kept his doors.

Chapter 3

Lola hadn't been down Tristan's low road since he'd saved her from the Rider three weeks ago. It looked the same as it had back then, all fresh white paint and sky-blue carpet, but the once-sturdy walls now rippled like fabric curtains, and the carpeted floor creaked loudly beneath her feet. The sound was especially ominous since Tristan had never been able to adequately explain exactly what his low road ran through. For all Lola knew, she was one misstep away from plummeting into the void between worlds.

Thanking her lucky stars she'd picked a small body for this venture, Lola eased down the hallway one step at a time, keeping as far from the walls as possible just in case that did anything. At least she didn't have far to go. There were only seven doors in the hall today. All of them looked the same, so Lola went for the closest, wrenching the brass knob with her little child hands to open the way into somewhere very dark.

It still looked safer than Tristan's rickety low road, so she plunged inside. It was only after she'd shut the door—which looked like rusty metal from this side—that Lola realized she was in an alley.

At least, it used to be an alley. It looked more like a cave now thanks to the massive chunk of collapsed Skyway lying on top of the crushed buildings. Water from the most recent snow poured down the cracks in the broken concrete, turning the ground into a slimy black river. Still more dripped down through the fissures in the collapsed roadway overhead, the drops landing like icy needles in her hair.

"Guess even the Living City can't fix everything in three weeks," Lola whispered to her sister's thread as she pulled up her child body's purple hood. "Come on. Let's go see where we are."

She inched her way forward, grateful yet again for her small body as she crawled under fallen electrical cables and wiggled around crushed dumpsters. The collapsed chunk of bridge was nearly a hundred feet wide, so it took a lot of creeping, but eventually she reached the place where the alley ended and the fallen Skyway gave way to open sky.

"Wow," she breathed, shielding her eyes against the sudden brightness. "That's something you don't see every day."

She was standing on a road in what had been the DFZ Underground, but the gray November sky was no longer blocked by bridges and buildings. All of that was gone, replaced by a chasm filled with twisting steel and concrete. The fissure actually started just a few feet in front of her, but when she leaned forward to peer over the edge, what she saw sent her scrambling right back.

Thanks to Queen Morgan's twenty-four-hour news habit, Lola had seen plenty of footage of Fenrir's destruction. But things never looked as big on camera as they did in real life, and the gorge in front of her was so massive it made her dizzy. The whole city from here to the Detroit River had been leveled, the superscrapers ripped up by the roots to reveal the network of buried electrical tunnels, sewers, and pipes below. Water was leaking everywhere thanks to the wet November snow, but while that would have been a problem in other disaster zones, here it was a feature, keeping the ground loose and pliable for the giant sewer pipes that tunneled through it like worms.

The Living City might have taken a hit, but she was definitely still alive. Like a forest after a fire, the ground teemed with motion. Water pipes, electrical cables, and brightly colored telecom lines spread through the wreckage like roots. Between them, the foundations of buildings sprouted like saplings, forming floors, windows, and staircases before Lola's eyes. The tallest, an apartment complex, had already risen past where the Skyway bridges used to be, its rooftop solar panels unfurling like spring leaves as the new building stretched up toward the dreary sky.

The roads were regrowing as well. Lola could already see the first marks of a new grid, but for some reason, they weren't on the ground level where she was standing. All the new roads seemed to be forming several dozen feet *below* the original Old Detroit streets, making her gasp in excitement.

"I don't believe it," Lola whispered, clutching her sister's thread. "I thought she was digging down because Fenrir had damaged her foundations, but I see it now. She's putting in another layer!"

It was more than that. The broken chunks of buildings weren't just lying at the bottom of the pit because they'd fallen there. They'd been sunk into the earth on purpose to serve as underground platforms, presumably for some kind of new transportation system.

Lola *really* hoped it was a subway. Traffic had always been terrible in the DFZ, but the last few years had been the worst she could remember. A subway would change all of that, though given how dedicated the DFZ was to her cars, it could also have been the start of an underground highway.

Whatever the new construction ended up being, seeing it lifted Lola's heart. She'd worried Victor had broken the DFZ for good with his play for godhood, but the city looked like she was bouncing back. Maybe not as quickly as everyone wanted, but she wasn't beaten yet.

"I can't wait to see what it looks like when she's done," Lola said, shifting her eyes to the narrow line of undestroyed buildings and Skyway bridges that still stood like a cliff to the north. Simon's hospital was up there somewhere, but it was a long walk for little legs, especially with a giant construction zone in the way. Her copy of Simon's phone included his ride-share apps, but the island of crushed buildings Tristan's door had opened into didn't look like it connected to the rest of the city anymore. If Lola wanted to reach the hospital before nightfall, she was going to have to try again.

Just thinking about going back into the rickety low road made her knees wobble, but Lola forced herself to turn around, slipping back through the crack beneath the collapsed Skyway bridge and up the flooded alley to the rusted door she'd come out of. She'd just wrapped her hand around the knob when she caught a flash of blue out of the corner of her eye.

She whirled around at once, but the alley was empty. It was also so dark that she couldn't have seen anything even if it had been there. A floodlight would have fixed that, but Lola's tiny body didn't have so much as a light bulb's worth of gossamer to spare, so she settled for breathing deep through her nose, searching the damp air for any hint of midwinter magic.

She was almost disappointed when she didn't find anything. Not that she *wanted* to get caught by the Rider, but being outside the bubble of Tristan's barrow made her remember the times that hadn't been so bad. Even when she was convinced Victor had abandoned her to die, Valente had been good company. Less so when he'd betrayed her, but still, she missed him.

Shaking her head at how pathetic that was, Lola grabbed the rusty doorknob and shoved her way back into Tristan's low road. The floor creaked just as alarmingly now as it had before, but Lola was tired of being timid. She charged ahead, grabbing the next knob in the line.

It took her four tries before she found a door that opened somewhere she deemed acceptable. It wasn't actually closer to the hospital than the first, but where that door had stranded her in the middle of the DFZ's pit of rebirth, this door opened into the familiar chaos of Riverfest, which was far more useful.

Like Lola herself, Riverfest was a temporary creation that had grown into something much, much greater. It used to be a weekend boat show and craft fair at the end of summer, but the floating market had been so popular that the organizers kept extending the dates until eventually the festival ran all year long. It had gotten way bigger, too, with hundreds of floating shops and restaurants tied to an ever-expanding network of piers and pontoon docks that jutted out into the wide neck of water where Lake St. Clair emptied into the Detroit River.

This put it directly below the northern swath of city that had escaped Fenir's destruction. Still on the totally wrong end of things from the hospital, but at least the roads here were intact. That was good enough for Lola's rapidly falling standards, so she double-checked her costume and stepped through the door, grabbing the garishly painted wall on the other side for support as her little feet landed on the gently rocking floor.

Tristan's door came out next to the restrooms inside Riverfest's biggest floating restaurant, the Dandy Lobster. Given the state of the city, Lola would have expected it to be deserted, but she should have had more faith. This was the DFZ, the city that didn't know the meaning of the word "stop." The place was packed to the rafters despite a huge banner on the wall announcing a thirty-percent disaster markup on all menu items.

It was classic DFZ price gouging, but it still cheered Lola's heart to see her city springing back. The thick crowd also made for nice cover as she darted toward the exit, dodging waiters carrying trays of lobster rolls and lobster ravioli and plates of vegetables shaped like lobsters until she made it to the gangplank that connected the floating restaurant to the docks outside.

Being one of the only intact shopping areas left in the city, Riverfest was *packed* with people, including tons of families. Kids were running everywhere, throwing things into the water and crowding the carts that sold light-up toy versions of the Hero's golden sword, dragon-themed candy, and all other manner of parent-wallet bait. There was a rowboat selling piles of old Fenrir merch that no one was buying, a giant I SURVIVED THE END OF THE WORLD sign you could take selfies in front of for five bucks, and flocks of street hawkers selling every kind of food that could be put on a stick.

It was flashing, crazy, changeling-friendly chaos, and Lola was so happy to see it she could have burst. She was wondering if she should pick up a present for Tristan as a pre-apology for the blood mage she was hopefully about to bring into his barrow—fairies *loved* gifts—when something slammed into her gossamer.

Lola stumbled on the dock as the punch of disbelief caught her from behind. It happened so fast, and there was so little of her, her magic almost slopped into a puddle before she caught herself. She was still struggling to hold things together with a hand latched onto her shoulder.

"Where are your parents?"

Lola looked down at the waterproof green carpet under her feet, hiding her face from the middle-aged woman who'd suddenly appeared behind her.

"What are you doing walking around by yourself?" the woman demanded, whipping Lola's little body around to face her. "Did you steal something?"

Lola couldn't even reply. Just like Jamie's, the woman's self-righteous confidence was as hard as a brick wall. It didn't matter if she thought she was dealing with a fairy or a shoplifter. She *knew* beyond the shadow of a doubt that Lola shouldn't be doing whatever it was the woman thought she was doing, and that absolute belief acted like a blowtorch on the spun sugar of Lola's gossamer.

She started melting immediately, her body going soft as taffy in the sun. The collapse was spreading even quicker than the time Frank had shot her, and with so little magic to work with, Lola had no way to hide it. Her shoulder was already oozing out from under the woman's fingers, causing her to snatch her hand back with a gasp.

"What is *wrong* with you?"

That was the last straw. Some people were simply intolerant of fairy magic. It was pure bad luck Lola had run into one here, but now that the woman's yelling had drawn the crowd's attention, more and more eyes were locking onto Lola's drooping body, and the harder they looked, the quicker she melted. She was about to lose structural integrity entirely when the woman who'd started this mess stumbled sideways with a grunt.

Lola had no idea why. Everyone else was standing back, and she'd been too busy melting to do anything. But while she didn't know what was going on, the middle-aged lady was definitely tipping to the left as if something had crashed into her. Was *still* crashing into her, because even when the woman got her feet back on the green carpet, her body kept going sideways, taking her right to the edge of the floating dock before tipping her over the rope and into the icy river.

The crowd exploded as she fell. All the people who'd stopped to watch a full-grown woman scream at a little girl were either rushing for the life preservers or pulling out their phones to film the chaos. This brought even more people running over to see what the commotion was, creating the diversion Lola desperately needed. The moment the crowd's eyes were off her, she bolted, darting down the maze of floating docks until her feet finally hit dry land.

She stopped with a gasp when she reached the gravel lot that fed into the main Riverfest gangplank. She was back beneath the Skyways now, standing in a big open square lined with bars, restaurants, and coffee shops that used to be the festival's parking lot. The cars had all been shoved farther back into the Underground as Riverfest became a permanent event, but there was still a big area for delivery trucks off to the side.

Squeezing her soggy gossamer like a wad of wet paper, Lola dove into the gap between two tractor trailers. This got her away from prying eyes, but the damage was already done. Her body was a wreck, and she wasn't sure she had enough unmelted gossamer left to fix it.

"Come on," she whispered, squeezing her eyes shut as she huddled in the shadow of the truck's giant tires. "Keep it together. You *have* to keep it together."

But it was no good. She'd whittled her magic so thin trying to dodge the Rider, there wasn't anything left to work with. Every time she got one limb stable, the other three just started oozing faster. Even when she dissolved her phone to get a little more, it wasn't a drop in the bucket of what she needed.

Lola squeezed her melting eyelids tight with a cruse. How could she have been so stupid? She'd been so focused on avoiding the Rider, she hadn't even considered what might happen if someone doubted her disguise, which was just plain dumb. Did she think she was immune to disbelief now that her magic was finally behaving? Even Tristan could turn into sea-foam if he let himself get caught doing something stupid in front of enough people. Had she forgotten *everything* she'd learned as Victor's monster?

Apparently so, because her very next thought was a wish that she still had her pills. That made Lola the maddest she'd been yet, because those damn pills had never helped anything. She'd never needed his bloody magic to be herself, and she didn't need it now.

With that, Lola hit the brakes on her runaway panic and forced herself to focus. She could do this. The gossamer body might be tiny, but it was still hers. This was the same magic that had brought her back from Fenrir. She *could* control it, she just had to believe.

That wasn't a cheesy line from a self-help poster. All gossamer—hers, Tristan's, even the Wild Hunt's—was powered by belief. That was why even non-magical humans were able to melt it, but it was also how Lola could put herself back together. She just had to reassert her own belief of how she should be over the mess the woman and the crowd had turned her into. That shouldn't be impossible now that she was alone, so Lola rolled what was left of herself into a ball, shutting out the fear and distractions to focus on her face.

Not the yogurt lady or Victor's redhead. Even if it was the little-girl version, the face she had on today—the face she'd worn *every* day for the last three weeks—was her sister's. It was the face that made her human even when she wasn't, because Lola was more than a changeling who'd lived past its purpose. She was a sister and a person, the monster who'd attacked the city and the heroine who was going to save the people she loved. She was a thousand times more than anyone gave her credit for, and she was *not going to melt here.*

The belief behind those words hit her harder than Victor's pills ever had. They turned Lola's whole body solid in an instant, flash-freezing her melting gossamer into place. For one long second, she was a hard-clenched rock of determination. Then, when she was certain nothing would move unless she allowed it, Lola released the pressure and started putting herself back together.

She started with her fingers, shaping what appeared to be melting wax mixed with monster fur back into the little girl's small, brown hands. She did her arms next, then her legs, then her feet, and finally her torso. Her face came last of all, even though it was the first thing she'd focused on. Faces were always what got you kicked the hardest when you got them wrong, so Lola waited until everything else was stable before shifting her features back into the younger version of her sister. The dark-haired, wide-eyed little girl Lola imagined she would have looked like if she'd never become the monster.

The process took way longer than she wanted, but eventually, Lola was back in the child's body with her big purple coat, sitting on the muddy gravel with a shadow hiding her from the crowds in the square beyond.

A man's large, dark shadow.

She jumped to her feet with a squeak. The gap between the trucks had been empty when she'd dived for cover. Now, though, there was someone blocking her exit. He was dressed all in black with a mirrored motorcycle helmet covering his face, not that it mattered. He could have been wearing a clown suit and Lola still would have known him from the wintery taste of the magic that hung over her like an ax.

"How did you find me?"

The Black Rider reached into his jacket pocket and pulled out his writing pad.

I pay very close attention to you.

"Forgive me if I'm not flattered," Lola said, pressing her small back into the truck's giant tire. "Seriously, though, how did you do it? I nearly killed myself cutting my magic down this small. Such a tiny fraction of my gossamer shouldn't even blip your radar, so how are you here?"

The Rider pressed the pad against the truck's door to steady it as he wrote down his answer. *I used my compass,* it read when he turned it back around. *I told you before, ever since I ate your dream, there's an arrow in my head that points only to you. All of you. Even when it's only a tiny portion, there's still a swing. I wanted to see you, so I followed it.*

"Well, that's just great," Lola said, easing her body toward the tire's outer edge. The gap between the bottom of the truck's cab and the gravel would be a tight squeeze for someone as big as the Rider, but her little body could fit through no problem. She was about to make a run for it when the Rider thrust his pad at her again.

I'm not here to hurt you.

Lola arched an eyebrow. "You get a choice in that?"

The Rider flipped his notepad to a new page and began writing furiously. *No. Victor's kill order still stands. But since the majority of you is somewhere else, I haven't technically "found" you yet, and I can't kill someone I haven't found.*

"That's a pretty weak technicality," Lola said, edging closer to her escape.

She had to get out of here. Valente might have found a way around killing her immediately, but he was still Victor's weapon. It'd been easy to forget that part when she'd been lonely and scared back in the flooded alley, but this was different. She wasn't even sure if she could thank him for slipping her Simon's location without risking Victor overhearing. When she turned to run, though, the Rider grabbed her shoulder.

He didn't do it hard. Lola knew he was perfectly capable of throwing her through the Skyways if he wanted, but his grip was only strong enough to keep her from vanishing under the truck as he dropped his pad on the ground and started writing on it with his free hand.

Please wait.

Lola sagged against his hold. Every second she spent with Valente was dangerous, but she couldn't say no to that, especially when he kept writing.

I'm not here because of Victor. I just wanted to tell you I'm sorry. I know that doesn't mean much at this point, but I might not get another chance to talk to you, and I couldn't let you go without saying I am so, so sorry about what happened that night.

"Me too," Lola said, reaching up to squeeze his gloved hand. "If it makes you feel better, I don't blame you for what happened. All of this is Victor's fault. I know you can't betray him—"

I will always betray him, the Rider wrote, his pencil moving in violent thrusts. *He's the one who made me turn against everyone I ever loved. I used to follow his orders without question because I thought I didn't have a choice, but after what happened with you, I realized that's not true.*

"What do you mean?" Lola asked with a surge of hope. "Have you found a way around your oaths?"

The Rider shook his helmet. *He's still my master. I can't refuse his orders directly, but I can abuse every loophole and technicality.*

"Like how you wormed your way out of killing me just now?"

Valente nodded. *I'm done being his slave. He can punish me all he wants, but I'm going to keep hammering every opening he leaves me until I find the one that brings him down.*

"Is that how you helped me before?" Lola asked, thinking back to the mysterious invisible force on the docks. "You used your gossamer to push that lady into the river, didn't you?"

The Rider's visor turned toward her, and even though Lola knew there was no face inside it, she could feel his smug smile.

Victor didn't order me not *to help you.*

"Thanks for the save," Lola said with a grin before her face slid back into a scowl. "But if your plan is to bide your time until Victor slips up, you're in for a long wait. He doesn't make many mistakes."

He makes them all the time, the Rider wrote. *You were his biggest, which is why he wants to kill you so badly. You showed him how weak his control really is.*

"Is that why you don't have your head?" Lola asked, moving closer despite her better judgment. "Victor took it, didn't he? He doesn't trust you anymore."

He shouldn't, Valente wrote angrily. *A fairy knight is incapable of killing his monarch, but I'm not one of them. I was born human, and I'm going to find a way. I'm going to kill him, Lola.*

He pressed down so hard at the end that his pencil tore the paper, but Lola couldn't shake her head fast enough. "Don't," she begged. "Victor's as petty as he is vicious. If you put him in a corner, he'll do everything in his power to take you down with him."

I'm fine with that.

"I'm not!" Lola cried, whirling around to grab the Rider's shoulders. "Maybe you're okay with dying for revenge, but I'm not letting Victor take anything else away from us. Forget about finding loopholes. Just keep your head down and do whatever you have to to stay alive until I figure out a way to set you free!"

Valente let her hold him for a long time before breaking away to pick his pad up off the gravel.

There is no way, he wrote. *I made this bed, Lola. I know there's no hope for me, but there is for you. I've already got a plan.*

She was afraid to ask, but, "What?"

The Rider turned his visor from side to side. He must not have seen whatever he was looking for, because he hunched over a second later, writing his answer in letters so tiny, Lola had to squint to read them.

Victor knows Alberich is coming for him. I don't know what he's planning because he didn't tell me stuff like that even back when he trusted me, but I do know he's depending on me to be his counter to Orlando.

Just reading the name made Lola shiver. She could already see Alberich's voiceless, bloodstained knight hammering the Rider with his giant sword again like he'd done in their first fight, but Valente wasn't finished.

Victor's got my head hidden somewhere even I can't feel, but he'll have to give it back if he wants me to have a chance. He's already ordered me to fight to the death if Orlando shows up, but he didn't tell me not to lose.

The writing grew stiff after that, the black pencil marks thick and sharp as if he'd been bearing down with all his weight.

I'm going to throw the fight.

"You can't," Lola said. "If Orlando beats you while you're wearing your head, you'll die for real."

That's the idea, the Rider wrote calmly. *Victor has a lot of tricks up his sleeve, but facing the entire Wild Hunt will be a stretch even for him. I'm supposed to guard his flank and keep Alberich's best weapon occupied, but if I let Orlando kill me right at the beginning, there'll be nothing to stop him from crashing into Victor's back. Once that happens, it'll be over.*

"So will you!" Lola cried, throwing her little arms around him. "Don't you dare do this, Valente. Don't you *dare* trade your life for Victor's. He's not worth it!"

I'm not doing it for him, Valente wrote, wrapping his arms all the way around her tiny body to keep writing over her shoulder. *I'm doing it for us. For you and me and Simon and everyone else that Victor's crushed. His death is the only way any of us get free.*

"Then we'll find another," Lola said, fisting her hands in the leather of his riding suit. "I'm not accepting a solution where you die!"

It's all I've got left, he wrote, his shaking hand wobbling all over the page. *I'm sworn to him for life. His or mine, whichever ends first. This is my chance to make up for all the evil I've done on his orders. I can't bring those lives back, but I can stop Victor from taking any more. My mind's made up.*

"Your mind's not even here," Lola said angrily as she pushed him away. "I'm not letting you do this. I'm going to rescue Simon, and then I'm coming back for you. I don't care about your noble sacrifice. I refuse to let you die!"

The notepad fell to the ground as Valente crushed her into his arms, curling his towering body around her small one with a silent shake. He was trying so hard, she realized. Trying to be brave, to make amends, to do the right thing. Of course he didn't want to die. He just didn't know any other way, but Lola would find one. It was the first thing she'd sworn when she'd gotten free, but she couldn't keep her promise if he was dead.

"Stay alive," she ordered, pushing back to look him in the eyes, even though she knew there was nothing under his visor. "I saved myself. I saved my sister. I'm going to save Simon right now. I'm coming for you next, so trust in me and wait. I swear I'll find a way to set you free."

The Rider didn't have an answer for that. He just knelt there with his pad forgotten on the ground. Lola gave him one more hug, pressing her face into his leather chest until she could feel the warmth she remembered beneath his cold magic. She gave herself five seconds to enjoy it, and then she walked away, striding back into the busy square before the mage whose blood she could still feel tainting the Rider's winter magic realized what she was up to.

Chapter 4

The nearest Skyway entrance was conveniently located one block away from the Riverfest gangplank. Lola had to remake her copy of Simon's phone to find it, though, because the metal staircase was bolted to the opposite side of a giant support pillar and thus completely invisible from the river. Not the greatest planning, but people who could afford to live up on the Skyways wouldn't be caught dead at an overgrown carnival like Riverfest anyway, so it could have been intentional.

At least the climb was educational. One side of the staircase was open with only a single metal railing to keep pedestrians from plummeting to their deaths, but the side that faced the support pillar was papered with recruitment posters for the Hero's Army. The advertisements ranged from classy all-text appeals to gory, full-color photos of goblins being ripped apart by blood magic. Clearly, Victor was aiming to hit as wide a spread as possible, and his efforts looked like they were paying off. Nearly every poster was missing at least one of the perforated information tabs along the bottom, and who knew how many people had tapped the LEARN MORE button the digital barcode promised to bring up in their phone's AR.

Lola supposed it was only natural. From the outside, Victor was the perfect DFZ champion: a downtrodden outsider who'd come to the city to forge a new life and ended up saving the world. His story wasn't that different from the Peacemaker's, and everyone loved the Dragon of Detroit. It only made sense that they'd love Victor, too. He'd made sure they never had a reason not to by funding food for the city's refugee camps out of his own pocket and paying a fair salary to any mage who joined his army, even if they had zero experience. Whatever their feelings about blood magic or how Victor's nightly speeches increasingly attacked *all* non-humans, not just fairies, it was hard to bite the hand that fed you, and at this point, Victor's hands were feeding most of the people left in the city.

"You always were good at bribery," Lola muttered, glaring up at the giant billboard of Victor that loomed over the stairwell's exit.

The Hero gazed benevolently back, his face so altered by the illusions he used to make himself young and handsome that he was barely recognizable, but Lola would always know. No matter how much magic he smeared over himself, nothing changed the cruel gleam in his blue eyes as his giant image smiled over the city he'd so generously saved.

Lola gave the billboard a rude gesture before putting her hands into her pockets to get walking. It was a long trek to the hospital, and now that she was out of the Underground, the wind off the lake was bitingly cold. Fortunately, gossamer didn't care too much about temperature. As a lone child walking down a busy road, she got a few worried looks from passersby, but nothing that stung too much. Traffic was light in any case with so many people forced out of town, giving her space to zone out and think about what had just happened.

It wasn't any less painful the second time. Victor was easy to rage against, but how did you stop someone who saw suicide by Alberich's bloody knight as his only way out? Valente was brave enough to actually go through with it, too, which was the most frustrating part. At this point, Lola almost wished the Black Rider *was* an urban legend. A mindless monster controlled by his stories would have been easier to deal with than this tragedy.

She brooded for a good five blocks before shoving the whole mess out of her head. Whether it was by his own hand or someone else's, Valente's doom wouldn't arrive for another few days at least. Simon needed her right now, so Lola pulled out her phone to bring up the map and work on her plan.

It needed to be a good one. Blood mages could heal themselves out of just about anything, so if Victor had decided Simon needed to be in a hospital rather than locked up in a warded cell, his situation must be pretty dire. If Lola had been thinking logically instead of just emotionally, she would have asked Valente for more information, but she'd already stormed out of that conversation, which meant she was flying blind. That was her least favorite way to do anything, but as Lola walked closer to her destination, she got a rare stroke of luck.

As expected from a place that catered to the Skyways' richest, St. Claire's was the picture of discretion. With its mirrored glass towers and lack of an ambulance bay, it didn't even look like a hospital from the outside. But despite these efforts to hide its true nature, St. Claire's was still a medical institution, and as one of the only DFZ hospitals that hadn't been crushed by Fenrir, it was mobbed.

Lola saw the line before she spotted the actual building. The hospital's front steps were a sea of people spilling out into the road, and what she could see of the inside through the windows looked even worse. What was clearly supposed to be a fancy lobby filled with indoor trees and sunlight was crammed tight as a sardine can with gobs of people all shouting over one another for news about their loved ones.

From the panic on the reception desk staff's faces, this was clearly a nightmare scenario, but Lola couldn't have asked for better. With so much chaos, no one noticed one more little girl wiggling her way through the revolving doors. She slipped through the lines next, tiptoeing past the fistfight that had broken out in front of the elevators to sneak into the emergency stairwell.

Valente had already given her Simon's room number. The building's public Wi-Fi was slammed thanks to the mess downstairs, so the searchable map was down, but with a little creative interpretation of the fire evacuation plans posted at every landing, Lola was able to determine that Simon was being held in the fifth-floor ICU.

This must have been one of the *really* expensive areas, because the hallway was empty and silent when Lola stuck her nose out the stairwell door. The lights had already been turned down for the evening, and the staff at the nursing station looked calm and relaxed, probably because there were only ten rooms on the entire unit. Simon's was all the way at the end, a giant suite with a frosted glass door and a glowing red sign that read *Private*.

Lola turned her eyes back to the nurses' station, taking a good, hard look at their scrubs before pulling back into the stairwell to make a set for herself. Even after dissolving her phone, she didn't have enough gossamer to do anything about her height, so she was a very short nurse, but everything else was perfect right down to the photo ID clipped to her pocket. Then, putting on her best "I absolutely belong here and you're wrong for thinking otherwise" face, she pushed open the heavy fire door and walked into the dim hallway, doing her best not to shake too noticeably.

There was no way to stop it completely. Lola had a lot of baggage when it came to hospitals. This one was infinitely nicer than the charity institution where Victor found her, but the smell was exactly the same, triggering so many bad, old memories that her gossamer started wobbling.

Lola crushed it ruthlessly back into place, nodding politely to the other nurses as she walked past their station toward Simon's door. It was locked when she reached it, but a quick swipe of her ID over the scanner fixed that, letting her into the biggest hospital room she'd ever seen.

It looked like a hotel penthouse. The place was absolutely enormous with its own living room, kitchen, and fancy tiled bathroom that boasted a rain shower and a Jacuzzi. There was a sitting area under the windows with a lovely view of the lake, real art on every wall, and a separate guest suite where visitors could spend the night. The only thing that looked remotely medical was the bed dominating the center of the main room.

Like everything else in this place, it was massive, but it was still a hospital bed with folding rails and a fleet of vitals monitors. It was separated from the rest of the room by a blue curtain that could be drawn on all four sides for privacy. Only the two back panels were closed at the moment, but the bed was so big that Lola still had to walk all the way to its side before she could see the man lying in the center, or what was left of him.

If she hadn't known him nearly all her life, Lola wasn't sure she would have recognized the skeleton lying under the sheets as Simon. His face was covered with a mask to help him breathe, and his dark skin was bruised and sagging. There didn't seem to be a single inch of him that wasn't covered in some kind of sensor, tape, or cuff, but the sight that hit Lola hardest was his expression. She'd been with Simon through a lot of horrible things, but she'd never seen him look as scared as he did now.

That made sense. Simon didn't talk much about his past, but Lola knew he'd been in a coma when Victor had found him because their master constantly threatened to put him back into it if he didn't do as he was told. It seemed Victor had finally made good on that, but seeing Simon like this was actually a relief. A coma was way easier to deal with than a full-body cast or any of the other horrors she'd imagined on the way over, especially since she was certain that Victor was the one who'd made him this way.

That might not have sounded like a hope, but Lola was
confident that anything Victor could do, Simon could undo. She
just needed to reach him.

Plan made, Lola got to work. Her first step was casing the
hospital suite for cameras and unwanted visitors. When she'd
made certain they were alone and covered the lone security
camera with one of Simon's blue privacy curtains, she turned off
all the lights and climbed up into the giant hospital bed beside him,
making her already tiny body tinier still until she was small
enough to fit into the gap between the plastic headboard and
Simon's pillow.

When she'd wiggled as far down as she could get, Lola
changed every color on her body to match the light blue hospital
sheets. It wasn't true invisibility—she was still working on that—
but between the color and her tiny size, she should be nearly
impossible to see in the dark, quiet room. Satisfied she wouldn't be
outed by a casual glance, Lola reached down to touch Simon's
head.

"Hey there, Mr. Wizard," she whispered, cradling the crown
of his tight-shaved head with her tiny, powder-blue fingers.
"Wiggle something if you can hear me."

She looked down hopefully, but Simon's comatose body
didn't budge. He only seemed to be breathing because of the
machines, which felt like a bad sign. The heart monitor assured
her that he was alive, though, so Lola bent down even lower,
curling around him like a fallen piece of curtain until her forehead
touched his.

Even as she closed her eyes, Lola was terrified it wasn't going
to work. Unlike Valente, Simon was one hundred percent human.
Entering his dreams was a power reserved for true fairies, not
hack jobs like herself. She was made from the same magic, though,
and she *had* been able to enter her sister's nightmare of Fenrir.

Under highly unusual circumstances, admittedly, but it still counted as proof that a changeling going into a normal human's dream was possible.

Even if it wasn't, Lola had to try. As she'd realized that night at the diner, Simon was the closest thing she had to actual living family. If anyone deserved a leap of faith, it was him.

"I hope you're not dreaming of anything embarrassing," she whispered as she tightened her grip on his head. "Because ready or not, here I come."

What happened next was a lot of fumbling. Despite reaching into her sister's mind practically every hour for the past three weeks, Lola's track record for entering a comatose human's dreams was not exactly stellar. But while she'd yet to have success on the sister front, she *had* been feeding Morgan several times a day. She knew exactly what it felt like when a fairy entered your mind, and she copied that feeling now, reaching, reaching, reaching with her magic for the dream she knew had to be there.

Please, Simon, she begged as she pressed her small, blue forehead against his cold, still one. *Please let me in!*

Minutes ticked by. Lola pushed every way that she could think of, but she still hadn't managed to touch anything but his physical skin. She was trying not to panic when the gossamer tendril she'd been trailing through the stillness of Simon's mind finally caught.

After that, everything happened in an instant. One second, she was crouched over him like a gremlin on the giant hospital bed. The next, she was falling forward, tumbling face-first into a nightmare.

Lola had shared a lot of dreams in her life, but she'd never had to wrestle one before.

Just like when she'd fed the Rider, Simon's dream had yanked her in. But while all she'd had to do to enter Valente's mind was open her eyes, Simon's was slippery as an eel. She had to fight to hold onto him, pushing against the heavy weight of his unconscious mind to keep her magic wrapped around the one bit that was still kicking.

When the dream finally relaxed into her grasp, the heaviness lifted like a blanket, and Lola opened her eyes to a familiar sight. She was back in Victor's mansion, in the stone cell that had been Simon's bedroom while he'd lived there. Simon himself was right in front of her, but not the man she knew. This was a version of Simon Lola had never seen before: a tiny, frail boy in a gray hospital gown kneeling on the cold stone floor, and standing in front of him was Victor.

Not the Hero. This was Victor from Lola's worst memories, the cruel monster of her childhood. Even now, the sight of him made her want to run and hide, but he wasn't looking at her. He was staring down at Simon, foot tapping impatiently next to a second boy, who lay at his feet.

She blinked in surprise. Unlike Simon, Lola was certain she'd never seen this person before in her life. He was pale and scrawny with dull, unfocused eyes. He lay still as a log beside Victor's leg, so still that Lola couldn't say for sure if he was breathing. She was about to lean down for a better look when Victor began to speak.

"It is very simple," the blood mage said, his cold eyes locked on Simon. "I am looking for an apprentice. This one has already disappointed me. I'm hoping you can do better."

He nudged the thin stranger as he finished, rolling the limp boy over with the toe of his polished shoe. The unknown child didn't even flinch at the motion, but Simon jumped back, his whole body shaking in fear.

"Use the magic I showed you," Victor ordered. "Prove you're worth my effort, or I'll send you right back into that coma."

"But…" Simon whispered, his dark eyes flicking between Victor and the unnaturally still boy. "If I use the magic on him, he'll die."

"I don't care," Victor said. "And neither should you. The first thing you must learn as a blood mage is that all lives are not equal. We are only as valuable as the effort we put in." He planted his foot on the smaller boy's shoulder. "This one has already revealed his uselessness. Now's your chance to prove you're better."

"But it will taint my soul," Simon argued. "Blood magic can't be taken back. It stains you forever. I can't—"

"But you've already done it," Victor said, his voice taking on a sinister smoothness. "You used blood magic on your brother. That's what startled your father into crashing the car, but your brother didn't die because he hit that tree. *You* killed him."

Simon's eyes grew wider with every word, but he didn't deny it. Lola wished he would. She wanted to throw herself in front of him and scream at Victor to stop lying, but she couldn't move, because this wasn't her dream. It was Simon's. His memory of a past he'd never told her about. That was when Lola knew that it was true, because unlike Victor, Simon wasn't a liar.

"That's why I saved you," Victor went on, his face curling into a coaxing smile. "When I saw your stain at the hospital, I thought, here's a young man with promise. Here's a soul like mine: someone whose first instinct is to go for blood. That's nothing to be ashamed of, Simon. Blood magic is humanity's weapon, the power we've been denied. I've been looking for someone I can share that with, someone who will help me in my great work, but

I have to know you're worth the investment."

He crouched down, grabbing Simon's shaking hands and placing them on the boy. "Show me you have what it takes."

Little by little, Simon's trembling fingers closed around the unknown child's shoulder. Even in the dream, Lola could smell the bloody magic rising around him like a knife, but it never struck. Time had slowed to nothing, leaving Simon trapped in this moment, because it wasn't a moment at all.

It was a nightmare. The worst decision of his life stretched out into an eternity. Even though the rest of the dream had stopped, Lola could see the eleven-year-old Simon panicking above the boy he would eventually kill to prove himself to the man he'd grow to hate. It was all there in this instant, the tipping point of his life, but Simon couldn't make a different choice, because this wasn't real. It wasn't even a true dream. Now that she'd adjusted to it, Lola could finally see this place for what it was:

A prison.

Every other dream she'd been in—whether she was sharing it with someone else or just dreaming for herself—had moved and shifted like a living thing, but this one didn't move at all. It was a stone box, a frozen slice of time that didn't go forward or backward.

Now that she knew what to look for, she could actually feel the blood that pulsed behind the walls. Simon's blood, because this whole place was inside Simon's mind. Lola was certain that Victor had built it—he was the only one cruel enough—but Simon had to be the one keeping it going, because he was the only mage here. But if he was the glue holding everything together, then he was the one who could break it.

"Simon!" she cried, shoving her way through the taffy-thick air of the frozen prison. "Simon, it's me! Don't listen to him! This is your mind. You can stop this!"

She kept pushing as she yelled, fighting forward until she was standing right in front of Victor. She would have kicked the hateful man over if she could have, but all the objects in the dream were as solid as the stone floor. They didn't move no matter how hard she shoved, which was only to be expected. The first mind any blood mage learned to control was his own, and while she knew Simon hated it, Victor had been right about one thing: he was a very good blood mage.

"He's tricking you," she said, crouching over the prone boy so Simon would be forced to look at her. "It's just like what he did to me with my pills. He's not actually strong enough to hold any of us by himself, so he fools us into building our own prisons. He struts and lies and pretends he's the master of monsters, but his posturing only works because we bow. All you have to do is stand up, and you'll be the one looking down on *him*!"

She finished with a beaming smile, but while she'd succeeded in getting Simon's attention, the boy was staring at her like she was a stranger. Lola shifted immediately, replacing her sister's face with the doll-eyed redhead Victor had made her wear through most of their childhood. It should have been the version of her that Simon knew best, but the boy's expression didn't change. He just turned away, ignoring Lola completely to go back to Victor and the horror of what he was about to do.

"Oh no you don't," she said, shoving her hands between Simon's and the boy. She didn't even know what the poor kid's name was. By the time Victor brought her to the mansion, Simon had already been his apprentice. She'd never known there'd been another, or that Simon had had to kill him. Simon had never told her any of this, and there, at last, Lola realized her problem.

She couldn't get through to this Simon because he hadn't met her yet. This had all happened before her time, which meant she had no place in this dream. If she was going to break through the horror, she needed to be someone he'd listen to, but the only faces Lola had that this Simon would recognize were Victor's and his mother's.

Their master was right out. Not only was he already here, Lola didn't think there was anything she could speak with his mouth that wouldn't make the situation worse. Victor was a liar, anyway. That made him useless for what she needed, but Lola didn't think turning into Simon's mom was a good idea either. Firstly, she'd only seen her as an old lady, not the young mother this Simon would know. Second, while she was certain that Simon loved his mom, their relationship had always been strained.

Lola had always assumed that was Victor's doing. Now, though, she wondered if it wasn't because of what had happened. Simon's mother was a kind and loving person, but how did you forgive one son for killing the other?

Thinking back to how she'd seen them act together, Lola wasn't sure she had. Also, this Simon was straight from the coma. Even if his mother would eventually forgive him, it hadn't happened yet, which meant a mom-costume was a terrible idea. What else was there, though? Who could Lola turn into that this version of Simon would listen to?

She looked down at his terrified face again. That seemed to be the core of the prison. By keeping him stranded in the horror of his worst decision, he never got the chance to think about anything else, like escape. It was a horrible, cruel trap, but at least the freeze-frame bought Lola time to think.

Not that thinking was easy with Victor looming behind her like an executioner, but this was no time for her own baggage. She was here for Simon, damn it. She just wished she knew what to do. Dreams she could handle, but this was a blood-magic prison. It needed a mage, or at least a real human.

The actual Simon would have been perfect. He'd have known exactly how to break himself out, which was undoubtedly why Victor had chosen this moment for his cage. It was the same reason Lola had been a child when he'd spoken to her in the Fenrir dream. Victor was only comfortable with the versions of them that he could control.

Ironically, that was the thought that made her realize what she had to do. Flipping her hands around to grab Simon's instead of just stopping him from touching the boy, Lola changed her shape again. It was a hard, slow change because she'd never taken this form before, and she had no mirror to check herself. She did have a lot of memories, though, providing her with a treasure trove of images to dig through until every detail felt perfect.

The next time Lola lifted her head, she was Simon. Not the little boy on the floor or the gawky teenager she'd grown up with or even the nervous young man who'd left Victor's mansion to start his own business. This was the Simon she'd seen at the diner: the fully developed mage who was confident in his power. She'd even kept his dark turtleneck and tired eyes, focusing on looking as real as possible as she stared down at his younger self.

"Hello, Simon."

If Lola hadn't been concentrating so hard, she would have given herself a high five. That was the best male voice she'd ever achieved. It really did sound *exactly* like Simon's, and the boy on the floor looked up at once.

"Who are you?"

"I'm you," Lola lied, positioning her Simon so that his tall body hid the specter of Victor looming over them. "I need you to listen to me. You can't change what happens tonight, but you *do* get past it. I'm proof of that."

For some reason, this motivational message made the boy look more distressed than ever.

"But you're a blood mage."

Lola blinked. She hadn't realized her Simon costume included his stained soul. This *was* the most perfect copy of a person she'd ever made, though, and they *were* inside Simon's mind. He could be picking up on the reality behind the image, or maybe he was just seeing what he expected to see. Lola wasn't certain, but either way, it didn't matter.

"You do become a blood mage," she said in Simon's calm voice. "But you're not like Victor. You use your magic to heal and help people. That's the sort of mage you become, and your sister's very proud of you."

The boy scowled. "I don't have a sister."

"You will," Lola-Simon promised. "And she will love you no matter what happens. All of your family does. We don't hold the past against you, Simon. Victor's going to steal a huge part of your life, but that doesn't mean he gets everything. There's still a future where we get free, but I need you to let go of this so we can make it there."

"But I haven't proven myself yet," the boy whispered, his voice cracking with fear as he grabbed the previous apprentice. "If I don't do this, he'll put me back in the coma!"

"He will," she said solemnly, "but it won't matter. You're good enough to get out of any prison he can make. You've already proven yourself to everyone who counts, so let's go back to them."

She smiled as she finished, a bigger, warmer smile than she'd ever seen on the adult Simon's face. "Your sister's worried to death about you."

That worked. Lola *knew* it would, because it had worked on her. That was the same smile the boy Simon had given her the first night she'd come to the mansion as a terrified, barely human seven-year-old, and it had the same effect on his younger self as it had on her. The moment she smiled, the boy smiled back, letting go of the poor, dead memory to grab her offered hands. And as he did, the horrible heaviness of the prison vanished.

Simon's old room vanished with it. Victor, little Simon, and the unknown boy all blew away like dust. Lola let her Simon costume go with them, putting her real face back on as she sank through the fading memory into what appeared to be the exact same room.

She landed with a stumble, looking around in alarm. It would be just like Victor to build a second prison around the first. But while this was definitely Simon's old room at the mansion, it was no longer a barren cell. There were travel posters on the walls and a tiny desk stacked with books in the corner. It looked like the version of Simon's room she remembered from just before he'd moved out, right down to the picture of the two of them at the Grand Canyon on the windowsill. The only thing that wasn't right was the color.

The entire room was tinted red. Not the awful bright crimson of Victor's death, but it was definitely a bloody color, especially around the life-sized portrait of Victor hanging on the wall where the door should have been.

That *definitely* hadn't been there the last time Lola was in Simon's room. It reminded her of the red-tone pictures that decorated the walls of Victor's death. It even had the same red thread dangling off the bottom of its ornate gilt frame, except this string didn't end in a bow. It ran across the stone floor and up to a stool placed in the room's far corner, where it tied around the neck of a lanky, dark-skinned man who was sitting with his head in his hands. A man who looked very much like—

"*Simon!*"

Chapter 5

Lola didn't know how she hadn't seen him sooner. The only reason she could think of was that he'd been sitting so still. He still hadn't moved even now that she'd called his name, but when Lola rushed toward him, he shrank back against the red-stained wall.

"Stay away!"

Lola skidded to a stop. It was Simon's voice, but she'd never heard him sound like that before.

"Simon?" she said tentatively. "It's me. It's Lola."

She'd thought that would snap him out of it. But while the man huddled in the corner did lift his face from his hands, his eyes were full of hate.

"I should have known you'd use her eventually," he said in a bitter voice. "But it won't work. I know it's not her. Lola would never help you break me."

"You're right about that," Lola said, taking a step forward. "Victor didn't send me, Simon. He doesn't even know I'm here. I found you and entered your dream on my own. This is a jailbreak. I'm busting you out of here!"

For a second, the fury on Simon's face faded. Then it came back twice as strong as he turned around on his stool, putting his back to her.

"You're going to have to do better than that."

"I'm not one of his tricks," she insisted. "It's really me!"

But Simon's back stayed turned, and honestly, Lola couldn't blame him. Blood magic was all about getting into people's heads. Of *course* Simon would trust nothing he saw here.

She looked around the red-tinted room in frustration. At least she was pretty sure where she was now. This must be Simon's death, the place where his soul and the world's magic connected. It wasn't a quarter as large as Victor's awful red lounge, but Lola spotted the hole in the ceiling that led to the Sea of Magic when she looked up.

It was the only exit she could see, but Lola didn't think they'd be getting out that way. She wasn't sure she could survive the black chaos without Fenrir's huge magic protecting her, much less escort Simon. Could humans even leave their death without dying?

Lola had no idea, but Simon wouldn't be sitting around in here if going out the top was an option. Something had to be holding him down, and looking at the blood-red thread tied around his neck, she had a pretty good idea what it was.

"How did Victor put that on you?"

"He didn't," Simon said quietly, reaching up to touch the thread only to stop an inch before his fingers reached it. "I tied this here."

Lola couldn't believe it. "*Why?*"

"Because he told me to," Simon replied, hunching his shoulders. "I was young, okay? And he was horrible." His shoulders hunched higher. "The real Lola would understand."

"I *do* understand," she said, moving closer. "But you're not that little boy anymore. You're a blood mage too. A good one, and this is *your* death. Your soul, not his. You can kick him out!"

He sighed at that, a long, bitter sound. "I don't know what your game is, but I'm not playing. Go tell your master that'll I'll sit down here until I die before I go back to him."

Lola threw her head back with a frustrated groan. "For the last time, Simon, Victor didn't send me! I can prove it, too. The last time we were together, I was dressed as your mother at Peach's Diner. You told me that night that humans make mistakes, and that sooner or later, Victor would too. Well, you were right. He *did* make a mistake. He underestimated me, and I wrecked his plans."

She walked right up to where Simon was hunched on the stool and placed a hand on his shoulder. "I got free of him," she said fiercely. "Now, I'm here to help you do the same. We're busting out of here—the two of us together, just like you wanted—and we're never looking back."

Those were his words. Words Victor couldn't know because he'd been in Alberich's barrow writing his bloody spellwork around her sister at the time, but Simon still shook his head.

"That proves nothing," he said, leaning away from her. "Jamie was there. She could have overheard."

Lola blinked. "Jamie was at the diner?"

He nodded, and Lola scowled. It wasn't that she didn't believe Victor's assistant would stoop to stalking, but she was surprised that she hadn't noticed. Jamie was normally impossible to miss. She was thinking back to try to figure out where the obnoxious blond had been hiding when she decided it didn't matter.

"Screw Jamie," she said, thrusting her left wrist between Simon's face and the red-tinged wall he was determinedly staring at. "I *am* Lola. I know you've never been able to see my sister's thread, but it's right there, and guess what? I found her, Simon! She's waiting back at Tristan's right now, safe and sound. You can be safe, too. We can *all* be! I just need you to—"

"*Enough!*" he snarled, covering his ears with his hands. "I'm not listening to another word!"

Lola stepped back with a huff. Under any other circumstances, she would have been proud of him for making such a valiant stand, but she didn't have infinite time. Her body was still back in the hospital room. She'd camouflaged herself pretty well, but if a nurse came in and freaked out over the tiny blue figure clutching Simon's head, Lola had no idea what would happen. They needed to get out of here, but she didn't know how to make Simon believe her.

"What can I say?" she asked, slumping against the red-tainted wall. "You were always the one with the plan, so you tell me. How I can convince you I'm not one of his tricks?"

Simon stiffened on his stool. He clearly didn't want anything to do with this, but her request must have kindled a little hope, because he eventually turned around to give her one of his classic Simon scowls.

"I never told Lola the truth about my brother," he said in a quiet, serious voice. "Or what I did to the apprentice before me. If you're really her, why aren't you horrified?"

"Because I know you," Lola said, looking him in the eyes. "Victor made all of us do terrible things, but that doesn't mean—"

"He didn't make me do this," Simon said, lifting up his hands.

Lola jerked back. Like everything else in the little room, Simon's hands were red, but it wasn't from the stain that permeated the air. They were *actually* bloody, his long fingers coated in a layer of deep scarlet as thick and glossy as fresh paint.

"Victor didn't make me a blood mage," he said quietly, looking down at his reflection in the glossy wetness. "I came into my magic at a young age. My parents were so proud, but my older brother couldn't stand it. He'd always been the best at everything. Then I tested positive as a mage, and suddenly I was getting all the attention. He was jealous, and he took it out on me. We fought all the time, but he was bigger, so he always won. Then, one night while we were driving home from my grandmother's, he started picking on me in the car. I was so sick of it. I wanted him to leave me alone, to just go away, so I..."

"You used your magic on him," Lola finished, reaching out to take his bloody hands. "I'm so sorry, Simon, but that still doesn't make you like Victor. You were just a kid. You didn't know—"

"I *did* know," Simon snarled, yanking his hands back. "The very first thing they tell you when you find out you're a mage is 'Don't do blood magic.' I knew what I was doing was wrong. I knew that it would kill him, but that's what I wanted. I *wanted* him to die." He dropped his head back into his hands. "I'm just as bad as Victor."

"No, you're not," Lola said. "You regret what you did, right?"

"Every day of my life."

"Then that proves it," she said confidently. "Victor's never regretted anything. He holds his sins up like trophies, but he punishes you by making you relive yours. If you were really like him, he couldn't have turned the night he made you kill that kid into a prison. Victor would have crushed that poor boy and moved on without a moment's hesitation, but you've been trapped in that cycle for three weeks precisely because *you're not like him!*"

By the time she finished, Simon was staring at her with new eyes. "It really is you," he whispered. Then his face grew horrified as he turned his back on her again. "I wish it wasn't. Wish you hadn't seen—"

"It's okay," Lola said, wrapping her arms around him. "It's okay, Simon. You're my brother, and I love you. There's no secret that's ever going to change that."

He shook his head furiously. "I'm not who you think I am. Do you know why I worked so hard at learning how to remove bad memories? It wasn't so I could help other people. I wanted to cut out my own crimes, to make myself forget what I'd done. I thought if I could erase my past, I'd remove the stain, but..."

He looked down at his bloody hands. "No matter how good I got or how many people I helped, I could never fix myself. The blood's always there, and the worst part is, it was so *easy*. That's why Victor picked me. It wasn't just because I'd already done blood magic. His other apprentice, the boy I killed to earn my spot, he was also stained when Victor found him. I was just better. 'A natural-born talent,' Victor said, and he was right. All I had to do was wish for my brother to die, and it happened."

He hunched over even farther. "It was the same for the other apprentice. I knew it was wrong, but I was so afraid of going back into the coma that I did whatever Victor said. I didn't even have to try that hard. All I had to do was touch him, and his soul ripped to shreds."

Lola sighed. "Simon…"

He shook his head, crossing his arms over his chest to hide his bloody hands as he curled over on himself. "You were right," he whispered into his chest. "We're all his monsters."

"No, we're not," she said firmly, grabbing his shoulders and wrenching him around to look at her. "I only thought that at the time because I was stuck in his bloody shadow. The moment I got free, though, I saw the truth. We were never the monsters. He was. You, me, and the Rider: we're the victims he forced to do his monstrous things. Even Jamie—"

"Jamie *is* a monster."

"Yeah, okay, she's awful," Lola agreed. "But the rest of us *aren't*. Why do you think Victor grabbed us as kids? It wasn't because he wanted to be a father. He needed us young and vulnerable because that's when he could screw us up. If we were actually horrible like him, he wouldn't have had to go through all that effort."

"Maybe not for you," Simon said coldly. "You were innocent. I was already a killer when he found me."

"That doesn't mean you're doomed to be one forever." She put a hand on his cheek with a smile. "You did things that you regret, but they're not who you are. I know that for a fact because the Simon I grew up with, *my* Simon, was the very best person I knew."

"I was the only person you knew," he said with an exasperated look. "He kept us locked up alone in that house for years."

"And I never would have survived it without you," Lola assured him. "Every day, I was terrified Victor would decide I wasn't worth the trouble and stop making my pills. You were the only thing in that place I wasn't afraid of, my one good person. That's why I can't sit here and listen to you say you're the same as Victor. You're the only reason I survived him."

"You would have made it without me," Simon muttered, but he leaned into the hand she was still pressing against his cheek. "He really messed us up, didn't he?"

"Abusers tend to do that," Lola said. "But we're not helpless kids anymore. I beat him. I don't even need his pills now. And if I could do it, so can you."

"How *did* you get free?" Simon asked, sounding more like himself as he finally straightened up.

Lola shook her head. "It's a long story. I promise I'll tell you everything later, but right now we have to get out of here before Victor catches us."

"That's the one thing he can't do," Simon said as he gestured at the red room. "Despite everything he's done, this is still my death. Victor can send visions to torment me, but he can't come in himself unless I allow it."

"Then how did his stuff get here?" Lola asked, looking at the giant portrait of Victor Simon's thread was tied to.

"I put that up myself," he replied with a shamed look. "Like I said, he messed me up."

"No judgment here," Lola said, waving her hand. "He had me swallowing my own leash twice a day for twenty years. But if you control your death, how did he trap you?"

"Because that's what he does," Simon said bitterly. "When I was a kid, he had me make all these mental constructions as part of my training. I was terrified of him, so I didn't question why. By the time I was old enough to realize I was building my own cage, it was too late to fix it."

Lola sighed. "Childhood traumas are the deepest."

"But you broke it," he said, smiling for the first time since she'd spotted him. "Victor knew he wouldn't be able to control my death once I grew up, so he built his prison to trap my conscious mind. I have zero control over that part of my brain when I'm in the coma, so even though I'm myself down here, up there, I'm still a terrified little kid who can't see past what he's about to do. I've had to watch myself relive that awful moment over and over, knowing I couldn't do anything to stop it. I thought I'd be stuck like that forever."

"Until you broke out," Lola said with a grin.

"Until *you* broke me out," he corrected, grinning back. "I saw everything you did. You made a really good me. Though, for the record, I would never be that sappy."

"It's a good thing I got there first, then," she said smugly. "You were clearly in need of some sap."

"I still don't understand how you were able to enter the dream in the first place," he said, ignoring that comment. "The way Victor had me make the prison, no one but him should've been able to get in."

Lola puffed out her chest. "Did you forget who you're talking to? I'm a changeling. No one can keep me out of anything."

Simon chuckled at that. Lola smiled at the sound for a moment, and then her face fell into a frown. "There's still one part I don't get. If you've been sitting down here this whole time, what was the reliving-your-worst-memory thing supposed to do? Was Victor just torturing you for fun?"

"He was trying to break me," Simon explained, looking grim again. "He's trapped me like this on several occasions over the years. I can feel everything that happens to my younger self, but I can't do anything to help. That's how the prison works. It forces me to sit down here reliving my worst night over and over until I can't take it anymore and beg Victor to let me out."

Lola sighed bitterly. "He always was a fan of making people beg."

"I wasn't going to do it this time," Simon swore. "I'd rather die than kiss his boots ever again. My plan was to run down the clock until my body gave up, but then you appeared." His face broke back into a smile. "You beat him, Lola."

"*We* beat him," she said, grinning wide. "I knocked you out of the loop, but you were the one who broke his prison, and now you're going to get us out of here."

"I'm going to get *you* out," Simon said, settling back onto his stool. "I'm staying."

"*What?*" Lola shrieked, grabbing his shoulders. "Are you crazy? I'm not leaving you with him!"

"You won't be," he replied, waving his hand at the red room. "It might not be much to look at, but I'm king inside my own head. It's one of the few tenets of blood magic I've always agreed with. Unless I let him in, Victor can't touch me here, and that's why this is going to work. He's still out there doing horrible things, right?"

Lola nodded frantically. "He's building an army of blood mages and has pretty much taken over the city. That's why I rushed over the moment I found out where you were. If I don't rescue you now, I might not get another chance."

"That's fine," Simon said. "I don't want to leave."

"What are you talking about?" she demanded, gripping his shoulders like she could force him to see how insane that sounded. "Weren't you the one who wanted to drive away and never look back?"

"I did want that," he said, "back when it was the only way to set you free, but you got there on your own." He touched her face with a smile. "You don't need me to rescue you anymore, Lola, so I'm going to do what *I* want. I'm going to take Victor down."

"No," she said, shaking her head wildly. "No, no, *no*, don't do this to me, Simon! This is our chance to get away! You can't—"

"The only thing I can't do is keep tolerating this," Simon said with a glare. "I'm not the first apprentice he's done this to. There were others. Other kids before us that he used until they broke. I can't just run away from that. Someone has to stop him, and thanks to you, I'm in the best position to do it."

"So what?" Lola cried. "This isn't our job, Simon! We've already given Victor enough. Alberich is coming to kill him in a few days anyway, so let it go. Let someone else—"

"There *is* no one else," he said angrily. "Do you really trust Alberich to beat him? You know Victor always has another plan."

That was the same argument Lola had made to Morgan just a few hours ago, but she still shook her head. "That doesn't mean we have to fight him!"

"That's exactly what it means," Simon argued. "Victor made my prison. He *knows* the only way I can get out of the coma is if I submit to him completely, but you broke his hold. Thanks to you, I can wake up on my own now, but he *doesn't* know that. If I come out now, Victor will think I'm his."

"Simon."

"I'm always most obedient right after I wake up," he went on, talking over her. "He has no reason to think this time will be different. If I go back to him now, he'll trust me, which means this is the best chance I'll ever get to stab him in the back. I can—"

"Simon, *stop!*" Lola yelled, making him jump.

He opened his mouth again right after, but Lola grabbed hold of his shirt.

"Just stop," she pleaded, wrapping the soft fabric in her fists. "You always have all these ideas to bring down Victor, and they *always* end with us losing. Maybe this time will be different, but I can't take that chance. I didn't fight my way down here to let you go back to him!"

"I'm not going back to him. I'm going back *for* him." He gave her a little smile. "Don't you see? This is my chance to—"

"*No,*" Lola snapped, beating her hands against his chest. "Do you have any idea how much I risked to save you today? I'm not letting you throw that away on some stupid revenge plot!"

He grabbed her clenched hands with a scowl. "You're the one throwing things away. Don't you want to stop him?"

"Not if it costs your life!" She stared up at him with her heart in her eyes. "*Please*, Simon, I'm begging you, don't do this. You know how Victor operates. It doesn't matter if he's expecting it or not. If you put yourself back in his power, he'll never let you go."

"He's not a god, Lola," Simon said, pushing her away. "I'm grateful you came to save me, but if we run now, we'll be running and hiding forever while Victor keeps doing whatever the hell he wants. That's not freedom. That's letting him win."

"This isn't about winning," Lola said in a disgusted voice. "Victor took everything from us. This is our chance to take something back! We can leave him behind. Let someone else—"

"There is no one else." He pinned her with a scathing look. "I won't trust our future to the fairy scumbag who helped Victor make this possible. For all we know, Victor and Alberich are still working together, and this whole 'coming to kill him' thing is just the next step in their plan. Even if they have truly become enemies, do you honestly believe our old master can be killed by someone as immature and thoughtless as the Nightmare King?"

Lola dropped her eyes. "Not really, but—"

"Then you understand." He reached out to squeeze her shoulders. "I can't say how much it means that you came to save me, but my mind's made up. I won't trust Victor's downfall to a stranger. I have to make sure he's dead with my own hands. That's the only way any of us get free."

Lola dropped her head. Then she dropped all the way to the ground, curling her arms around her legs with a sob. "I really hate you right now."

"I love you, too," Simon said, getting off his stool to hug her.

"You'd better not lose," she said, hugging him back like she was trying to strangle him. "If you die because of this, I'll kill you."

"I'm not going to lose," he said confidently as he helped her stand back up. "Have a little faith in your fellow monsters."

"Don't throw my own words back at me," she grumbled, scrubbing her eyes. "I assume you have a plan."

"Always," Simon said with a sly smile. "I'm sure this comes as no surprise, but killing Victor is something I've put a *lot* of thought into. I can't tell you the details because I'm going to need him to believe I came crawling back legitimately, and that'll be a lot easier if we're both ignorant. You're just going to have to trust me."

"I do trust you," Lola said without hesitation. "It's just…"

"Just what?"

She rubbed her hands over her face with a groan. "I just can't believe I made it all the way down here and now I'm leaving without you. That makes me zero for two today."

Simon frowned. "Zero for two?"

"I couldn't save the Rider, either," she explained. "He's still trapped by his unbreakable knighthood oaths. Victor took his head away, too, so even if I did think of something, I couldn't…" She trailed off, eyes growing huge. "Wait, you're about to trick Victor into thinking you're his loyal apprentice again, right?"

"That's the plan," Simon said. "Why do you ask?"

"You could find his head!" Lola said in a rush. "Valen—the Rider wants to beat Victor as badly as you do. He's going to let Alberich's knight kill him just so Victor will be left without a defense. But if you steal his head, he won't be able to die even if he loses! He'll just respawn like he always does!"

"Won't that mess up his plans?" Simon asked with a scowl. "It sounds like he's already got a solid strategy. I don't think he'd thank me for—"

"Dying is not a strategy," Lola snapped. "The two of you might be ready to throw yourselves away to spite Victor, but I'm not giving that bastard another thing. He doesn't deserve any of our lives, so you'd better come back to me, Simon, and you'd better be carrying the Rider's head."

"I'll always come back to you," he promised, pulling her into his arms one last time.

"I'll hold you to that," Lola whispered, squeezing him extra tight before she stepped back. "If you're really not coming with me, then it's time for me to go. I left myself in a precarious position on your hospital bed."

"At least I'm in a hospital this time," Simon said cheerfully. "The last time Victor put me in a coma, he left me passed out in the basement."

"That's not funny."

"It wasn't meant to be," he said, holding out his hand. "I'll toss you up. Get your body and get out of there. I'll follow in an hour to make sure Victor has no reason to suspect I had help. I'll contact you as soon as I've got something, and Lola…?"

"Yeah?" she said, grabbing his fingers.

His face split into a huge grin. "Thanks for riding to my rescue."

She was opening her mouth to say it was no more than he would have done for her when Simon swung his arm up. The move launched her into the air, sending her flying up, up, up through the heavy quiet of his still-unconscious mind before exploding back into the real world.

She came back to herself with a gasp, nearly knocking the little blue body she'd conjured to hide herself off the hospital bed. She grabbed one of the monitor wires at the last second, hauling herself back onto Simon's pillow with slow, groggy jerks. She was still shaking off the shock of being tossed from death into life when a man's surprised voice sounded across the room.

"What the—"

Lola froze, her shrunken body going still as her eyes flicked to the knot of men sitting in front of the hospital suite's biggest TV.

There were four of them, all in their shirt-sleeves with their red coats—the same red coats featured in every Hero's Army recruiting poster—thrown haphazardly over the back of the sofa. Two pizza boxes lay empty on the coffee table in front of them, along with a forest of beer cans and several guns. Three of the men were still watching the football game on the screen, but the fourth one was staring straight at her.

Lola flattened herself against Simon's pillow with a curse. She was such an idiot. Just because the room had been empty when she'd arrived didn't mean Victor had left Simon unguarded. The mages must have been out getting dinner when she'd come in. It was pure luck they hadn't noticed her body while she was inside Simon's mind. Now that she'd moved, though, they were all turning to stare, their disbelieving gazes doing more damage to her gossamer than their guns ever could.

"What *is* that?" asked the farthest, putting down his beer to squint in Lola's direction. "A cat?"

"It looks like one of those paintings people do of sleep paralysis," said another. "You know, where they draw the little demon crouching over the guy's head to show—"

"Shut up," ordered the man who'd spotted Lola first, grabbing his red coat and shoving his arms back into it as he walked toward the bed. "Did you idiots listen to nothing the Hero said? It's obviously a fairy."

Lola's gossamer went stiff. She'd been struggling to hold her magic together under their scrutiny, but the moment the red-coated mage named her, everything changed. She was no longer in danger of being melted by their disbelief. As soon as the man invoked the Hero's name, every human in the room believed in her completely.

The iron hand of their conviction had already grabbed her gossamer, molding her body to fit their expectations just like the coliseum crowd's belief had molded her poor monster. When it was done, the tiny blue shape Lola had made to blend in with Simon's sheets had morphed into something that looked more like a goblin than actual goblins did. She was still recovering from the shock of having someone else twist her magic when the red-coated mage popped something into his mouth. He swallowed whatever it was with a grimace, and then he threw out his arm like he was throwing a punch from across the room.

The magic that hit her next felt *exactly* like Victor's. Lola knew he'd been gathering blood mages, but this was ridiculous. Even Simon's magic didn't feel this close. If the man in the red coat hadn't obviously been a stranger, Lola would have sworn it was Victor himself pummeling her down.

It was certainly Victor's style. The blast of magic hit her like a truck, filling her mouth with the horrible, metallic taste of her pills, but the real victim was her gossamer. It shattered on impact, which made no sense at all. Gossamer was the essence of flexibility. It was gooey and liquid, more likely to bend than to break.

Too bad no one had told the mage that. The moment his magic touched her, Lola cracked like a dropped dinner plate. It wasn't until she actually started falling apart that she finally realized what was happening. This wasn't some crazy new spell that broke the fundamental nature of gossamer. It was the bane. She'd just been smacked with the blood magic bane Queen Morgan was always ranting about, and *wow*, was it living up to the hype. The stupid mage hadn't even hit her with that much magic, but the blow had gone through her like a baseball bat made of fairy kryptonite. At this rate, she was going to splinter to dust before the guards even made it to the bed.

There was nothing else for it. If Lola didn't want to die here, she was going to have to get out of this body. Luckily, the blue goblin was only a tiny fraction of her total gossamer. Cutting it off wouldn't hurt nearly as much as the car she'd sacrificed to the Rider. She'd even left her remaining magic in a convenient Lola shape for precisely this sort of emergency. As she closed her eyes to make the switch, though, Lola quickly realized that, unlike the rest of her fairy powers, moving between pieces of herself was one skill the removal of Victor's blood seemed to have made *worse*.

She didn't know if Tristan's barrow was just too far away or if the fake personality she'd crafted for her doppelganger was clogging the path, but Lola couldn't bridge the gap between her separated chunks no matter how hard she tried. She couldn't even feel what the other her was doing. By the time she'd accepted that escape wasn't happening, Victor's goons were right on top of her.

"What are we gonna do with it?" one of them asked, poking Lola's cracking blue flesh with a tongue depressor from the nurses' stand.

The man whose magic had shot her down grinned. "Take it to the Hero, of course. He's been looking for something to kill on camera, and this one's nice and ugly."

Panic seized in what was left of Lola's chest. No, no, *no*, she couldn't let them take her to Victor! She'd rather crumble to dust. At least then she'd only be dead. Her former master wouldn't be nearly so kind. She *had* to get away, but the bane had left her gossamer so fragile that she couldn't even crawl without risking total collapse. She was frantically trying to believe herself back together like she'd done between the trucks when Lola felt something lift its head inside her.

There was no other way to describe it. In the darkness behind her perception, something huge was moving. A growl came next, rumbling through her like an earthquake as anger curled beneath her skin, itching with eagerness to tear the humans apart.

It was a terrifying feeling, but unlike every other part of her, there were no cracks in these sensations. The growling anger was whole and strong, steady as iron in its determination to bite the ones who'd done this.

Lola wanted to bite them, too. She was sick of always being the one on her knees, sick of being weak. She wanted to be the person looking down for once. It was just a thought, a fearful fantasy, but the moment it crossed her mind, the thing inside of her leaped.

Suddenly, Lola wasn't a beaten little goblin crumbling into powder. She was as tall as her normal body again, then even taller, towering over the mages with a growl that rattled the medical equipment. Her skin prickled with the feeling of growing fur, and her jaw unhinged to make room for all her new teeth as she fixed her eyes—her beady, colorblind, inhuman eyes—on the terrified men.

They bolted the second she looked at them. They'd been happy to gloat over a dying goblin, but they couldn't even stay on their feet in the face of a real monster. Their leader tried, hurling handfuls of bloody magic at the thing Lola had become, but his spells rolled right off the monster's shaggy fur. His face went gray when he realized the bane wasn't working, but that was only to be expected, because Lola wasn't a real fairy. She was a changeling, a monster, and no magic had ever worked on her.

The beast roared again as it grabbed the mage with its massive paws and hurled him across the room. The others had already made it back to the table where their guns were, but bullets had never bothered Lola even in her normal shape. They didn't so much as tickle the monster now, but as the shots flew through her to lodge in the room's rear wall, Lola felt a new sensation.

Hunger.

She was starving, hungrier than she could ever remember being, but not for any of her usuals. Even the lingering smell of pizza didn't tempt her, and Lola *loved* pizza, but the men smelled delicious. Not their flesh or blood. Their *fear.*

The monster breathed it in, sucking the delicious smell deep into its body. Ah, that was it. *That* was what she wanted.

The lead mage was screaming now. Being thrown into the wall must have broken something important, because he was pulling himself across the hospital floor with his arms, bellowing at the others to help him. His screams were a siren call to the monster. It followed the noise like a hawk zeroing in on an injured rabbit, opening its fanged mouth so the man's sweet fear could flow into its maw. It was about to take a huge, delicious bite when Lola screamed.

STOP!

The monster froze, its curved claws barely an inch from the man's quivering back.

The other mages took this as their chance to run. They bolted for the door, shoving each other out of the way. Their leader screamed at them not to leave him, but no one listened. He was pulling himself across the floor on his belly when Lola finally wrestled the monster's attention off of his wailing cries and back onto herself.

That's it, Lola said, keeping a firm grip. A grip on what, even she didn't know, but she held it tight, forcing the monster backward until its shaggy body was pressed against the cold glass of the hospital windows.

It growled in frustration, looking longingly at the downed mage, but Lola jerked it back. *That's not what we do,* she said firmly. *Alberich might have made us, but that doesn't mean we're him. We don't eat fear.*

The monster didn't agree. Food was right there, food that would make them strong. Hadn't she just wished to be strong?

Not like this, Lola said, forcing their eyes away from the screaming man. *If we eat him, we really will be a monster.*

But that was what they were. They'd always been a monster. Even she called them that.

I'm sorry, Lola said with a mental wince. *I don't think that anymore. It's just... I used to be so afraid of you.*

The monst—creature—snorted. How could she be afraid? They were one and the same.

I know that now, Lola said, reaching out to her other self. *And that's why we can't eat him. The whole point of getting free was that so we'd get to choose what we are, not them. And if it's up to us, then I want to be something we can be proud of. Something good, you know?*

The creature did know. From their earliest days in the hospital, it had always wanted to be good. To be loved, or at least not feared.

I'll love you, Lola promised. *I was only afraid of you because of Victor. He taught me to hate you, but I felt your feelings inside of Fenrir that night. You were trying to save her. Trying to help, just like me.*

She looked down at their long-clawed paws. *I'm sorry I called you a monster just now. That was wrong. It's always been wrong, because you were never my enemy. You've only ever tried to protect me like you did right now, but it's okay. They're gone. You can go back.*

The creature whimpered. It didn't want to go back into the dark. It was scary and lonely down there.

Then stay with me, Lola offered. *Victor kept us isolated, but I say we never have to be alone again. We'll wake up our sister and be a family just like we always dreamed.*

The creature's murky vision went to the silver thread on its giant furry wrist, and Lola nodded.

She's waiting for us. But you have to give me back our body so I can get us out of here.

The creature was all right with that. Now that the mage on the floor had passed out, taking his intoxicating fear with him, it was horrified by what it had almost done. Horrified and confused. It never used to like being scary.

It's okay, Lola said. *Alberich's powers are running strong at the moment. That's bound to cause some issues, but we'd be dead right now if not for you. You saved us.*

The creature didn't agree. The hospital room was wrecked, and its sensitive nose had picked up several more humans running down the hall. It had rampaged and ruined everything. Now they were going to be caught and—

You haven't ruined anything, Lola insisted. *You did your part. Now it's time for me to do mine. I've got this. Just let me have control.*

The creature gave it gladly, its fur and claws retracting until Lola was herself again, standing in the little girl's body with her back still pressed against the freezing window.

She took a moment to clench her hands in pride. That was the second time she'd come back from her other shape on her own, but she was certain now that she could do it again. Victor had always told her that the transformation was something that needed to be held back at all costs, but that had been a lie like everything else. Her creature wasn't her enemy. They were two faces of the same magic, the same soul. That was *her* strength that had thrown the mage through the drywall, and it would protect her just as she'd protected it.

Assuming she didn't get them killed by standing around.

Lola dropped into a crouch. Even her human ears could hear the rush of people coming down the hall now, and she dove behind the hospital bed just in time as a squad of private security guards in riot gear burst through the door. The nurses ran in next, going straight for the red-coated mage who'd passed out on the floor. Everyone was shouting over one another when Lola heard someone give the order to call the Hero.

That was her cue to book it. In all the chaos, no one had noticed the little girl squatting behind the bed yet. She took advantage of the blind spot to shift back into the short nurse she'd used to get in, standing up slowly under the guise of checking Simon's vitals.

But while there were more than enough people crammed into the room for her to slip away unnoticed, she couldn't leave things like this. If Victor arrived to stories about a furry monster mauling one of his mages, Simon's plan to win his trust was doomed. She couldn't let him wake up to a bomb like that, so Lola leaned over his bed, using the privacy curtains to hide her hands as she tossed a small glob of gossamer at the ceiling.

It cost her more than she could really afford to do it. By the time she finished, her nurse, who was already questionably short, no longer had a lab coat or an ID, but at least now Simon would have a heads-up before he had to face Victor. Lola didn't know if it would be enough, but it was the best she could do. The head nurse was already on the phone with someone who sounded a lot like Jamie, signaling Lola that it was time to go.

Still pretending she was checking on Simon, Lola waited until the orderlies came in with a spinal board for the mage on the floor. As the flood of new people and equipment poured into the room, Lola took her chance and slipped out, trusting her scrubs to make her invisible as she walked past the frantic nurses' station toward the stairwell.

Chapter 6

Simon had told Lola he'd give her an hour to clear out before he woke up, but he started rising the moment she left.

Part of this was practicality. Best he could tell, he'd been in the coma for at least three weeks. It took time to put the body back in order after that sort of disruption. Mostly, though, it was impatience.

Ever since his childhood, Victor had been kicking him down. His apprenticeship had been nothing but bullying and abuse as he struggled to please a man who was only ever pleased with himself. From the first moment he'd been made to bow his head, Simon had dreamed of revenge. Revenge that, thanks to Lola, was now nearly in his reach.

How could he not leap to grab it? Lola was barely out of his death before Simon charged after her, shooting up through his soul so quickly that even Victor would have been impressed. He pulled on his magic as he climbed, drawing in power not just from the normal ambient magic of the DFZ like legal, unstained mages did, but also from the deepest reaches of himself.

That was a tough thing to do when you were already at the bottom. Now that Lola had destroyed the memory prison that separated him from his physical body, though, Simon could feel the pulse of his own blood again. He felt the strength of his bones, the slow grinding of his organs. He felt the microorganisms and complex internal ecosystems that formed the throne upon which the human consciousness sat.

But Simon was not here to sit. He came back into his body like a conqueror, seizing the quiet systems struggling to keep him alive and forcing them into full production. They screamed as he pushed, flooding his first flickers of consciousness with pain. Some parts failed to start entirely, languishing like dead meat inside him, but Simon forced them back to life, pushing his comatose body toward consciousness like a coachman flogging an exhausted team of horses up a hill.

This was the most important lesson Simon had received from his master, the technique that separated Victor and his students from all the thoughtless, crimes-of-passion blood mages the Paladins hunted down. It was the defining element of the Conrath method, the masterstroke that had kept his master alive for so many years:

Total mastery of the self.

This wasn't some cheap, self-help-book enlightenment. Victor had taught Simon how to control every aspect of his being, from the death that waited at the pit of his soul to the cells that made up his fingernails. With enough practice, a Conrath-trained blood mage could turn off pain responses from entire portions of his body, or tell his liver to filter twice as fast.

Simon didn't normally mess with such delicate internal systems, but there was no point being cautious now. He'd miss what might be his only shot at Victor if he didn't hurry, so he went in swinging, forcing his organs back into full service one by one until he was finally able to open his eyes.

The hospital room was bright but quiet. He could hear the hum of the monitors and the slow pump of the breathing machine he no longer needed. He was attempting to pull the mask off his face with his weakened fingers when he saw words glittering on the ceiling panels above him.

Made a mess, the writing said. *V's mages caught me when I came out. Got away, but they'll tell him they were attacked by a fairy monster. You'll need a good story when V comes. Damage is three spooked, one w broken back. Sorry and see you soon.*

There was no signature, but Simon didn't need one. There was no one else who used that particular shade of sparkling purple for her secret notes. The words faded as soon as he read them, leaving him staring at the white and gray of the drop ceiling. He was still contemplating what he was going to do when he heard a familiar voice in the hall.

Simon snapped his head toward the sound, cutting off his pain receptors as the sudden movement caused his stiff muscles to seize. He knew he'd regret that later, but Simon couldn't afford to be distracted. He was already sitting up in the bed, folding his thin hands over his emaciated legs as a handsome man wearing a golden sword led a troop of red-coated mages into the room.

If Simon hadn't known the sight of Victor's stain so well, he wouldn't have recognized him. His master had always covered himself in illusions, but never to this degree. He looked twenty years younger, and his skin glowed with a radiant brightness, as if he were walking under a spotlight that shone only for him.

The mages behind him were even stranger. They weren't wearing illusions, so Simon had to assume they were actually as young as they looked, but that made no sense. Every one of the six red-coated people walking behind Victor was as deeply stained as he was. They looked like they'd been doing blood magic for decades, which shouldn't have been possible for people in their twenties. Simon was still trying to figure it out when Victor stepped in front of him.

The illusion of Victor's dark eyebrows lifted when he saw his apprentice sitting up. He turned and pointed at the hallway next, signaling the oddly-stained mages to wait outside. They did so at once, bumping into each other in their rush to obey. When the last one out shut the door, Victor walked over to stand at the foot of Simon's bed, staring down at his apprentice like a hungry hawk.

"What happened?"

He pointed at the man-sized hole in the drywall. Simon took the chance to break eye contact, pretending to examine the destruction as he scanned the weirdly huge hospital room for cameras. When he saw that the only one had already been blocked with his curtain—Lola's work, no doubt—he took her ball and ran with it.

"I did," he said, looking his old master dead in the eyes.

Victor's eyebrows went up again. "*You?*"

"I was confused when I woke up," Simon lied through his teeth. "I thought the mages were threatening me, so I took control of their minds and filled their heads with monsters until they ran."

Victor scowled. "Must have been quite the vision. One of them is downstairs with three cracked vertebrae."

Simon lifted his bony shoulders in a careless shrug. "You know what a mind can do when it's properly convinced."

His master actually chuckled at that. "You always did have talent," he said, taking a seat on the end of Simon's bed. "It's the only reason I continue to put up with you, but I must say I'm surprised. Jamie was convinced you weren't going to come out this time."

"I did feel that way when I went in," Simon said, not even having to fake the bitterness in his voice. "But things look different when you're standing on death's doorstep."

"There is nothing more terrifying than death," Victor agreed, giving him a measuring look. "Does this mean you're ready to behave?"

Rather than give him an answer to dissect, Simon just bowed his head. It was the same show of submission he'd made the last time he came out of the coma, and it had the same effect.

"Wonderful," Victor said, his voice bright with malicious joy. "I do so love it when you come back to me, Simon. You're always much more agreeable after a break."

"I didn't break this time," Simon said, taking a deep breath. Here went nothing. "I'm ready."

His master went still, his blue eyes boring through the illusions covering his face. "Don't lie to me."

"It's not a lie," Simon said with real frustration. "I was sitting down there under the prison, wondering how much more I could take before my body gave up, when I realized things didn't have to be this way." He met Victor's stare with a hard glare of his own. "You always said I'd get tired of losing eventually. Well, congratulations, you were right. I'm sick of fighting the same fight over and over and never getting anywhere. I want to be on the winning side for once, so..." He bowed his head again. "Please teach me, Master."

If Victor had looked delighted before, he looked euphoric now. "You don't know how long I've waited to hear those words," he said, reaching out to seize Simon's gauze-covered hands. "You were always my greatest frustration. You had the most potential I'd ever seen in a student, and yet you insisted on squandering it. I thought I'd lost you for good this time, but the only way to unlock that prison is to submit to me entirely."

He thought a moment longer, and then he leaned forward, wrapping his arms around Simon in a fatherly embrace. "I knew you'd see it my way eventually," he whispered. "Welcome to real power."

"Thank you for waiting so long," Simon replied, forcing himself to hug the blood mage back.

"I am nothing if not patient," Victor said as he let go. "But I also didn't get this far by taking people at their word." He held out his hand. "You don't mind if I test your sincerity."

It wasn't a question, but Simon was ready for this. He took Victor's hand without hesitation, opening his mind as his master's magic flooded in.

If they'd been anybody but who they were, this was where Simon would have failed. There was no one better at searching minds than Victor, but there was no one who knew his blind spots more thoroughly than his apprentice. He came into Simon's mind like an invading army, but rather than trying to hide what had happened in the prison between Lola and his younger self, Simon shoved a different memory at him: the one from his actual past of the first time he'd submitted.

As always, the memory of that night made him feel dirty as nothing else could, but Simon didn't hesitate. He embraced the awful feeling, embellishing the old scene with new layers of greed and resentment that he was not the one looking down. Each one was an echo of the feelings he'd picked up from his master over years of servitude, but that just made them even better, because the only person Victor had never doubted was himself. All Simon had to do was mirror his own feelings back at him, and the old man accepted them without question, embracing Simon again with open arms.

"You really are ready," he said, squeezing him tight. "I always knew this day would come. That's why I tolerated your continued disobedience. I was certain my efforts would pay off in the end, and I was right." Simon felt Victor's face move below his illusions as his master broke into a grin. "I was *right!*"

"You're always right," Simon said, pulling back to meet Victor's smile with a nasty one of his own. "That's what finally did it for me. A man can only be wrong so many times before he has to accept that he's the problem. But I've realized my stupidity, and I'm eager to make up for lost time. Now, what did I miss?"

"Too much to bother repeating," Victor said, bursting into motion now that his apprentice's loyalty had been confirmed. "The important part is that I've got five thousand new blood mages who've sworn their loyalty and no time to train them."

"Five *thousand?*" Simon repeated, glancing at the red-coated figures he could see waiting just outside the room's frosted-glass door. "How did you get so many? And why isn't the DFZ crushing you?"

"A great deal has changed while you've been coming to your senses," his master explained, pacing the room grandly. "Thanks to my efforts, the world has reversed its opinion of our art. We're finally on the cusp of the golden age of blood magic I've been working toward all these years, but there are still a few hurdles that must be overcome before I can truly claim victory."

"What kind of hurdles?"

"It's more of a singular large one," Victor said casually. "For petty reasons of his own, Alberich, the Underground King, has decided he wants to kill me. I'm perfectly amenable to this since his attack will give me another chance to play the Hero, but that plan only works if I survive his assault. If it was just him alone, there'd be no question, but Alberich and his entire court have been feasting on fear for the better part of a month, which makes things more challenging."

Lola had already told Simon that much, but he still managed to look appropriately shocked. "Isn't Alberich the fairy you were working with?"

"Ours was always a marriage of convenience," Victor replied with a dismissive shrug. "It was useful in the beginning, but we're both working to build worlds in which the other has no place. So, naturally, it has come to war."

"And how do you mean to win?" Simon asked, genuinely curious. "Blood magic manipulates humans, but with the exception of the pills you made for Lola, I've never heard of it doing anything to fairies."

"The changeling's pills were actually what gave me the idea," Victor said, looking delighted by a chance to explain his brilliance. "Just like spirits and their concepts, fairies are slaves to human belief. All I had to do was spread the rumor that blood magic was their weakness, and it was done."

Simon couldn't believe it. "How did you get so many people to buy into something so absurd?"

Victor's face split into a grin. "Because the average human has no idea what blood magic actually does. They know it only as forbidden power, dark magic, which made the lie even easier. Humans are naturally self-centered. It was no stretch at all to convince them that anything so dangerous to us that it's been banned in every country must also be deadly to our enemies."

As much as he hated to admit it, Simon was impressed. Even so. "How are you *actually* going to beat them, though?" he asked. "Even with five thousand mages abusing a weakness, Alberich is a king, the biggest of his kind. You can't just go head-to-head with—"

"My dear boy," Victor interrupted with an indulgent smile, "you must learn not to question your master. There is no contingency you can imagine that I have not already foreseen and prepared for. I will, of course, be happy to explain all the details of my plan to defeat Alberich when we have more time, but now that I've responded to the hysterical calls about monsters at the hospital, I must move on to my meeting with the DFZ."

Simon didn't have to fake his surprise this time. "The DFZ?" he repeated, eyes wide. "*You* have a meeting with the spirit of the Living City?" When the other mage nodded, Simon began to sputter. "*How?* She hates blood mages."

"Maybe before," Victor replied smugly. "But everything's different now that I'm her Hero."

He said that last word as if it were the secret to everything. Simon still didn't understand, but he was sure Victor would make good on his promise to explain. His master never could pass up an opportunity to brag.

"Good luck, then," he said, remembering to bow at the last second. "What would you like me to do in the meanwhile? Should I keep resting here or—"

Victor scoffed. "I didn't teach you how to rebuild your body from nothing so you could *rest*. Did you miss the part where I have five thousand mages to train?"

Simon frowned. "Do they need training? I saw the stains on the ones you brought with you. They look like they're already quite familiar with blood magic."

"Looks can be deceiving," Victor said, reaching into his pocket. "The idiots accompanying me today didn't even know they had a death inside them before last week. The reason they look as they do now is because of these."

He held out a familiar-looking orange bottle. Simon took it gingerly, unscrewing the plastic cap to shake a blood-red pill into his hand. It looked the same as all the medicines Victor made for his clients, though not as strong as the pills he'd made for Lola. Simon didn't think a human could take one of those and survive, but he wasn't sure what this one did. The magic inside felt very complex as he rolled the pill around in his palm, feeling out the spell Victor had coiled under its shiny surface.

"Is it a teacher?"

"It's *the* teacher," Victor said proudly. "Blood magic is a challenging art. Even a gifted student like yourself took six months to master the basics. My new army doesn't have that kind of time or talent, so I took everything I needed them to know and put it in there."

He took the pill back from Simon, squeezing it between his fingers like a tick. "This pill contains a curated copy of my own skills. One dose is enough to bring even the most talentless mage up to my level, at least for a few minutes."

"But what about their own magic?" Simon asked in horror. "It takes years to build up the conditioning necessary to use the higher-level techniques without damage. If you give a bunch of untrained mages your skills, what's to stop them from accidentally obliterating their own minds?"

"Nothing," Victor said. "But that's what's so wonderful about my new recruits. They're here because they want power, and I give it to them. Honestly, the fact that my magic is so dangerous only makes them want it more. Everyone knows *real* power always comes with a price."

"But what are you going to do with them all?" Simon asked. "Unless you actually give them training, an army like that can only be used a few times before it disintegrates."

"That's not a problem," Victor replied casually. "If everything goes as planned, a few times should be plenty. The real problem is making enough doses for everyone before the Wild Hunt arrives, which is where you come in." He handed the red pill back. "Do you think you can copy that?"

Simon had no idea. Victor had never trusted him enough to let him make pills before. If he was doing so now, then Simon's lie must have worked even better than he thought. Either that, or his master really was so pressed for time that he had no choice but to delegate. Whatever the reason, it was exactly the sort of opening Simon had been looking for, and he couldn't nod fast enough.

"I won't let you down."

"Make sure that you don't," Victor said. "Even if you've seen the error of your ways, you have a lot to make up for. Jamie told me what happened when she caught you, how you denied me in favor of the changeling, who, by the way, is dead."

That lie was so bold, Simon had to remember to look surprised instead of furious. "Lola is dead?"

"Slain by Alberich's monster," Victor said with a sad sigh. "Not that it could have ended any other way. Fairies always eat their own in the end."

Just like you, was what Simon wanted to say, but he was deep in his role now, and he managed to keep his face blank. Victor, however, wasn't finished.

"You need to be on your guard," he cautioned, lowering his voice. "She was Alberich's changeling before I found her, and while our Lola is gone, the Underground King is capable of making others that look and act just like her. If one should approach you, she is the enemy. Do you understand?"

Simon nodded, not trusting himself to speak. Even knowing what a liar Victor was, it was hard to believe he could say all of that with a straight face. A good apprentice didn't speak back to his master, though, so Simon quickly moved on to less dangerous topics.

"When would you like me to start on the pills?"

"Immediately," Victor said, striding toward the door. "You couldn't have come back at a better time. I'll need eight thousand more doses before the end of the week. That should give us enough for the battle against Alberich plus extra for all the other incidents that are bound to crop up before then. Jamie will come by later to check you out of the hospital and get you set up at my new building. She'll also bring you a change of clothes. We have an image to maintain."

"Yes, Master," Simon said with a bow.

Victor waited until his head actually touched the sheets before he left, marching out of the room through the crowd of red-coated mages, who leaped to follow him.

<div align="center">~~~</div>

When Victor said Jamie would be by later, Simon had assumed he meant in the next few hours, but she didn't actually arrive until nearly midnight.

That suited Simon just fine. Even if the coma had been magically induced, forcing his body to go from complete immobility to relative functionality in less than an hour was not without its price. He was utterly exhausted, and the moment he relaxed his control over his pain responses, every muscle in his body began to complain. He was perfectly content to lie in bed while the nurses rolled him to a room that didn't have a man-sized hole in the wall.

The doctors were amazed by his recovery, which was only natural since it had literally been miraculous. The Hero had already ordered his discharge, but they still wanted him on bed rest, which, again, suited Simon just fine. He spent the time catching up on the news he'd missed over the last three weeks, which turned out to be even crazier than Lola or Victor had made it sound. No wonder his Tinker Bell had looked so wrecked.

But while the Hero seemed to be taking the human world by storm, Simon felt Victor was deluding himself about his chances against Alberich. Despite what the pro-Hero channels were desperately trying to spin, it was obvious the Wild Hunt was running roughshod over every effort to control it. Even with an army of blood mages jacked up on pills, facing the Nightmare King head-on sounded like suicide, which Simon would have been fine with if he hadn't been so convinced that his master had something else up his sleeve.

Victor might be an egomaniac, but he wasn't a fool. If he was pitting himself against such extreme odds, he must have a secret strategy, something no one else would think of to make sure he landed on top. Simon was picking apart the pills to see if the spell inside did anything extra besides just transferring Victor's expertise when Jamie finally strolled in.

"Well, well, well," the statuesque blond said in a singsong voice. "If it isn't the turncoat come crawling back. I told you you'd regret it."

"You did say that," Simon replied tightly, scooping the pills back into their orange bottle as Jamie plopped herself down on the end of his hospital bed.

It was a lot harder to keep the rage off his face with her than it had been for Victor. Simon's hatred of his master was bitter and complicated, but Jamie was a petty sellout, which made her easier to despise.

She was also not alone. There were two women in the red coats of the Hero's Army with her. Both looked like blood mages, but their souls were freshly stained, not the deep crimson he'd seen on the mages who'd accompanied Victor earlier. New recruits, then, which was perfect. Sensing when someone was using blood magic was a lot easier than doing it yourself, but these mages were so inexperienced, they didn't even flinch when Simon's magic touched them, filling their minds with a command so subtle, they probably thought it was their own idea.

See nothing.

"I still can't believe you came back," Jamie said, completely unaware of her escorts quietly leaving the room. "Victor's acting like he always knew it would happen, but he didn't see you in the diner. You were ready to die to protect that fairy monster. And here I thought I was the one with bad taste in crushes."

"You are," Simon said flatly, putting the bottle of pills aside. "Can we get on with this?"

Jamie shrugged and pulled out her phone. "Victor wants you brought in at the top level," she said, flicking her fingers through the complex augmented reality haze lists and spreadsheets that only she could navigate. "He's giving you access to his own workshop, and I've got a team working on setting up a bedroom for you just down the hall from the Black Rider's."

Simon arched an eyebrow. "He gave the Rider a room?"

"More like a closet. Not that the Rider ever has a chance to use it. Victor's been keeping him on a tighter leash than usual ever since…"

Her eyebrows wiggled suggestively as her voice trailed off, and Simon's scowl sharpened. "Ever since what? I've been in a coma for three weeks, remember?"

"Yeah, yeah," she said, snickering at him. "It's just funny. I mean, you were *so* into her. Now you're back to being a team player, and you don't even know."

"Know *what?*" he asked through clenched teeth.

Jamie leaned closer with a wicked grin. "That your precious changeling slept with the Black Rider."

Simon went still.

"I heard it happened the same night you went into the coma," Jamie went on, eating up his silence. "She didn't even wait three hours after you were gone to jump on that ride. Kind of makes you wonder if she ever cared about you at—"

"Shut up."

Jamie froze like someone had pressed her pause button. Simon fell back into his bed a second later, his forehead drenched in sweat. His body hadn't been ready for that much magic just yet, but Jamie always knew how to get under his skin.

He'd have to be more careful in the future. For now, though, the outburst worked to his advantage. He'd blasted Jamie's mind wide open, leaving the suspiciously beautiful woman empty-eyed and silent as Simon pushed himself back up.

"You are never to speak of Lola's love life to me again," he instructed, pressing on Jamie's mind until she nodded.

He didn't have to do it hard. As expected from Victor's oldest servant, Jamie's mind had been invaded so many times it was practically paved smooth. He'd have to take care to leave no trace since Victor was clearly in here constantly. For now, though, Simon settled back against his pillows to take advantage of the opportunity he'd always been too afraid to seize before.

"Tell me what really happened while I was gone."

The magic fell from his lips like bloody drops, filling his throat with bile. This was the sort of blood magic he'd always avoided. Doing it now made him feel dirtier than ever, but desperate times, desperate measures, and the fact that it was Jamie definitely made things easier.

Unfortunately, she didn't have much to say that he was interested in. He learned all about the media promotion strategy for Victor's new Hero persona as well as tons of random other information, like the fact that Jamie had turned seventy-five yesterday. He'd had no idea she was so old under the beautiful face she'd sold her soul for. But while Simon would definitely be throwing that back at her later, Jamie was infuriatingly ignorant when it came to the stuff he actually cared about.

Since she'd helped Victor pay for the movie, she didn't believe the story they'd told the rest of the world about Fenrir being the first wave of the Wild Hunt's invasion, but she didn't know anything about how the giant wolf had been created or where it had gone. The only piece of new information she was able to give him was that Victor had been furious about how the battle went. He'd passed off Fenrir's walking away from him as part of his strategy to the cameras, but Jamie had talked to him right after it happened, and his anger had terrified her. Even she could tell he'd lost, which was why she was working so hard to promote his Hero now. She'd thrown all-in with Victor. If he couldn't recover from this, she was done for.

"It's always about you, isn't it?"

"Yes," Jamie answered immediately, too locked under his control to even blink her eyes, which were now dry and red. Simon blinked them for her with a disgusted shake of his head. Truly, she and Victor deserved each other. But while this hadn't been nearly as informative as he'd wanted, there was still one piece of information he hoped to scoop up before he released her.

"I'm going to ask you one more thing," he said in the calm, monotone voice that was most effective when talking to people in this state. "You will answer to the best of your knowledge, and then you will forget we had this conversation. Understood?"

"Yes."

Simon nodded and leaned closer, pushing Jamie's mind as hard as he could without breaking it as he asked his final question.

"Where is the Rider's head?

Chapter 7

The night sky—visible from everywhere in the city now that most of the Skyways had collapsed—was lightening toward dawn by the time Lola finally made it back to Tristan's creaky hallway.

It wasn't her fault. The moment she'd cleared the mess outside Simon's hospital, she'd booked it down the icy sidewalk to Riverfest. A cab would have been faster, but she didn't have enough gossamer left to make a phone anymore. It was only a few miles in any case, but when she finally made it back to the door by the bathrooms inside the Dandy Lobster, it had opened into a broom closet.

This sent her into a panic. Lola didn't know if her doppelganger had worked too well and Tristan had moved the doors without realizing she wasn't inside, or if he *had* realized and locked her out as punishment. That felt a little harsh, but Tristan was a fairy. A gallant one, but still a trickster famous for being easily offended, and he had specifically told her not to leave.

Whatever the reason, she wasn't getting back without him. She was sneaking over to the waiters' station to call him on the restaurant's phone when Lola realized she didn't know Tristan's number. The card he'd given her with his info had been lost ages ago, and Lola hadn't thought to ask him for a new one, since, until today, she'd never left his barrow. It hadn't even crossed her mind, and now she was stuck out in the city with no way to get back.

Calling herself every type of idiot, Lola shoved her way back through the crowded restaurant and locked herself in the bathroom to focus on her gossamer. She still couldn't transfer her consciousness back to her decoy body, but nothing could stop her from feeling the magic that was her literal largest piece. She could sense the big lump she'd left behind as clearly as she could feel her tiny body's bony fingers. That should have been as good as a compass, but the whole reason she was staying with Tristan was because it was impossible to get a solid location on a fairy barrow. She knew it was somewhere to the west, but every time Lola thought she had a solid direction, her other self would slide away, leaving her spinning in circles.

She ignored the people hammering on the door for thirty minutes before she gave up. Clearly, following her magic wasn't going to work, but while she couldn't get a handle on her own power, Tristan's was another matter. The door she'd come in through was gone, but Lola doubted he'd cut himself off from the DFZ entirely. There had to be another door to his barrow here somewhere, so Lola let herself out of the bathroom to find it, waving apologetically to the now *very* long line as she ran out of the restaurant with her nose in the air to catch the scent of Tristan's sea-salt magic.

She kept her nurse outfit on the whole time. Even with what Lola felt was an unbelievably short height, people didn't notice someone in scrubs walking alone like they would've noticed a child. She'd learned the hard way back when she'd worked for Victor that kids were a total no-go in most situations, especially after dark. Even in the DFZ, people cared about that sort of thing, but a nurse out and about at weird hours was totally normal.

It worked like a charm this time, too. Lola didn't feel so much as a second glance as she walked out of the festival area into the Underground proper, sniffing like a bloodhound at every intersection as she worked her way methodically through the empty streets.

The lack of people was more unnerving than she'd expected. The DFZ was normally a hive of activity at all hours. She hadn't noticed it in the bustle of Riverfest, but once Lola got out into the more normal areas of the city, the crowds had thinned to nothing.

Lots of businesses were open, but no one was inside, and traffic was so light that she could have walked in the street. It was eerie and unnatural, but at least the lack of distraction made it easier to follow Tristan's scent.

It still took nearly all night before she found what she was looking for. Fifteen blocks west of Riverfest, down a terrifying hallway in the basement of a collapsed motel, she finally caught wind of the concentrated power that was the surest sign of a low road. Getting to it meant climbing down a stairwell covered in a waterfall of slimy black water, but to Lola's fairy nose, the mildew and grease were overwhelmed by the clean, cold scent of the northern sea. It blew most strongly from the door at the back, a stained, rust-covered metal slab that looked exactly like the sort of thing you screamed at horror movie characters not to open.

Lola was a bit nervous about opening it now. Unlike the doors she'd used earlier, this one was locked, which was a problem. Not because she couldn't get around a deadbolt, but breaking into barrows was a quick way to get yourself dropped into something unpleasant, like a troll den. She'd never found out if Tristan kept any trolls, but it'd be just her luck to stumble into one now.

She supposed she could have just knocked, but then Tristan would know for sure that she'd disobeyed him, and Lola wasn't ready to stick her head into that hornets' nest unless she absolutely had to. Besides, what was the point of being a changeling if you couldn't slip into places you weren't supposed to be? She'd already gone through the trouble of finding his door. Might as well go all the way as she transformed her pointer finger into a lock pick and got to work.

Thankfully, Tristan's disguised barrow door gave her no more trouble than a real cheap deadbolt. Barely a minute after she'd started wiggling the pins, the lock clicked, and the rusty door swung open to reveal the pristine white-and-blue hallway. Lola was still celebrating her unexpected victory when she realized the slimy black water from the hallway was rushing into the hole she'd just made. Cursing at the disgusting mess, Lola threw herself inside, slamming the door behind her before she flooded Tristan's low road. This cut off the water, but the impact caused the already rickety hallway to start swinging like a collapsing rope bridge over a ravine.

Fortunately, the entrance to Tristan's apartment was only a few feet away. Lola charged toward it, grateful yet again that she'd chosen a small, light body as the blue carpet began to sag under her feet. She could already feel the supports giving way when she burst into the barrow's living room.

The swaying stopped the moment she was through the door. She still slammed it for good measure, pressing her back against the wood as she struggled to catch the breath her gossamer body didn't actually need, but couldn't stop fighting for so long as some part of Lola considered itself human. She was still calming herself down when her panicked eyes spotted the windows.

The sweeping view of the Alaskan wilderness she'd been staring at for the last three weeks was gone, replaced by a white-sand beach lined with palm trees that were currently being lashed by a terrifying tropical storm. It didn't look like much of an upgrade, but at least Lola understood now why the doors had shifted. Tristan must have moved his barrow while she was out.

That wasn't unusual in and of itself. Tristan had moved his home dozens of times over the years she'd known him, but that was back when food had been plentiful. Not being a real fairy, Lola didn't understand the particulars of barrow magic, but even she knew that moving was expensive. If he'd done it now when food was so hard to come by thanks to Victor's bane, there had to be a reason. Probably a bad one.

Lola shed her nurse costume like a banana peel, switching back to a miniature version of her usual body as she ran past the ever-present magical banquet table—which was now laden with piles of tropical fruit and coconut pastries—toward the guest room. She threw open the door with a bang, then sagged in relief when she saw her sister in the bed like always. She was walking over to touch the girl's warm skin just to reassure herself everything was actually fine when she heard someone clear their throat.

Lola whirled toward the sound to see her doppelganger. Her other self was still sitting where Lola had left her, only instead of being slumped over the chair watching trashy TV on her phone, she was sitting up at a card table playing what appeared to be an intense game of cribbage with Tristan.

A very beleaguered-looking Tristan. The knight was dressed for battle in a full suit of armor that had probably been gleaming silver at one point. Now, though, every piece was scraped and dented, and the old Welsh longsword he'd stabbed into the floor next to his chair looked even worse. Its hilt was broken on one side, and the heavy blade was so full of notches it looked like a saw. Even the spots where it wasn't broken were pitted from what looked like acid, and the lower half was completely covered in a sticky black substance Lola recognized as dead gossamer.

"What happened to you?" she cried, running over. "Are you okay?"

"Oh, I'm fine," Tristan replied, giving her a needle-sharp look from beneath his dented helmet. "We were just enjoying a game. Weren't we, Lola?"

"I'm not enjoying this game," her doppelganger replied bluntly. "There are too many rules, it takes too long, and the stupid fairy keeps cheating."

"She's very forthcoming with her opinions," Tristan said. "Also with your location, what you intended to do there, and why you made her." He arched a dirt-smudged eyebrow. "If you're going to go to the effort of making an impostor, you might want to teach it to lie."

"I hadn't realized you were planning an interrogation," Lola said sheepishly, looking down at her small feet. "I wasn't trying to trick you. I just didn't want you to—"

"Know you'd run off to do *precisely* what I asked you not to?"

"Worry," she finished, dissolving her grumpy doppelganger into a rainbow pile of magic that she immediately pulled back into herself.

Coming back together felt even better than Lola had anticipated. She was savoring the feeling of having actual toes again instead of foot-shaped lumps when Tristan dropped his cards on the table with a sigh.

"I'm not going to bother asking how you got into an untethered low road that shouldn't have been accessible to anyone but me," he said, turning to face her. "I've long accepted that your magic doesn't obey anything like normal rules. All I want to know is did it *work*?"

"Did what work?" she asked, sinking into the Lola-shaped depression her copy had left in the padded chair.

"Don't be cute," he warned, propping his elbows on the card table to glare at her properly. "I came in to ask for a dream to replace my lost gossamer and ended up chatting with your oh-so-charming copy for an hour. How did you even make her, anyway? That was a true conjuration. I didn't know your gossamer had gotten *that* good."

"Being away from Victor does wonders," Lola replied, puffing up at the unexpected praise. "And I had to do something with all the magic I was leaving behind. A copy seemed like good cover, though I mostly made her because I didn't want to leave my sister alone."

She glanced longingly at the girl on the bed. Tonight was the longest they'd been apart since Lola had ripped her out of Alberich's golden bed at the bottom of Fenrir's pit. She'd hoped the change would trigger something, but her sister looked exactly the same as she had when Lola left, still quiet as a corpse beneath the guest bed's fluffy comforter.

"Well," Tristan said, leaning back in his chair, "Seeing as you're here sighing over your pet human and not mounted on a spike in front of Victor's new office tower, your ruse must have worked at least a little. Did you see the Rider at all, or were you able to give him the slip?"

"Definitely not the slip," Lola said, looking down at the bad hand of playing cards her double had left on the table when she'd vanished. "I left as much of my magic behind as I could, but the Rider still found me in under five minutes. The only reason I'm not toast is because he was able to wiggle around Victor's kill order on a technicality."

"He got around a direct order?" Tristan looked impressed for a moment before his scowl snapped back into place. "Good for him, but I'm very disappointed in you, Lola-cat. I know you're fundamentally incapable of following directions. Normally, I'd say that's your best feature, but this is serious. You know what we're up against. Did I not *specifically* tell you not to give the blood mage any more weapons?"

"I was trying to *take* his weapons," Lola said, slumping into her chair. "I didn't whittle my gossamer down to a nubbin and risk the Rider for kicks. I was trying to rescue Simon."

Tristan's eyebrows shot up. "The blood mage's apprentice? He's still alive?"

Lola nodded.

"And?"

"And I don't want to talk about it."

The fairy gave her a scathing look, but Lola just slumped harder. She really didn't want to discuss what had happened, and not just because she was still mad at Simon for staying with Victor instead of coming home with her. She didn't want to tell Tristan because his queen was counting on the Hero to weaken Alberich. If the fairies knew Simon was planning to betray his old master, they might decide he was a risk to their strategy, and even in her current skeletal state, Morgan wasn't someone Lola wanted to drop on Simon's head.

"What about you?" she asked, blatantly changing the subject. "Why did you move your barrow? And why do you look like you just got back from losing a war?"

"Oh, this is nothing," Tristan said flippantly, brushing a smear of dead gossamer off the giant dent in his silver shoulder plate. "You should see the other guys."

Lola gave him a serious scowl, and he settled back into his chair with a wince. "I was searching for Alberich's head."

"Isn't he already wearing it?" Lola asked. "I mean, I know fairy heads are normally super-secret, but Alberich has been galloping his Hunt in front of the entire world for weeks. That's a lot of scrutiny to endure, so I just assumed…"

Her voice trailed off at Tristan's beleaguered look. "Trust me," he said. "If Alberich was wearing his head, you'd know. You're seeing the Nightmare King at his finest thanks to an endless feast of human fear. People believe in him again, so he doesn't have to worry about being melted out of the sky like you or I would, but this is actually one of the better-case scenarios. When the Underground King puts on his head, that's when we should *really* be afraid."

"So why hasn't he done it?" Lola asked. "Not that he needs the extra power since he's already riding circles around everyone, but Alberich never struck me as the holding-back type."

"He's not," Tristan agreed, finally removing his battered helmet. "But a fairy's head is a double-edged sword. Wearing it allows us to reach our fullest potential, but it also gives the enemy something to swing at. Normally, gossamer is immune to pretty much everything except disbelief. We can't be stabbed, shot, crushed, burned, or blown to bits. We also can't be drained of magic or banished like spirits. Dragon fire does sting a smidge, but only when they're using their life's fire, and I've yet to meet the dragon who was willing to burn itself to a crisp to defend a few mortals."

"The blood magic bane hurts," Lola pointed out, rubbing her arms at the memory.

"And that's why it's such a big deal," Tristan agreed. "It gives humanity a weapon that can actually hurt us, a fact Victor Conrath is currently leveraging to the hilt. But even if his cursed magic shattered every fairy on the planet, Victor could never destroy us fully unless he found our heads. They're the only way true fairies can *actually* die, which is why Alberich will never put his on no matter how powerful it makes him. Even he's not that reckless."

"If that's the case, how'd you get so banged up?" she asked, frowning at the trickle of rainbow gossamer blood leaking down from his temple. "If you weren't trying to take Alberich's head off his shoulders, how did you get those injuries?"

"From his barrow."

"Wait, you actually got in?" Lola said, sitting up. "I thought fairy barrows were impenetrable strongholds!"

Tristan gave her a flat look. "Says the changeling who just broke into mine."

"Exactly," she said. "I'm a changeling. Nothing's ever known what to do with me, but you're a real-deal fairy. If you could just walk into Alberich's barrow this whole time, why didn't you do it sooner?"

"Because I don't enjoy being eaten," Tristan snaped, lifting his arm to show her the giant teeth marks that had turned the delicate plates of his silver armor into crushed scrap metal. "Just because I can't technically die so long as my head is safe doesn't mean I can't be brought right up to the edge. The only reason I risked it is because Alberich and his court were distracted by cities full of terrified humans. My queen and I thought it'd be a quick search through an empty house, but Alberich had a lot more monsters left over from the old days than we anticipated, and even I can get outnumbered."

Lola looked at his dented armor with new horror. "How many did you fight?"

"Too many," Tristan said, tilting his bleeding head toward the window where the tropical storm was still scouring the unfamiliar beach. "I had to move my barrow to the other side of the planet just to get away, and for zero reward, I might add. I barely managed to make it halfway down before Alberich's monsters forced me out, and I didn't catch so much as a whiff of his head."

"But you *do* think it's there," Lola confirmed.

"Without a doubt," he said fiercely. "A barrow is a fairy's absolute domain. There is nowhere safer, which is why I took the risk. A very expensive risk, it turned out."

He conjured a white handkerchief to wipe the blood off his temple, but Lola was tapping her fingers on the table.

"Could you try again?"

"Not on your life," the knight huffed. "Do you not see me bleeding?"

"I didn't mean right now," she said quickly. "But getting a fairy's head means you control that fairy, right? That's what Victor did to Morgan."

"It'd be much more than that," Tristan assured her. "For all his delusions of godhood, Victor's only human. All he could do with Morgan's head was lock it in a box. If my queen got her hands on Alberich's head, she'd eat it in one gulp, take command of the Wild Hunt, and this whole idiocy would be over."

That was grislier than Lola had imagined, but she shouldn't have been surprised. All fairies, even Tristan, got their power from eating other fairies. Lola normally found that gross in the extreme, but she would have paid money to watch Morgan eat Alberich right now, and from the gleam in his eyes, so would Tristan.

"Want me to try going in?" she offered. "You've seen how good I am at sneaking into barrows. His monsters attacked you because you're an invader, but I'm one of them. They probably wouldn't even notice me."

"Absolutely not," Tristan said, pointing at his battered armor. "What part of how I look right now makes you think this is something you want to do?"

"Want has nothing to do with it," Lola said angrily. "You just told me that if we steal Alberich's head and feed it to Morgan, we could turn this whole thing around. Without the Wild Hunt, Victor's got nothing to fearmonger against. People will stop listening to him, which means his Hero act will stop working, including the bane. If we move fast enough, we might even be able to stop this before Alberich reaches the DFZ!"

Tristan looked appalled. "Why would you want to do that? Keeping the Wild Hunt from biting our heads off is one thing, but don't you want Alberich to kill Victor?"

Not if it meant Valente died, too.

"The only thing I want is for all of this to stop," Lola said, reaching out to grab his hands. "Don't you see? Alberich's head is our ticket out of this mess! If you know it's in his barrow, let's go get it!"

Her hopes rose like a rocket as she spoke. This was the solution she'd been searching for. If she could get her hands on the king's head, the Wild Hunt would be over, which meant no one had to die! There'd be no fight for Valente to throw, and while Simon would still be stuck, Lola was sure Victor wouldn't kill him until he'd completely given up on his apprentice embracing his dark ways, which he never would because Victor's entire schtick was that he *never lost.*

That was what made this plan so perfect. She'd already accepted that she couldn't beat Victor at his own game, but she *could* remove his chance to play. Heroes were useless if they had no one to fight. It was the same trick she'd pulled when she'd walked Fenrir away, only better, because this time she could actually save people! She was feeling dizzy from all the possibilities when Tristan burst her bubble.

"You can't sneak to Alberich's barrow."

"*What?*" Lola cried. "Why not?"

"Because you're made from his gossamer," the knight explained, giving her a look that said this should be obvious. "He'd freeze you before you even found the door."

Given how many times Alberich had appeared out of nowhere and done just that, Lola couldn't say he was wrong, but there was no way she was throwing in the towel yet. "Then I'll feed you dreams until you're well enough to go back in," she said stubbornly. "We can't give up!"

"That's not your call to make," the knight said firmly, extricating his fingers from her grasp. "I serve my queen, and she's already decreed that we were only trying this once. We always knew it was a long shot, but while I appreciate your willingness to be my battery, I can't allow myself to get this injured again. Alberich's Hunt will be arriving any day now. If I'm not in fighting shape when it does, we lose all hope of beating him."

"You won't have to beat him if we get his head," Lola argued, clasping her hands together. "*Please*, Tristan! Just give it one more—"

"*No*," he said sharply, his voice harder than Lola had ever heard it. "I know what a coup getting his head would be. That's why I risked myself in the first place, but it *didn't work*. Alberich's Hunt might be riding through the sky, but his Underground Kingdom is still enormous and filled with monsters, including ones big enough to eat me down until I'm nothing but a head myself. I won't make that sacrifice. Not when I finally have my queen back, and not for a fear-drunk fool like Alberich."

Lola dropped her eyes. She couldn't blame Tristan for not wanting to die over this, but it was just so bitter. She hadn't even realized Alberich *had* a head twenty minutes ago, but now she felt like she'd lost everything all over again. She tried telling herself that it was fine, that nothing had really changed, but her mouth still tasted like ash when Tristan finally hauled himself out of his chair.

"I have to go to bed," he said, yanking his black-tarred sword out of the carpet so he could use it as a crutch. "Please don't leave the barrow again."

Lola went still. Tristan had told her once that fairies only slept when they were on death's door. If he was going to bed, he must be even more injured than he looked.

That wouldn't do. Tristan was her friend, not to mention his barrow was the only thing keeping the Rider from hauling her back to Victor. Fortunately, this was the one problem Lola did have the power to fix. Her dreams were fairy superfood. That was the whole reason Tristan had come in and discovered her doppelganger in the first place. But when she opened her mouth to make the offer, Tristan was already shaking his head.

"Not to sound ungrateful, but I'm afraid I must decline," he said, stabbing his sword into the floor again to push himself to his full height. "Even wounded fairies have their standards, and given the way you're looking, I don't think you have any dreams I'd enjoy eating at the moment."

Lola flinched like she'd been burned. It wasn't that she didn't understand his logic—one of the reasons she'd always liked Tristan was because he *didn't* feed on fear and misery—but the rejection still stung. She knew she wasn't exactly a ray of sunshine at the moment, but Tristan didn't look like he was in any state to be turning down food.

Maybe that was the reason, though. Tristan had always said her dreams were peaceful, but between losing her chance at Alberich's head and her worry over Valente, Simon, her sister, and everything else, Lola's mind was anything but. For all she knew, eating her dreams in this state would make Tristan's injuries worse, not better. He was just looking out for himself by turning her down, but that didn't make her feel like any less of a failure as the knight limped out of the room.

"Seems like no one wants my help tonight," she muttered, turning back to her sister. "But I am going to save you. I don't care how long it takes. I *will* figure out how to wake you up, and then we're going to work together to make this right. We're going to save everyone, just you wait and see."

She finished with a smile so forced it was more like a grimace, but her sister remained as still as ever on the mattress, her breaths rising and falling silently below Buster, who was sleeping in a ball on her chest.

Chapter 8

The Black Rider stood in the wreckage of what had been a perfectly nice hotel room in Troy, Michigan, his reflective visor flicking in and out of the light from broken fixture swinging overhead. At his feet was a journalist, one of the thousands who'd flooded the ring of suburbs around the demolished DFZ since Fenrir's rampage. The difference was that *this* journalist had had the poor judgment to write a piece critical of the Hero. Now, he was a stain on the hotel carpet, another victim of the Rider's reign of terror.

Valente turned his helmet away from the sight. He couldn't remember how he'd gotten to this particular room or how the man had died. That happened sometimes when he fought his oaths. He could refuse to come along for the ride, but his body always obeyed, leaving him blinking in the aftermath of atrocities he didn't remember committing.

He wasn't sure which was worse, knowingly doing Victor's dirty work or waking up to the evidence, but he hated himself harder each time it happened. He'd killed more people in the past three weeks purging the Hero's critics than he ever had back when Victor was merely a blood mage.

The Black Rider's rampage would have been major news even outside the DFZ if the Hero and the Wild Hunt hadn't been dominating every headline. But just because the talking heads weren't talking about him didn't mean people weren't paying attention. Valente had already noticed that no one whipped out their phones for selfies when he rode by anymore. These days, they mostly just ran, usually screaming for the Hero to save them. The same "Hero" who kept his Rider busy 24-7.

If only they knew, Valente thought bitterly, stepping away from the red wetness that was rapidly spreading through the carpet. No one would follow Victor if they could see what he really was. But while the evidence was certainly there, the voices willing to call it out were growing fewer and fewer thanks to Jamie's PR push and Victor's media allies.

That pressure was enough to kill most stories, and for those reporters who still managed to slip a scoop through the cracks, there was the Black Rider. He paid a visit to anyone who dared speak the truth, keeping the Hero's image bright and shiny in the public's eyes. Their glorious savior, just as Victor liked it.

Shaking his helmet in disgust, the Rider went into the tiny bathroom for a towel to scrub the blood off his clothes. He always cleaned up before leaving a job, but his old habit was just that these days—a habit—because no matter how hard he scrubbed, the blood no longer came off.

That was only natural. His leather riding suit wasn't actually clothing unless he was wearing his head. Without it, his body was just a shadow. All shadows were cast by something, though, and Valente knew from the dark blotches he could see even against the black leather of his gloves that he was stained beyond redemption.

His only comforts were that it'd be over soon, and that Lola wasn't around to see him like this. Valente could scarcely stand to look at himself, turning away from the bathroom mirror as he removed his empty helmet to clean the blood that had dripped into the visor. He was vowing to stay in his head and make it less messy next time when the summons roared into his mind.

Come!

The command landed so hard he stumbled. He caught himself on the bathroom counter and pulled out his phone, which was buzzing wildly as a stream of text messages came in.

Get back here now.

My office, front receiving room.

Don't be seen.

Valente put his helmet back on with a silent sigh. This was the third emergency summons he'd gotten this week. For an all-powerful Hero, this Victor sure seemed to need the Rider's services a lot more than the old one. He was pushier, too, yanking the oaths in Valente's mind to send his Black Rider scrambling out of the hotel room and into the hallway full of terrified people peeking through the cracks in their doors to see what the screaming had been about.

Their stares dug into Valente's corrupted gossamer, but everyone believed in the Black Rider these days, so he barely felt it. He was just grateful no one tried to stop him as he ran down the fire escape and hopped onto the silent motorcycle he'd summoned by the exit, tearing off through the rows of emergency shelters Homeland Security had set up in the hotel parking lot.

Like everywhere that touched the DFZ's border, Troy, Michigan, was crammed with refugees who'd lost their homes to Fenrir. Even with his magical bike, the streets were barely passable, forcing Valente to ride on sidewalks and over parked cars. The moment he crossed the city limit, though, a ramp rose out of nowhere to meet him.

Valente took it with a heavy heart. He still didn't understand how things had ended up this way, but the Living City absolutely belonged to Victor now. Even with fallen highways still lying on top of her neighborhoods and only a quarter of her population back in their homes, she always found time to make straight roads for the Hero's servants. The shortcuts were the only reason Valente had been able to keep up with Victor's increasingly insane demands, but he still felt bad every time he took one. It just didn't seem right that a spirit as free as the Detroit Free Zone should be bent to Victor's will.

She'd even built him a skyscraper. None of the other reconstruction had made it past the old Skyways yet, but the Hero's Tower shot out of the ruined city like a gleaming, golden sword. It was as tall as the Dragon Consulate used to be, but much more heavily fortified. The walls were made from solid granite covered in gold-painted steel plates, and every window opened so that the mages inside could attack the Wild Hunt in the sky if needed. There was even a giant square out front specifically designed so the Hero could battle the city's enemies without causing further damage, though it was mostly used for Victor's press conferences and greeting his adoring public.

There were a lot of them. The streets around Hero's Tower had been turned into a tent city for Victor's die-hard fans, and not just the ones who thought they owed him their lives. The grateful crowd was still there, but Victor's constant preaching about no longer bowing to spirits and dragons had won over a new sort of follower. The kind that packed his square with HUMANITY FIRST signs and anti-dragon symbols that hadn't been seen since Algonquin ruled the city.

Even this early on an icy November morning, the crowd outside Victor's tower was already two blocks deep. That would have been a problem for the Rider, but as ever, the city put the Hero's needs first. Valente barely caught a glimpse of the people waving signs before the ramp he'd been following suddenly dipped underground, leading him down an orange-lit tunnel that definitely hadn't been there yesterday.

The new ramp dropped him straight into the tower's underground parking deck. He vanished his bike as soon as he arrived, striding up the stairs that connected the parking level to the elegant lobby. This put him shoulder to shoulder with the crowd of red-coated mages that seemed to get thicker every day. But unlike normal DFZ citizens who cowered at the sight of the

Black Rider, Victor's minions didn't even notice him. Their eyes passed right over, nudged away by the pills that gave them their power. They would have walked right into his chest if Valente hadn't been so quick on his feet, dancing through the packed lobby to the key-carded, warded elevator that would take him straight to Victor's office on the top floor.

The command to get to his master's side was pounding through him like a migraine by the time he finally made it to the penthouse level. He was tempted to charge straight in just to make it stop, but he'd been ordered not to let himself be seen, so he kept to the secret paths, slipping through the hidden door just off the elevator lobby to the secret security room on the other side of the two-way gilt mirror that looked into Victor's office.

As he stepped up to the glass, Valente saw why his master had yanked his leash so hard. In the palatial room on the other side of the mirror, Victor was sitting at his desk in front of the window that overlooked his fawning masses in the square, and standing before him were two dragons in their human forms and a middle-aged human woman with gray-streaked brown hair.

Like any resident of the DFZ, Valente recognized the shorter dragon immediately. With his bright green eyes and boyish face, it could only be the Peacemaker, the famous Dragon of Detroit. That meant the other green-eyed dragon next to him—the giant one with an equally enormous sword strapped to his back—must be Justin, his fearsome brother-slash-bodyguard.

The Rider took a step back at the sight. Whatever his master might think, Valente was under no illusion that he could take a dragon, much less two. The human he was less sure about. She had to be a mage of some sort given all the spellwork on her clothing, but Valente was too busy staring at the dragons to pay her much attention. He could already feel Victor's grip on the magic that connected them telling him to get ready, but it wasn't the dragons who moved first. It was the woman.

"We will not tolerate this," she said, continuing what was clearly an ongoing complaint. "I don't know how you tricked the DFZ into taking your side, but you don't fool us. The Merlin Council doesn't exist just to protect humanity. We also protect the spirits from tyrants like you! Your proposal to ban all non-blood mages from the city is completely insane. No one will stand for it!"

The cat on her shoulder meowed in agreement, which was a shock since Valente hadn't realized there *was* a cat until that moment. He still wasn't entirely sure, because while the thing with its tail wrapped around the woman's neck was definitely cat-shaped, its white body was semitransparent, like a ghost's.

Victor certainly didn't like it. The moment the cat moved, he'd grabbed Valente's oaths like an emergency brake. But while his grip was hard enough to choke his knight, Victor's voice was, as ever, perfectly composed.

"I am not yours to tolerate, Archmage Novali," he replied dryly. "As for how I 'tricked' the DFZ, I assure you I did no such thing. Everyone knows that the soul of a city is her people, and the people's hearts belong to me."

He turned in his chair as he spoke, waving at the window overlooking the chanting crowd in the square below. "I'm their Hero," he said smugly. "The man who saved their city and the entire world, and the only one they trust to do it again. The Wild Hunt is on its way to the DFZ as we speak. So far, I'm the only mage whose magic has proven effective against the Nightmare King's forces. Do you really need to ask why the Living City chose me over you?"

"She didn't *choose* anything!" the archmage yelled. "You hijacked her! You think I believe it's coincidence that you just 'happened' to show up with your golden sword not two weeks after her Merlin—her sworn *protector*—died? The Fenrir movie had been out for months! If the Wild Hunt was going to launch an attack, why didn't they do it in the summer, when Fenrir's popularity was at its height? Why did they oh-so-conveniently hold off their invasion until the DFZ was at her weakest?"

Victor arched the Hero's perfect eyebrow. "Are you implying that I somehow triggered this heinous attack?"

The archmage didn't reply, but a wind began to rise in the room. It blew right through the walls, so cold that even Valente's icy gossamer shivered. Even Victor leaned back in his chair a fraction when the woman with the ghost cat on her shoulder stepped forward.

"Merlins are the voices and defenders of the Mortal Spirits," she said in a voice as cold as the wind. "I don't know if you had a direct hand in this or merely seized an opportunity, but Fenrir wasn't the only thing that attacked the city that night. You waited until the DFZ was alone and took advantage of her weakness. Now, you're kicking out the rest of us to isolate her further, but we will not let you! The Merlin Council *will* do its duty!"

The wind was howling by the time she finished, but Victor didn't raise his voice at all.

"That is not for you to decide," he said, smiling placidly as if the furious archmage were just another unruly client. "There's a whole world of spirits out there who I'm sure are happy to take your orders, but this is the DFZ. She's always done things her own way, and she's clearly decided she has no more need for you."

"Only because you rabble-roused," the archmage snarled, but before she could get going again, the Peacemaker raised his hand.

"I can't speak for spirits or mages," the dragon said in a surprisingly soft voice, "but my pact with the DFZ isn't something that can be revoked by changing her mind. You've convinced her to flip her laws completely, allowing blood mages while banning every other sort of magic, but you can't make her ban dragons.

Our allegiance was sworn on my life's fire. This is *my* territory, Mr. Conrath. Your human rules have no bearing over dragon affairs."

"Tell that to the city you let down," Victor snapped, his temper coming out at last as he rose from his seat. "She trusted you, her *Peacemaker,* to defend her peace, and you failed. You couldn't do anything to stop Fenrir. I could. That's why I'm the Hero, and you're just another monster."

"Watch your tongue, mortal," growled the tall dragon with the big sword.

"You'd do better to say that to *him,*" Victor said, pointing at the Peacemaker, who looked angrier than Valente had ever seen him, even in the pictures that were supposed to make him look scary. "The age of dragons and monsters is over. It's humanity's time now. We're the ones who make the Sea of Magic churn and create the spirits you're all so fond of speaking for. The only reason any of you have power is because we allow it, so maybe it's time for the serpents to watch their snouts. Don't you agree, archmage?"

The woman clenched her hands into fists as the cat on her shoulder arched its back. "I will *never* agree with such a self-serving, egomaniacal—"

She cut off when the Peacemaker caught her arm. A second later, Valente felt why. The whole tower had started to vibrate, shaking the metal plates that paneled the outside like a rattlesnake's tail. Valente hadn't been a mage even before he stopped being human, but he still felt the warning loud and clear. Everybody did, and Victor's smile grew insufferable.

"That's right," he said, his blue eyes shining. "This is *my* city now, so unless you wish to face the DFZ's wrath, I suggest you remove yourselves from her presence." He sat back down in his chair with a smirk. "Thank you for visiting. I shall take your opinions under consideration."

The big dragon tightened his grip on his sword. The terrifying wind was still howling, sending chills through Valente like someone was stomping on his grave. Victor's hand tightened on their link as the tense silence stretched, and for a moment, Valente was sure his master was about to order him to charge right through the glass.

He was already planning to take the mage down first. She was the smallest target, but arguably the most dangerous. The dragons would just smash him, but that wind felt like it could erase him from existence. He wasn't looking forward to any of it, but at least he didn't think he would survive. That was a win by Valente's current rock-bottom standards, but just when the doomed fight seemed a foregone conclusion, the Peacemaker turned and started walking away.

"The DFZ has been my friend, home, and ally for twenty-five years," he said, not even bothering to look back at Victor as he marched toward the door. "I will not let you goad me into fighting her. We will find another way, but this is not over, blood mage."

"That's where you're wrong, little dragon," Victor said. "It's been over for weeks. But do give my regards to your mother. Unlike you, she can read the shifts in power, and she's been quite eager to do business with the new Hero of humanity."

It was hard to see from behind the two-way mirror, but Valente could have sworn the Peacemaker's jaw twitched at that. He didn't say anything, though. Just walked out of the room.

His furious-looking brother followed a few seconds later, stomping and spitting smoke the whole way. The archmage left last, glaring at Victor with the fury of something much bigger than herself. In the end, though, she followed the others, slamming the huge door to leave Victor alone in his office.

He slumped onto his desk as soon as it was over. Behind the mirror, Valente paused. He'd never seen his master look so spent, but he'd never seen Victor go face-to-face with two dragons and an archmage before, either.

"Stop lurking and get in here."

The command landed hard enough to make Valente jerk. The pain that followed made him miss the days when Victor would just text his orders. He never used to hammer like that for every little thing.

Valente supposed he'd brought that on himself when he'd become "disobedient." His only regret on that score was that he hadn't done it sooner, but he wasn't sure how much more of this he could take. Victor had already pried him out of his hiding place and marched him into the room, forcing every movement until Valente's gossamer was quaking.

"Fetch my pills."

Valente turned and walked to the safe set into the opposite wall, his bloodstained gloves moving silently as he opened the key-coded lock to reveal an orange prescription bottle with Victor's name on it. This, too, was new. He'd never seen his master take his own pills, but Victor looked as desperate as Lola used to. He actually got up from his desk to meet his Rider halfway, snatching the bottle out of his hands like an impatient child.

"We need to move faster," he muttered as he ripped off the cap and tapped a pill—a golden one, not red—into his palm. "The mob's love is strong but fickle. Everything *must* be in place by the time Alberich arrives. If we miss this window, I won't have enough time left to line up another."

Valente went still at that, and his master sneered. "Don't get excited," he ordered as he slapped the golden pill into his mouth. "You tied your fate to mine a long time ago. I held up my end of the bargain. I freed your family, or what was left of them. Now it's your turn."

He paused to pour himself a glass of water from the carafe that was always on his desk, and then he went back to the window, looking more like the dazzling Hero with every step as the golden pills worked their magic.

"Miracles don't come for free," he said, taking a sip from his glass as he watched the crowds piling up in the square below. "You used to understand that. You used to be grateful. But the changeling ruined you as she ruins everything. It's the nature of her cursed kind. They do nothing but show you what you can never have, but you should know better than anyone that dreams change nothing."

He glanced back at his Rider with a Hero's smile. "There is no escape for you. Your only future is at my side, so I suggest you put more effort into helping me ascend. Because if I fail, you'd best believe I'm taking you down with me."

He narrowed his eyes to sharpen the words, but Valente did nothing. His master often threatened him like this, never realizing that the Rider didn't fear death as he did. If Valente had had his head and the voice that came with it, he would have told Victor to hurry up and do it. That sort of comment might have ended him up like poor tongueless Orlando, though, so Valente embraced the silence, staring at his master with the Rider's eyeless gaze until Victor turned away.

"Jamie's already sent the next list of targets to your phone," he said, sliding his pill bottle into the pocket of his red jacket. "Try to do a better job with this batch. I know the Hero's hard to compete with, but you need to catch more headlines. Sending a message doesn't work if no one reads it."

Valente didn't know how he could be more terrifying than he already was. But the orders were still coming in at maximum strength, and his body bowed before he could stop it, spinning

Valente toward the door like a leaf on a string. But just before his consciousness was overwhelmed by the knight's compulsion to obey, Victor stopped him short.

The Rider jerked to a halt. Then he spun again, his body bolting back to its master's side. He made it with less than a second to spare before the door opened, and Simon walked in.

If Valente had had his head and the eyes inside it, he would have sworn they were broken. The last time he'd seen Simon was when he'd visited his house with Lola. Later, when everything was over, he'd heard that Victor had locked his apprentice in a mental prison that had only two exits: total obedience or death.

Valente had been certain the mage would choose death, yet here he was, walking right into Victor's office like he belonged. His face was gaunt as a skeleton's, but his dark eyes were as sharp as ever as he placed a red pill on Victor's desk.

"That was quick," Victor said, sounding impressed despite himself as he picked up the pill to examine it. "When did you arrive?"

"Just now," Simon said, not even looking at the Rider as he took a seat on the edge of Victor's desk to spare his emaciated body the effort of standing. "Jamie was late getting me discharged, so I made that one in the hospital and thought it'd be better to bring it straight to you. What do you think?"

"Not bad," Victor admitted, rolling the crimson pill between his fingers. "But I expected no less from my protégé. It's still not quite right, though."

Simon scowled. "What's wrong about it?"

"It'd be easier to show you myself," Victor said. "Follow me to the workshop. I'll guide you through it step-by-step."

"I look forward to the lesson," Simon replied with a humble bow. "Thank you, master."

Valente was so shocked he couldn't even move to follow Victor as the two mages started toward the door. It just didn't seem possible that Simon—*Simon,* the man Lola had worked herself to tears trying to save—would be acting like one of Victor's bootlicking mages. He was still staring stupidly when Victor glanced back at him over his shoulder.

"You are dismissed," he told the Rider casually. "I will be with my apprentice for most of the morning. I expect you to have cleared your list by the time I contact you again."

If Valente hadn't already been speechless, that would have done him in. Fortunately, his body, ever obedient, nodded for him, keeping his vision locked on the ornate carpet until his master and his apparently reformed apprentice vanished through the door separating Victor's penthouse from the normal, non-secret elevators.

Chapter 9

Lola spent the next three days trying to reach her sister.

It wasn't any more successful than the last three weeks, but she was so desperate to save *someone* that she threw herself all-in. She tried shaking. She tried yelling. She tried dousing them both in ice water. She tried sleeping with her body pressed up against her sister's to see if she could spark a shared dream like the one she'd had the night she'd slept with Valente. She used her gossamer to turn the entire room into a replica of Fenrir's pit to see if she could re-create the circumstances that had let her slip into her sister's mind the first time.

She tried everything she could think of, and none of it worked.

"I don't get it," Lola moaned, flopping down on the bed beside her sister, who still hadn't moved so much as a finger. "I've stuck my magic so far down her throat that I've tickled her toes, but she doesn't even twitch." She pressed her face deeper into the guest room's ridiculously soft sheets. "Maybe Alberich really did eat her soul."

"That's not how it works and you know it," Tristan said from the chair in the corner, where he was drinking a mug of something green and foul-smelling that he claimed was an old fairy cure-all. "Human dreams are like milk. You can suckle at the teat until it runs dry, but you can't climb inside the udder and drink milk that hasn't been made yet."

Lola grimaced at the disgusting comparison, but she was glad Tristan was up and about. This was the first time she'd seen him since he'd gone to sleep after his raid on Alberich's barrow. He still looked exhausted, but he'd traded his banged-up armor for a white leather bomber jacket, sheer white mesh tank top, skin-tight acid-washed jeans, and a pair of silver-studded boots, which seemed like a sign of recovery.

"She's probably just dug down deep," he said, holding out his mug so one of his low creature servants—who looked like frogs wearing top hats today—could refill it with another ladle of sludgy green liquid. "She's spent her entire life in a magical sleep. Perhaps she doesn't understand yet that waking up is an option?"

Lola had worried about that as well. "Have you ever seen this happen before?"

The fairy pursed his lips. "Depends on what you mean by 'this.' Preserving humans by enthralling them in enchanted slumber used to be common practice. I once kept a princess asleep for a hundred years to help her avoid a particularly upsetting marriage, but I've never heard of putting someone under as a baby and keeping them that way for their entire life."

"Why not?" Lola asked bitterly. "Seems like it works pretty well."

"But it doesn't," Tristan insisted. "The whole point of keeping humans around is to feed off their dreams. Enchanted sleeps are normally used to suspend a mortal's life until you're ready to use it, kind of like putting your dinner in the freezer. But a human who's been asleep her entire life would be useless." He nodded at the girl buried under the blankets. "Even if the body grows, a mind that's been kept isolated in slumber is basically still a newborn, and baby dreams hardly count as food."

Lola pushed herself up with a sigh. "Maybe that's what's wrong. What if she's not waking up because she's stuck as a baby?"

"We'd absolutely hear something if that was the case," Tristan said. "Have you met a human infant? They're not what anyone would call quiet."

"I'd be happy if she started screaming at this point," Lola said, rubbing her hands over her face. "If she doesn't snap out of this soon, she won't be able to resist Alberich when he shows up to take her back."

"I don't think that's going to make much of a difference," Tristan said darkly, staring into his cup. "Awake or asleep, no human is a match for the Nightmare King. I just hope Victor really is as dangerous as you're always insisting. We're going to need him to take a very big bite out of Alberich if any of us are to have a chance at surviving this."

The bleakness in his voice made Lola wince. Tristan hadn't exactly been peppy since he'd come back from his disastrous search for Alberich's head, but she'd never heard him sound so worried. Not that any of them had reason to be optimistic at the moment.

Morgan had been out hunting on her own since Alberich had told them he was on his way, so Lola wasn't sure what her status was, but unless the queen had eaten enough to ramp herself to godhood in the past three days, it wasn't looking great. She hadn't heard a peep from Simon since she'd left his death, either, but she'd spotted him standing behind Victor during the Hero's evening address, so his plan to worm his way back into their master's trust must still be a go.

That was good, Lola supposed, but even knowing that Simon was setting him up for a backstab, she didn't like that Victor was getting more help. He certainly didn't need it. Thanks to the news media's breathless coverage of everything Hero, Lola knew Victor's blood mage army was getting bigger every day. The US, the dragons, and the Merlin Council were making all kinds of noises about curbing his rogue military power, but so far as Lola could tell, no one was actually *doing* anything. Meanwhile, the situation in the city was deteriorating by the day. Victor's followers controlled practically the whole DFZ now, but the one

Lola was really worried about was Valente.

Even the Black Rider couldn't grab headlines from the Hero, but the few stories Lola had managed to catch whenever she was forced to take a break from beating her head against the silent wall of her sister were insane. They made Valente sound like an absolute monster. She wasn't sure if there was any truth to the bloody tales or if Victor was just trying to give people more reasons to cling to his Hero, but she hated it. She hated all of this.

Her already clenched fists twisted tighter in the bedsheets. She'd focused all of her efforts on her sister because she loved her and because she was the only person Lola could still reach. But she'd pushed harder than she'd known she could these past three days, and it hadn't changed a thing. She still felt just as doomed as she had when Alberich first showed up, or when Valente told her he was planning to die, or when Simon insisted on going back to Victor. The only difference was that, back then, she'd still had time to work on a fix. Now, though, Lola had nothing.

If *only* they'd been able to get their hands on Alberich's head, but that ship was long sailed. The only reason she hadn't completely lost hope was because Simon was still out there. If he could find the Rider's head like she'd asked, there was still a chance they could keep Valente from dying when Orlando showed up. It wasn't much, but it was the only hope Lola had right now, and she clung to it with rabid determination. She was about to ask Tristan if he was feeling well enough to open the barrow for pizza delivery since she was almost at the bottom of her emergency Cup Ramen stash when Lola felt something buzz in her pocket.

She rolled off the bed with a jolt, landing on her butt on the carpet as she wrestled the sleek, slippery phone out of her gossamer and up to her ear.

"Hello?"

"It's me," Simon said.

Lola clutched the phone with a relieved breath so sharp it cut. "You have no idea how happy I am to hear your voice right now."

"I'm happy to hear you, too," he said, sounding very pleased with himself. "But I need your help. I'm at the ruins of Tristan's old apartment, but I can't find the door to his barrow. Can you—"

"Wait, you're *here?*" Lola interrupted in a panic. "Like in person? What about—"

"Victor's asleep," he said, sounding even smugger than before. "He still has to do that sometimes. I already made sure I wasn't followed, so can you ask the fairy to me in? I've got something for you."

Lola promised she would and hung up, looking pleadingly at Tristan, who just arched an eyebrow.

"I thought you said you weren't able to rescue Victor's apprentice?"

"I said I didn't want to talk about it," Lola reminded him. "I made it to Simon no problem. He just didn't want to come back with me."

"I can see why you wouldn't want to talk about that," Tristan said, taking an unhurried sip of his disgusting tonic. "So why is he scratching at my door now? What's he been doing that merits an audience with the lady whose help he so caddishly rejected?"

"Pretending to be Victor's loyal servant so he can stab him in the back."

Tristan choked on his green drink. "You should have led with that," he said, hauling his stiff body out of the chair. "Which door is he at?"

"Your old apartment," Lola said, sticking to the fairy's heels as Tristan hobbled into the living room. "I know it's destroyed, but I didn't tell him where any of your new doors were, so it was the only place he knew to go."

"That's fine. Low roads are a specialty of mine." He got to the hallway door and paused, looking over his shoulder. "You might want to wait here. I'm not exactly at my best right now. I wouldn't want to accidentally drop you in the ocean."

Lola backed off at once, putting up her hands as Tristan limped into the blue-carpeted hallway and closed the door. She felt the whole barrow tilt like a ship going over a wave a second later. The floor was still settling when Tristan came back in, and walking right behind him was Simon.

Tears sprang to Lola's eyes. She couldn't help it. It was just such a relief to see him on his feet again. Even the horrid red coat he was wearing couldn't detract from the healthy glow of his skin and the fullness of his face, so different from the skeletal corpse she'd seen at the hospital.

"I'm *so* glad you're okay!" she cried, running over to throw her arms around him. "I've been worried sick!"

"It's been a worrying time," Simon agreed, hugging her back with only one arm, because the other was holding a large metal box.

Lola's breath caught when she saw it. "Is that—"

She was interrupted by a loud *bang* followed by the overwhelming smell of flowers. When she turned to see what had caused it, Morgan was standing in the middle of Tristan's living room.

Lola took an awed step back. She hadn't seen the fairy queen in days, but her hunts had clearly been going better than Tristan had led her to believe. Like Simon, she'd transformed from an emaciated skeleton into a glowing picture of health.

She was seven feet tall and perfect as a Renaissance painting with her alabaster skin, leaf-green eyes, and waterfall of golden hair that trailed behind her like a veil. Her dress was a tapestry of sweet-blooming lilies, and her head was crowned with a garland of fragrant fire-red honeysuckle. Wherever her bare feet touched the floor, wildflowers sprang from the polished hardwood, filling Tristan's barrow with the scent of a summer morning.

"Wow," Lola said, batting the butterflies and honeybees that suddenly filled the air away from her face. "Someone's feeling better."

"I've been working hard," the queen informed her in a voice as sweet and rich as the scent of her flowers. "It's been quite the uphill battle, but that's the lovely thing about humans. Even when the world is ending, there's always someone willing to open their heart." She flashed a knowing smile at Tristan. "Or at least their legs."

The wounded fairy had a good laugh at that while Lola's face turned scarlet. She didn't know what else she'd expected from the queen of Tristan's court, but the gleam in Morgan's eyes made her knight's constant flirtations seem innocent by comparison. It got even worse when Morgan turned her predatory smile on Simon, whose eyes were now the size of golf balls.

"Hello, handsome," she cooed, leaning closer to his spellbound expression. "What have you brought for me?"

"He didn't bring it for you," Lola said irritably, shoving herself between the queen and Simon, who was still staring at the flower-covered beauty in awestruck wonder. "Stop enthralling my guest."

"I'm not enthralling him," Morgan insisted, looking insulted by the very idea. "What you're seeing is the natural reaction to my restored glory. He's merely showing his good taste, which is lucky for him, since he's not *your* guest. My knight was the one who bade him enter. That makes him ours."

Lola shot a furious look at Tristan, who just shrugged and sat down on the couch. Fortunately, the fairy queen didn't seem interested in feeding off Simon. Her green eyes were locked on the box under his arm as she gestured for him to hand it over.

"Uh…" Simon said, shaking his head like he was trying to clear it. He glanced nervously at Lola next, but she just sighed and motioned for him to go ahead. There was no point making a stink when they were all on the same team, and she was as eager as Morgan to see what was inside.

"It's not often I allow a bloodstained man into my presence," the queen informed him as she took the box from Simon's trembling hands. "The changeling believes you can be trusted, but I'm not so sure. You reek of fresh blood."

Lola jerked. She'd been so excited to see Simon up and walking around, she hadn't realized how much he smelled like Victor until Morgan pointed it out.

"Oh, Simon," she whispered, pressing a hand to his red sleeve. "What did he make you do?"

"Nothing," he said, finally shaking himself free of the fairy queen's bedazzlement. "This was my own work."

"But you swore you'd never—"

"Victor wouldn't have believed I was serious if I'd kept refusing to do his magic," Simon said in a hard, practical voice. "I did what I had to, but I promise the results will be worth it." His face split into a smile. "I've got him, Lola."

Lola was already opening her mouth to ask how when Morgan stepped in front of her.

"Explain," the queen demanded.

"Victor's army isn't actually what it looks like," Simon said, tilting his head back to meet the tall queen's gaze head-on. No small feat without a changeling's immunity to protect him from her glamour. "He's got willing victims coming out his ears, but blood magic is more than just shoving your hand into someone else's soul. The spells he needs to make his army effective take years to master. That's way longer than he's got, so, as usual for

Victor, he's cheating."

"How?" Lola asked.

"Same way he did with you," Simon said. "He's feeding them pills packed with his magic. One dose is enough to make someone who normally struggles with high-school-level spellwork into a mage on par with Victor himself, at least for a few minutes. That's how he's suddenly able to field thousands of well-trained blood mages. They're not actually trained. They're just doing what the pills tell them."

The queen snapped her fingers. "*That's* why my spies kept reporting smelling Victor all over town. I was worried he'd figured out the spirit trick of appearing in multiple places at once, but those weren't actually Victor at all. They're just normal people riding on his borrowed power."

"That doesn't make them any less dangerous," Lola said nervously. "One Victor is bad enough. If he's figured out how to make an army of himself, we're in big trouble."

"We would be," Simon agreed, "*if* he was actually in control." His lips curled into a smirk. "Unfortunately for Victor, he's stretched himself too thin. Making the number of the pills necessary to turn thousands of power-hungry idiots into competent blood mages was more than even he could handle alone. So, like everything he doesn't have time to do himself, he shoved the job off onto me."

Lola couldn't believe it. "He's trusting *you* to make his pills?"

Simon nodded quickly. "That's why I went so hard into his blood magic. I've been churning out pills nonstop for the last three days, and you'd better believe I've made some changes to the recipe. Nothing big enough for Victor to catch, but when the Wild Hunt arrives, his blood mage army is going to suffer a critical malfunction."

"Simon," Lola said in awe, "that's *brilliant*."

"Very brilliant," the fairy queen agreed, though she wasn't smiling. "Just make sure you don't pull the rug out from under him too early. If fighting Victor doesn't cut Alberich's riders down by at least half, we'll just be trading one disaster for another."

"Don't worry," Simon said, pushing up the sleeve of his red jacket to show them the brand-new spellwork tattoo wrapped around his forearm like a snake. "I've made sure I'm in absolute control of the kill switch. Every pill has a fault that can only be triggered by my blood. Nothing goes down until I say so, and only when the time is exactly right."

"Wisely done," Tristan said, hauling himself up from the couch. "As you humans say, 'When you swing for the king, you'd best not miss.' I'm happy to see you've thought this through, but what of the present you've brought?"

They all looked at the box that was still waiting unopened in Morgan's hands, and Simon's smile widened. "That's also part of the plan," he said, looking proudly at Lola. "If you're going to kick someone's feet out, you don't go for only one leg. Victor's strategy to hold onto power includes a lot more than just blood mages, so I *persuaded* Jamie to tell me where he was hiding the Black Rider's head."

Lola was giddy by the time he finished. Morgan wasn't moving quickly enough, so she went for the box herself, grabbing its top to peek inside. But she'd barely gotten her fingers under the lid when Tristan slammed the metal back down.

"Have you looked inside this box yet?" he asked Simon.

"Of course not," Simon said testily. "I was Victor's right-hand man for twenty years. I know what the Rider's head does to humans who aren't his master, but I'm certain that's it. Jamie's been with Victor even longer than I have. She knows where all the bodies are buried, and this is the only fairy head she knew about."

He smiled at Lola. "He was hiding it under his bed back at the mansion."

Lola stared at him in awe. Victor's bedroom at the top of the golden tower was the only place in their old home that she'd never been. The wards he'd installed around it were so nasty that even she'd never dared trying sneaking through. Simon had really stuck his neck out for this, but Tristan's expression had her worried.

"Why are you making that face?"

"Because I fear you're about to be gravely disappointed," the knight replied as he lifted the lid.

Lola rushed to shield Simon's eyes. She was about to yell at Tristan for reckless endangerment when she caught sight of the head in the box. A head that was most definitely *not* Valente's, or even human-looking.

The thing nestled inside the metal box looked like it had been cut off a sheep the size of a horse. Its wool was white and fluffy as fresh snow, too perfect to be real. It looked like someone had decapitated a stuffed animal, at least until you got to the rainbow gossamer that was still dripping from the stump of its severed spine.

"What is *that?*"

"It's Lamb," Morgan said, her voice delighted as she reached in to grab the head by its wool. "Lamb, my darling! Wake up!"

The fluffy head twitched between her rosy fingers, and then the giant sheep opened its eyes, staring at Morgan with horrified, side-slitted pupils. "My queen!" it bleated piteously. "The blood mage betrayed me!"

"Of course he did, you silly thing," Morgan scolded, petting the sheep's soft wool. "He betrayed us all."

The head began to weep after that, but Lola was too confused to feel sympathy. "Wait," she said, dropping the hand she'd slapped over Simon's eyes. "Who's Lamb?"

"One of my court," Morgan replied, cradling the crying head in her arms like a baby. "And Victor's lover, at least until he betrayed her."

"I never loved him!" the sheep's head insisted. "He's a rotter!"

The queen arched a golden eyebrow. "That wasn't what you said last time. You claimed he was a genius and I just didn't understand."

The sheep lowered its sideways eyes sullenly, but Lola was still gawking.

"Victor's lover was a sheep?"

"She's not a sheep all the time," Morgan said with a laugh. "You're just seeing her at an unflattering moment."

"You mean as a head," Lola said, her eyes going huge as she realized what that meant. "Victor kept his murdered lover's severed head in a box under his bed?"

"Makes sense," Tristan said. "His skill with blood magic might be at the top of his species, but no human can use gossamer. I always wondered how he was keeping that stolen barrow of his from falling apart, but now I see. Lamb was still in there."

Lola felt like a fool. She'd never questioned how Victor kept his house up. She'd simply accepted it as another facet of his seemingly limitless strength. Like everything else about him, though, it was a lie, an illusion built on someone else's stolen power. But if this was the fairy that he'd killed to get his barrow, then—

"Where's the Rider's head?"

"I don't understand," Simon said angrily. "I had complete control of Jamie's mind. She couldn't lie to me, and she said this was it."

"I'm sure she thought it was," Morgan said, tucking Lamb's fluffy head under her arm. "Since we keep our true forms hidden, most humans have no idea whose head is whose. Did she say it was the Rider's specifically?"

Simon opened his mouth then closed it again. "No," he said at last. "I asked her where the Rider's head was, and she replied that Victor kept the fairy's head in a safe under his bed. It never occurred to me there could be *two* heads. I just assumed..." He trailed off in frustration. "I'm sorry. I may have just tipped our hand."

"Don't worry, darling man," the queen replied with a dazzling smile. "This is the best mistake you could have made! Despite how she looks at the moment, Lamb is quite powerful. A bit of a wool brain, but you'll never find anyone with more skill at spinning gossamer, which I'm sure is why the blood mage pursued her. Getting her back now puts a much-needed ace in our hand. I even give you permission to blame the break-in on me when Victor finds out. If I'd known she was still in such good condition, I would have gone after her myself."

Lola wouldn't have called being a head in a box "good condition." Considering how she'd found Morgan, though, she supposed it was all relative. But while she was happy to rescue anyone from Victor, she didn't understand why everyone else was acting like this was over.

"We have to go back," she said. "The Rider's head is still in there! If we don't get it, he's going to die."

"That's not certain," Tristan said in a cajoling voice. "Victor's Black Knight might be an abomination, but he's no slouch. He went toe-to-toe with me after taking a beating from Orlando. Granted, I was queenless at the time, which put a serious damper on my abilities, but he's not going to just roll over for the Wild Hunt."

"Yes, he will," Lola said, clenching her fists. "Simon's not the only one planning to betray Victor. The Rider's going to lose to Alberich's knight on purpose so he can send Orlando crashing into

Victor's back."

The room went silent as she finished. Lola thought that was because they were horrified, but then Tristan's face broke into a proud smile.

"That brave boy," he said, laying a hand on his heart. "He really was a knight after all."

"Very noble," Morgan agreed. "I just hope he times it right. Orlando's a powerful weapon, but he's not a precise one. With our luck, he'll kill the Rider and go for one of Victor's copycat mages because he's too stupid to tell the difference."

She turned to Simon. "You work with him. Can you ask the Rider to hold off until after Alberich lands? My husband never could resist a good gloat, so I know he'll go straight for Victor. It would be best if the Rider waited until then to die. That would ensure Orlando stays on target, though it might mean you'll have to finish him off yourself, knight."

"I look forward to it," Tristan said, dropping a hand to the sword he was suddenly wearing. "I have a score to settle with that tongueless bastard."

The fairies both nodded as if this were a very good plan indeed, but Lola couldn't believe what she was hearing.

"Why are you all acting like this is okay? Valente's planning to *die* for something that might not even matter anymore!"

"It matters very much," the queen objected, flashing a dazzling smile at Simon. "Just because your brilliant mage has found a way to sabotage the Hero's Army is no guarantee that Victor himself will perish. Throwing Orlando at him is the perfect solution. Even with our unfortunate new bane for blood magic, Alberich's Red Knight is a killing machine who feels no pain. He'll rip Victor apart before the old fool's magic can shatter his gossamer."

"But at what cost?" Lola demanded. "Your plan was to use Victor to weaken Alberich, but there's no way he's sending the Rider into that fight without his head. That's why we have to steal it *before* he faces Orlando. If we don't, the Black Rider's done for!"

She'd thought that much was obvious, but the rest of the room was looking away from her, leaving Lola with a sinking feeling.

"You don't care," she said, stepping back. "You don't care if he dies!"

"It's not that we don't care," Morgan said. "It's just that this way is better."

"How is him *dying* better?"

"Because he's already doomed," the queen snapped. "Knights are tied to their monarchs unto death. Even if you did manage to save his head, there's no future for him without Victor. He'll just diminish like Tristan did without me, only much faster since he was never a true fairy to begin with. Putting him out of his misery is the kindest option, and this way he gets the satisfaction of taking Victor down with him."

"It really is for the best," Tristan told her gently. "The Rider's story has always been a tragedy. Giving his life to defeat a tyrant is a far better ending than any of us thought he'd get. It was his idea to do this, wasn't it?"

Lola nodded glumly, and Tristan nodded back as if that settled things. "Then let him have his victory. Let him die a hero so he won't have to die a—"

"*No!*" Lola shouted, stabbing her finger at Simon. "If he's got a kill switch on the Hero's Army, then there's no reason for the Rider to fight. I wasn't going to let him die even if it would kill Victor. I'm definitely not letting him do it for *nothing.*"

"It's not for nothing," the queen insisted. "The Rider's sacrifice is a critical move that will ensure—"

"He's not a chess piece for you to move around!" Lola yelled. "He's a *person*!"

"Who is doomed," Tristan reminded her, but Lola wasn't having it.

"You think I don't know what that feels like?" she cried. "I was Victor's monster too. I know *exactly* how hopeless it is to think you've got no future without him. That your only choices are to die alone or be his slave forever. But the Rider didn't abandon me when I was turning into Fenrir, and I'm not going to abandon him now. I don't care if it's his decision. You can't make real choices under Victor because with him it's always 'serve or die,' but I found a way out. I have to believe the Rider can, too, because apparently no one else here is willing to give him a chance."

Tristan sighed. "Lola-cat—"

"Don't 'Lola-cat' me," she snapped. "You act like you're some all-knowing God of Knighthood, but even you were impressed when I told you how the Rider dodged his oaths to avoid killing me. You *know* he's not a bad person, so don't stand there and act like the Rider killing himself is some kind of noble victory because that's what's convenient for your queen."

The fairy looked horribly affronted, but Lola didn't care. She didn't even care if Victor lived or died at this point. Her only concern was getting her people out of his blast radius. Simon sounded like he was already covered, and while Lola didn't know how she was going to save the Rider yet, she was determined to keep trying even if she had to do it alone. Valente had done no less for her.

With that, Lola took matters into her own hands, turning her back on the others as she marched back into the guest room and slammed the door.

<div style="text-align:center">~~~</div>

"Don't follow her."

Simon hadn't even started to move yet when the queen spoke, but that didn't mean he did as he was ordered.

"I owe it to her," he said as he walked toward the door Lola had just slammed. "I'm the one who got her hopes up and then brought the wrong head."

"You do yourself a disservice," the beautiful fairy replied, moving in a swirl of flowers to block his path. "You're good at hiding it, but I'm the Queen of Desire. I know what you want, and I know how you get it. Victor's Black Knight is as good as dead, which means all you have to do is be patient. The changeling will forget about him soon enough, and then it will be your turn."

"I'm not doing this to get my *turn,*" Simon told her in a disgusted voice. "Now, if you'll excuse me, I need to get to Lola before she does something crazy without my help."

The queen rolled her eyes, but Tristan looked impressed, which made her roll them even harder.

"Have it your way," Morgan said as she carried the sheep's head out of the room. "I must see to Lamb. Don't let him do anything that might endanger our plans, knight."

"Yes, my queen," Tristan said, wrapping an arm around Simon's shoulders. But instead of marching him back into the strange hallway full of doors, the fairy waited until his queen was out of sight before steering Simon straight toward Lola's door.

"What are you doing?"

"What I want," Tristan replied with a dazzling smile. "Contrary to what Victor may have led you to believe, a knight is not a slave. I respect my queen and obey her orders, but that doesn't mean I have to agree with everything that comes out of her mouth."

Simon arched an eyebrow. "But didn't she just specifically tell you not to do this?"

"She ordered me not to let you endanger our plans," the knight said. "And I don't intend to, but that doesn't mean I wasn't touched by your noble act."

"My noble act?"

"How you rushed to Lola's aid despite the fact that it would mean helping your rival," the fairy explained, pulling Simon closer as he lowered his voice. "My queen is very powerful, but she's only interested in desire. True love, the sort where you place another's happiness above your own, is too bitter for her palate."

"But not for yours?"

"I find it the most delicious thing in the world," Tristan purred, leaning in until his lips were a hair's breadth from Simon's ear. "I didn't become a knight because I enjoy taking orders. A fairy's life is too long to live without purpose, and I decided centuries ago that my purpose was to be a champion. Normally, that means serving my queen. Right now, though, I'm championing *you*."

Simon pushed him away with a huff. "I don't need a champion."

The fairy gave him a knowing smile. "Don't you? The changeling's heart is not easily won. Believe me, I've tried. But you seem a good sort of man for a blood mage, and she obviously cares for you very much, so I think you'll do nicely."

Simon was about to point out this wasn't something Tristan got a say in when the knight slapped him on the shoulder.

"Go to her!" he commanded. "Be her knight! Help her feel she did all she could, and maybe when this is over, I'll no longer have to taste sadness in her dreams."

"You shouldn't be eating her dreams at all," Simon said. "But… thank you. You know, for not kicking me out."

"What are co-conspirators for?" the fairy replied with a wink. Then his face grew serious. "Just make sure you don't shake things up *too* badly. If the blood mage ends up surviving this because I distracted you with a girl, the queen will have my head."

"Don't worry," Simon told him darkly. "Victor's not going to survive."

"Then we have nothing to worry about," Tristan said, giving him one last slap on the back. "Good luck!"

The words were still hanging in the air when the fairy vanished like sea spray, leaving Simon standing alone in front of Lola's door.

Chapter 10

Lola burst into her room like a misfiring bomb. The door slam startled Buster so badly that he fell off the bed. He ran behind the chair next, meowing angrily at Lola as she began violently pacing the room.

A plan. She needed a plan. A fast one, because she'd wasted too much time already. Alberich's Hunt could arrive any time now, but what was she going to do? Her best idea to sneak out of the barrow had already tanked, and she didn't think the Rider's loophole extended to looking the other way while she ransacked all of Hero's Tower, assuming Valente's head was even there. She was sure Victor would keep it close, but that could still mean any number of—

Her whirling thoughts were interrupted by the click of the doorknob, and Lola's hands balled into fists. "Go away, Tristan."

"It's not Tristan."

She glanced up at the sound of Simon's voice, and her face split into a beaming smile. "You stayed!"

"You didn't think I was letting you do this alone, did you?" he asked with a smile of his own before turning to stare at the woman on the bed. "Is that your sister?"

"That's her," Lola said proudly. "I've been trying to wake her up since the Fenrir disaster, but as you can see…"

She trailed off with a shrug, and Simon's face fell into a thoughtful scowl. "Have you tried—"

"*Yes*, Simon," Lola said with a frustrated huff. "If it exists, I've tried it, but nothing *works*." She flopped into the chair Buster was still cowering under. "Apparently, I'm garbage at rescuing people."

"It's never as easy as the movies make it seem," he told her gently, taking his own seat on the foot of her sister's bed. "They always show you the last-second save, but you never get to see what comes after, like how many people end up in traction because Superman got thrown through their building."

"Now I remember why I stopped watching movies with you," Lola groused, then she smiled again. "But I am *very* happy you're here."

"I'm just sorry I messed up," Simon said guiltily. "We wouldn't be in this situation if I'd gotten the right head."

"You did more than I could," Lola assured him. "But we have to keep trying. Whatever the fairies say, the Rider's one of us. I know you don't like him, but—"

"It was never him that I disliked," Simon said. "I thought he was an extension of Victor, a mindless puppet. It never occurred to me that there was a person under that helmet until I saw how he acted around you."

"He is a person," Lola said with a warm smile. "A good one who doesn't deserve this. Tristan always acts like the Rider's situation is his own fault because he's the one who swore the knighthood oaths, but we both know how Victor puts you in a corner."

"I know," Simon said, his eyes getting that haunted look that she'd seen inside his death. "So, what's our plan?"

"I'm not sure yet," Lola admitted, slumping down in her chair. "But it's going to have to be something crazy. The Rider's still under orders to kill me, and he can trace my gossamer anywhere I go. He also doesn't know where his head is. It was the first thing I asked about."

"And you believed him?"

Lola gave him a scathing look.

"I had to ask," Simon said, putting up his hands. "Just because he's not Victor's mindless puppet doesn't mean he's free to tell us the truth. For all we know, Victor ordered the Rider to tell you about his head so you'd go looking for it and fall back into his clutches."

Lola froze. She hadn't even considered that possibility, which was *stupid* because it was exactly the sort of trap their master would lay. A few moments later, though, she decided it didn't matter.

"Even if it was a lie, that doesn't change anything," she said fiercely. "Head or no head, I'm not leaving him in Victor's clutches."

Simon chuckled. "I knew you'd say that." Then his face grew grim again. "I just wish I knew how we were going to do it. If we were looking for anything other than a fairy head, I could do a tracking spell, but the Rider's almost as resistant to human magic as you are."

"But not immune," Lola said, thinking back to their fight with the Paladins. "I think I've got an idea, but we'll have to get inside Hero's Tower to pull it off."

"Why the tower?"

"Because Alberich's Hunt could arrive any time now," she explained. "Victor knows the Rider can't fight Orlando without his head, so I bet he's keeping it close. You know what a coward he is with his own life."

"Makes sense," Simon said. "The tower's a big place, though, and Victor had the city build it custom just for him. It's got secret rooms all over."

"I'm sure I can find it if I get close," Lola said, tapping her nose. "The Rider's magic has a very distinctive smell."

"So long as you don't need me to help you search," Simon said with a sigh. "I've still got a thousand more pills to make before Alberich arrives."

"All you have to do is sneak me in past Victor's legions of followers," Lola assured him. "Once I don't have to worry about getting melted by some wannabe blood mage who can't tolerate fairy illusions, I can handle the searching on my own."

"Okay, but how am I sneaking you in?" he asked. "I've got clearance, but even if he's found a way not to kill you on sight, I doubt the Rider will be able to ignore you waltzing into Victor's penthouse."

"That's exactly what I'm counting on," Lola said, her face splitting into a grin as she told him the plan.

~~~

Thirty minutes later, Simon walked into Hero's Tower carrying Buster's cat crate. Victor had already informed his faithful that Simon was his apprentice, so none of the red-coated mages said a word as he marched through the elegant lobby and took the special elevator that went straight to the casting workshop.

It had been Victor's personal workshop until just a few days ago, and it still had the look. Not only was it only one floor down from the Hero's penthouse, everything inside the huge room still reeked of his blood despite the sterile laboratory aesthetic. Even the gleaming stainless-steel casting circles couldn't hide the dirty, deathly feeling the place exuded like a smell, and the drains placed at discreet intervals in the cement floor definitely weren't helping.

Having already worked here around the clock for the past three days, Simon walked through the horror-movie setting without a second look, placing the plastic cat carrier on the large steel table that served as his desk. Since this had been Victor's private casting room, there were no security cameras inside, but that didn't mean he wasn't being watched. Case in point, Jamie stormed in barely half a minute later, her lovely face blotchy with
~~~

terrified fury.

"Where have you been?" she demanded. "I've been looking for you for an hour! Why did you turn off the tracking on your phone, and what is *that?*"

"A cat," Simon replied as he moved the plastic carrier away from Jamie's accusing finger.

"I can see that," she snapped, leaning down to glare at the plump animal cowering at the back of the cage. "But why do *you* have it? I thought you were allergic."

"I am," Simon said, pulling up his computer's augmented reality field to look over the day's assignments. "But it seems that, before she died, Lola paid for her cat's boarding using my account. The vet wouldn't stop calling me, so I took some personal time to pick him up."

The blond didn't look convinced, but Jamie had always put her own problems above everything else, and right now, she was clearly too freaked out to care.

"Whatever," she said, pulling out her phone. "I need another batch of pills. The Hero's speech brought in a bunch of new idiots last night, and I need to give them all a test dose to make sure the sudden surge of blood magic doesn't pop their brains before Victor wakes up."

Without looking away from his work, Simon reached into the sleek white cabinet behind him and pulled out a glass jar full of bright-red pills.

"That's my entire supply," he warned as Jamie grabbed it. "I won't have any more finished for another hour."

"You might want to work faster," Jamie advised, tapping her manicured nails against the glass pill jar like a machine gun. "Our sources report the Wild Hunt left France late last night. I don't know how long it takes nightmare horses to fly across the Atlantic Ocean, but—"

She cut off as the door behind them slammed open, and the Black Rider marched into the room. Jamie nearly dropped her pills at the sight. She snatched them back against her chest at once, scuttling out of the workshop without another word. The Rider waited until she was gone to approach the desk, slamming his gloved hands down right next to where the cat carrier was sitting.

"Can I help you?" Simon asked.

The Rider's body tensed as he pulled his writing pad out of his jacket pocket. He grabbed one of Simon's pens off the desk next, his gloved hands moving in angry jerks as he scribbled a note and shoved it in Simon's face.

Why did you bring her here?

"I don't know what you're talking about," Simon said, leaning back in his chair.

Don't lie to me, the Rider wrote furiously. *I know Tristan already picked up Buster.* The writing grew messy as his gloved hands began to shake. *You know what he's ordered me to do. Why would you bring her here to die?*

Simon leaned forward with a smile, beckoning the Rider closer so he could whisper into his reflective helmet.

"A better question would be, 'Why do you think that's what I did?'"

The Rider jerked as Simon grabbed his notepad and tore off the incriminating page, crumpling it in his fist as he pushed off the desk to roll his chair out of the way. That was the only warning the Rider got before a grand piano made of lead fell out of thin air above his head, crushing him instantly.

<center>~~~</center>

"A lead piano?" Simon said as he rolled his chair back over. "*That* was your big attack?"

Lola was panting so hard from the effort of spinning so much gossamer so quickly that she couldn't get a reply out for a solid thirty seconds.

"It was… a calculated risk," she huffed at last, transforming her paw into a hand just long enough to let herself out of Buster's carrier. "Glamour is strongest when it's in context, and cartoons have taught us that everyone, no matter how tough, gets flattened when you drop a piano on their head."

She was just glad it had worked, especially since she'd had to nix the sound effects. A giant crash would have made the gossamer piano even more believable, but it would also have alerted everyone in the building, which defeated the purpose of a sneak attack. The other senses must have made up for it, though, because when Lola dissolved the broken piano back into her body, the only thing left of the Black Rider was a crushed helmet.

She breathed a sigh of relief at the sight. Stupid as it might be, that piano had been the most concentrated lump of gossamer she'd ever created. Given how many times the Rider had shrugged off her cars, Lola had been seriously worried he couldn't be killed with gossamer. She was a lot better now than she'd been back then, though, and much more determined. She'd only been trying to get away from the Rider before. This was a premeditated attack backed up by everything she'd learned about her magic since she'd gotten free of Victor, and it had *worked*. Now she just had to hope the streak continued for all the other parts of the plan.

"We don't have much time," Simon said, shoving the broken helmet into the white drawer he'd taken the pills out of. "It usually takes less than an hour for the Rider's body to reappear next to his head. Can you feel where it is?"

Lola sniffed the air with her cat nose, grateful she'd brought all of her gossamer along this time. With so much power to pull on, she could smell every bit of magic in the building. Not surprisingly, it was almost entirely Victor's. But while the reek of blood was so thick it made her gag, she still managed to catch the cold, clean scent of Valente's midwinter gossamer filtering down from the floor above.

"Got him," she said, hopping her fake Buster off of Simon's desk. "Looks like Victor's keeping him in the penthouse."

Simon shook his head with a huff. "I should have known that's where he'd be. Victor's too paranoid to let the really important stuff out of his sight, and his private rooms are the only place he could keep something without Jamie knowing."

"Is she going to be a problem?" Lola asked, looking at the door with a nervous flick of her tail. "She did see us with the Rider."

"If she is, I'll take care of it," Simon assured her, hopping up from his chair. "But you need to get going. I don't think the Rider will blab about my part in this unless Victor specifically asks, so we need to make sure he has no reason to be suspicious."

"Don't worry," Lola said. "I'll make sure Victor knows I acted alone as I'm skedaddling with the Rider's head. You just stay in here and keep working like a good little drone."

"I'll have to work if I'm going to make enough sabotaged pills for everyone before the Hunt shows up," he said, rubbing his hands over his tightly shaved black hair. "If Alberich is really as close as Jamie said, it's going to be down to the wire."

"You can do it," Lola said confidently. "No one pulls off a rush job better than you."

"I don't know if I should take that as a compliment or not," Sumon grumbled, opening the workshop door for her with a worried smile. "Good luck, Tinker Bell."

"You too, Mr. Wizard," Lola said, ducking her furry head low as she scuttled into the hallway.

She dumped her Buster costume the moment she was around the corner, trading her baby boy's adorably round body for a bony stray with dark, indeterminate fur. A mouse would have been even better, but despite all the progress she'd made, Lola still wasn't able to squeeze her gossamer down that small. Medium-sized cat was the best she could manage, but while this form wasn't as inconspicuous as she would have liked, it had its advantages. People didn't scream when they saw a cat the way they did for other feral mammals, and no one tried to ask an animal questions like they would a human disguise. On the downside, cats couldn't operate elevators, which was where Lola ran into her first big problem.

Being in such a prestigious position just one level down from the Hero's penthouse, Simon's workshop shared its floor with only one other office: Jamie's. Lola didn't want to risk running into her in any shape. Without Victor's secretary, though, she found herself alone in front of a wall of elevators with multiple cameras watching the doors.

Clearly, this way was a no-go, so Lola went on the prowl, slinking along the baseboards until she found an air vent that was far enough away from the security cameras. After a quick, catlike look over her shoulders, she pushed her not-actually-solid body through the protective grate, oozing into the brand-new duct on the other side like the rainbow-sludge monster she secretly was.

Movement got much easier from there. With no cameras to watch her or people to startle, Lola was free to do truly impossible things, like replace her cat paws with sticky gecko feet so she could walk up the vertical duct's metal walls. There were still wards to get past, but that was nothing for a changeling. She slipped right through the spells with barely a shiver, climbing through the ventilation shafts as fast as her sticky feet could go. But while it took her less than five minutes to reach the floor with Valente's icy scent, Lola could find no direct path into Victor's private living area.

She padded around the ducts for a good fifteen minutes before she finally realized what was going on. The suspicious bastard had put his penthouse on its own separate ventilation system. The closest Lola could get was the elevator lobby outside his office, which had even more cameras than the floor below. Even worse, the only vent not in the camera's direct line of view was the one in the ceiling.

There was nothing else for it. Lola oozed through the ceiling vent as quietly as possible, trusting people's belief that cats always landed on their feet to cover her tail as she dropped right in front of the cameras. She ran for cover the second her paws hit the ground, scrabbling across the polished marble toward the first hiding place she saw.

There were plenty to choose from. Just like the castle he'd made for himself inside poor beheaded Lamb's barrow, Victor's private floor took "ostentatious" to new extremes. Even the elevator lobby was packed with side tables, floor lamps, and wall hangings that looked like they'd been stolen straight out of a museum.

Given that he'd completely taken over the DFZ, that might actually be where they'd come from. Stolen or not stolen, though, the wall hangings made an excellent shield as Lola skirted the lobby's edge. She was still figuring out how she was going to tackle the heavy wooden door to Victor's office when one of the elevators behind her dinged.

Lola froze, pressing her bony cat flat against the floor. When the polished brass doors rolled open, though, the person who came out wasn't one of Victor's red-coated mages. It was a thrall.

Lola stood back up with a grin. She hadn't even thought about Victor's thralls since she'd seen his last batch break free during his disappearance, but it made total sense that he'd still have them. It went against Victor's nature to give up perfect servants who did exactly what they were told, happily worked themselves to death, and were mentally incapable of betrayal. No matter how badly they clashed with his current "Hero of the people" persona, he'd never be able to let them go, and that was Lola's ticket in.

She shot out of her hiding spot and ran straight at the thrall's feet, meowing expectantly as she rubbed her furry body against the young woman's ankles. It took several seconds for the sounds to penetrate the haze Victor had placed over the thrall's mind, but once the meows got through, the empty-eyed woman gave Lola an indulgent smile as she dutifully opened the office door.

Lola trotted inside with her nose in the air. Thralls might be perfect lackeys, but all that magically enforced obedience left them pretty bad at critical thinking. Other than specific orders given by their master, all of their decisions—going to the bathroom, navigating stairs, opening doors—were made on a thoughtless, mechanical level.

This left them incredibly susceptible to suggestions that matched typical human behaviors, such as opening the door for a meowing cat. Thralls didn't stop to think, "Is this right?" or "Should a cat even be here?" They just automatically did whatever fit the stimuli and went back to their assigned task, which in this thrall's case meant carrying a large box of mail.

Lola left her to it, loping across the carpet to start sniffing her way around the palatial office, but she already knew Valente's head wasn't here. Despite the big desk with all its locked drawers and the fancy safe set into the far wall, this room was clearly just a front, somewhere impressive for the Hero to meet with all the people who needed more delicate interaction than speeches from a podium. It was too shallow for any real secrets, so Lola ran back to the thrall, almost tripping the woman as she carried her box of mail through a side door that she'd opened with a security card tied to her wrist.

Lola darted inside as soon as the gap was wide enough, racing along the wall for cover until she realized there were no cameras in here. She'd just entered the core of Victor's private domain. Even for his own security, he'd never allow video evidence of this place, because the entire room was packed with thralls.

It looked like a love child between Victor's old casting workshop and a celebrity's mailroom. The floor was covered with dozens of interlocking magical circles surrounded by a ring of folding tables piled high with letters. The wall Lola was hiding against was stacked with a mountain of hand-labeled packages, gifts sent to the Hero by his fans all over the world.

She sniffed the cardboard boxes curiously. Even if he was just using thralls to sort his mail, it stuck her as odd that Victor bothered at all. She would've expected him to send his fan mail straight to the incinerator, but the thralls were opening each envelope and package with care, sorting the heartfelt letters and children's drawings into plastic bins. Once full, these bins were picked up by yet another set of thralls, who emptied them into the center of the room's largest magical circle.

Lola's ears went flat against her head. She didn't know enough about Victor's magic to say what was happening, but she was certain it wasn't good. Every time the thralls dumped a new load of handmade cards and lovingly knitted scarves into the circle, the intricate spellwork written in Victor's precise hand flashed blood red. The objects vanished a second later, leaving behind a drop of golden liquid. It shone like a dot of pure sunlight on the stone floor, but it had the same bloody smell as Lola's pills. The scent only got stronger when one of the thralls collected it with an eyedropper and carried it to a basin that was already half-full of golden, viscous fluid.

The lovely, sunny light filled Lola with dread. She'd never seen golden blood magic before, but she could feel the awful power cutting into her gossamer. It was the same pain she'd felt when the Hero had sliced Fenrir with his golden sword. Not the wound itself, that had been tiny. What had hurt was people's belief that the Hero could kill her. Belief that was clearly still being harvested and turned into…

Lola wasn't sure, exactly, but she was positive that basin of golden liquid figured heavily into Victor's plans. She'd kept him from reaching critical mass when she'd walked Fenrir away, but he'd clearly found other ways to harness the Hero's power. Power that would only get stronger if he succeeded in defeating Alberich and saved the DFZ from the Wild Hunt.

Shuddering at the thought, Lola hopped her cat to the top of the nearest mail pile to get a look at the magical circles from above. She didn't have time right now to do anything about them, but she got a good mental snapshot to show Simon later. Maybe he could tell her what the golden liquid was for and how to stop it.

Lola was tempted to go ahead and knock the basin over. That was sure to throw a wrench in Victor's plans, but it would also get her caught. Thralls weren't *that* dumb, and strange as it felt to say, she wasn't here for Victor. She'd come to save Valente, whose magic she could already smell getting stronger.

That lit a fire under her tail. Lola had never actually seen the Rider re-form, but from the way the icy magic was condensing, she knew it wouldn't be long. If she didn't find his head before his body returned, they'd be right back to square one. Lola wasn't cocky enough to think she'd get away with dropping a piano on him twice, so she forced herself to ignore the golden liquid and jumped back to the floor, shooting between the thralls' feet as she raced through the busy mailroom toward the hallway on the other side.

There were thralls there, too. Normal domestic ones running what was clearly the Hero's private apartments. As expected from a penthouse suite, it was absolutely enormous: a maze of entertainment rooms, sitting areas, and a full kitchen staffed by glassy-eyed cooks. None of them so much as glanced at Lola's cat as she raced over their feet with her nose in the air, following Valente's midwinter scent to the place where it was strongest.

This turned out to be a room at the very center of the building. It was so small, she thought it was a closet at first, especially since it had no windows. Hardly any furniture, either, except for a bed, but that fit the Rider's MO. Her cat eyes could even make out a body lying beneath the blankets. She was worried she was already too late when the man rolled over, and Lola saw that he had a head. One that definitely wasn't the Rider's.

Fear sent her little body flat against the carpet. That was Victor. *Victor* was sleeping in the tiny bed. She'd been so focused on tracking Valente, she hadn't even smelled him. Now that she'd realized what she was looking at, the reek of his bloody magic hit her like a boot to the face, and it wasn't alone. Valente's icy gossamer was here, too, gathering like a cold front on the floor at his master's feet.

That must have been where the Rider's body was about to appear. But if he was reforming next to Victor, then his head must be…

Lola's eyes snapped back to the man under the blankets. Of *course*. Victor had already hidden one fairy head. Why not bury Valente's in the same place he'd stuffed Queen Morgan's? Even the Rider couldn't get into the blood mage's hideous red death, but Lola was a different story. She'd already been to the pit of Victor's soul once. By accident, admittedly, but she'd gotten into Simon's death just a few days ago. And if she could do it to him…

Her claws dug into the carpet. Lola knew now what she had to do; she just *really* didn't want to do it. Slipping through Simon's mind was one thing. She trusted him, and he'd also been in a coma. Victor could wake up at any moment, and she didn't even want to think about what he'd do if he caught her in his death.

The only reason she'd made it out last time was because he hadn't been there, which was strange now that Lola thought about it. A human's death was the root of their soul, the place where the physical and magical connected. That didn't seem like the sort of thing you could just bop out of, but there was no way she and Morgan could have escaped if Victor had been there, so where had he gone?

Lola had no idea, and she didn't have time to worry about it. She could already feel the Rider's gossamer thickening in front of her, so she coiled her cat body just like she'd seen Buster do and leaped onto Victor's bed. She was about to sneak up the mattress to his head when she realized it wasn't going to work.

Not getting into Victor's dreams. Lola was pretty certain she could do that. But, as she'd discovered back at the hospital, her gossamer didn't go into the dream with her. If the Rider came back while her mind was still inside, he might melt her body, or worse, wake up his master before she got out. Lola had no idea what would become of her if that happened, but she had a terrible feeling she might get stuck inside Victor's head forever.

That would absolutely be a fate worse than death. She had to find a way to protect her gossamer while she was under, and fast. From the way the temperature was dropping in the room, the Rider's arrival was only minutes away, so Lola hopped back off the bed to try the only solution she could think of.

Just as she'd done back at Tristan's, she divided her gossamer into two pieces. One was as tiny as the cat she was still pretending to be, while the other was practically all of her. It was the most uneven division she'd ever made, but that was the point. Valente had already said he paid close attention to her, which meant Lola's only chance was to give him a target *so* big, he wouldn't even notice the scraps she'd left behind.

Once she had her two pieces stable, Lola took the larger portion and spun it into the same replica she'd made of herself last time. With so much of her magic crammed inside, this doppelganger was even better than the first. Aside from the silver thread, which was still wrapped around the actual Lola's paw, it practically *was* her, right down to the worried expression on her face. She was already opening her mouth to say something when the real Lola cut her off.

"Valente's going to reappear any second," she whispered, rising up on her hind paws to make the tiny voice that came with her now very tiny cat easier to hear. "I need you to go back to the thrall room and cause a distraction."

"Okay, but why?" her copy whispered back. "He's going to realize pretty fast that I'm not you."

"He won't," Lola promised, looking down at the crumb of gossamer she'd left herself. "I'm made of less magic right now than I'd usually use on a shoe. There's no way he'll think you're not the real me."

"Yes, he will," the double insisted. "He'll know."

Lola opened her mouth only to close it again. Why was her double so sure when Lola herself wasn't? On that same note, why was she still "Lola" even though practically all of her magic was somewhere else? As she'd been told many, many, *maaaaaaaaany* times, changelings didn't have souls. She was just a fabrication, a child-stealing spell gone rogue, and yet Lola knew with absolute certainty that she was here in the cat, not in the body that looked like hers. It didn't make any sense as she understood her own magic, but she had no time to figure it out.

"Just go break stuff," she ordered. "Whether we fool him or not, the Rider can't allow his master's plans to be disrupted, but Valente's a kind guy. I bet he won't turn you into ice chunks like he did the troll."

That would be wonderful, because Lola had left herself a very small lifeboat. She was reasonably certain she could regenerate any amount of gossamer given enough time, but she'd never tried coming back from a piece this small before, and as much as she loved cats, she didn't want to be stuck as one.

"I'll come back as fast as I can," she promised, hopping up onto the headboard of Victor's bed. "Just keep the Rider off me."

"I can't beat him," her doppelganger warned. "The only reason your piano worked earlier was because he wasn't expecting it. That's not going to happen twice."

"You don't need to win," Lola assured her. "You just need to buy me time. Now go cause a ruckus."

Her double nodded and crept out of the room, slipping through the wards on the doorway Lola hadn't even noticed as easily as a real changeling. Beaming with pride at what her gossamer could do, Lola slipped silently down onto the mattress. She was so small now that she could hide her body completely behind Victor's pillow. She used this to get closer to her old master than she'd ever dared, creeping forward until she was nose to nose with Victor's sleeping face.

It felt *incredibly* weird, and not because she was a cat. Before this moment, Lola had never actually seen Victor when he wasn't awake. No surprise considering his obsession with control, but he looked so… different this way. He was still smothered in the illusions that turned him into the handsome Hero, but his face looked hollow and empty in a way even magic couldn't hide. His body also seemed much smaller than she remembered, curled up under the blankets like a little old man's.

He looked so vulnerable that Lola seriously considered covering his face with a pillow and ending it all right here. The only reason she didn't was because she was pretty sure Valente's head would be lost forever if Victor died with it still inside. That, and she no longer had enough gossamer to form the hands she needed to hold the pillow down.

Shaking her head at the missed opportunity, Lola curled her little cat body around Victor's scalp. She'd just pressed her tail against his ear for even more contact when she heard the *thunk* of the Rider's brand-new body hitting the floor.

Everything was a scramble after that. Lola pressed herself as flat against the pillow as she could get, hoping the dark and all the gossamer she'd sent out as bait would keep Valente from spotting her as she plunged herself like a spear into Victor's dreams.

Chapter 11

Diving into Victor's dreams was like falling into a vortex. As with everything involving her former master, he dragged her down, sucking her through his suffocating red darkness. It went on so much longer than her descent into Simon's dream that Lola was staring to worry he'd trapped her in some kind of eternally falling loop when her feet landed on something that didn't give.

She stopped with a stumble, looking around to see what sort of dream she'd landed in. No matter how hard she squinted, though, there was nothing to see. There was no movement, no people, not even any lights, just red-tinged darkness stretching out forever in every direction.

Lola planted her feet with a frown. She waved her hand in front of her face next. As expected, it was too dark to see it. She could feel it was a *hand*, though, and not a paw.

Her frown deepened. She must have reverted back to her normal shape sometime during the fall. That shouldn't have been possible given how little gossamer she'd left herself, but dreams didn't follow normal logic, and Lola was certain that this *was* a dream. It had the right feel, though she found it odd that Victor would dream of nothing. Not that she'd wanted to see his twisted dreams, but it was very weird.

Since her normal body seemed to be back, Lola held out her hand to make a flashlight only to think better of it at the last second. She didn't know what sort of dream this was yet, but shining a light around a sleeping man's head seemed like a sure-fire way to wake them up. This would all be for nothing if Victor came to and kicked her out before she'd done anything, so Lola settled for groping her way forward, sliding her feet blindly along the ground as she started searching for a way down.

There had to be one. Thanks to Simon, Lola knew that Victor went to his death quite often, and when you went somewhere a lot, you made a path. If Lola could find Victor's, she should be able to walk right down to the creepy red room she'd busted into when she'd freed Morgan. It was a beautifully simple plan, but as ever, Victor made things difficult.

She walked through the dark for what felt like hours, but her groping hands never bumped into anything. Same went for her feet. Even when she took off the sneakers she hadn't realized she was wearing until her lace came undone, the floor here all felt the same: a smooth, flat nothing.

It went on for so long, Lola began to worry she'd been wrong before. Maybe Victor wasn't dreaming after all and she was wandering through the darkness of his unconscious brain. Lola didn't know if that was possible, but she liked it better than the other explanation, which was that she'd fallen into a trap.

Given whose head she was in, it wasn't unthinkable, but Lola had never heard of a human who could shape his own dreams. Not lucid dreaming where you took over what was already there, but true control where *you* determined what appeared. If anyone could do it, though, it would be Victor. She was worrying she'd already doomed herself when she heard something slosh.

Lola stopped with a jerk, reaching down to feel the ground with her fingers. Everything here was body temperature, so she hadn't even noticed she was walking through a puddle until she heard it. Sliding her bare feet around her in a circle, Lola determined she was standing in a shallow lake of some kind of viscous liquid.

Her stomach curdled instantly. Everything in here already reeked of Victor's magic, so she couldn't smell it, but she knew it was blood. It was *always* blood with Victor. But while that thought made her want to gag, at least the blood was something. If this part of the darkness had a blood lake, then it must be different from the rest.

Trying her best not to think about what she was walking through, Lola paced the shallow lake to get a measure of its size. She'd only heard the splash a few seconds ago, so she reasoned she couldn't be that far in, but no matter how far she walked, Lola couldn't find the pool's edge. It seemed to be everywhere, an ocean of blood filling his entire mind. And while that was *very* Victor, it didn't give her much to work with. There was no trail, no tunnel, no spot in the lake that was deeper than the rest. It was just a bunch of blood lying on the ground.

Just thinking about that made Lola want to throw up. Even if it wasn't doing anything but sitting there, she had a lot of trauma involving Victor's blood, particularly in large pools. But as hard as she was trying to keep those memories at bay, they actually gave her an idea. A terrifying one, but nothing else was working, so Lola stopped walking and got down on her knees.

The blood started seeping into her clothes immediately, covering her in a sticky, heavy, *familiar* feeling. The only thing missing was Victor's hand shoving her down, but Lola breathed through the anxiety and bent lower, curling her body over until her nose was touching the pool's oily surface. Simon had said that a person's death was the deepest part of themselves. This whole time, Lola had been groping around on the surface, but the last time she'd gotten into Victor's death, she'd had to sink.

That thought was enough to make her dry-heave. She'd rather fight the Rider blind than plunge her face into yet *another* pool of Victor's choking, disgusting blood, but she couldn't think of any other way. Her double wouldn't be able to keep Valente occupied for long. She needed to suck it up and do what she'd come here to do, but the blood was so *thick*. Her face wasn't even in it yet, but Lola could already feel it coating her lungs and eating her screams.

Every bit of her was begging not to do this. As ever, though, Lola couldn't run away. Before, that had always been because Victor was holding her down. Now, though, Lola was the one forcing her face forward, because she'd promised. She'd *promised* Valente she'd save him. If she broke her word now after making such a fuss, she'd be as big a liar as Victor.

That was just horrible enough to get her over the edge. Quickly, before she lost her nerve, Lola plunged her face straight into the blood. This should have ended in a broken nose since the puddle was barely deep enough to cover her feet, but—just like when Victor had slammed her face down in the Fenrir dream— Lola didn't crash. She *sank*, falling into the shallow puddle like she was falling down a well.

Blood poured into her nose as she plummeted. If she'd screamed, it would have filled her completely, but Lola didn't scream this time. She didn't fight, didn't let him in. She just curled her body into a ball and went with the flow, sinking like an anchor down, down, down through the red darkness until it wasn't darkness anymore. It was just red. A blinding, overpowering crimson that filled her senses before condensing into the monochrome room she remembered.

She landed on the crimson carpet like a meteor. Her balled-up body unfurled when she hit, leaving her gasping on her back. Lola swore she could still feel the blood all over, but her hands were clean when she brought them up. She was running them over her face to make sure the blood was really gone when she noticed the room was bigger than she remembered.

A *lot* bigger.

Lola went still, hands falling back to the carpet as she stared up at the cavernous space. It was still red and weird with its modern furniture and creepy blood fireplace, but the crimson carpet was now the size of a football field. The porthole to the Sea of Magic she'd escaped through last time was so far away she could barely see it, and the red chandelier that lit the place looked like a distant star, but the biggest change by far was the room's walls.

They'd grown exponentially just like everything else, but unlike the ridiculously huge carpet, all of their extra space had been crammed with pictures. So, *so* many pictures packed together in a grid that it looked like the walls were tiled.

There'd been pictures on the walls last time too, but this was ridiculous. There had to be thousands of them now, acres and acres of people's fearful faces going up as far as Lola could see. They were all done in the same red-only monochrome as the portrait of Victor she'd seen inside Simon's death, but that painting had been life-sized and full body. These were much smaller, little eight-by-tens that showed no more than the subject's head and neck.

Each one was framed in a simple black rectangle with a red thread hanging off the bottom. But where the thread in Simon's death had ended in a noose around his neck, these were all tied off with neat little bows, like presents waiting to be unwrapped.

That struck her as important, but Lola hadn't come to gawk at Victor's creepy magic. Despite its growth spurt, the red room still had the same layout as last time, which meant the red safe with Valente's head should be behind her. That was where it had been when she and Morgan had broken out, but when Lola finally made the trek across the field of carpet, the table the safe was supposed to be on was empty.

She grabbed it with a curse, pulling the ugly red thing off the wall to check behind and under it. It was pointless because she could already see there was nothing, but this didn't make any sense. Victor's death was the only place he could put the Rider's head where even Valente wouldn't be able to feel it. It *had* to be here.

Roaring with rage and fear, Lola began tearing the room apart. She overturned the couches and ripped off their pillows, stuck her head over the fire to look up the chimney. She even tried to pry the pictures off the walls, but there was nothing to find. The safe they'd broken out of last time simply wasn't here.

Too defeated even to scream, Lola stumbled back to the fireplace, pressing both hands against the red mantel as she stared down at her bare feet. What did she do now? She'd been so sure that Valente's head would be here, but she'd realized halfway through her violent search that she couldn't smell a whiff of his midwinter magic. She'd told herself that was because everything here was soaked in Victor's bloody stench, but now…

Lola's fingers curled against the blood-red bricks. If the Rider's head wasn't here, then this had all been a waste of time. She'd put Simon in danger and dropped that piano on Valente for *nothing*. Victor would be waking up any second, and she had zilch to show for it. She didn't even know how she was getting out of—

Her whirling thoughts stopped with a jerk as a pair of black, glossy shoes, the only thing besides herself in this place that wasn't bleedingly red, stepped into her vision. She was still gawking at them in uncomprehending horror when a familiar smug voice sounded practically in her ear.

"Hello, my monster."

Lola closed her eyes with a hiss. "How long have you been here?"

"I'm always here," Victor replied. "This is my death, after all."
Of course.

"I felt your first intrusion as well," he informed her casually.
"I was too busy with more important matters to act on it back
then, but I didn't want you thinking I hadn't noticed."

"I don't care," Lola said, hands balling into fists. "Where is
the Rider's head?"

"Is all you're here for?" He sounded disappointed. "I thought
you'd come to kill me."

"You're not worth the trouble," Lola snarled, yanking her
head up at last. When she turned to bare her teeth at him, though,
the sight of his face stopped her cold.

The man beside her was definitely Victor, but in a form Lola
had never seen. He'd always covered himself in illusions, especially
since he'd become the Hero, but there was no magic on him now.
Just his own face, which was so saggy and ancient it looked like he
was about to crumble to dust before her eyes.

"Surprised?" Victor said, turning his chin to give her a better
look at his sunken cheeks. "You shouldn't be. Mortality is a tyrant,
and I've been doing this for a *very* long time."

Lola knew that. He'd appeared to her as a middle-aged man
in the hospital twenty years ago. If the image he'd presented then
was even remotely true, he'd have to be in his sixties by now, but
this Victor looked way beyond that. She'd never seen a human so
withered who was still alive.

"Now you see why I wear the illusions," he said when she
couldn't stop staring. "People pay less attention to you as you get
older, which is ridiculous. Experience *is* power. I could try to fight
the stupidity, but it's so much easier getting people to swallow a
story when it comes in a handsome package, and heroes are
supposed to be young."

He lifted his thin arms, old joints creaking inside his sagging red jacket as he cupped Lola's cheek with a skeletal hand. "But we've never needed pretensions, have we, my monster? You've always seen me for exactly what I am."

"Are you delusional?" Lola cried, jerking away. "You've done nothing but lie to me my entire life!"

"Did I?" Victor asked, tilting his skull-like head. "The first day we met, when I saved you from that hospital, I told you I was the hero, and here I stand. I told you you were the monster, and there you are. I told you you could save your sister, and so you did."

He smiled. "You've always liked to paint me as the architect of all your suffering, but I've never needed to lie to one so far beneath me. I've always been and done exactly what I said. You were the one who needed to believe differently."

"*No*," Lola snarled, scrambling farther away. "You don't get to do this to me. You don't get to reshape the past into a story where you're not a lying abuser. I saw what you did to Simon, and I know what you did to Valente. You're the monster here, not me. All I ever wanted was to get *away* from you!"

"And yet here we are, closer than ever." His wrinkled face twisted into a terrifying version of the smug smile she knew so well. "You crow and strut about how you're free, but you've spent the last three weeks hiding in someone else's barrow. You seduced my knight, and yet the moment I returned, he knelt right back at my feet. Even your darling Simon came back to my fold. And yes, I know he intends to betray me, but that's how it always goes between a blood mage and his apprentice. I wouldn't respect him if he didn't try, but it's not going to work. His efforts, like yours, will always end in failure. You know why that is, don't you?"

Lola turned away, refusing to answer, so Victor did it for her.

"Because I always win."

"Is that all this is about for you?" she spat, glaring at him with a lifetime of hate. "Winning? Gratifying your arrogance?"

"Arrogance is the core of humanity's strength," he said proudly. "We have always been weak and short-lived. If we meekly accepted our lot, we'd be nothing but grass trampled beneath the feet of greater powers. It is our daring, our *arrogance* that has lifted us out of the mud we were born into. That is what blood magic is about. *That* is humanity's power, and it's why you can never beat me. Because I know exactly what I am capable of, and it is far greater than you."

Lola clutched the edge of the fireplace. She wanted to call him out, to scream that he was a narcissistic liar, but it was hard to say anything when Victor's magic was burying her like a landslide. Logically, she knew that was because they were inside his death, the one place in the universe where Victor actually was a god.

There was no way he wouldn't be stronger than her here. But no matter how many times Lola told herself that was the reason, a small traitorous voice whispered that Victor had been stronger *every* time she'd faced him. The only time she'd ever been able to go toe-to-toe with him was when she'd taken over Fenrir, who was also his creation. Every other time, though, *every other time* she'd defied him, she'd lost. Why should this time be any different?

"There, there," Victor said, reaching out to pet her hair. "It's not your fault. You've always been a stupid little monster, but I'm strong enough to forgive. Come back to my side. Kneel at my feet again, call me master, and all of this will be forgotten."

Lola yanked her head away from his touch. "I'd rather—"

"Die?" he finished with a smirk. "You're so quick to throw that threat around, but is it really your choice to make? You're not a true fairy, after all. Your gossamer belongs to Alberich, not you. And while that might seem like an advantage at the moment, the fairy king's attack isn't going to go the way he thinks. I'm sure Morgan and her foppish knight have already written me off, but that's how it is with immortals. They always think we're weak. That's why they lose, but you're different. You've known from the start that I *always* win, which is why you're the only one who gets a second chance."

"Even if that was true," Lola said, taking another step back, "even if Alberich does die and take me with him, what makes you think I'd ever come back to you?"

"Because you're a survivor," Victor said. "Your ability to cling to life no matter what has always been your greatest strength. But when I crush Alberich and his Hunt—and I *will* crush them—the gossamer that forms your body will cease to exist. There will be no more second chances after that, so if you don't want to vanish with the king who's already written you off, I suggest you reconsider."

He fisted his skeletal hand as he finished. When he opened his fingers again, the smell of fresh blood hit Lola like a punch. Sure enough, when she glanced down, there was a red pill sitting like a jewel at the center of his withered palm.

"Take it," Victor ordered, "and all will be as it was before."

He sounded so sure, so confident she'd do what he said, it gave Lola great joy to turn her face away. As ever, her defiance infuriated him, causing the magic roaring through the room to tighten as Victor grabbed her head with his free hand.

"Do you not see the great mercy you are being offered?" he snarled. "I am the only hero you will *ever* have. The only one who can save you and the girl at the end of your precious thread from oblivion. She will die in that dreamless sleep, and it will be your fault." He shoved the red tab against Lola's hard-pressed lips. "*Take the pill!*"

She couldn't tell him no without letting the pill into her mouth, so Lola lashed out with her foot instead, kicking Victor's legs as hard as she could, but it didn't work. He might have looked like a walking skeleton, but his body was as hard as stone, probably because it wasn't actually his body at all. It was a manifestation of his consciousness, and Victor had always had an iron will.

Lola certainly wasn't strong enough to break it. Even if she'd had all her gossamer here to pull on, she didn't think she could have made him budge. He really was a god in this place, just like Simon had said.

The truth of that knocked the fight right out of her. She never should have come here. She'd been just as arrogant as Victor, thinking she could beat a blood mage in his own death. He was already cramming the pill between her lips, filling her mouth with the hot metallic reek of—

Pain exploded across Lola's gums as her teeth shot out like spikes, forming a razor-sharp wall between the pill and her tongue. Something growled inside her at the same time, staring out of her at Victor with colorblind eyes full of rage.

She welcomed it with open arms. There was no hesitation this time, no fear. The moment her creature rose to the surface, Lola threw herself into the change. It happened so quickly, she didn't even feel the claws growing over her fingers until they lashed out, slicing at the mage's exposed chest like a fan of scythes.

For the second time ever in Lola's memory, Victor looked surprised, his wrinkled brows shooting up to what was left of his wispy hairline. For a heart-stopping moment, it looked like she was going to cut him in half. Then Victor stepped back as smoothly as ever, letting Lola's swipe pass cleanly through the empty air where he'd just been.

"You see, this is why you need your pills," he said, shaking his head. "Just look at what you become without me."

Lola roared in reply. There was no more separation between her and her creature as there'd been at the hospital. She could feel the sharp claws shredding the red carpet like they were her own toes. Just like in the days before Victor found her, they were one body again, only much, *much* bigger.

No longer was she a terrified lump hiding under her bedsheets from the nurses. This Lola towered over her old master, her roars so powerful, they rattled the pictures on the walls. For one glorious moment, she was huge and strong, a primal force that could tear through anything. And then Victor shook his head.

"Disgraceful," he said, rolling up his sleeves. "I thought you were better than this. But if you insist on acting like an animal, then I have no choice but to treat you like one."

He flexed his fingers as he spoke. The bloody magic twisted in reply, but not toward Lola. He was reaching out to the pictures, which were suddenly reaching back.

All over the towering walls, the figures in the frames started moving. They bowed their heads and lifted their previously not-pictured hands up toward Victor like worshipers. As they offered him their open palms, the threads tied to the bottom of each portrait shot out to loop around Victor's fingers.

Within seconds, his hands were wrapped completely in red. When he moved them next, the whole room moved with him, closing around Lola like a fist.

She pushed back with a roar, slashing at the pictures as they got closer. For once in her life, though, her monster couldn't wreck things. Her giant claws slid harmlessly off the red walls, leaving her stuck like a snatched rabbit as Victor smirked up at her from where he was still standing beside the untouched fireplace.

"Did you really think this would change anything?" he asked, closing his red-wrapped fingers to tighten the room's grip. "Though I must admit, I didn't expect you'd be able to bring that thing in here with you." He flashed her a cruel smile. "You must be even more monstrous than I thought."

Lola's answer to that was to start chewing on the red walls that held her prisoner. Like everything else, they tasted horribly of Victor's blood. They were also strong as steel, but her jaws were stronger. It cracked a few of her teeth to do it, but she managed to dig her fangs into one of the portraits whose thread was tied to Victor's hands.

The man inside screamed when her teeth sank in. Blood came next. Real, hot, bubbling life's blood that tasted only slightly of Victor. Lola spat it out at once, and Victor started to laugh.

"I told you you couldn't win," he said, waving his hand at the pictures. "Even if you kill them, I have more. There's no end of greedy fools ready to trade their souls for the Hero's power. Even if you chew my walls bare, I'd just bring in a new batch, but by all means, keep going. You've already killed thousands as Fenrir. What's a few more?"

He finished with a taunting smile, but Lola kept her mouth stubbornly shut. Victor lied as easily as he breathed, but she'd tasted that blood. Even if they were psychos who'd sold their souls to a blood mage, she'd spent her whole life trying *not* to be a monster that killed people. She wouldn't be one for him now, especially since she knew Simon's portrait was up there somewhere as well.

"Such a soft-hearted monster," Victor crooned as she backed off. "Though for the record, it wouldn't have made a difference. Whether you kill them all or not, you can't escape me. I am your master, body and soul. No matter how far your run or how deep you hide, you will always be *mine*."

He clenched his red-wrapped hands as he finished. The room followed the motion, crushing Lola between its walls like a paper cup in a trash compactor. The pressure snapped her bones like twigs, which was a shock because Lola hadn't realized she had bones in this form until they broke. The cracking filled her with dread like nothing else so far, sending a wave of panic through her creature as both of them realized the truth.

They were going to die here. Victor's red death was going to grind them both into pulp, and then they'd be stuck drowning in his choking blood forever. But while that was terrifying enough to make Lola freeze up, her creature went absolutely crazy.

It broke away from her with a terrified squeal, leaving her tumbling inside its giant body as it clawed at the closing walls. Victor watched its struggles with a look of cruel amusement, staying just far enough away that its gnashing teeth couldn't reach him, but not so far that he missed any of the show.

The sight of him enjoying this so much was infuriating enough to kick Lola out of her panic. She *had* to get control back, if only to save her other self from his mockery.

It certainly wouldn't be to escape. She'd already accepted there was no chance of that, but at least she could make sure Victor didn't get to laugh at them while they died. But as she was struggling to grab enough of their magic to make the terrified creature listen, Lola heard a sound from high, high above.

Lola Daniels!

Her head shot up. That wasn't a human voice. It sounded more like a car horn that had just happened to form words, but she couldn't see anything but Victor and his terrible crushing walls. She was about to dismiss the whole thing as a panic-induced hallucination when Victor looked up as well.

"*You,*" he hissed, his cracked lips curling into a snarl.

Hope surged inside Lola's chest. She wasn't sure what was going on, but anything that made Victor angry was aces in her book. If nothing else, it was a good distraction, buying her some breathing room as she struggled to regain control over her panicked creature. She was actually making some headway when the fist of crushing red walls gapped open a little, and she finally caught a glimpse of what was going on over their heads.

High above them, way, way at the top of Victor's enormous death, a hand was reaching through the hole that led to the Sea of Magic. Not a human hand. It looked like a sculpture made from pipes and electrical wires, its finger joints clicking like ratchets as it reached down toward them.

Lola! the strange voice cried again as the hand made of junk grew. Its fingers stretched down like snakes, the wires and plastic knotting around each other to form a rope that slid between the twisted red walls until they were dangling right above her creature's shaggy head.

Grab on!

Lola was desperately trying to. She seized her creature with everything she had, shaking it out of its panic as she screamed at it to lift their arm. She'd nearly gotten their paw up to their shoulder when a golden light flashed in the redness, cutting the dangling rope in half.

It cut Lola too, causing both her and her creature to scream in pain as the light seared their collective flesh. When she turned the creature's head to see where the strange burning had come from, Victor was holding the Hero's golden sword in his red-wrapped hands.

He swung it again as she watched, slicing the strange hand with a roar of fury. The fingers shattered when he hit them, raining pieces of broken plastic and metal down on Lola's creature's flat face. It looked like a pretty effective attack, but no matter how much of it Victor cut off, the hand never seemed to get any smaller. Every time the sword smashed through it, more pieces came down from the top, rebuilding the damage instantly as the junk-sculpture hand reached down to grab Lola's creature by the scruff of its neck.

"*No!*" Victor roared, swinging his sword wildly as the giant hand picked her up. "You cannot escape! *I'm* the god of this place! *You will not take what is mine!*"

Under any other circumstances, Lola would have believed that entirely, but the hand didn't seem to care. It just flew back up toward the hole in the ceiling where the Sea of Magic was churning like a washing machine packed with the chaos of the universe, taking Lola and her creature with it as it vanished back into wild, pounding dark.

Chapter 12

Are you okay?

Lola twitched inside her creature's shaggy body. Its weak eyes couldn't see anything in the churning darkness, but she didn't smell Victor's blood anymore. That seemed like a good sign, so Lola let her terrified creature run away, leaving herself human again—at least in looks—as she peeked her head up.

Sure enough, she was back in the Sea of Magic, only this time she wasn't being bounced around like a pinball. She could feel the primal currents rushing just a few feet away, but there was a glowing barrier between her and the chaos. The light was nauseatingly orange and glaringly bright, reminding her of the DFZ's streetlights.

A second later, Lola realized there was no "reminding" about it. There *was* a DFZ streetlight shining directly over her head, and standing beside its sticker-and-graffiti-covered pole was a small figure wearing a black hooded coat that glistened like wet pavement.

"Who are you?" Lola asked, scooting as far away from the very strange stranger as she could without leaving the streetlight's protective circle.

Instead of replying, the figure pushed its hood back to reveal a gaunt face that could have been a girl's or a boy's. But while her sunken features were painfully human, her eyes were an unnatural bright orange, shining out of her face with the same glow as the streetlight overhead, which answered Lola's question.

"You're the Spirit of the DFZ."

And you're Lola Daniels, the spirit of the Living City replied happily, her divine voice filling Lola's head. *Car enthusiast.*

Lola frowned. Of all the reasons the city god might know her, that wasn't the one she would have picked.

Of course, I know you, the DFZ said, orange eyes shining merrily. *I'm your city! You've lived in me all your life. I've always known who you are, though I admit you've been much more in my attention lately.*

Lola winced. "I'm *really* sorry about Fenrir," she said in a rush. "I would have stopped him sooner, but Victor—"

If Victor Conrath could be stopped by trying hard, none of us would be in this mess, the spirit said with a huff like the blasts of hot air that came up through her sidewalk grates. *But I'm afraid we'll have to pause this conversation. The blood maniac is waking up, and he is* not *happy I helped you. If we don't get you to Fenrir's vessel ASAP, I don't know if I'll be able to keep holding on.*

Lola shot a terrified look at the deadly swirling magic and scrambled back to the street lamp.

Good to see you can keep it together in a crisis, the city said, looking around. *Now, which way do we go?*

"You mean you don't know?"

The spirit of the DFZ shrugged. *He's your bad doggo.*

In no universe would Lola ever call the city-sized, world-ending wolf a "doggo," bad or otherwise. It was the rest of what the spirit said, though, that made her panic.

"But I don't know how to get back!" she cried, clinging to the streetlight for dear life. "Victor made Fenrir, not me! The only reason I was able to get in last time was because of my sister."

The orange-eyed spirit tilted her head in confusion. *You have a sister?*

Lola was struggling for a way to explain her situation that wouldn't take up too much of their very limited time when she felt a familiar tugging on her wrist. After three weeks of nothing, the movement made her jump. Sure enough, when she looked down, her sister's thread was pulling hard against her skin, the silver thread shooting off like an arrow into the dark. It was the same thing that had happened the last time she was here, which didn't make sense at all. She'd left her sister sleeping safe in Tristan's barrow. Not—

Is something wrong?

"No, it's just…" Lola trailed off, pointing at the silver line. "Do you see that?"

The spirit squinted her glowing eyes. *See what?*

"Never mind," Lola said, grabbing the glowing thread with both hands. "This way."

The city stuck right by her elbow, keeping them both inside the protective circle of her streetlight, which floated along behind her like a pull toy. If Lola had had any spare mental capacity, she would've had a billion questions about that, but pulling herself along her sister's thread was taking all of her concentration.

It was much, *much* harder this time, but that was only to be expected. The last time Lola had jumped into the Sea of Magic, Fenrir had been the most feared thing on the planet. Of course doing this by herself would be harder. If the DFZ's light hadn't been keeping them safe, the currents would have ripped her to pieces. But while the city spirit hadn't been good for directions, she was great at providing cover, buying Lola the space she needed to crawl down the silver thread into a big black hole that looked an awful lot like Fenrir's pit.

It wasn't exactly the same. This crack at the bottom of the Sea of Magic wasn't a tenth as big as the one she'd gone into with Morgan. That made sense, given that the whole world was no longer watching Fenrir act out a monster movie on live TV, but Lola still couldn't understand why her thread had led them *here*. She'd busted her butt to save her sister from Fenrir. The glittering line should be pointing up toward the surface or wherever her sister's soul was, not going down.

Too bad the thread didn't seem to realize that. It went straight into the depths like a silver anchor chain. Not knowing where else to go, Lola followed it, yanking herself hand over fist all the way down to the pit's floor, which was the same uneven black stone she remembered from her first time here. It even still had the clawing finger marks left by all the people whose fear Victor had harnessed to dig the place out. But while her silver thread was lying in huge coils all over the ground, Lola didn't see anything else.

Hey, that wasn't so bad! the DFZ said cheerfully as her waterproof boots hit the ground next to Lola. *Now, where is...*

Her strange voice faded off like distant traffic. When Lola turned to see why, her bare feet froze on the rough stone.

There, rising over them like a mountain in the dark, was Fenrir, or what was left of him. The giant wolf was clearly dead, and had been for some time. His rotting corpse was already collapsing like roadkill in the sun, the black fur peeling off his flesh in huge, house-sized chunks. The only good thing Lola could say was that at least he didn't stink. But while she wasn't sad to see the demise of Victor's doomsday monster, the DFZ looked devastated.

Oh, man, she groaned. *I hate it when she's right.*

"She who?" Lola asked, more confused than ever.

Archmage Novali, the DFZ replied, frowning when this didn't seem to ring any bells. *Head of the Merlin Council? Most powerful Thaumaturge in the world? Has a glowing cat?*

"Sorry," Lola said, shaking her head. "I don't know much about human magic." At least, not the sort that didn't involve blood. "But how did the archmage know about Fenrir?"

Because she's the best, the city replied proudly. *She figured out what Victor was up to the moment Fenrir reared his ugly head. She saw right off the bat that he was a manufactured spirit. Unfortunately, knowing what he was didn't make him any easier to fight. We thought we were really screwed there until you took over and walked him away.*

Lola's jaw fell open. "You know about that?"

Well, we didn't know it was you specifically, the DFZ said. *But the archmage postulated that Victor, being a blood mage, would have used a human death as the foundation for his spell. There's no other way he could have controlled such a huge spirit, but blood mages are great at controlling people. That's why she asked me to go out and find you. We were hoping that you could do it again.*

There was no way Lola had heard that right. "You want me to bring Fenrir *back?*"

I'm not exactly thrilled about it, the city said with a grimace. *But we're kind of up against the wall here. A city's heart is her people, and Victor's flooded mine with his rabid followers. Their devotion means I can't crush him with any of the objects I would so dearly love to drop on his stupid head. The only reason I'm still free enough to stand around talking to you is because the rest of the world still sees me as the Detroit Free Zone, and the DFZ bows to no one!*

She finished by shaking her defiant fist at the swirling dark above their heads, and then the god's shoulders slumped. *It won't last, though. The longer Victor stays in power, the more people stop seeing me as an independent city and start seeing me as his. Once that happens, I'm finished, which is why I'm willing to take another wolf to the face to stop it. I don't know what let you take control last time, but if you can get Fenrir back on his feet, the archmage thinks it'll be enough to kick Victor and his red-coated cronies out of the city before the Wild Hunt arrives. That last bit is super important. We've seen how much power people were willing to give Victor just for standing up to Fenrir, even though he didn't win. If he actually manages to defeat the Wild Hunt, he could become unstoppable.*

That was exactly what Lola had been saying. It was so gratifying to finally hear the same sense from someone else. Unfortunately…

"I can't do it," she said, shaking her head. "I'm all for feeding Victor to his own wolf, but I can't control Fenrir."

Sure you can! the DFZ said, throwing up her scrawny arms. *I know he looks kinda dumpy right now, but that's only because he was never a real spirit to begin with. There's nothing wrong with his vessel, though. This place is huge! Maybe not as big as it once was, but there's still way more magic here than Victor could stop even with his stupid sword, especially since his blood magic bane doesn't work on spirits. We just have to figure out how to get your puppy back on his feet, but you're the mage Victor used to kick off this place, right? Once you retake control of your death, Victor will be dog food!*

She sounded so excited, it broke Lola's heart to tell her the truth. "I'd love to help you," she said, shaking her head. "But I'm afraid I'm not a mage. I'm not even human. I don't know how you missed it considering I was a giant furry monster when you saved me, but I'm a fairy, a changeling. I don't have a soul or a death to take over."

But she knew who did. The proof was right there on her wrist. *That* was why the silver thread still led back here even after she'd gotten her sister out. This wasn't just Fenrir's vessel. It was her sister's death. *She* was the foothold Victor had used as the starting line for his monster. Fenrir's birth had turned into a horrible black pit, but before humanity's fear had strip-mined it into a yawning chasm, this place had probably been a little room just like Simon's, which meant…

Lola didn't even take the time to finish the thought. She was already whirling around, putting her back to the city spirit as she grabbed her thread with both hands. She still wasn't able to move it, but she could follow where it led, tracing the loops and tangles that lay all over the ground like abandoned fishing line until she found the one thread that didn't circle back on itself.

She broke into a run as soon as she spotted it, tripping over the uneven ground as she sprinted across the gigantic pit. The DFZ followed right on her heels, both of them charging through the dark until the silver trail they'd been following came to an abrupt end.

Huh, the DFZ said as Lola stumbled to a stop. *Who's that?*

Lola's throat was too tight to answer. There, lying like a dropped sock on the stone floor, was her sister. She looked exactly the same as she had back at Tristan's, right down to the fuzzy pink cat pajamas Lola had bought her off the internet. Even the silver thread was right there on her wrist, but of course it would be. She had more right to be here than Lola did, because unlike the changeling who had replaced her, she was human.

A human soul inside her death.

Lola had hoped that'd mean she'd find her sister waiting for her as Simon had been. But while she was still frustratingly asleep, her chest was rising and falling just like it did in the real world, giving Lola hope.

"Hey!" she yelled, dropping down to grab the unconscious woman by her shoulders. "It's me! It's Lola, your sister! I'm here to rescue you! Open your eyes and look at me!"

She punctuated every word with a shake, but her sister didn't react any more now than she ever had. Lola tried again, even louder this time, but as always, it didn't work.

"I don't understand," she said, her voice cracking as she reached up to touch her sister's beautiful black hair. "I'm finally here. I found you just like I promised. *Why won't you wake up?*"

That last part came out as a scream. She was about to start shaking her again when a gentle hand landed on her shoulder.

I'm so sorry for your loss.

"Don't say that!" Lola snapped, glaring over her shoulder at the god she'd completely forgotten was here. "My sister's not dead!"

She couldn't be. Even in this place, her chest still moved with the breaths that had always kept Lola's hope alive. That should have been proof enough for anyone, but the DFZ was looking at her with that awful pity, and a cold lump formed in Lola's throat.

"Why do you think she's dead?"

Because that's an empty corpse, the spirit said sadly, pointing at the girl in Lola's arms. *I'm the god of a major metropolitan area. Thousands of people die inside me every day. I know what human souls look like, and there's not one in there.*

"You're lying," Lola snarled, clutching her sister to her chest. "If she's dead, why does she still feel warm? Why is she breathing?"

I have no idea, the spirit replied, frowning as if that *really* bothered her. *I'm home to three major magical universities and I have the highest per capita mage population in the world. There's not a lot of magic I haven't seen, but this is a new one on me. We're inside the Sea of Magic. Physical bodies have no place here. Fenrir's corpse made sense because he was a spirit, even if he was a fake, but how is there a dead human lying on your floor?*

She sounded completely baffled, but Lola wasn't listening. She'd already curled over her sister's body. It couldn't be true. Her sister couldn't be dead. There had to be another explanation, something Lola could fix. She couldn't lose her one and only family. Not when she'd already lost everything else.

I know you're hurting, the city said gently. *But we don't have time to mourn right now. The Wild Hunt will be arriving any minute. If we're going to keep Victor from using them to finish what he started three weeks ago, you* have *to get Fenrir moving. If you could just—*

"I can't," Lola said bitterly, pressing her face into the fuzzy fabric of her sister's pajamas. "Fenrir was her dream, not mine. She's the one Victor used."

And killed. Lola hadn't wanted to believe it was possible, but now that the DFZ had confirmed her worst fears, everything made a horrible kind of sense. Her sister wasn't waking up because of something Alberich had done. This, like everything else, was Victor's doing. Lola had rescued her body, but not before the blood mage had blown her soul into... into *this.* This wasn't

Simon's cozy bedroom or even Victor's gaudy crimson hall. It was a pit. A huge empty hole with nothing inside it but a rotting corpse.

"He killed her," Lola whispered, her voice thin as a fraying thread. "I was too late. He killed her!"

But it's not too late to stop him from killing anyone else, the DFZ said desperately, getting down on her hands and knees and pressing her cheek against the ground so she could look Lola in the face. *I'm not entirely sure what a changeling is, but if you grew up in the DFZ, you're one of mine, and we never say die! Even if the mage that started all of this is dead, Fenrir's vessel is still here, and where there's a vessel, there's a spirit! We can still use that to stop Victor before—*

"There is no stopping Victor!" Lola yelled at her, baring her teeth, which were sharpening into knives again. "You're the city of second chances! It's easy for you to have hope, but I've been fighting Victor my entire life. The only time I even got close to winning was because of her." She shook the limp girl in her arms. "She's the one you want. She's the reason I made it back, the thread that held me together, and you just told me she's *dead*!"

Worse than dead. If she'd died like a normal person, the death gods could have found her. They would have rescued her soul and taken it somewhere safe, somewhere better. But Victor had ruined that just like he ruined everything.

No wonder she'd felt like an empty shell. Victor had turned her soul into a void. If the DFZ was right, she was the one who could have beaten him, but they were too late. Just like always, Victor was one step ahead. He'd already used and discarded Lola's sister just like he did everything else. Now her only family was gone forever, and Lola hadn't even gotten to tell her how much she loved her.

Don't look like that, the DFZ pleaded as Lola began to shake. *I heard the blood mage talking before I broke in. He was trying to get you back under his control, right? I've gotten to know Victor Conrath a lot better than I've wanted to over these past few weeks, and I don't think he would have bothered if you didn't still have the power to hurt him. I'm sorry I was insensitive about your situation earlier, but we really need you to—*

"I can't hurt him," Lola whispered, turning her face away. "Just leave me alone."

The DFZ's orange eyes flashed, but whatever she'd been about to say was buried by a crushing wave of power. The moment Lola told her to go, the pounding magic she remembered from the last time she'd been inside Fenrir's vessel crashed down like a mountain. Even the Living City couldn't hold up under so much pressure. Her image collapsed like a demolished building, leaving Lola alone in the dark with two corpses: one breathing and one not.

<div align="center">~~~</div>

Twenty minutes earlier.

Valente didn't know it was possible to delay his re-formation until he tried it. The moment he felt himself coming back together, he pushed in the other direction, swatting and kicking the different pieces of his magic apart. He wasn't sure if it made a difference, but it felt like it took longer than usual before his headless naked body condensed out of the shadows.

He sat up in confusion. The pitch black of the windowless room didn't hamper the fairy vision that was his only option without his head, but Valente still wasn't sure where he was. It wasn't until the mental compass that always pointed at his master snapped into position that he realized he was sitting on the floor of Victor's bedroom.

That shouldn't have been a surprise. Victor had kept his head under his bed for years before he'd trusted his Rider enough to let Valente store it in his own apartment. Unlike back then, though, Valente still couldn't feel his actual head anywhere. He should have formed right next to it, but the only gossamer he felt was Lola's.

If everything hadn't been so terrible, that would have been a lovely thing to wake up to. But while he could feel her warm, sunny magic all around him like a blanket, he couldn't pin down the source. The compass in his head kept spinning in broken circles, swinging wildly between this room and the hall outside.

His knighthood oaths surged in response. Their desperation to please their king grabbed Valente's body like a fist, forcing him to his feet. They dressed his body in a freezing gossamer version of his usual riding clothes next, snatching the magic tight as a straitjacket around him.

The feeling made him jolt in surprise. Valente couldn't normally make things out of gossamer, but the oaths were another story. Anything that was technically within his power, they could make him do in service to his master, and Victor had made his wishes very clear. His body had already spun itself around, jerking like a puppet toward the bed where the tiny bit of Lola glimmered like a sunbeam.

Valente had to dig his new boots into the carpet to keep from grabbing her. He already knew there was no stopping the oaths. If he refused the compulsion, they'd take over his body and make him do it anyway, so Valente appeased the beast instead, tearing his attention off the small but blindingly bright gleam of Lola on Victor's pillow to focus on the larger but dimmer mass of her magic he could feel somewhere down the hall.

It was still difficult to get out of the bedroom. The oaths weren't actually intelligent, but Valente had learned he couldn't keep tricking them the same way for long. They were already wising up to his "I haven't found all of her so I can't kill any of her" excuse, making his limbs drag like lead as he stumbled into the hall.

Valente came back with the thought that the majority of Lola's magic was in the thrall room. His master had stressed over and over that whatever was going on in there was of critical importance and absolutely not to be interrupted for any reason. Surely, obeying that order was more important than investigating the tiny piece of Lola that was still in Victor's bedroom and possibly waking his master up in the process, something Victor had also ordered his knight never to do.

This logic appeased his oaths somewhat, but Valente could still feel them twisting like snakes inside his brain. A very strange feeling since he was truly headless at the moment. He didn't even have a new helmet ready since he hadn't expected to wake up in the middle of Victor's private suite.

Fortunately, the only other people in this part of the tower were thralls, and they didn't care about anything except what they were told to. Case in point, one of them was walking down the hallway toward him right now. The woman's glossy eyes slid right over the empty space at the top of the Rider's collar, ignoring him completely in her rush to deliver Victor's freshly pressed laundry to his dressing room.

Valente grabbed her arm when she came in range, reaching for his notepad only to remember he'd left it on Simon's desk right before Lola had crushed him with a piano. He *still* couldn't believe she'd done that. Not the crushing part—that was totally acceptable self-defense—but why a piano?

He was dying to ask. Dying to talk to her for any reason. But Valente didn't get to enjoy things like that anymore, and the thrall was pulling so hard against his grip that he was afraid she was going to dislocate her arm.

He let her go at once. He'd wanted to find out what was going on in the mailroom before he went in, but the thrall couldn't listen to a man who couldn't talk, and Valente didn't have time to find another notepad. He could already hear crashes coming from the workshop, kicking up the compulsion he'd triggered by reminding his oaths how important protecting that room was.

Shaking his neck at the mess, Valente turned and started jogging toward the room where Victor "processed" his mail. The crashes got bigger as he got closer. He didn't hear any screaming because thralls didn't do that, but the whole place was in chaos by the time he finally burst through the door.

It looked like a tornado had blown through. All of the sorting tables had been knocked on their sides, leaving the thralls who worked at them waving their hands uselessly through the air like factory machines on an empty assembly line. The inlaid magical circles looked like they'd been pried out of the floor with a crowbar, and the bowl of golden liquid Victor painstakingly collected every day had been splattered in an arc across the ceiling. Pieces of mail were flying everywhere, thrown into the air by the girl who was still kicking her way around the room like the bags of letters were piles of leaves raked up specifically for her enjoyment. She did seem to be enjoying herself, too, her pretty face beaming with Lola's huge smile.

"This is fun!" she cried as she punted a package at one of the hanging lights. "I should be a distraction more often!"

Valente ran a hand over the spot where his face should have been. The girl kicking the mail was made of Lola's gossamer, but it definitely wasn't her. She looked more like a Lola doll that had come to life. He wasn't entirely sure how that worked, but the knighthood oaths were screaming at him to make her stop, so Valente stepped forward to grab her by the arm.

"Hey!" she said, tugging against his grip. "What gives?"

Valente let go of her just long enough to grab one of the flying letters out of the air. He stole a pen next, snatching it right out of a reply-writing thrall's fingers. Both actions together couldn't have taken more than five seconds, but by the time Valente turned back around, the girl-who-was-almost-Lola had spun her gossamer into a mallet and was swinging it over her head to smash the track lighting out of the ceiling.

He grabbed her again, taking her mallet away and tossing it on the floor to free his hands as he wrote a question on the back of the envelope he'd snatched out of the air.

What are you?

"I'm Lola," the girl who was obviously not Lola said proudly. "Go on, ask me a question!"

What are you doing? he wrote next.

"Causing a ruckus to keep you distracted from the real Lola."

Valente couldn't help himself. *Aren't you not supposed to tell me that?*

The fake Lola shrugged and shaped up another mallet. She was already swinging for the lights again when Valente pinned her arms behind her back, holding her wrists together with one hand while he wrote furiously with the other.

What did she want you to distract me from?

"She's going into Victor's dreams to find your head."

Valente was so stunned that he let her slip from his grasp. The double seized the opportunity to grab *both* of her mallets and charge straight into the giant stack of packages in the corner. The sounds of destruction were so loud that even the thralls looked up, but Valente was frozen in place, his gloved hands fisting tighter and tighter.

This couldn't be happening. Lola was supposed to be safe. He'd bent over backwards to keep her out of this, to keep her away from *him*. Now she was going into Victor's dreams, plunging headfirst into the monster's mouth, and it was all his fault.

The panic that shot through him at that was enough to make even the oaths go quiet. He never should have told her about his head. Never should have gone near her at all, but he couldn't bring himself to die without telling her he was sorry, and now that selfishness was going to get her killed. He couldn't let that happen, not after she'd finally gotten free. Killing Victor was supposed to be his atonement, the one thing Valente could still do to make up for all the evil he'd done as his knight. It wouldn't bring anyone back, but at least he'd be leaving the world a better place. A better place for *her*.

Lola was a huge part of why he was doing this. She was the only person who'd seen him, all of him, and hadn't despised him. Even Valente despised himself, but Lola never had. Even after Victor had ordered him to kill her, she'd embraced him and said she didn't want him to die. Valente had no words for how much that meant, but he hadn't thought she'd actually do it. Even if she did find his head, a knight had no life without his monarch, which meant Lola was putting herself in danger for *nothing*.

The double was still merrily smashing boxes when Valente grabbed her again, shoving the envelope, which was now scribbled all over, into her face.

How do I make her stop trying to save me?

"Oh, you can't stop Lola," the girl assured him. "She does whatever she wants. Just look at me! According to Tristan, changelings shouldn't even be able to make gossamer that can think for itself, yet here I am!"

She smashed another package flat before leaning on the handle of her mallet to grin at him. "You might as well give up and let her save you, because Lola's not going to stop until she does."

But it's impossible, Valente wrote, his hands shaking so badly that the letters looked like squiggles. *I'm a knight. Only death can free me from Victor.*

"That doesn't matter," the double informed him casually. "Her sister's dead, too, and Lola hasn't stopped trying to save her."

Valente jerked. *Her sister's dead?*

"Well, her body's technically alive, but there's nothing inside. Tristan's known for weeks. He just hasn't said anything yet because it would make Lola upset."

But he said something to you?

"He was interrogating me," the double said, lifting her chin as if this made her terribly important. "There's something going on with Lola's magic that he doesn't understand. See example number one: myself! He's always known she wasn't a real changeling since actual changelings don't dream. He thought that was due to Victor's human blood, but that stuff's been out of her for weeks and she still—"

She cut off as Valente grabbed another letter to start writing again, reading it carefully when he shoved the note under her nose.

What do you mean Lola's not a real changeling?

"Hey, I'm just telling you what Tristan told me," the double said, raising her hands. "But it does make sense. I mean, if Alberich could just make a changeling with dreams as delicious as Lola's, why would he need to steal babies? All the food he needed would already be right there."

When Valente tilted his headless body to think that over, Lola's copy made a break for her mallets again. He smacked them out of her hands before she got six inches, pinning her arms behind her as he wrote his next question.

What else did Tristan tell you?

"Not much," she said with a sigh. "He mostly wanted me to tell him stuff. I have all of Lola's memories up to the point where she spun me off, so I'm a great source of information."

Again, she sounded smugly proud about that, and the Rider hunched his shoulders like a scowl. *Shouldn't you be more loyal?*

"I am loyal!" the copy cried, looking terribly hurt. "But Lola made me in her image, and she doesn't care about secrets. All she wants is for everyone to be happy and safe. And for Victor to die in a fire, but that's a distant second. She mostly just wants to set you all free. That's why she's fighting so hard to find your head. She was never going to sit back and let you sacrifice yourself even if it would kill Victor. You're way more important to her than he is."

She's important to me too, Valente wrote in shaky letters. He stared at the words for a long time, and then he crumpled the scribbled envelope in his hands, reaching down to snatch a fresh one off the ground to write a new message.

I need you to do something for me.

"I know, I know, it's 'die,'" the double said with a dramatic sigh. "I *told* Lola I wasn't strong enough to fight you, but she said that was okay, so I guess you can go ahead and melt my gossamer or whatever. Can I smash a few more things before you do it, though? Lola has a lot of pent-up rage, and breaking Victor's stuff is *really* satisfying."

I think you already broke it all, Valente wrote, waving his pen at the destroyed room. *But I'm not going to kill you.*

She looked confused. "Don't you have to kill Lola?"

You're not her, he wrote. *But you are made from a lot of her gossamer. I'm pretty sure she's going to need that back, so I'm letting you go. In return, I want you to deliver a message for me.*

"Sure, what is it?"

Valente's body moved in a silent breath. This was the most selfish thing he'd ever done, but just like that wonderful night by the lake, he couldn't bring himself to stop. Lola always did this to him. Even when she wasn't here, even when he knew it was all doomed, she still somehow made him hope. It was a stupid, self-indulgent feeling Valente knew he didn't deserve, but he couldn't stop his hand as the words appeared on the page.

Tell her I'll wait, he wrote in tiny letters, turning his back to make sure the thralls didn't see. *I can't promise I'll survive the Wild Hunt, but if she's brave enough to go into Victor's dreams for me, the least I can do is try.* He tightened his fingers on the pen. *I won't throw the fight with Orlando. As long as I can, as long as it takes, I'll do my best to stay alive until she finds a way to set me free.*

"That will make her very happy," the double promised, wrapping her arms around his chest. "Don't die, Valente!"

The sound of his real name spoken in Lola's happy voice shook him to his core. By the time he got control of himself again, the copy had vanished like the morning dew, leaving him standing alone in the chaos as the tower's alarms began to blare.

Chapter 13

Lola didn't know how long she sat in the dark. It felt like a lifetime, or maybe an afterlifetime. She wasn't sure if changelings counted as mortal, but it sure felt like she'd fallen somewhere people never came out of.

When she wasn't staring blankly into the nothingness, Lola spent her time studying Fenrir. The rotting corpse wasn't exactly pleasant viewing, but it was easier to look at than the empty human behind her. She couldn't even turn her head that direction without bursting into tears.

She knew it was stupid, mourning so hard for someone she'd never even met, but that didn't stop the loss from cutting to the bone. Normally, when Lola felt this hopeless, she'd grab her thread and tell her sister that everything would be okay. Even when it was a blatant lie, just having someone to put on that brave face for had made Lola feel like maybe it could be true.

Now, though, she had nothing. No sister, no plan, no hope. Even if she'd known how to get out of here, Valente and Simon were probably already dead, which meant there wasn't anyone for her to go back to.

That set her off all over again. She was bracing for another long cry when Lola heard something thump in the darkness. It was the first noise she'd heard since the DFZ had disappeared, but when she lifted her head off her knees to see if the city spirit had come back, her sister was spasming on the ground.

Lola shot to her side with a yelp. The girl looked no more conscious than she ever had, but her body was bucking like a landed fish. Even worse, the spasms were slamming her head against the stone floor, threatening to crack her skull wide open.

"*Stop!*" Lola screamed, wrapping her arms around her sister's shoulders to keep her from hurting herself. "Just *stop it!* Hasn't she suffered enough?"

She didn't know who she was yelling at, but they didn't listen. Her sister just kept right on thrashing, whipping her body back and forth like she was possessed. Lola tried to hold her down, but for someone who was supposedly an empty corpse, her sister was freakishly strong. Stronger than Lola had ever been even when she'd spun herself muscles.

"Please," she sobbed, clinging to the convulsing girl with all her might. "Don't do this. Even if it's empty, her body's all I have left. Don't destroy my last piece of—"

"*Lola!*"

Lola's head shot up, her eyes blinking against the brightness that was suddenly everywhere. She was still wrapped around her sister, but they were no longer at the bottom of Fenrir's pit. They were lying on the bed in Tristan's guest room. Even stranger, Lola had almost all of her gossamer back. She could still feel the cat she'd left with Victor, but the rest of her magic was here.

She let the cat go at once, slicing the tiny bit of gossamer free as she climbed off her sister, who'd fallen still the moment they arrived. Lola was leaning over to check the girl's head when her magic rippled. For a horrible moment, Lola thought it was Alberich, and then her doppelganger stepped out of her gossamer.

"Thank goodness you're back!" the other Lola sobbed, throwing her arms around the original. "I was so worried!"

Lola pushed her right back off. "How did you do that?"

"Valente told me to give you your gossamer back," her double replied tearfully. "But I didn't know how to get it to you! I was shaking and shaking, but—"

"*You* were the one shaking her?" Lola asked sharply,

whipping her head back toward her sister, who was indeed lying askew in the middle of the bed.

"It was the only way I knew to reach you!" the other her wailed. "I'm only made of gossamer! I couldn't follow where you went!"

Lola covered her face with a groan. She supposed she should be happy that her sister's death was still connected to her physical body, but the hope was just reflexive at this point. She had no actual expectation anymore that the empty girl on the bed would ever wake up, but the rest of this didn't make any sense. How had her double pulled her out by shaking her sister's body? And how had she given Lola's magic back without Lola's say-so? She was *supposed* to be a spell who only did what she was told.

"I thought I told you not to gain sentience."

"But this is *important*," her doppelganger insisted. "The Wild Hunt just arrived in the DFZ!"

Lola flinched. And here she'd thought today couldn't get worse. "Who's winning?"

"They're not fighting yet," her double reported as the real Lola pushed past her into the living room. "Alberich's vanguard is still circling Victor's tower, but that's not what's important. I have a message I have to deliver from—"

She cut off with a squawk as Lola pulled her gossamer back in. She couldn't deal with whatever was going on with her copy right now. She'd much rather get her news from Tristan, but the knight and his queen were nowhere to be found. There was, however, a note waiting for her on the coffee table.

Lola-lion, it read. *Gone to war. If you've got any aces left up your sleeve, now would be a good time. -XOXO, Tristan.*

Lola tossed the note away and grabbed the remote. She was trying to remember the right combination of buttons that would turn on Morgan's wall of televisions when her doppelganger smacked the controller out of her hand.

"Would you knock it off?" Lola snarled, whirling to face her mirror image, who was suddenly standing right beside her. "If you want to rebel against your creator, do it tomorrow. I've been through too much today already, and I can't take it."

"I'm not rebelling," her double insisted, glaring at her with Lola's own scowl. "I'm *trying* to help. There's something very important that I need to—"

She was interrupted by a roar of sound as the entire wall of televisions came on all at once. Lola took the chance to yank her back in. She tied her gossamer in a knot this time, locking herself up tight as a drum to keep out interruptions before turning her attention back to the screens.

Morgan had left them tuned to news channels all over the world, but while the announcers were all speaking different languages, every TV was showing the exact same image: the Hero's Tower rising from the destroyed DFZ like a golden sword, and the black cloud of riders swirling through the sky around it.

~~~

"And you didn't *stop* her?" Victor shouted.

Valente shrugged his shoulders, giving his master the hardest "you brought this on yourself" glare a headless body could muster.

"Days of work," Victor groaned, running a hand through the Hero's perfect hair as he gazed mournfully at the mailroom Lola's double had destroyed. "Vital efforts, *ruined*!" He whirled back to his Rider. "You think I have time to fix this? Alberich's riders are already swarming the city, I've got the DFZ wailing in my ear about her bloody peasants, and you just let that menace waltz in here and smash the most critical piece of my infrastructure!"
~~~

The Rider bent down to grab one of the Hero's trampled fan letters off the floor. He was pulling the pen he'd found earlier out of his pocket when Victor slapped the envelope out of his hand.

"I don't have time for your nonsense," the blood mage snarled, grabbing the collar of the Rider's motorcycle suit where the shadows curled out of his headless torso like wisps of smoke. "We're finishing this right now. Go get your head!"

Valente jerked. The knighthood oaths were already hammering at him to obey, but he genuinely didn't know where his head was. If he did, he would have told Lola and saved her the trauma of going into Victor's dreams. Since his master was awake and yelling at him, he assumed she hadn't been successful, but that just made the order even more confusing. *Had* she stolen his head, and Victor wanted him to go get it back? Or was this some kind of test to—

His racing thoughts swerved off the road when his arm started moving of its own accord. The oaths didn't usually take over his body this quickly, but the magic must have gotten fed up with his inaction, because it was moving Valente like a puppet, shoving his gloved hand down the empty hole where his neck should have been.

Valente stumbled in horror as his arm pushed in up to the elbow, practically dislocating his shoulder as his hand rooted around inside his chest. Then, with a jerk of triumph, his arm yanked itself back up, dragging something freezing out with it.

The feel of that icy lump sliding through his empty neck made Valente want to vomit. If he'd still had a mouth to open or a stomach to empty, he absolutely would have. Being the headless monster that he was, though, all he could do was stagger silently as his hand popped free of his neck and shot out to show Victor its prize.

Valente already knew what he'd see. That didn't stop his eyeless gaze from locking onto the thing he hated most in the world, even more than Victor. The face he still couldn't help but love.

Even after all these years, the fairy's severed head was as lovely as a snowflake. Despite the gray skin and blue lips making him look like a frostbitten corpse, he was still more beautiful than any creature—alive or dead—had a right to be. Beautiful enough that he almost didn't need the cursed magic that poured down from his face like a waterfall, making anyone who laid eyes on him ready to kill for the prize of his attention.

Valente was no exception. Even knowing what was coming, one look was all it took to collapse his convictions, leaving him nothing to hold on to as he slid into the maw of the dead fairy's gossamer.

He wasn't the only one. The whole time Victor had been yelling at him, the mailroom thralls had continued their business, quietly cleaning up the mess the fake Lola had made. When the head came out, though, every human in the room snapped to attention, their eyes locking onto the dead fairy with the worshipful attention that was normally reserved for Victor. They looked at Valente next, baring their teeth as they crept closer.

Valente fell into a crouch in reply, ready to kill if that was what it took to keep the fairy for himself. It seemed impossible that he'd ever cared about anything else. But just as he was forming a hammer of invisible gossamer to protect his prize, Victor said, "Stop."

Everyone in the room froze. Then the magic crashed on top of them, pushing the thralls to their knees as Victor replaced the dead fairy's enthrallment with his own, far bloodier version. It pushed Valente down as well, forcing him to the ground as Victor said, "Put it on."

Valente didn't need his oaths to obey. As much as he hated everything about this, for once, Victor was the lesser evil. *Nothing* could be worse than the sticky, decaying infatuation pouring off the dead fairy like plague water. At least when it was on his shoulders, the fairy's head couldn't enthrall him, so Valente shoved it down, letting out a soundless scream as the icy gossamer dug its fangs into what was left of his humanity.

He'd never get used to how much that hurt. The head clamped onto him like a crocodile, filling him with all the things being headless normally muted. Exhaustion, sorrow, rage, and physical pain took turns pounding through his body in waves, leaving him gasping on the mail-strewn floor.

When it finally receded enough for Valente to stand back up, the thralls were gone, leaving the wrecked room empty save for Victor, who was waiting in the doorway with his fingers drumming impatiently on the hilt of the Hero's golden sword.

"Took you long enough."

"You didn't let me put it on for almost a month," Valente reminded him, wincing at the feel of the fairy's inhumanly smooth voice inside his raw, newly-formed throat. "The cost builds up."

"And whose fault is that?" his master snapped, tossing Valente a fresh copy of the Rider's mirrored helmet. "If you hadn't been such a disobedient swine, I wouldn't have had to take such drastic measures."

He paused like he was waiting for an apology, but Valente just slid the helmet over his head. "How did you hide it inside me?"

"Clever, wasn't it?" Victor said with a smirk. "Though, technically, your head was never 'inside' of you at all. Like all the fairy monsters, you're made of gossamer. Any attempt to hide your head inside your body would've been the same as letting you wear it. To keep it truly safe, I had to put your head somewhere no one but me could reach, so I hid it inside the last part of you that's still human."

"My heart?" Valente guessed.

"Your death," Victor replied, his eyes shining with triumph inside the handsome illusion of the Hero's face. "It was quite the feat. Seeing as you haven't been fully human since you were a teenager, your death had grown extremely fragile. One wrong move was all it would have taken to scatter the last remnants of your mortal soul, but this is me we're talking about. I was able to tuck your head away without you even knowing what I'd done."

He looked incredibly pleased with himself, but Valente narrowed his glowing eyes. "If it took a master blood mage to hide it, how did you make me get it out? I'm not even a mage."

"That's what made it so brilliant," Victor informed him proudly. "When I performed the spell that merged his gossamer with your human body, I tucked your soul *inside* the fairy's head. Not only did this enable you to become functionally immortal, it meant the only way to reach your death was through your head. But since your head is just a lump of gossamer rather than flesh, I could take it into the realm of magic with me just as I took Morgan's."

His face split into a grin. "It was the perfect hiding place! Only someone possessing your head could reach your death to place the head inside. Once it was in position, you became a closed circle, an infinite loop that only you could break. This should have meant your head was lost forever, since, as you just observed, you're not a mage, but you *are* my knight. Anything you are technically capable of, the oaths can force you to do at my command. And since every human is capable of moving magic at least subconsciously, all I had to do was order you to fetch your head, and you broke the lock yourself." He grinned wider. "Is that not genius?"

Valente stared at him with the Rider's heavy silence until Victor rolled his eyes.

"Pearls before swine," he said, pulling a set of earbuds and a small microphone out of the pocket of his red jacket. "I'd explain further because this triumph deserves to be appreciated, but Orlando will be here any moment. I've already notified the press, so get down there and earn your keep."

"The press?" Valente couldn't believe it. "You're revealing me to the public?"

"I have no choice," his master said casually as he inserted the earbuds into his ears. "Heroism requires an audience, and while you're not a patch on Fenrir, a good fight still draws in the rabble." He clipped the mic onto his collar next, tapping it a few times to be sure it was on before he asked, "How long until we're ready?"

"Fifteen minutes," Simon's harried voice replied, the sound bleeding through the earbuds so softly that only the Rider's gossamer-enhanced senses could have picked it up. "I'm bringing the last batch of pills down now. As soon as I distribute them, your army will be ready."

Victor cut off the conversation with a smile. "You heard my apprentice," he said as he tugged his red jacket straight. "I don't care if you die. I don't care if it destroys you. You *must* hold the Wild Hunt back for fifteen minutes."

Valente looked down at the letter-scattered floor. If he was still following his old plan, that order would have ruined everything, but he wasn't throwing himself away for this pig of a man anymore. He'd made a promise, and for once in his life since the fairy had appeared at his door, Valente was going to keep it.

"Did you hear me, slave? I—"

"I heard you," the Rider said, lifting his mirrored visor to Victor. "And I'll do more than just hold them back. When this is over, I'll have Orlando's head."

The Hero's perfect eyebrows arched suspiciously. His knight's new eagerness must not have interfered with his plans, though, because Victor just waved him away.

"Then get down there and do it," he said, glancing out the window at where the dread riders were galloping past like leaves in a tornado. "Just make sure you don't make your entrance from my tower. I have a reputation to maintain."

Valente supposed it would look bad if the serial-murdering Black Rider came marching out the Hero's front door, but he didn't care about Victor's plots. When he ran down the Tower's fire escape as fast as a streak of shadow, Valente did it for Lola. For the arrow in his head that still pointed steadfastly at her light. She was still alive, still fighting, and so long as she was fighting, he would fight with her. He would fight *for* her as she'd fought for him, and maybe, just maybe, they'd win.

That hope put wings on his boots as he raced through the tunnels that ran under the Hero's Tower and up the hidden ladder Victor had ordered the city to build beneath the giant square outside. The secret door was disguised as a storm drain covered with a locked steel grate. Valente didn't have the key, so he broke the lock with a slam of his invisible gossamer, pushing the metal cage up with his shoulder.

He'd tried to be quiet about it, but spotlights still found him the moment he cracked the lid. The crowds that normally mobbed the front steps of Hero's Tower had cleared out the moment the Hunt showed up, leaving only the flock of news drones buzzing through the air. The AI-driven cameras locked onto the Rider's helmet the second it emerged, nearly driving Valente back down the ladder as hundreds of TV spotlights flashed over from every angle to smack him in the face.

If physical eyes were all he'd had, the glare would have left him completely blind, but the Rider's vision had always been only partially based on normal sight. The magical half of him had never needed eyes to see, and it didn't need them now as he climbed out of the drain to stand in the middle of the square. The kick of disbelief that came next, however, was a lot harder to handle.

Valente's gossamer wasn't as vulnerable as Lola's. Thanks to the stories Victor had spread, so long as he acted like the Black Rider, people generally believed in him just fine. This meant when he did get hit, it was always a sucker punch, and right now, the world was clearly *not* expecting the Black Rider to come crawling out of the ground like a rat.

Their surprise whacked him like a mallet, causing Valente's normally ice-hard gossamer to become soft and stretchy. He wasn't in danger of melting, but if Orlando caught him like this, the fight would be over before it began. He was scrambling to get himself back together when a word shot through his mind.

Hold.

The order washed over him like a tide. It took a lot for Victor to command him from a distance like that, but it worked. The moment his monarch spoke, the oaths obeyed, locking Valente's gossamer in place until the storm of disbelief subsided.

It did so surprisingly quickly. Valente didn't know if people had just accepted his appearance as part of the insanity or if Victor had gone on TV and justified his presence, but something was definitely happening. All the remote news drones were swarming like flies for a shot of Valente as he braced his resolidified legs. He lifted his head next, his mirrored visor shining white in the reflected glare of the TV lights as he turned his face toward the cloud of horsemen swirling overhead.

It was an especially apocalyptic sight for Valente. With his eyes closed to keep out the spotlights, there was no veil of illusion to hide the true horror of the Wild Hunt. Just gleaming eyes and flashing teeth as the riders circled in and out of the gray clouds.

It must really have been only the vanguard, because he didn't see the monster that was Alberich's true shape anywhere. None of the hunters were attacking yet, either. They were only here to stir terror in the hearts of everyone watching, which would then serve as fuel for the actual assault.

It was the same strategy they'd used on every city. Valente was wondering why Victor had sent him out so early since all the attention he generated would only make Alberich's main attack even stronger when he heard something heavy land on the pavement behind him.

There was no need to look. There was only one fairy with that sticky, rotten taste. That said, when Valente finally did turn around, the monster waiting for him was nothing like the one he remembered.

The first time he'd faced Orlando, the fairy had looked like a pile of rusted armor. Now, Alberich's knight was sharp and shiny as a brand-new knife. He'd always been enormous, but he must have been feasting nonstop these last three weeks, because he'd grown even bigger, his huge body covered in armor that gleamed like a mirror under its syrupy layer of fresh blood.

Seeing him this way, Valente finally understood why Tristan had called Orlando "The Red Knight." He'd been more of a rusty brown before. Now, though, Alberich's killer was blindingly, glossily, lewdly red in the blazing TV lights. Only his voice was still the same, rattling like an angry pile of chains behind the flat visor of his helmet as he aimed his giant sword at the Rider.

Valente cracked his real eyes open in reply, focusing all of his senses on the enemy as he gathered the mountain of gossamer that came with his head. The lights were so intense, he could actually see his normally invisible magic shimmering around him like a blue ghost. If Orlando noticed what he was doing, though, the knight clearly didn't care. He just charged straight at Valente, his rattle rising to a hungry, tongueless roar as he swung his sword to take his enemy's head.

The wide swing should have been easy to block, but when Valente grabbed it with his invisible gossamer, the Red Knight's sword—which was now as sharp, shiny, and red-coated as the rest of him—sliced straight through it, forcing the Rider to jump before he got sliced in half.

He danced backward across the square, his boots sliding over the dropped signs and other trash left behind by the Hero's fleeing crowds. But while he was moving faster than last time thanks to his master no longer being lost, Orlando was even better. He shot after Valente like red lightning, his tongueless voice revving like a chainsaw as he stabbed his huge sword straight into the Rider's chest.

Valente blocked with his gossamer, engulfing the sword and shoving it back out before it could cut deeper than his leather jacket. But while he'd avoided getting skewered, the force of the blow still sent him flying into the huge front doors of the Hero's Tower. He went through the bulletproof glass like a cannonball, wrapping himself in gossamer just like he'd seen Lola do to keep from getting shredded as he crashed into the marble wall of the elevator lobby.

He pushed himself out of the wreckage with a groan, brushing the dust off his helmet, which had cracked when his head hit the wall but done its job of keeping his skull intact. The relative darkness of the empty lobby was a relief after the blinding TV lights, but he knew he couldn't stay, and not just because Victor wouldn't let him hide. It was obvious now that he wasn't the only one who'd put on his head for this fight, which meant if Valente was going to keep his promise to Lola, he was going to have to get creative.

Shaking his head, Valente pulled in all of his gossamer except for one tendril, which he used to smash the lobby's lighting control panel and plunge the already dim room into total darkness. This panicked the fleet of camera drones that had flown into the lobby after him, but not nearly as much as what he did next would have. The moment the lights went out, Valente sank into the floor, his body dissolving into invisible gossamer before racing back across the square into the shadow cast by his gloating opponent.

It was the only place he could come up. The dissolving-and-moving thing wasn't one of his stolen fairy powers. It belonged to the Black Rider, and in all his stories, he always appeared right behind you.

This was the first time he'd ever done it voluntarily. Valente hated being the Black Rider. He hated scaring people, hated being the thing in the night. He'd only played the monster because Victor had made him during the years when he'd been trying to make his knight into an urban legend he controlled.

Much to his master's disappointment, Valente had never managed to make the jump. He still had some of the Rider's powers, though, and unlike gossamer, they worked better with an audience. All he had to do was embrace people's horrible expectations of him, and the Black Rider did the rest, letting him rise silently out of the giant's shadow with a spike of frozen gossamer already ready to stab into Orlando's back.

The Red Knight howled like tearing metal when he drove it in. As his magic tore through the bigger fairy's, Valente felt something slide around his spike. Something hard and round, almost like there was a rock floating inside of Orlando's otherwise gelatinous magic.

The feeling vanished when Orlando yanked himself off the Rider's invisible blade. Valente caught him by the shoulder as he moved, clenching his magic to freeze the other knight's gossamer and shatter him to pieces. He'd just about wrapped his bitter cold around Orlando's neck when the tongueless knight made a sound like a thousand hornets and blew apart, scattering into a spray of bright red and silver droplets that flew across the square to recondense a dozen feet away.

But not without cost. The fairy who came back together was as red and shiny as ever, but the blood on his armor this time was his own. It ran down his faceless visor like wet paint and turned his rasping voice into a gurgle.

For a soaring second, Valente thought this meant he was winning. Then he saw that the fairy's shimmering redness wasn't spilling like normal blood. It was gathering, welling in pools inside his armor as Orlando whipped his hand forward, throwing his bloody gossamer like a hail of swords straight at Valente's face.

There were no shadows to sink into this time. As soon as he saw the red blades flying toward him, Valente turned and ran. His silent motorcycle appeared by the second step, condensing out of thin air between Valente's legs to send him racing forward. It wasn't actually faster than the flying blood, but the bike made it easier to maneuver, letting him use the rest of his gossamer to knock away the blades he couldn't dodge.

He still couldn't avoid them all. By the time he made it to the other side of the square, three of the bloody swords had found their marks: one in his leg, one through his arm, and one just under his shoulder blade. If he hadn't been wearing his head, that would have been enough to poof him. With his head, though, it was almost worse, because he couldn't get away. He just sat there bleeding real human blood, not the bright-red Halloween-store gossamer kind Orlando was spewing like a fountain as he readied his next volley.

Valente slumped over his handlebars. He was starting to think he hadn't injured the fairy at all with that backstab. He'd seen the blood and gotten excited, but Orlando wasn't fleshy like him. He was *all* gossamer, a bag of tricks to terrify and fool humans like Valente into mistakes exactly like this. The flying swords weren't as big as the one in the knight's hands, but they were much harder to dodge, and they still did the job.

Too good a job. From the dark spots swimming across his vision, Valente knew he couldn't take another stab. He was going to die if he kept letting the knight hit him. That would have been great if he'd still wanted to lose, but it hadn't even been ten minutes yet. Victor had ordered him to hold out for at least fifteen, but while the oaths could and would force Valente to fight to the death, they couldn't force Orlando to lose. The other knight was already launching another volley, forcing Valente to ride like hell or be skewered under a volley of gossamer spears.

He drove like he'd never driven before, condensing his invisible gossamer into a thick shield over his back since knocking the blades away was useless. Maintaining such a heavy defense while driving took all of his concentration, but while Valente should have been paying attention to the fight, all he could think about was Lola in the alley between the trucks, begging him not to die.

He could still feel her somewhere far to the west. She was probably back in Tristan's barrow, watching him on TV like everyone else. Would she think he was still losing on purpose?

Still throwing his life away despite everything she'd done?

That was the thought he couldn't stand. Valente had never been afraid of death, but the idea of Lola thinking he was throwing himself away when she'd faced her greatest fear to save him—or worse, that she'd blame herself for his death because she hadn't been able to get his head in time—was an ending he could not face. He could not lose here, not yet.

Valente slammed on his brakes, bouncing the rest of Orlando's blades off his shield as he spun his bike around. He ran his hands over his wounds next, stopping the bleeding with a freezing layer of gossamer. Across the empty square, Orlando threw out his giant arm again, sending another volley of blood-red swords flying at him, but the Rider didn't run this time. He planted his feet on the ground instead, gunning his silent bike straight toward his enemy.

The red swords turned in an arc as Orlando opened his arms to greet him, clearly intending to crush the Rider between his body and the flying blades. Valente hit the gas in response, putting on a burst of speed as he aimed his motorcycle dead center at the giant's chest. Then, when he was too close for either of them to dodge, he let go of his bike and launched himself straight up into the air.

Just like everything else it did, the black motorcycle made no sound as it crashed into Orlando. The impact didn't even force the huge fairy to step back, because the Rider's bike had never been anything but gossamer and shadows. The flying swords that had been chasing the Rider landed next, pattering against their creator like red raindrops. Neither seemed to bother Orlando in the slightest, but they did distract him from Valente as the Black Rider fell straight on top of his head, his arm already stretched down to slap his gloved hand flat against the top of the Red Knight's bloody helmet.

He fired his magic like a shotgun blast the second he made contact, flash-freezing the gossamer that formed Orlando's skull. This caused the knight's helmet to splinter, but that wasn't actually Valente's target. He already knew from his earlier stab that the fairy's head wasn't on his shoulders.

It was in his chest.

The hard lump that had rolled off his spike earlier was the only piece of the knight's unbeatable gossamer body that was different. It was also the only thing Orlando had bothered to move out of his way, so Valente plunged his arm down, shattering through the Red Knight's frozen helmet as he dug his way into the giant's body to search for his prize.

He must have been on to something, because for the first time ever, Orlando went on the defensive. With a roar like a giant table saw, he swung his huge sword straight up, carving off a piece of his own chest in his rush to slice the Rider off of him. But Valente had already seen it coming and dropped down the Red Knight's back, using his opponent's massive size against him just as he'd done with the troll he and Lola had fought. While Orlando chopped through his own neck in a frantic effort to catch him, Valente's hand was already melting through the armor between his shoulder blades, his gloved fingers sliding through the gossamer like hot nails through wax until they found the solid lump he'd felt before.

It slid away the second he touched it. Orlando was thrashing beneath him, chopping his own body to pieces in his frenzy to reach the Black Rider. Valente had to fend off the wild swings with one hand while reaching with the other, his fingers scrambling after the hard lump that was darting around inside the bigger fairy's body like a fish.

It couldn't stay that way forever, though. As Orlando cut himself smaller and smaller, the lump had fewer and fewer places to run. It was just a matter of time before Valente cornered it. Just a little more and—

There!

He seized the wiggling lump in his fist and launched backward, yanking the thing out of Orlando like a plug. The fairy screamed as it tore free. A real scream, not a buzzsaw whine, because the lump Valente clutched in his hands wasn't a lump at all. It was a head. A boy's small head carved from a knotty piece of pine wood with a little tin soldier's helmet nailed to the top.

The sight was so unexpected that Valente almost dropped it. The head opened its eyes as he watched, huge amber things that wept sticky sap. It opened its mouth next, chomping at the Rider with rows of splintery wooden teeth that did indeed have no tongue between them. He was trying not to lose a finger when Orlando's giant body turned and took a swing at him.

It was much, much slower without its head, but still alive enough to be a threat. Valente had to drop the head to grab the blade before it crashed into his shoulder. The head landed between his boots with a clatter and immediately started rolling away, leaving its body to keep the Rider busy while it made its escape.

It had nearly made it to the open grate the Rider had climbed out of when its journey was cut short by the side of a polished black shoe. This was swiftly followed by a gallant crimson-coated body as the Hero stepped into the spotlights, swinging his golden sword in a gleaming arc to slice the fairy's head in two.

Orlando's body collapsed the second it happened. One moment, it was pushing Valente to his knees. The next, it had melted into a pile of rainbow-sheened ooze, bubbling and popping like hard candy tossed into a frying pan until it boiled away completely.

Valente watched it disappear with frantic breaths, too wound up to believe it was really over, that he was really still alive. Dimly in the distance, he could hear people cheering and shouting, but not for him. They were shouting for the Hero as Victor walked across the empty square, his golden sword gleaming in the TV lights as he held it up to show everyone the last of the fairy's bubbling blood.

The crowd started cheering more wildly than ever, but Valente could barely stay on his feet as his master approached. He'd thrown everything he had into melting through Orlando. His weakened gossamer was already sliding off his stab wounds, allowing them to start bleeding again. The resulting dizziness sent him to his knees, which should have been a good move. Victor loved nothing better than to see people kneeling before him, but there was no smile on the Hero's face as he came to a stop above his Rider.

"And thus do the dogs turn on each other."

Valente froze. He could see Victor's lips moving, but his voice was coming from all directions. *Speakers,* his pain-numbed mind realized belatedly. Victor wasn't talking to him. He was speaking into his mic, addressing everyone in the city and all the millions more watching at home as he pointed the tip of his sword at Valente's cracked helmet.

"I see now why the Black Rider was able to terrorize this city for so long," he announced dramatically. "He's no urban legend. He's just another fairy monster defending his feeding grounds."

He moved the golden sword closer. "Didn't want to share the fear from your murder spree, did you, monster? Or perhaps you thought you could avoid my blade if you proved yourself useful?"

He paused like he was waiting for an answer, but before Valente could say a word, the Hero charged on.

"Unfortunately for you, I don't believe that the enemy of my enemy is my friend. Monsters have no place in the world *I* protect, which means your days of killing without consequence are over, Black Rider."

A wild cheer went up at this, but Valente could only stare. This couldn't be what it seemed. People couldn't actually be *buying* this garbage, could they?

It was ridiculous, but when Valente finally managed to tear his eyes off of Victor, he saw the Hero's fans pouring out of the side streets and buildings they'd fled into, their faces red with fury as they screamed at the Hero to do his job. Kill the monster! End the Black Rider's reign of terror!

Victor waved at them with an indulgent smile, and then his hand went up to his collar to cut his mic. The Rider's hand shot out at the same time to grab the Hero's golden sword, but the blade burned right through his glove. He was still gasping from the pain when his master leaned over him.

"You should be grateful," he said in his normal, unamplified voice. "I'm giving you what you've always wanted. Today's the day you finally get to be free."

"No," Valente whispered, backing away. "Not like this. I won't... You can't..."

"Be quiet."

The order landed like a sledgehammer, though not nearly as hard as the next one.

Hold still.

Valente's body froze. He was still inside it, still watching, but he couldn't even close his eyes. His oaths held him like a calf on the slaughter block as Victor raised the Hero's golden sword. He paused at the top, looking around to make sure all the cameras were watching before he swung it down to slice straight through the middle of Valente's head, killing him instantly.

Chapter 14

"Someone come clean this up."

Victor's order came through Simon's earpiece crystal clear. Through the monitors in the Hero's central command office underground, he saw the red-coated medical team scramble to obey. They grabbed a gurney and raced for the ramp where the rest of the Hero's Army was waiting to deploy. They were about to head outside when Simon came down the metal stairs.

"I'll do it."

"Are you sure, sir?" the mage in the front asked nervously. "Aren't you supposed to be overseeing—"

"I said I'll do it," Simon repeated, adding a bit of magic to his voice this time.

A real blood mage would have scoffed at such a small push, but these idiots weren't real. They were fools dazzled by Victor's promise of easy power. All their knowledge was borrowed from a pill that specifically did not include resistance training. Add in Simon's implied authority as Victor's apprentice, and their minds were easier to manipulate than the average non-mage's. They got out of his way at once, practically groveling as they passed Simon the wheeled gurney and opened the door to let him outside.

The mages watched nervously as Simon pushed the gurney up the ramp the DFZ had built specifically for today. The one that was supposed to allow the Hero's Army to flood into the square and shoot the Wild Hunt out of the sky.

Well, the fairies were here, but—in a surprise to everyone except Simon—no order had come down from their Glorious Leader. The whole time the Rider had been fighting Orlando, the mages in the command center had been arguing over whether or not they should go out and help. One had even had the guts to call

Victor, who'd told him to shut up and wait for orders.

The poor guy had looked like his dad just told him Christmas was canceled, but Simon hadn't been surprised in the slightest. From the moment the TV lights hit the Rider, he'd known what Victor was planning. He hadn't expected the Rider to win—that had been a legitimate shock—but what came after had been classic Victor, which was why he was racing to his master's side. Victor must need this kill very badly to sacrifice a tool as valuable as the Rider, which meant Simon would do whatever it took to make sure he didn't get it.

The square was overrun with drones by the time Simon reached the top of the ramp. He'd overheard Victor and Jamie organizing the media blitz yesterday, but that still hadn't prepared him for the sheer volume of coverage. Every news outlet in the world—especially those who'd missed out on last month's Fenrir disaster—was here in force, filling the square in front of Hero's Tower with camera drones, AI-piloted news vans, even actual living reporters in warded body armor.

That last one sounded like a suicide mission, but it wasn't Simon's business if someone decided a scoop was more important than their life. He was glad the media was here. They kept Victor distracted, as did the crowd cheering from the square's edge. Those idiots' faith in the Hero was so strong, they thought they could stand on the sidelines of a war zone like it was a football game. Victor ate it up, though, so Simon said nothing, keeping his head dutifully down as he ran the gurney toward the scene of the world's most televised murder.

"There was no need to come out yourself," Victor said as Simon rolled up. "We have people for this."

"Your 'people' couldn't handle it," Simon replied, which wasn't even a lie. Now that he was out in the open, he could hear the terrifying thunder of the Wild Hunt's hoofbeats above his head. Their screaming horses circled like a cyclone in the grim evening sky, filling the square with the howling wind of their fury.

"Isn't it beautiful?" Victor whispered, the dazzling illusion of his Hero's face suffused with wonder as he stared up at them. "It almost makes me glad that Fenrir was such a debacle. This scene is so much grander."

He grinned as he looked back down at Simon. "Let this be a lesson to you, apprentice. There is no failure that a clever man can't transform into opportunity."

Simon nodded grimly, keeping out of the cameras as he started moving the Rider's body onto the gurney. This was his first time actually touching Victor's experiment. Simon knew that his gossamer was supposed to be icy, but it didn't feel right that his body was already this cold. Life under Victor might have numbed him to blood and violence, but even Simon's hands were shaking as he gathered the two halves of the Rider's head and placed them on the gurney's white plastic surface.

"Good work," Victor said as Simon pulled the sheet over the Rider's broken helmet. "His corpse would have distracted from my victory."

Simon nodded and seized the gurney handles, eager to get away now that he had what he wanted, but Victor grabbed his arm. When he turned to see why, his master was looking at him with an odd expression.

"I'm proud of you, Simon," he said, his voice surprised, as if he couldn't believe he was saying it, either. "Of all the apprentices I've had, you were by far the most interesting. Your scheming mind helped me push my own limits. I'm grateful to you for that, so I hope you won't be too disappointed."

An icy tendril curled in Simon's stomach. "Disappointed about what?"

Victor flashed him the Hero's smile and turned his attention back to the Hunt. It was his typical game—saying something cryptic to make you beg for more—but Simon didn't have time. Anything that came out of that man's mouth was only ever for his own benefit, anyway. Whatever he was hinting at, Simon was sure he was better off not knowing.

With that truth firmly in his mind, he turned his back on Victor to focus on wheeling the Rider away from the battlefield. There was a medical station set up in the parking deck of Hero's Tower, but Victor's whole army would be watching if Simon went that way, so he shifted course, pushing the Rider's body toward the front of the Hero's Tower instead. It was tricky getting the gurney up the stairs without help, but Simon made it work, shoving the cart through the gaping hole the Rider had left in the tower's glass doors.

The dark lobby was a relief after the blinding lights outside. All the news teams were fixated on the Hero, so Simon didn't even have to worry about drones as he parked the gurney at the back of the tower's marble atrium and got to work. He grabbed a piece of glass from the shattered windows and sliced it across his palms, first his right, then his left. When his hands were good and bloody, he took a deep breath and flipped back the sheet to reveal the two halves of the Rider's head.

The floating, dazzled feeling that hit him next was almost a relief. He'd worried it was too late, but if the Rider's head still had enough oomph left to enthrall him even a little, that was something Simon could work with. As he'd learned from Lola, fairies were incredibly tough. For all that they called it "gossamer," their magic was more like ballistic gel. Human souls were far more fragile, but the Rider hadn't been fully human for a long time. If this was going to work on anyone, it would work on him.

After taking a good, hard look at both pieces of the Rider's face, Simon squeezed his eyes shut to block out the rapidly weakening enthrallment and used his bloody fingers to push the Rider's head back together. When he was certain he had everything lined up correctly, he turned his attention inward, focusing on the magic inside his own body: the living connection between soul and flesh that gave blood magic its power. *His* power, tyrannical and strong as he turned it on the Rider with a single command.

"Live."

The word came out of him like a gong. The lingering magic of the Rider's human soul thrashed in response, fighting his grip like a wounded animal. This only made Simon hold on tighter, squeezing until he could feel every drop of the Rider's blood like it was his own.

This was an area of blood magic that even Victor didn't toy with. Not because bringing people back from the dead was taboo, but because his master was simply too selfish to care about any life that wasn't his. The closest he'd ever come was the first time he'd pulled Simon out of the coma, but Simon had spent a lot of time inside his death. He knew exactly what sort of collapse the Rider's soul was experiencing as it detached from the physical anchor of his body, exactly where to grab to hold the crumbling walls of his death together.

It was an unnatural invasion, an unforgivable breach of another person's mind, but Simon told himself he didn't care. He pushed through the overwhelming wrongness, pulling the Rider's soul back inch by inch up the bridge he'd made from his own blood. He did the same for the Rider's body, commanding the broken cells to heal just as he'd done for his own in the hospital.

When both soul and body were under his total control, Simon shoved them back together. The gossamer he trusted to stick on its own, concentrating all of his attention on the Rider's human parts: the cracked bones and bleeding flesh and the soul that bound them together into a person rather than a sack of meat. That was Simon's specialty, and he worked faster than he'd ever worked before, weaving the dead man like a tapestry until the Rider's severed skull fused back together, and he opened his glowing eyes with a gasp.

"Easy," Simon said, reaching under the gurney for the medical tape, which he used to bind the Rider's split helmet back together over his face before the fairy's rapidly returning magic could enthrall him for real. "Coming back from the dead is a traumatic experience. You've got to let it flow through you, or the pressure will make you crack."

He wasn't sure if the Rider heard him, but eventually his frantic hyperventilating slowed to normal gasping. He collapsed back onto the gurney next, lifting his bloody gloves to his helmet-covered face in wonder.

"I'm alive."

His deep voice was as captivating as ever, causing Simon to lean closer before he caught himself.

"You are," he said, taking a step back from the once again very dangerous man. "How do you feel?"

"Incredible," Valente said, turning his cracked helmet toward Simon. "You saved me."

"Don't call it salvation," Simon warned, sinking to the ground as the exhaustion of holding all that magic finally caught up with him. "If you weren't already a monster, you'd be an abomination right now. I just infused every part of you with blood magic. You're so stained now that even Victor would be shocked."

"That's not all you did," the Rider said, his deep voice awed. "You broke it."

"Something's still broken?" Simon asked, pushing back up in alarm. "Where is it? I thought for sure I got all—"

"That wasn't a complaint," Valente said as he climbed off the gurney. "You broke my oaths."

"Your what?"

"The knighthood oaths," he said excitedly, grabbing Simon by the shoulders. "They've always been wrapped around me like a fist for years, but now—"

"You died," Simon finished, his eyes flying wide as he realized what was happening. "You were bound to Victor unto death, and he killed you." His face split into a grin. "He broke his own oath."

"And you brought me back," Valente said, his deep voice shaking with joy. "You set me free. I'm not his knight anymore!"

Simon gasped as the Rider lurched forward and crushed him in a hug. He was struggling to breathe when Valente suddenly let go and stepped back, his deep voice hesitant as he asked, "Why?"

"Because I wasn't going to let him win," Simon replied, reaching into the trauma kit under the gurney for a roll of gauze to bind his bleeding hands. He was still picking the piece of tape off the end when Valente fell to his knees.

"I owe you my life."

"Get up," Simon said irritably as he finally got the gauze unraveled. "Delighted as I am to free anyone from Victor, I didn't do this for you. I just couldn't stand the thought of that ass taking credit for slaying the monster he created. But things are about to get even better."

He shot an evil smile at the glaring TV lights outside. "The Hero killed you in front of the entire world. When people see you alive again, it'll put an enormous crack in Victor's image. Maybe not enough to bring him down, but there's no way it won't hurt, and that's good enough for me." His smile faded as he looked down at the gauze he was wrapping around his hands. "I also did it for Lola. She cares a lot about you, and I care a lot about her."

The Rider shifted uncomfortably. "I'd think that'd be a reason *not* to save me."

"Then you know nothing," Simon snapped. "I don't care what you are to Lola, but I know what she is to me. The only thing I've ever wanted is for her to be happy. If that means dragging your soul back from the Sea of Magic with my teeth, I'll do it in a heartbeat."

"I'm very glad you feel that way," Valente said, lowering his head. "Thank you, Simon."

"Stop that," Simon grumbled, turning away. "I hate being bowed to. It makes me feel like Victor."

"You want me to go out there and kill him?" the Rider offered, lifting his helmet eagerly. "There are no orders in my head anymore. I can probably even enthrall him now that he's not my king." His bloody gloves clenched into shaking fists. "I can do anything. I can finally make him pay for—"

"No," Simon said as he finished bandaging his hands. "You might be riding high emotionally, but you were dead not two minutes ago, and your body is still a mess. You couldn't fight the normal version of Victor right now, much less *that*."

He tilted his head back toward the square where Victor was still standing with his golden sword, his body shining brighter and clearer than even the TV lights could account for.

"What's happening?" the Rider asked, tilting his cracked helmet.

"Exactly what he planned," Simon replied with a sigh. "He's got the whole world believing he's the only thing standing between them and Alberich's Hunt. All he has to do now is win, and he'll become the Hero for real."

"What does that mean?"

"It means exactly what it sounds like. Humans instinctively pour magic into anything they value or fear. That's how spirits are born. That's how Victor made Fenrir, and now he's doing it to himself." Simon narrowed his eyes at the golden man in the square's center. "He's angling to become something no modern person has ever seen: an immortal spirit with a human's freedom of will. Think Hercules or Maui or any other demigod, though I'm sure Victor intends to ditch the *demi* part."

The Rider shifted nervously. "Can he actually do that? Become a god, I mean."

Simon shrugged. "Magical historians are still arguing over whether transcendent humans actually existed or if they're just stories, but if anyone can make the jump, it's Victor. He's been working toward this his entire life, and he's got advantages the ancient heroes could only dream of."

He pointed at the swarm of camera drones that was still circling Victor's head. "There are thirty times more humans alive today than there were the last time magic flooded the world. All those people can be manipulated into pouring their magic into whatever bucket you want, given the right context. Victor already tried and failed to harness that power the night he fought Fenrir, but he's learned from his mistakes. This time, he's made himself the center of the story, but that just makes it easier for me to pull the rug out from under him."

"How?" the Rider asked.

"Because he isn't a god yet," Simon said, pointing up at the sky full of nightmares. "He's put himself in a catch-twenty-two. To become a god, he has to do something divine. That's why he built an army and drugged them with his power. He can't actually defeat Alberich's Hunt by himself, so he's rigged the game to make it *seem* like he can. All he has to do now is keep the farce up until enough people swallow his lie to actually make it real. It's the ultimate fake-it-till-you-make-it, but the trick only works if people buy it, which is why I'm going to make sure Victor stumbles at the most critical moment."

"How?" the Rider asked again. "Not that I doubt your skills, but what are you going to do when he's out there and we're in here?"

Simon fished one of the red pills out of his pocket. "I sabotaged his pills. Not enough for him to notice. They had to still work or Victor would have realized something was up too soon. I even took one in front of him to prove my version was legit, but there's a change that Victor didn't see."

He rolled back his sleeve to show the Rider the new spellwork he'd tattooed onto his arm. "I added a kill switch. A hidden key tuned to my blood and my blood only. As soon as the Hunt comes down, Victor will give the word for his army to drug up, but the moment my pills go into their mouths, I'll hit the trigger and freeze their bodies in place. Forget using blood magic. They won't be able to blink, leaving Victor standing alone out there like an idiot."

He rolled his sleeve back down with a smirk. "After that, the Hunt just has to do what it does best, and our Victor problem will be over."

The Rider shook his head. "It can't be that simple."

"It wasn't *simple* at all," Simon snarled. "Do you have any idea how difficult it was to come up with a change that Victor wouldn't notice? If I hadn't been his apprentice for twenty years, I never could have done it, not to mention the thousands of pills I had to make *by hand*."

He whirled back to the Hero standing alone in the square. "The fact that I pulled any of this off is a miracle, but that's what it takes to beat the miracle seller. Even with all the pills in position, though, we're not in the clear until his mages actually take them, so if you really want to thank me for saving your life, watch my back. If I don't get the timing exactly right on this, it'll all come to nothing."

The Rider nodded and stepped away, giving him his space, though what Simon really needed was a glimpse into the future. For all the effort he'd put into his kill switch, the underlying spellwork was still Victor's. Once he froze the Hero's Army, he'd only be able to hold them like that for a few seconds before Victor realized what was happening and reasserted control. That should still be enough time to break what was always an incredibly delicate operation and turn the tide against his cocky master, but only if Simon did it at the exact right—

A bloodcurdling screech cut through his thoughts. Up in the sky, the swirling mass of the Wild Hunt shifted like a flock of starlings and began to dive. The whole world shook with the thunder of their hooves as they poured down from the clouds, falling onto the city like a screeching ax.

It was the same sight Simon had seen on the news of the Wild Hunt's attacks on other cities. That only made it even more terrifying, though, because he'd also seen the aftermath. The Wild Hunt didn't just eat people's fear. It ate their flesh and their bones, their buildings and their weapons. It destroyed for the sake of destruction, demolishing people's sense of safety so Alberich's court could keep feeding on their fear even after the attack was over.

That endless fear was also why the Hero had been able to rise so quickly. Alberich really had given him the perfect villain. All Victor had to do was stand firm and raise his sword against the charge, and the whole world threw their hopes like flowers at his feet.

It was happening right now as Simon watched. The moment the Hunt began its descent, Victor's Hero flashed brighter than ever, his iconic golden sword glowing like the sun. The signal came through Simon's earpiece at the same time, ordering the waiting army to take their pills.

"*Simon,*" the Rider hissed.

"Not yet."

A muffled roar rose up as the army hidden beneath the tower's foundations obeyed their Hero. Simon could feel the pills he'd made activating as they slid down five-thousand-eight-hundred-and-seventy-two throats, and then the floor shook under his feet as the mages began their charge. He could already see the front line coming up the ramp at the edge of the square, but he didn't do it yet.

Not yet.

Not yet.

Now.

When the first red-coated soldier was nearly to the Hero and the Wild Hunt was only two dozen feet from the ground, Simon clenched the muscles beneath his new tattoo, sparking a chain reaction that spread through the blood he'd sneaked into every pill. The magic shot through the Hero's forces like lightning, scrambling the intricate framework that allowed the amateur mages to pull on Victor's masterful expertise. The disconnect hit them like an electric shock, stunning their nervous systems and leaving the whole army stumbling in their tracks.

Simon stumbled with them. An unwelcome surprise, but not wholly unexpected. He'd also taken the pills: once in front of Victor to prove they weren't poison, and then several more over the following days as he tested the batches to make sure everything was perfect. He hadn't taken one today, but a good chunk of Victor's spell must still have been lingering in his system, because the blowback hit him like a truck. He knew the stun would only last ten seconds at best, though, so he wasn't worried. At least, not until he looked up.

When Simon recovered enough control over his muscles to lift his head, he was no longer standing in the shattered lobby with the Rider. He was back in the red-tinged version of his old room at the mansion. Back in his death.

That wasn't right. There was nothing about the pills or the sabotage he'd slipped into them that should kill the user. The shock of so much blood magic risked causing a hemorrhage the first time, but once they adjusted to the dosage, the pills should have made the user *more* resistant to death, not less. This especially applied to an actually trained blood mage like himself, but there was no denying where he was. Simon was still trying to figure out what had gone wrong when he realized he wasn't alone.

"Hello, apprentice."

Simon whirled around. He knew he shouldn't have been surprised, but nothing could stop his gasp when saw Victor standing right beside him. Not the Hero from this morning. This was the Victor of Simon's childhood, the one from the portrait that was now hanging empty on the wall.

The shock was enough to make him stumble backward. It couldn't be possible. This was *Simon's* death. Victor had made him install that portrait when he was too young to realize he could say no, but the moment Simon had learned to fully control his magic, he'd kicked his master out. With the exception of Lola—whom he always welcomed—no one should have been able to get in here. *Especially* not Victor, yet there he was.

"So," his master said, folding his hands behind his back as he looked Simon up and down, "you sabotaged my pills. I thought that was your plan when you jumped on the chore of making them, but I never did manage to find what you'd changed." His smile widened. "It must have been very clever, but I'd expect nothing less from my best."

"How did you get in here?" Simon demanded, grabbing Victor by the shoulders. At least, he tried to grab him. His hands had barely moved when the red thread that was still around his neck—the one that was tied to the empty portrait Victor had stepped out of—tightened like a choke chain.

"Such a disappointing question," Victor tsked as Simon clawed at the red string cutting off his breath. "You changed my spellwork so expertly that even I couldn't find the flaw, and yet you still haven't realized its true purpose. Come on, Simon. I thought you were cleverer than *that*."

Simon couldn't answer with the thread crushing his windpipe, so he settled for giving Victor a murderous look, which his master apparently found hilarious.

"Don't look so sour," Victor said with a superior smirk. "As I told you just now in the square, I'm actually quite proud of what you've accomplished. Betrayal is the natural course between a blood mage and his apprentice. I'd have been gravely disappointed if you hadn't tried to bring me down, but it was never going to work. As clever as you've become, you still haven't learned to see what's in front of your nose."

He fished one of the red pills out of his pocket, holding it up for Simon to see.

"This pill was never a vessel to give the unworthy my power. That was just the gilding, the bait to make those idiots bite. What I *really* needed was for them to welcome a piece of myself into their deepest hearts, as I am now in yours."

Simon stopped struggling against the thread to blink in shock. Of *course.* How could he have been so blind? The point of the pills was never the spellwork, it was the blood. Victor's blood gobbled down by thousands of greedy idiots who coveted his power, but were too ignorant to kick him out when he made himself at home in their deaths.

"That's right," Victor said at his horrified look. "Every man and woman who's taken one of my pills is having this same conversation inside their own deaths with me right now, though you're the only one with the strength to talk back." He reached out to touch the red noose around Simon's neck, loosening it just a fraction. "Let's hope you have something interesting to say."

Simon gasped as the air rushed back into his lungs. The red thread was still tight around his neck, but it was no longer cutting off his windpipe, leaving him enough breath to snarl at his master.

"Are you insane?"

Victor rolled his eyes. "Surely you can do better than that."

"What else is there to say?" Simon wheezed. "You've taken over five-thousand-eight-hundred mages who can't even cast blood magic without you pulling their strings. Those idiots have no power to give you, and the Wild Hunt is practically on top of your head. An army with your power at least made sense, but this is madness!"

"Oh, Simon," Victor said, shaking his head. "As always, you lack vision. Do you really think it was enough to be the leader of the army that saved humanity? Of course not. Heroes are great because they stand alone. Right now, all over the world, billions of people are wishing for me to win with all their hearts. They pray to me, beg me, put their faith in me. The Hunt hasn't even landed yet, but I'm already a god in every way that counts save one: capacity."

He wrapped his hand around the red thread that went to Simon's throat. "For all my talents, my soul is still frustratingly mortal. Even with the legend of the Hero expanding my death to enormous proportions, there's a limit to how far a human can stretch. It doesn't matter how much magic the world pours into me if I lack a container big enough to hold it. In order to possess the power of a god, I need a vessel the *size* of a god's, not a man's. Understand?"

Simon didn't want to flatter him by answering that, especially since it didn't matter. Victor was too much of a braggart not to tell him, and sure enough, a few moments later, his master continued.

"As I said, there are limits to how far a human soul can stretch," he said, pacing in front of his choking apprentice like a lecturer. "But, as I proved with Fenrir, there's no rule you can't break with enough magic. The problem is getting there. If I had the sort of magic Fenrir was wielding, I could do anything: expand my death into a true spirit's vessel, make myself immortal, destroy the fairy menace, all of it. Unfortunately, actually handling that much power would have instantly shattered my mortal soul.

"That's why I used the changeling. Being gossamer, she was flexible enough to hold all that magic. My plan was to let her take the brunt and then simply step into Fenrir's vessel once it was finished. It was a brilliant strategy, but I failed to account for the changeling's resilience. That's the frustrating thing about fairies. For all that they melt at the first skeptical look, they never seem to *die*."

He blew out an irritated breath, and then his smug smile snapped back into place. "But a true blood mage never accepts defeat. Disheartening as it was at the time, the changeling's rebellion turned out to be a blessing in disguise, because this plan is *so* much better. Instead of a winner-takes-all gamble for control of one giant vessel, I've got fifty-eight-hundred smaller ones that have already been willingly given."

Simon's eyes went huge as he realized what that meant. "That's... what you were after?" he wheezed against the still-too-tight thread. "*That's* why... why you gathered an army? So you could use... use their..."

"Use their deaths," Victor finished impatiently. "Naturally. They're certainly not good for anything else. Sharing my victory over Alberich would have defeated the entire purpose. With this method, though, I get everything."

Simon shook his head. "You still... have to... win. Not... a... god yet."

"It's only a matter of time," Victor said, reaching into his pocket again to pull out an orange prescription bottle with his name on it. He popped the plastic lid with his thumb and turned the bottle to show his apprentice the pills inside, which were as golden as his sword and glistening with potential.

"I've been collecting the power people have been throwing at the Hero for weeks," he explained, putting the lid back on. "It's nowhere near what I was wielding when I was linked to Fenrir, but I don't have to be a god just yet. I only need to wield the power of one long enough to defeat the Wild Hunt. Once I've destroyed the enemy no one else could stop, even my skeptics will have to admit I'm the genuine article, and the belief of a grateful world will flow into the network of deaths I've assembled to catch it. They'll bear the brunt while I ride the swell, sailing past the limits of mortality to become the Hero for real. For*ever*." His smile widened to a grin. "Is that not brilliant?"

It was. As much as Simon hated him, even he had to admit Victor had pulled off one hell of a triumph, *if* it worked.

"Of course it's going to work," Victor said, reading the doubt right off his face. "You're still here because I trained you, but the rest of those fools never had a chance. They've already surrendered their deaths entirely to my control. Tiny spaces to be sure, but everything counts in large amounts."

He put his hand on Simon's head. "Thank you for listening, apprentice. It would have been wiser to let you hang, but I couldn't transcend mortality without telling you first. You're the only person in the world with the knowledge to appreciate the incredible feat I've accomplished. That's why I took you back despite knowing you would betray me. It's no fun being right unless someone understands how you did it."

He smiled at Simon one last time before reaching down to touch the string again. The noose tightened when his fingers brushed it, cutting off the tiny bit of air that had been keeping Simon conscious. He kept trying to fight it, kept trying to remember that he was the one who was actually in control of this place, but Victor had always been his weakness. The traps he'd laid in Simon's mind had been set so long ago that they were part of his foundations. Nothing he did now could get around them, leaving him choking on the floor as Victor stepped back into his portrait frame.

"If it makes you feel better, I meant what I said about you being my best apprentice. You put up a fantastic fight for what you were, it just wasn't enough. There's no shame in that. After all, you should know better than anyone." He turned to flash the dying man one last smile. "No one beats me, Simon."

Simon's hands twitched. But even if he could have managed a spell, it was too late. Victor had already vanished into the bloody background of his painting, leaving Simon alone in the death that was no longer his.

Chapter 15

"Master?"

Victor opened his eyes. From his perspective, he'd spent hours taking over people's deaths. Simon's had been his last stop specifically because he'd known it would take the longest. When he looked around now, though, it was as if barely a second had passed. He was still alone in the center of the empty square with the world's eyes upon him and the Wild Hunt charging straight at his head. The sight was every bit as horrifying as Alberich had promised, but Victor Conrath was not afraid. How could he be when he was now fifty-eight-hundred times greater than any human before him?

"*Master!*"

Jamie's voice was a flea in his ear, so tiny and terrified compared to the hugeness of his new self, but she was right. Now was not the time for standing still. Everything he'd built was finally in position. All he had to do now was light the fuse.

Keeping his hands close to hide what he was doing from the cameras, Victor reached into his pocket and dumped the entire contents of his pill bottle into his cupped hand. When he was sure he had all of them, he lifted his palm to his lips, pretending to be awed by the sky full of monsters as he pressed the fistful of pills into his mouth.

Just like the ones he used to make for Lola, the golden pills dissolved instantly on his tongue, flooding his body with the feeling he remembered from the night he'd fought Fenrir, but smoother. Stabler, because he was not fighting for his vessel this time. All the space he needed was already his, allowing the golden magic he'd collected to rage through him at full force as he lifted his sword to the enemy.

He let the first riders get close enough to ruffle his hair before he swung. With three weeks of Hero worship flowing through him and more still coming in from the people watching at home, it wasn't even hard. All he had to do was wave his sword in the enemy's direction, and a giant scythe of magic—his own beautiful, bloody magic—turned the screaming fairies to dust.

The next attack was even bigger, and the next, and the next. Not because he was trying to outdo himself, but because with every fairy he cut down, humanity's belief in the Hero grew stronger. It no longer mattered that his army was lying unconscious on the pavement or that he was only one man against the monstrous horde. Victor had already shown the world that he was all they needed. He was the one who shone like the sun, the man whose magic could kill any monster. Victor was the savior humanity had been waiting for since the return of magic eighty-five years ago, the man who couldn't die and never lost. The only person brave enough to stand against the tide of monsters that threatened to wash the world under. The only hero who could save them from death.

It was the mantra he and Jamie had been teaching the world with every interview, article, and advertisement. But no matter how well you laid the groundwork, seeing was the only true believing, so Victor showed them. He cut the enemy to dust, arcing his bloody magic up so high and bright that it could be seen for a hundred miles. He *needed* them to see, because the more they saw, the more they believed, and the more they believed, the greater his power grew.

By the time he started taking out the big riders in the back lines, Victor had reached the point where even fifty-eight-hundred deaths were no longer enough to contain the magic inside him, but that was very close to not mattering. With all of humanity cheering him on, he was finally reaching the critical mass necessary to transform his mortal soul into something greater. He was *finally* becoming what he'd taught them to see: a hero, a champion, a god to be worshiped. The only thing left was a finishing blow, a final burst of power to take him over the edge.

It wouldn't be long. Alberich relished his displays of terror, but he'd never been patient. The moment Victor stabbed his sword into Orlando's head, he'd set the clock ticking. That was why he'd taken his pills at the beginning rather than wait. He hadn't actually needed the Hero's power to destroy the rank and file thanks to the blood magic bane he'd so cleverly saddled all fairykind with, but the Underground King was different. He was also a god to his people, and he arrived like one, riding down from the sky on his screaming black horse to land with a thunderclap in front of Victor.

"Hello, old friend," he said, his voice ringing like a trumpet through the suddenly silent square. "You chose a flashy way to die."

"The same could be said of you," Victor replied, pointing his golden sword at the king's face, "monster."

The name had never fit him better. A month of abject terror had been a heady thing for Alberich. He still clung to his childish guise, but his body was as tall as Victor's now, and his smiling lips no longer bothered to hide the razor-sharp teeth behind them.

Seeing him like that filled Victor with joy. The Nightmare King was *such* a better opponent than Fenrir, who, despite all of Victor's efforts to make him terrifying, had still looked like a dog. No matter how much he destroyed or how many people he ate, a not-insignificant portion of humanity would always see Fenrir as an animal and therefore worthy of sympathy, but Alberich got no such leeway. His cruelty was written all over his face. He was the hunter who'd treated the world as his prey, and humanity uniformly despised him for it.

Hatred was a much sharper sword than fear. Victor's original plan had cast him as humanity's savior, but Alberich had given him the chance to be its vengeance. Where before he'd had to struggle to be worthy of the world's attention, all he had to do now was be a vessel for its rage. Their fury had already filled him to the brim, making his sword glow like molten gold as he pointed it at his old ally's throat.

"Really?" Alberich scoffed, pushing the glowing blade aside with one finger. "You think you can threaten me with the sword *I* made? You might have dazzled it up, but it's still my gossamer. All I have to do is snap my fingers and…"

His brassy voice trailed off. His fingers were still pressed together from the snap, but the golden sword remained firmly in Victor's grasp. The king tried again, shoving his hand at the weapon as he snapped and snapped. When nothing happened, he slammed his foot down hard enough to crack the pavement.

"What did you do?"

"What humans always do," Victor replied calmly. "Take over. You might have made this sword, but the moment I used it to rally the world against your kind, it became mine. Because I am human, and humans take."

"You *are* human," Alberich sneered. "As in mortal. *Weak!* Food for my—"

"It is humanity that makes me strong," Victor said, tilting his chin down to make sure the mic on his collar was picking up every word. "You came to this plane to hunt us, but we are no one's prey. We are the source and purpose of this world's magic, and you will learn what it means to face our wrath."

A cheer went up from the darkness surrounding the brightly lit square. The sound made Alberich jump, and Victor leaned closer, switching off his mic so the world wouldn't hear him whisper, "You should have listened to Morgan. She warned you this behavior would raise the wave of humanity's defenses against your kind. Well, it did, and I've ridden it all the way to the top."

"So I see," Alberich spat. "And you call me a parasite. But you're delusional if you think this Hero nonsense will let you beat me. I'm older than the stories you've hitched your star to, little mage. Old enough to know that for every triumphant hero, there's a hundred more who get eaten just like everybody else. Are those really the odds you want to play? It's still not too late to bow."

"Humanity will never bow," Victor replied, his voice taking on its own larger-than-life quality as he flipped his mic back on. "We are the masters of this world, and we will never grovel before the likes of you!"

He thrust his sword into the sky as he finished. The golden power was pounding through him like thunder now, and not only from his pills. Just like the night he'd faced down Fenrir, all of humanity was pouring its magic into him, only this time, Victor was the one in control. He took that power, all of it, and swung it like a scythe. Not at the mocking king in front of him, but at the host above, the rest of the Wild Hunt that was still riding in circles over the city like vultures.

It almost killed him to do it. Even with thousands of extra deaths and the expansions he'd made to his own soul, humans were simply not made for spirit-level magic, but he didn't have to hold it forever. He only needed to keep himself together for the few seconds it took to sweep his sword in a circle above his head, letting out a wave of power not felt since the night magic returned. It burned through the fairies' ranks like a golden filament, and everywhere it touched, the enemy died.

"*No!*" Alberich roared, but his booming voice was drowned out by Victor's shout of triumph.

Cutting down the fairies earlier had built him up, but it was no more than his own mages had done when he'd sent them to help contain the Hunt in Europe. Burning the entire host out of the sky, though, *that* was power on a whole other level. That was something no human could do, and the moment they saw it happen, people stopped hoping Victor would win and started *knowing.*

It was that absolute faith that catapulted him over the final threshold. Victor could actually feel his mortality burning away as humanity placed him on its pedestal, lifting him above them.

Making him a god.

No, Victor thought with a cackle as the Wild Hunt's ashes rained down around him. Gods were still bound by the prayers that created them. Even the DFZ was a servant, forever chained to the whims of her precious population, but Victor was different. He was a Hero in the oldest sense of the word, except this was no longer the ancient world. There were no jealous gods above him, no masters to pull his leash. He was free as a man ought to be, a god subject only to himself, and there was no longer anything anyone could do to stop it.

"I suppose you think you've won."

The words were so loud, he didn't recognize them as Alberich's until he lifted his head. The fairy king must have cast off his glamour while Victor was celebrating, because the thing standing over him no longer looked even the slightest bit human. There was no more boyish grin, no more charm. This was the Underground King as he truly was: a towering monster with a hide of smoking black rock, huge beady eyes meant for seeing in the dark, and a bristling maw of sword-sharp teeth that dripped with molten gold.

Through the connection to his faithful, the Hero knew it must be a terrifying sight, but it was all Victor could do to keep from laughing. If Alberich had been covered in shaggy fur instead of stone, he would have looked exactly like Lola's sad little monster.

"I finally see the family resemblance," he said, grinning up at the king. "Go on, then. Tell me how I'm losing despite destroying your entire court in a single attack."

"I need no court," the Underground King rumbled. "I allowed them to ride with me because it was entertaining, but I've never needed anyone to make me king."

Molten spittle scored the stone at Victor's feet as the monster loomed closer. "That's what makes us better. My kind earns our power by killing and eating, but your strength doesn't even belong to you. It's given by others, which means it can be taken away." He reached down to encircle the Hero with his giant claws. "The world might love a victor, but they'll turn on you the moment you start losing."

"Then I'll never lose."

Alberich laughed at him. Then he stopped, the smile falling off his hideous face as he realized Victor was serious. And in that moment of hesitation, the Hero ran him through.

Just as with Fenrir, the golden sword was far too tiny for the job. Even hunched over, Alberich's true form was the size of a building. That didn't matter, though, because the Hero's sword had never been just a sword. It was a symbol of humanity's belief that monsters could be killed. In the hands of Victor's new divinity, there was nothing it couldn't slay, and the Underground King was no exception. The moment Victor stabbed the golden blade into him, he fell like all the others, collapsing to his knees in the same place the Rider and Orlando had fallen. His giant body melted as he went down, vanishing like smoke while the whole world cheered around them.

Their cries pounded inside Victor's body, the only pulse he had now. He savored the feeling for a moment before lifting his arms to the sky, kicking his feet through the last of the fairy's rapidly melting gossamer with a whoop of joy. As the ashes of Alberich scattered, an army of reporters charged the now peaceful square from all directions, pushing each other down in their rush to be the first to interview the victorious Hero.

~~~

"He won."

The words fell out of Lola like lead balls. Victor's smug face smiled back at her from every screen as all the news networks crowded in for what was sure to be the interview of the century. Their fawning questions made her sick, but Lola couldn't turn them off. All she could do was sit there, her body going stiffer and stiffer as she struggled to process the truth.

Victor had won. She'd always said he could, but it still didn't feel real. Alberich and Morgan and Tristan, all the ancient powers who should have known better had said it was impossible. Even Simon had been so certain his plan would work, and yet…

And yet…

Lola buried her face in her hands. She'd thought it couldn't get worse when she'd realized her sister was dead. Then she'd thought it couldn't get worse when she'd watched him kill Valente. As always with Victor, though, there was no bottom. Even through the cameras, she could tell that he was no longer mortal, which meant it was over. Everything was over.

"No, it's not."
~~~

Lola jumped a foot off the cushions. She clenched her fists as she landed, whirling to face her doppelganger, who was standing behind the couch with her arms crossed stubbornly over her chest.

"How do you keep doing that?" Lola demanded, yanking her gossamer.

"Because you need me!" her double cried, yanking it back. "You made me to be you, and you'd never let yourself go through this alone!"

"That doesn't even make sense," Lola snapped. Then she fell back into the couch. "But it doesn't matter. Nothing matters anymore." She covered her face with her hands again. "Just do what you want."

"What I want is for you to get a grip," her double said, stomping around the couch to pry Lola's hands away. "Valente gave me a message before he sent me back. He told me to tell you he wasn't going to throw the fight. He said that he believed in you, and that he'd stay alive as long as it took for you to set him free."

"And that's supposed to make me feel better?" Lola cried, staring at the other her in horror. "Valente is *dead*! I know I didn't give you much of a brain, but how can you possibly think telling me this now would—"

"Because he kept his word," her double said fiercely. "Did you not see how hard he fought against Orlando? All he had to do was try a little less, and he could've died just like he'd planned, but he *didn't*. He fought with everything he had and *won* because you gave him hope."

"And look where that got him," Lola said, slumping harder into the sofa. "Victor betrayed him in front of the entire world, and no one even cared."

"Victor betrays everyone," the other her said in a stubborn voice. "That doesn't make what the Rider did any less amazing."

"But it still came to nothing," Lola muttered. "Valente tried his hardest, but he's still dead. So's my sister, and I'm pretty sure it's only a matter of time before Simon is too, if he's not already." She closed her eyes, too defeated even to cry. "There's nothing left. It's done."

"Only if you let it be."

Lola didn't think she had it in her to be mad anymore, but some part of her must have still been kicking, because that statement made her growl. "Why does everyone keep saying that? You and the DFZ both act like giving up is some kind of moral failure, but I've tried my whole life to beat Victor, and I just *can't*."

"That doesn't change what you have to do," the doppelganger said stubbornly. "Hope is what let Valente win even though Orlando was stronger. That's why I gave you his message, because if you lose hope, if you stop fighting, then Victor doesn't just win today. He wins forever."

"So I'm just supposed to keep beating my head against the wall?" Lola yelled. "Keep beating myself bloody and putting people in danger even though nothing I do ever works?"

"Yes," her double said without a trace of irony.

Lola flopped over on the couch. She didn't know what she'd done wrong to make her copy so delusional, but she could see reality just fine. Even if there was something she could do at this point, it wouldn't change anything. What was the point of soldiering on when everyone you'd been fighting for was gone?

"You're not gone," her double said, reaching down to squeeze the wrist where Lola's thread still gleamed. "Valente believed you could beat Victor. The DFZ believed you could beat Victor. While you were inside Fenrir, the whole *world* believed you could beat Victor. The only one who never believed it was you."

Lola glared at her suspiciously. "How did you know what I was thinking? And how do you know what the DFZ said? You were supposed to be off being a distraction."

"I know because you know," the doppelganger told her with a smile. "I'm made from your magic. That's why I *know* you can do this."

"Then tell me how," Lola begged. "What's the secret? What am I missing?"

The double shrugged her shoulders, and Lola scowled. "If you don't know any more than I do, how are you so sure?"

"Because you're the only one that's left," her other self said simply. "It doesn't matter how you feel about it. If you give up now, Victor gets away with everything, and you're not going to let that happen, are you?"

Lola scrubbed her eyes with a long, tired breath. She supposed it made sense that her doppelganger would know exactly what to say, but wanting to do something wasn't the same as doing it. If he'd actually done what it looked like he'd done, then Victor was basically a god now. Lola had no idea how to even start with that, but her idiot copy was right about one thing: if she didn't do something, then her sister and Valente and probably Simon had all died for nothing.

That was the thought that finally got her off the couch. Even if it was stupid, even if it failed, she couldn't leave things like this. She was racking her brain to think of something, *anything* Victor might have overlooked when her gossamer gave a sickening twist.

Her double vanished with a surprised yelp. Lola wished she could do the same, but her body was no longer hers. She couldn't even move her arm two inches to grab the couch as her magic turned itself inside out, transforming her into the sickening tunnel she always felt right before Alberich appeared.

He did so with a crash, falling out of her body into Tristan's coffee table with a splatter of rainbow gossamer. He was back in his boy form, not the towering monster she'd seen on TV, but that didn't make him any less scary. His face was all sharp teeth and fresh blood as he pushed out of the broken glass and turned on the frozen changeling with a snarl.

"Where is my treasure?"

Lola might have been defeated in every other way, but this was one hill she would always die on. "For the last time," she hissed through clenched teeth, "she's *my sister.*"

The bloody king rolled his eyes, but Lola wasn't having it. "Why are you even here?" she demanded, tugging against his hold until she was looking him in the eyes. "Your only redeeming quality was the fact that you were supposed to be able to beat Victor, but you *lost.* Shouldn't you be slinking back to your barrow after getting your butt kicked in front of the entire—"

"I did not lose!" the fairy roared. "You think a mere human could best me? *Me?* The Mouth in the Dark? The King of the Hunt?" He scoffed. "I have not yet begun to fight. You'll see, little changeling. You'll *all* see."

He started stomping toward the guest room the moment he finished, but Lola got in his way, vaulting over the back of the sofa to block his path. Alberich bared his teeth and grabbed her gossamer to shove her aside, but the fight with Victor must really have taken it out of him, because Lola was able to hold her ground. She was straining to keep it that way when the room burst open.

That wasn't hyperbole. Tristan's entire barrow opened like a flower, leaving Alberich, Lola, and the sleeping human girl in the guest bed stranded in the middle of a wide-open battlefield. The trampled grass was littered with dead trolls and the glittering bodies of headless fairies, the largest of which still had Tristan's silver-armored boot planted on its chest. Beside the knight was a beautiful woman Lola had never seen before, but assumed must be Lamb from the curly white hair and side-slit sheep eyes. Both fairies were covered in the shimmery gossamer blood of their enemies, but neither held a candle to Morgan.

She stood at the center of the battlefield like the ancient queen she was, towering and terrifying with a brace of severed heads hanging from her golden girdle like a string of onions. Yet another dangled by its dark hair from her fist, a lovely head with ridiculously large teeth that Lola recognized at once.

"Is that Alva?" Alberich said, letting go of Lola to give Morgan an approving smile. "About time you cleaned house, wife."

"Victory requires timing," Morgan replied as she added Alva's head to the rest of her collection. "Your battle with the blood mage provided the perfect opportunity to take back my barrow. I thought I'd be eating these traitors to bolster my strength for the battle against you." She turned to give Alberich a scathing look. "I never imagined you'd lose."

"For the last time, *I did not lose!*" Alberich bellowed. "That traitorous dog set me up! He thinks he's so clever, but this isn't finished. That blood mage is about to learn what true fear looks like!"

"I was afraid you'd say that," Morgan replied as Tristan and Lamb came over to flank her. "Stand down, husband. It's over."

"Nothing is over until I say!" the king snarled, baring his sharp teeth. "You think I'm weak like you? That I will roll over and hide from the humans just because they spilled a little of my blood? *Never!* I am the Nightmare King! I fear nothing, and I will not be pushed around by—"

"Enough," Morgan said, handing her string of heads to Tristan. "You had your chance, and you failed. Even your treasured human is nothing but an empty shell." She nodded at Lola's sister lying on the bed. "She has no more power to feed you, little king. Your only choice now is to retreat with us and regroup."

Alberich narrowed his golden eyes. "I do not run."

"Then I will drag you," the queen snapped, losing her temper at last. "I thought the changeling was delusional when she said you could lose. I foolishly assumed that you were still the great king I'd married, undefeatable by any save myself. Clearly, those years in Victor's box left me blind, because I never even considered that the Nightmare King could be beaten by a human. A *human*, Alberich!"

"He beat you first!" Alberich bellowed. "Victor took your head, but you don't see me rubbing that in your face, because there is no shame in losing to a treacherous backstabber who refuses to fight as monarchs should! But I won't fall for his treachery again. The next time I fight him—"

"There won't be a next time," Morgan snarled, baring her own teeth. "Open your eyes, you old fool. Victor Conrath's got all of humanity behind him now. Even if we fought him together, we wouldn't stand a chance. Our only shot at survival is time. Mortal love is fickle. The mob will tire of him eventually, and when it does—"

"That's not going to happen," Lola said.

All the fairies turned to look at her, but she just stared right back. "Victor never stops," she said. "Just because he finally got his godhood doesn't mean he's going to sit around enjoying it. He's going to take this victory and use it to launch his next campaign, and the next, and the next. He's going to keep punching higher and higher until there's no one left above him."

"All the more reason to crush him now," Alberich said.

"Except for the part where you can't," the queen reminded him, her beautiful lips curling in disgust. "You already blew your shot, and now the rest of us have to clean up your mess, as always."

"Oh, *of course*," Alberich sneered. "You're such a responsible monarch, leading our people deeper and deeper into their holes while our prey walks all over us. This is why my court was always bigger than yours, because I did not ask my subjects to cower before worms!"

"And now your subjects are worms' food," Morgan replied icily. "But your opinion in this matter means nothing." She waved an elegant hand at the bloody battlefield surrounding them on all sides. "You're in my barrow now, Nightmare King, and I say you will not leave this place to face the blood mage again."

As she spoke, Lola felt the queen's gossamer tighten around them like a net. Alberich must have felt it too, but all he did was sneer.

"You're not the queen of me, wife," he proclaimed, crossing his arms stubbornly over his chest. "We both know there's still one way to defeat Victor, and you will not keep me from it."

The queen's fair face grew pale. "You can't be serious."

When Alberich didn't reply, she pulled herself to her full, spectacular height. "*I forbid it*! If you put on your head to fight, you won't just be giving the blood mage the chance to slay you again. You'll be destroying an entire fairy kingdom! The Wild Hunt can be rebuilt, but your barrow is the largest stronghold we have left. If you let Victor cut your head, the Underground Kingdom will be lost, and all of *us* will be weaker for it!"

"I don't care about the rest of you," Alberich replied haughtily. "You have no right to tell me what to do, because unlike you sniveling cowards, I still remember what we are. We are the hunters, not the hunted! And frankly, if it's come to the point where a fairy king wearing his head can't beat a human, our species deserves to die."

The queen's lovely face turned crimson with fury, but before she could say another word, Alberich threw out his hand. Lola doubled over as he did, gasping in pain as the king spun her gossamer into a bubble around them, blocking out Morgan and the others. Tristan countered immediately, but he'd never been able to take over Lola's gossamer even back when she was Victor's, and he couldn't do it now. His sea-smelling magic rolled off of hers like water off a duck's back, leaving him banging soundlessly on the invisible wall as Alberich walked toward the bed where Lola's sister was sleeping.

"Stop!" Lola cried, fighting his hold. She'd resisted it before, but yelling at Morgan must have fired the king up, because his grip was back to its usual strength. She couldn't do more than wiggle feebly as Alberich whipped the blanket off her sister's body.

"Please no," she begged. "I know my sister fed you before, but she has nothing left to give. If you need dreams to get your strength back, you can have mine. Just leave my sister alone!"

"I'm afraid that's not possible," Alberich said, giving he a cruel smirk. "Silly little changeling, just where do you think my head is?"

Lola went still in his grip, and the king burst out laughing.

"Surely you didn't actually think a *human* was my treasure?" he goaded, reaching down to pinch her sleeping sister's cheeks. "It's true her delightful dreams are the only reason I'm alive, but that starvation ended as soon as I broke out. What you see now is just a box. My *real* treasure's hidden inside it, and you're the one who helped me keep it safe."

He leaned to the side, grinning around the frozen Lola at Morgan, who was still screaming soundlessly on the other side of the bubble. "That's right, wife! You're always so quick to call me a fool, but I got one over on you this time. I knew you'd send your White Knight to scour my barrow the moment I was out of it, so I hid my head in the last place you'd look: right under your nose! Even the blood mage didn't realize what I'd done because the changeling's gossamer and mine are identical. Of course, if I'd known your precious Tristan couldn't handle a few old trolls, I wouldn't have gone through the trouble."

He paused to savor Morgan's look of fury before turning his grin back to Lola. "They still might have found it if not for your guard dog routine. Such a *marvelous* little irony, but I'm afraid the joke is over. The time has come to put that uppity blood mage in his place, so if you'll excuse me..."

Lola screamed as the king stabbed his hands into her sister's stomach. Then she screamed again, writhing against his grip on her gossamer. She might not have been able to enter her dreams, but she could feel Alberich's fingers digging into her sister's flesh like it was her own. The thread on her wrist lurched at the same time, plunging straight down so hard that Lola's arm dropped with it despite Alberich's lock on her gossamer. She'd never felt anything so heavy, but she knew what it was.

It was death. Lola was feeling her sister's physical death through their shared connection. The pull grew heavier still as Alberich dug, plunging his hands into her sister's stomach to the wrist as he searched her insides. It got so bad that her sister actually made a sound, an involuntary gasp of pain as Alberich killed her. Lola could feel every agony through the thread, but so long as Alberich had control of her gossamer, she was helpless to stop him.

Hopelessness welled up inside her like a tidal wave. Her sister's empty body was the last thing she'd had left. Now the king was ripping her open right in front of her, and Lola couldn't do a thing. She was a failure to the end. A hopeless weakling who hadn't been able to save any—

"*No!*"

Lola couldn't move her head, but she managed to twitch her eyes over just enough to see her doppelganger appear beside her. The copy's gossamer was so runny it was spilling down her sides, making her look like a melting candle, but she still had enough structure left to grab Lola's shoulders.

"*You can't give up!*"

"What is that?" Alberich asked, removing his bloody hand from Lola's sister to snap his fingers at her double. "You there! Get back in line."

Her copy started melting even faster at the king's command, but she didn't let Lola go. "Remember what happened between the trucks," she gurgled as her body collapsed. "Remember what happened in the hospital. Your gossamer depends on *your* belief, no one else's! That's why you can't give up. If you let yourself believe it's over, then it really is, but it doesn't have to end this way!"

Her hands fell apart as she finished, but her voice had always been Lola's, and it was screaming in her ears.

"For the love of all of us, Lola, *fight him!*"

It was on the tip of Lola's tongue to say that she *was* fighting, she just wasn't winning, but her double collapsed before she could say a word. And weirdly enough, that was what got through to her, because with Alberich gripping her like this, her doppelganger shouldn't have been able to move any more than Lola, but she had. She'd defied the king who supposedly controlled all their gossamer, and if a brain-dead spell like her could do it, then maybe Lola could, too.

With that, she shoved her despair away. She threw it all away—the hopelessness, the fear, the failure—and focused on what she *could* do. Yes, Alberich had her pinned, but he only controlled her gossamer. That was the only part of her that belonged to him, the only thing holding her back, so with a roar that shook the foundations of the queen's barrow, Lola cut it away.

It was a thousand times worse than when she'd cut off her wrecked car to escape the Rider. The little coupe had been only a fraction of her total magic, but Alberich was everything. There was no part of her that was not also part of him, but Lola had never been just a changeling. Even with Alberich digging into her stomach, her sister's thread was pulling on Lola's wrist. Her human, *mortal* sister, who was now falling into a very *mortal* death.

Lola didn't know if that would be enough to make the difference, but unlike everything else in her life, her thread had always been her own. It was her constant, the one thing that never changed no matter what shape she took. Not even Victor had been able to break it, so Lola put all her faith in it now as she cut herself free of Alberich's control and lunged at the king's throat.

There was barely anything left of her by the time she got there. She was even tinier than the cat she'd left on Victor's bed. That should have made it easier for Alberich to stop her, but the Nightmare King was hardly at his best, and tiny wisps of gossamer took a lot more control to grab than big ones. He still tried, lashing at her with his bloody hands, but Lola was faster, spinning what was left of herself in a circle to wrap her silver thread around his neck.

The king had a much easier time grabbing that. Just like Victor, he'd always been able to move her thread, but that was back when the other end had been tied to a living person. Now, thanks to the bloody hole he'd put in her sister, Lola's silver thread had the weight of all mortality pulling on it, giving her the strength she needed to drag the king down with her to the place all humans eventually went.

Down into death.

Chapter 16

"What did you do?"

Alberich ripped himself out of the silver noose Lola had wrapped around his neck, stumbling across the uneven ground as he gaped at the endless darkness that now stretched over their heads. He turned to stare at Fenrir next, his golden-tanned face turning purple as he realized what had happened.

"You dragged us under the Sea of *Magic?*"

Lola was as surprised as he was. The whole thing had been her idea, but she was still shocked that it had worked. She was back in the darkness of her sister's death. She was even back to her normal size, wearing the standard t-shirt and leggings combo she always defaulted to when she wasn't paying attention. That attack couldn't have gone better if she'd had a month to plan it.

Her only regret was that her sister had had to die to make it happen. But while Lola would have traded every bit of Alberich's gossamer for even one more of her sister's breaths, she wasn't unhappy with this ending. Alberich was the one who'd stolen her sister in the first place. It was only fair that she should be the one who ended him for good.

Lola was still smiling at the fittingness of that when Alberich's sharp fingers dug into her shoulder.

"Take me out of here," he ordered, his golden eyes burning like embers. "*Now.*"

Lola looked down her nose at him as she said the best word in the universe.

"No."

"Do you not understand what you have done?" he roared. "Your little stunt left my head unguarded in Morgan's barrow! You're *my* gossamer! If she eats me, you're dead too!"

"I don't care," Lola said, shoving him away. "You killed my sister's body. You helped Victor kill her *soul!* I wouldn't normally consider you or Victor worth anyone's life, but I've already lost everything, so I don't care anymore. I hope Morgan does eat you! At least then something good will have come out of this."

"You think Morgan is good?" Alberich scoffed. "She married *me.*"

"At least she was smart enough not to help Victor become a god," Lola snapped back. "But none of that matters anymore, does it? Even if Morgan decides to mount your head on her wall, you're never leaving this place. The only way I've ever gotten out of here was through my sister, and you killed her."

"I wouldn't be so sure," Alberich said, tapping his curled-toe boot on the ground. "I might not be human, but I understand enough of their magic to know that deaths don't stick around for long after the body gives up the ghost. Since this place isn't crumbling beneath our feet, there must still be some life in that corpse yet. Life she'll quickly lose when Morgan goes digging after my head."

Lola's hopes skyrocketed for a moment before she got a hold of herself. "Even more reason to keep you down here," she said stubbornly. "If my sister did survive your murder attempt, I'd much rather leave her in Morgan's hands than yours. Unlike you, the queen understands finesse. I bet she could get your head out without hurting my sister at all."

"To what end?" Alberich snapped, losing his patience again. "We're still talking about an empty shell. Only an idiot would throw their life away for that."

"Then I'm an idiot," Lola said, crossing her arms over her chest. Then she smiled. "Which makes you the fool who got killed by an idiot."

She expected Alberich to rage at that—it was a big part of why she'd said it—but the king just pinched the bridge of his nose.

"I never figured you for the revenge-over-survival type," he said, sounding legitimately frustrated. "But before you gloat too much about feeding my head to my oldest enemy, I'd remind you that Morgan will not kill the blood mage. Even after consuming my fantastic power, she's too much of a coward. She's not like us."

"I'm *nothing* like you," Lola snarled, but the king just rolled his golden eyes.

"Don't be stupid. I saw your doppelganger. Now that you've made a life, even that silly little one, you know perfectly well that they *are* us. Just as she came from you, you came from me. You're my gossamer, my magic. All of your rebelliousness, your tricks and clever plans, they're all reflections of mine. That must be why Morgan's taken such a shine to you. You remind her of me."

Lola wasn't dignifying that with a response when Alberich's look turned sly. "I've always respected myself," he said, his eyes gleaming like golden knives as he crept closer. "So how about this? You get me out of here before the corpse upstairs finishes kicking the bucket, I'll get my head out the slow way that doesn't involve tissue damage, and then we'll go kill Victor together. Doesn't that sound like fun?"

"It sounds like stupidity," Lola told him bluntly. "You heard what Morgan said. Even if you put on your head, you can't beat Victor."

"You only think that because he's been brainwashing you to think he's invincible your entire life," Alberich argued. "I'm sure all that 'I never lose' garbage sounds like truth when you're stuck in his matrix, but anyone with actual power knows that's not how it works. Nobody wins forever. Like everything else about him, Victor's godhood is a scam. He's playing the whole world for fools, but I can break his ruse. He got his power by slaying me, but if I show up again stronger than ever, everyone will see his hero act for the paper-thin sham it is. That's the difference between a true king and a false one. My power doesn't go away when I get beaten. You're the living proof of that, so why don't we help each other out?"

"Because I'm not giving Victor another damn thing," Lola said, planting her feet stubbornly on the scratched-up stone. "Maybe your grand return could knock him off his pedestal, but if you put on your head and *lose*, Victor gets to add an entire fairy kingdom to his kill sheet. There's no way I'm handing him a victory like that. Even if your win was guaranteed, though, I still wouldn't help you." She bared her teeth. "You're the monster who stole my sister."

"Sister, sister, sister!" Alberich cried, throwing up his hands. "You know perfectly well that's not what she is, so stop acting like a martyr and use your common sense. That thing you call 'sister' never even knew you existed. You think her emptiness is a new thing? She's been that way for decades, and I would know. I'm the one who hollowed her out."

Lola went stone-still, staring at him as the ringing in her ears got louder and louder.

"You're lying."

"I can't lie," he reminded her, pointing at his sharp teeth. "Actual fairy, remember?"

"It has to be a lie," Lola insisted, clenching her fists. "Maybe she's empty now, but I know what I felt. I *know* she was there when—"

"You felt what you wanted to feel," Alberich said dismissively. "The petty imaginings of a lonely, desperate child, but what else did you expect? You're a changeling. You were made for delusion."

"She was *there*," Lola insisted, throwing up her hand so the king could see the silver thread that still, even now, glowed like moonlight around her wrist. "I've felt her my entire life! I took control of Fenrir by entering her nightmare! How was that possible if she was already empty?"

"Because it was never *her* nightmare," the king replied with a sly smile. "Would you like to know what you actually felt that night?"

That was a trap if Lola had ever heard one, but she couldn't stop herself from wondering, and from the gleam in his eyes, Alberich knew it.

"I can feel your curiosity," he taunted in a sing-song voice. "How about we make a bargain? I'll tell you the truth about your sister, and then we'll revisit how you feel about helping me kill Victor."

"It won't change anything," Lola warned. "I can't possibly want to kill Victor more than I do right now, but I'll never trade my sister for him."

"We'll see about that," Alberich said, taking a seat on the ground and patting the stone beside him. When Lola didn't move, he shrugged and started talking.

"A little over twenty years ago, I was languishing under my wife's most unjust imprisonment when a human mage suddenly appeared in my court. I was bored out of my skull, so instead of feeding him to my trolls, I agreed to hear him out. He told me he knew about all the changelings I was making to keep my kingdom fed through the barrier of my wife's cruelty, and he had a proposition. I would give him a changeling of his own, and in return, he would help me escape."

"I already know that part," Lola said impatiently.

"No, you don't," Alberich said. "You've never met another of your kind, so you assume all changelings are like you, but that's highly incorrect. Changelings are stupid: lumps of magic given just enough intelligence to imitate a baby. Most never even learn to speak, and why should they? Their only purpose is to distract busy parents from realizing their actual child's been stolen until it's too late."

"But—"

"If they hadn't been the only spell I could squeeze through Morgan's barrier, I wouldn't have bothered," the king said right over her. "Have you ever tasted a baby's dream? They're disgusting. Nothing but base-level instincts. You might as well feed off a dog."

He stuck out his tongue with a retch and continued.

"Because the sustenance provided by changelings was so meager, I had to send out hundreds to keep my kingdom functional, and I put no more effort into each one than was absolutely necessary. Of course, I wouldn't have had to make such massive batches if I'd been able to establish a breeding population, but thanks to my *darling* wife's betrayal, my barrow had been pushed so far away from the human plane that all the children I did manage to bring back inevitably died within the first few years."

"Wait," Lola said, voice shaking. "They *all* died?"

"I didn't do it on purpose," the king told her with a callous shrug. "Not that I care about human lives, but given how labor intensive it was to sneak them in, I wanted my stock to live as long as possible. Alas, their little souls just couldn't hold on when taken so far from the Sea of Magic. It wasn't a huge problem—there are always more humans—but it was just so much *work* for so little reward."

He sighed dramatically. "I thought I'd be stuck on the changeling treadmill forever, but the blood mage offered a unique solution. He would take one of my tragic charges back to the living world with him and use his unique control over human souls to merge its dying life with the changeling that had replaced it. That way, I'd still have access to all its life-sustaining dreams while Victor got a gossamer slave to use as he saw fit. It was the perfect answer to both our problems, and do you know who that little hybrid was?"

Lola clenched her jaw.

"*You!*" he cried, throwing his hands over his head as if she'd just won a game show. "No longer did I have to choke down toddler nightmares about potty training. I had my very own blood-magic enhanced super changeling who grew and cried and feared just like a real human. Better than human! Your gossamer-tinted dreams were stronger than anything actual mortals could produce, and you were so *afraid*. Your intense terror of Victor kept my court fed for years. You're the one who gave me the strength to create the Fenrir nightmare and broadcast it out to millions of people. Truly, none of this would have been possible without your help. That's why it hurts so much to see you turn against me. I'm the closest thing to a father you've got."

Alberich gave her a mournful look, but Lola just squeezed her fists tighter. "What about the girl?"

"What girl?"

"*My sister!*" she yelled. "The girl you hollowed out! I remember being in the hospital before Victor found me. You said real changelings were brainless, but my thread was my treasure even back then. I *know* my sister was on the other end! What did you do to her?"

"You *are* her, stupid," Alberich said, rolling his eyes. "What part of 'merge' did you not understand? We took the oldest child I'd stolen that was still viable, scooped out her soul, wrapped it in blood magic, and then Victor carried it back to the real world, where he mashed it into your gossamer. The only reason you think you have a sister is because Victor made her up. We needed to give you something to believe in so you'd reinforce the bond back to your human body, which was still locked up in my barrow. I also needed a way to access your dreams."

Lola looked at her gleaming thread in horror. "*This* sent you my dreams?"

"Like sipping cider through a straw," Alberich assured her with a lick of his lips. "You wouldn't believe how much magic I pulled through that silver wire, though I did also have to suffer your trite emotional babble." His face shifted into a mockery of her own. "Oh, sister, I promise I'll save us! Everything's going to be okay!"

He was crying huge fake tears when Lola snapped. "If she was never real, why did my thread move when I talked to her? Why did her hand close around mine?"

"Because you wanted it to," Alberich said as his face morphed back to its usual boyish smirk. "There was never any sympathizing soul on the other end. That was *your* body reacting to *your* stress. Anything more was pure fantasy on your part, but that's a good thing! Now that you know you are your own sister, you have no reason not to help me."

Lola gaped at him. "What part of that story was supposed to change my mind? If what you're saying is true, then that's *my* body you were sticking your hands into! If I wasn't okay with you kidnapping my sister and feasting on her fear, what makes you think I'd be fine with you doing it to me?"

"Because it gets you what you want," the king replied, hopping nimbly back to his feet. "All this time, you've been a brave knight fighting for your innocent, fairy-stolen sister, but that delusion's over. Now that you know your life is the only one at stake, you're free to choose how you want to spend it, and with everyone you love already dead, you've got no reason not to help me destroy the man responsible."

That was horrible logic, but Lola couldn't look away. "Could you…" She stopped to swallow against the tightness in her throat. "Could you really kill him?"

The fairy king's lips peeled back to show his dagger-sharp teeth, which Lola realized for the first time were just like her creature's. "Give me my head, and I will rip him to pieces."

Lola took a deep breath. She'd never wanted anything like she wanted Victor to suffer for what he'd done, but this was asking a lot. She wouldn't have even considered it back when she'd thought her sister was depending on her, but now…

She glanced over her shoulder at the tangle of silver thread that was lying on the ground exactly as it had been when she'd come here with the DFZ. She followed the gleaming trail with her eyes, tracing it back to the small shape she could just make out lying motionless in the dark. Back to herself, Lola realized with a jolt. That was *her* human side lying collapsed on the stone. *Her* soul waiting inside *her* death, just like Simon's had been.

That thought reminded Lola of the argument they'd had when she'd tried to convince Simon to leave with her. She'd been so mad at him for telling her no, but now Lola understood. Simon hadn't turned her down because he was bent on revenge. He'd done it because what she'd offered wasn't rescue. She'd been running away.

Shame began to burn on Lola's cheeks. All this time, she'd told herself she was being brave and selfless, ignoring her hatred of Victor to focus on saving the people she loved, but that wasn't how this worked. She'd said it herself to Morgan just a few minutes ago: Victor was never going to quit. It didn't matter how far they ran or how well they hid. If Victor wasn't stopped, nothing would change. He'd proven that when he'd tried to shove the pill into Lola's mouth back in his death. So long as he was alive, none of them would ever be free. He would just keep stomping on them—stomping on *everyone*—for*ever*.

Alberich was no better. Even if he did beat Victor, he'd just go right back to terrorizing the planet. Any way she looked at it, they were screwed, but for the first time in her life, Lola had something she could do about that.

"Sorry," she said, not sounding sorry at all, "but the answer is still no."

Alberich looked at her like she was insane. "You can't be serious. Were you even listening to me just now?"

"Oh, I listened," she said, crossing her arms. "You said we'd revisit how I felt about killing Victor after you told me the truth. Well, I've heard it, and my decision remains the same. No, I will not let you out of here. No, I will not take you to your head. And no, I will not help you kill Victor."

Alberich's face grew more furious with every word. "You don't think I can do it," he snarled. "Or maybe you're just afraid to die."

Lola rolled her eyes. "If that was true, we wouldn't be here, but it doesn't matter. Whoever wins the fight between you and Victor, the rest of us lose."

"What do you care if I feed off a bunch of cities you've never even been to?" Alberich asked scornfully. "They're just humans."

"*I'm* human."

She'd only meant to undermine Alberich's stupid argument, but as soon as Lola said it, the truth of her word struck her like a gong. She *was* human. An actual, legitimate human standing tall inside her death.

Lola looked up at the dark pit in new wonder. No wonder the DFZ had been so convinced she could help. Lola didn't know how big her death had been to start, but Fenrir's birth had stretched it into a canyon. Maybe not as big a one as it'd been when the monster wolf was rampaging, but it was still easily a hundred times larger than Victor's overgrown red room.

Lola wasn't a blood mage, so she didn't know how to take control of the space like Victor had, but surely she could do something with all of this. Even Simon, who hated blood magic, had always insisted that humans were gods inside their own souls, which explained why Alberich was wasting his time cajoling instead of threatening. He couldn't threaten her anymore, because *she* was king here.

"I don't like that look," Alberich said, narrowing his eyes. "I don't know what you're fantasizing about, but you being human changes nothing about our current situation. You might not approve of my Wild Hunts, but at least all I do is kill. You're the one who said Victor wasn't going to stop until there was nothing left for him to conquer. Look at it from that perspective and I'm by far the lesser evil. I've certainly done less to you. Victor abused you for twenty years, whereas you didn't even know I existed until a month ago. Surely, you're not going to waste your last breath spitting at me when you could have the blood mage's head on a platter?"

"Of course I'd rather have Victor," Lola said. Then she smiled. "But you're the one I've got. A lesser evil is still an evil, and you *are* the one who sold my soul to a blood mage as a child. I think that's enough to count this as a win, so I suggest you get comfy, your majesty, because neither of us is going anywhere."

"You speak as if that's a decision you get to make," Alberich growled, dropping into a crouch. "But just because I invited you to help me doesn't mean I'm incapable of getting out of here on my own."

"What are you going to do?" Lola taunted, pointing up at the blackness. "As you just helped me figure out, this is *my* death. I have it on good authority that makes me the boss around here, and I say you're staying."

"Unless I kill you," the king replied with a feral smile.

Lola scoffed. "You can't kill someone inside their own death. That doesn't even make sense."

"Are you sure about that?" he asked, creeping closer. "Maybe you didn't listen to the part of the story where I said you're not fully human. Half of you is still my changeling, and where there's gossamer, fairy rules apply."

Lola stepped back nervously. "Fairy rules?"

"If I eat you, I get your powers," Alberich explained, closing the distance she'd just made. "Including the one that links you to your body back in the physical world."

"Or you could get my mortality and end up trapped down here forever."

The fairy king's lips pulled back in a sharp-toothed smile. "I'm ready to take the risk."

He lunged the second he finished, flying at her like a golden hornet. It was a far cry from the appearing and disappearing he usually did, but it was still faster than Lola could move. She barely managed to get her hands up before the fairy knocked her to the ground.

His teeth were lodged deep in her arm by the time they landed. When Lola finally managed to kick him off, he took a chunk of her with him. She screamed in pain, slapping a hand over the hole to stop the flow of bright red blood pouring down the inside of her elbow.

Her blood.

Lola froze. All the life she could remember, her body had been a wobbling blob of rainbow gossamer. Producing realistic blood normally took concentration and reference photos, but the stuff running down her arm looked as red as Valente's when he put on his head.

"Not so cocky anymore," Alberich taunted, shooting out an inhumanly long tongue to lick her blood from his lips. "Looks like this place brings out your mortal side. I wonder how long it will take to bleed you—"

He cut off with a squawk as a giant paw lashed out at him from the shadows. Lola jumped as well, because that wasn't *her* paw. Her body had never felt more human with all that mortal blood dripping through her fingers. When the attacker finally shuffled out of the darkness, though, Lola's face split into a triumphant smile.

It was her creature. The giant furry shape she used to fear so much was standing on its own right in front of her. She'd never actually seen it from this angle, or much at all. Even when she'd lived that way all the time as a child, she'd avoided mirrors like the plague. Staring at it now, though, Lola realized her fairy half wasn't nearly as scary as she used to think. The rest of the world would probably still consider the twelve-foot-tall pile of fur and fangs absolutely terrifying, but as she watched Alberich back away, all Lola could think was that it looked like a hero. *Her* hero.

"You can do it!" she cried, waving her arms as much as she could without letting go of her wound. "Get him!"

Her creature roared in reply, reaching down to crush the fairy king between its massive paws. It had just gotten its claws around Alberich's throat when the king's human illusion melted away.

"You think you're the only monster here?" he snarled, sending Lola's creature staggering back as the stone-skinned, molten-gold-drooling giant that was his true face burst out of its hold. "Arrogant child! I was eating bigger things than you before humans came out of caves. How do you think I got to be king?"

"It certainly wasn't your winning personality," Lola said, ripping a strip off her t-shirt to bind her bleeding arm. "But you're the one being arrogant. Victor already beat the snot out of you, and it's two against one."

"I like my odds just fine," Alberich rumbled, digging his claws into the ground. "The King of the Wild Hunt versus a changeling who bleeds like a human and a half-breed beast that can barely see. Should I tie one hand behind my back to make it more sporting?"

He turned to flash his knifelike teeth at her, leaving his back wide open to her creature, who snarled and leaped. It was about to dig its thick claws into him when Alberich whirled and caught it in midair.

Lola hadn't even seen him move. He was clearly much faster in this form than he'd been as the boy. Faster and *bigger*. He grew a foot as she watched, swelling up through the darkness as he dangled her now much smaller creature in front of him.

"How are you doing this?" she cried in a panic. "I saw Victor burn you down to nothing!"

"I was regenerating while we talked," the king explained with a jagged smile. "Not that my offer to team up wasn't legitimate, but you have to learn to pay attention to more than one thing at a time."

He threw her creature as he finished. It hurtled across the cavern, landing with a horrible crunch at the foot of Fenrir's corpse. Lola was already running before it hit, but when she made it to her creature's side, the black stone floor beneath it was slick with bright red blood.

The sight made her go still. Her creature had never bled before. Even when the nurses at the hospital tried to draw her blood, nothing ever came out. It had to be because they were inside her death, but if her creature had the same weaknesses as Lola, there was nothing to stop Alberich from bleeding them *both* out and eating them at his leisure.

Lola couldn't let that happen. Her poor creature had suffered enough, but she had no idea how they were going to stop him. This was supposed to be her place of power, but Lola had only figured out she was human a few minutes ago. She knew nothing about human magic or if she was even a mage, and Alberich wasn't giving her a chance to experiment. His ugly monster had already leaped across the cavern like a praying mantis, landing on her creature with a horrifying *crunch*.

"*No!*" Lola cried, grabbing his stone body, but she couldn't pull him off. She wasn't sure how she'd kicked him off earlier, but trying to move him now felt like pushing a mountain. Alberich didn't even bother knocking her away as he leaned down to sink his dripping fangs into her creature's chest.

It roared in pain, thrashing against his teeth as its dark, shaggy fur grew soggy with blood. Lola screamed with it, scratching her fingers bloody as she clawed at Alberich's stone hide. No matter how hard she tried, though, nothing worked.

Her bloody fingers went limp as she sobbed. It was happening again. Even here in her death where she was supposed to have all the power, she couldn't win. She couldn't beat Alberich. Couldn't save her creature, couldn't—

"*Stop that!*"

Lola jumped a foot in the air. When she whirled to see who had spoken, a familiar face was staring back at her.

"*You!*" she cried.

"That's who I am," her double agreed cheerfully.

Lola blinked in confusion, and then her bloody hands clenched into furious fists. "I don't have time for jokes!" she snarled, stabbing a torn-up finger at her creature, who was still trying to kick itself off of Alberich's teeth. "I don't know how you're here, but if you've got enough gossamer to manifest, get in there and help! Turn into a tank and shoot him or—"

"I didn't come here to be a tank," her doppelganger said patiently. "You need to stop panicking and listen to me."

"*Do I look like I have time to listen?*" Lola shrieked as Alberich ripped a chunk out of her creature's stomach and began chewing it with horrible, wet crunches. "He's killing us!"

"No, he's playing you," the other her insisted. "You just said you're the boss of your death, so why are you letting him kick you all over it?"

"Because I don't know what I'm doing!" Lola wailed, looking at the monster in despair. "Because he's too strong, and I'm not—"

"What's strength got to do with anything?" her copy asked, grabbing Lola's chin to turn her head back around. "You're a changeling, not a troll. Your power has never relied on brute force."

"But—"

"Victor wouldn't have wasted his time trying to cram a pill into your mouth if you were actually weak enough to get kicked around by a one-percent Alberich," her doppelganger said in a frustrated voice. "You must know that because *I* know it, so stop fighting with yourself and *look*."

Lola didn't want to look, but her double still had a clamp-grip on her chin, turning her head like a pivot back toward the horrible fight.

It was even worse than when she'd turned away. Alberich's monster was as big as he'd been when he fought Victor on TV now. Her creature, on the other hand, was looking more pathetic than ever. It was losing blood by the bucket thanks to all the bites, and its claws weren't even large enough to dent Alberich's stony hide now that he was the size of a building.

The hideously uneven scene made Lola quake. Whatever point her double was trying to make, it wasn't working. If anything, she felt even more doomed than before. But when she yanked out of the doppelganger's hold to tell her disobedient spell that she was wrong, the other Lola was grinning wider than ever.

"Did you see it?"

"I saw that we're screwed."

"Exactly!" the other her said excitedly. "Alberich's head is lying unguarded in Morgan's barrow as we speak. If he doesn't get back there before she eats it, he's toast, so why is he wasting time beating up your creature? You're the one he has to kill to get his ticket out of here."

That was a very good point. Why *was* Alberich focusing on her creature and not her? And why was he taking his sweet time about it? As big as he'd grown, he could probably eat what was left of her creature in three bites, but he was still toying with it like a cat with a half-dead mouse. And while Lola absolutely believed that was the sort of thing the Nightmare King did for fun, she didn't understand why he was wasting his very limited time on it *now*.

"Because he wants you to feel exactly how you're feeling," her double said, gripping Lola hard. "He needs you to panic and despair because he's a fairy who *feeds on fear.* How do you think he got so big? It's not as if there's anything else here for him to eat."

Lola gaped at her copy in awe. "I'm sorry I called you brainless," she said, reaching up to squeeze her double's hand. "You're smarter than I am."

"I'm *exactly* as smart as you," the doppelganger said proudly. "I was made from your magic. If I'm smart and brave, it's because you are. Now get in there and stop him before he eats any more of us!"

She finished with a shove, sending Lola stumbling back toward the blood-drenched battlefield as she vanished into thin air. Lola felt her gossamer rush back as she did, which was a wonder in and of itself. Not just because she'd already regenerated so much after slicing herself down to nothing, but because she'd never been able to bring her gossamer with her to this side before.

The thought had barely crossed her mind before Lola realized it wasn't actually that remarkable. She hadn't been able to bring her gossamer with her into Simon or Victor's dreams, but the first time she'd come to this place after Victor had turned her into Fenrir, her gossamer had made the jump just fine. This time was the same. She hadn't sneaked in here through someone else's head. She'd ridden her own death straight down. Ridden it into her own *half-fairy* soul, which explained why her creature was here. She'd already accepted that the monster was part of her, but now that she'd seen it here with her own eyes, Lola believed it to her core, and with that belief came power.

She might not know anything about human magic, but Lola was pretty good at being a fairy. Now that her doppelganger had talked her down, she could feel what Alberich was doing. It was the same trick she used with her own costumes. He wasn't sucking magic out of her. She'd given it to him herself with her belief. She'd *believed* he was a terrifying monster, and that was what he'd become. That was how *all* gossamer worked, and now that Lola had realized that, she was able to look through the illusion into the truth beneath. See him for what he really was:

A fairy king without a head.

"Alberich!"

The monster stopped chewing on her creature long enough to give Lola a beady-eyed glower. "I don't recall giving you permission to use my name so informally."

"I don't need your permission," she said, stabbing her finger at the bloody mass of fur beneath him. "Let go of my other half this instant!"

Her creature's battered face lit up when Lola acknowledged it. Then it was sent flying as Alberich tossed it aside. The king rushed at her next, skittering across the pit like a wave of shadows until his giant body was looming over hers.

"Or what?" he whispered, his dripping teeth glistening just above her head.

Lola swallowed. He truly was terrifying. Even knowing that was the point, the sight of his sharp fangs was enough to make the wound in her arm start throbbing. She supposed nothing less would do for the Nightmare King, but Lola couldn't let him keep control. This was *her* death, dammit. He was trapped down here with her, not the other way around. But when Lola reached inside herself to gather enough gossamer for the cement truck she was planning to slam into his face, her hand bumped against something sharp.

She jerked away with a hiss. There was something in her stomach, which didn't make sense because Lola had never had a real stomach. Or, at least, that was what she'd always thought. Down here in the place where the physical and the magical met, though, it was slowly occurring to her that the old assumptions were no longer true. She had a human body now, which meant a human stomach. The same human stomach Alberich had started all of this by plunging his hands into.

And just like that, a plan burst into her mind. It was a stupidly risky one, but Morgan was taking forever, and Lola wasn't sure she could keep not being afraid of something as scary as Alberich long enough to stop him from eating them. Her creature already looked half gone, and Alberich was big enough now that he looked ready to start doing the same to her. His teeth were already brushing against her hair, daring her to scream and run, to fear him. Each scrape sent a wave of terror roaring through her, so Lola did the only thing left that she could think of.

She grabbed her thread.

In all the millions of times she'd done this exact same motion, Lola had never tried to go inside it. The possibility hadn't even entered her mind since she'd always seen the silver line as a binding tie, not a tube, but that wasn't how Alberich talked about it. He'd made her thread sound like a highway for magic, so that was the image Lola pictured as she shoved her gossamer into the silver filament.

It worked much faster than she'd expected. The king must not have been kidding about pulling gobs of magic though her. Despite its tiny size, the thread took Lola's gossamer with room to spare, letting her reach up, up, up into the body that belonged to her alone.

For a blinding second, she was back in the physical world. She actually caught a glimpse of Tristan's worried face as he fussed with the very expensive-looking spellwork bandage he'd conjured to bind her wound. If she'd pushed a little farther, Lola could have touched him, but she wasn't here to go back. There was no way she was leaving Alberich unattended inside her soul. She was only here for the sharp thing she'd bumped into before. The lump of throbbing magic she could now clearly feel inside her human stomach.

As Alberich had taunted, it was identical to Lola's gossamer. Other than the sharp edges, Alberich's head was practically invisible, but her own magic had never bitten her like that. The sharpness made it easy to find the edges. Painful, but easy to wrap her actual magic around it, pinching the king's gossamer out like a splinter and dragging it back down the silver thread into her waiting hands.

When Lola opened her eyes again, she was holding a furry black head with beady eyes and a jaw full of long, knife-sharp teeth that were perfect miniatures of the ones hanging above her.

"How did you get that?"

Alberich's voice was low, tight, and, Lola realized with a smile, tinged with the slightest hint of fear.

"It wasn't hard," she said, clutching the king's head between her palms. "You told me exactly where to look. You even gave me the idea for how to get it down here when you bragged about sucking up my dreams."

"Give it to me," he demanded, lurching forward until his dripping teeth were inches from her face. "Give to me *now*, or I'll kill you."

He looked like he was going to kill her no matter what she did, but Lola was done giving him power. That was *her* magic making his giant teeth gleam, and now that she was holding his life in her hands, she had the leverage to yank it back, banishing the lie of the monster to leave Alberich's little body plummeting to the ground.

"*No!*" he screamed, righting his fall just before he landed on his face. "You dirty little *thief!*"

But Lola wasn't listening. She'd already run over to her bloody creature, who was moaning pitifully where Alberich had thrown it.

"I'm so sorry," she said, tucking the fairy king's head under her arm as she used her reclaimed magic to summon a giant version of the same expensive bandage she'd just seen Tristan wrapping around her own stomach. "This is all my fault. I'm the terrified idiot who let him get that big, but it's over now. I'm here, I've got you."

Lola could feel the creature's relief like it was her own as she wrapped it up. She hadn't even realized how scared her other half was—how scared it *always* was—until she stopped pushing it away. So much of that fear came from her, but while Lola couldn't undo all those years of self-hate, she could help her other self now.

She was still bandaging the bite wounds when something shot up from the ground by her foot to make a grab for the fairy king's head. Lola batted it away with a flick of gossamer, sending Alberich flying as she snatched the head back into her arms. The king might not have been a giant monster anymore, but he was still clearly dangerous as he landed neatly on his feet, his hands coming up like claws.

"That belongs to me," he growled, creeping closer. "You have no right to steal my treasure!"

"And you had no right to steal my body," Lola snapped.

But Alberich had already leaped, jumping on her like a rabid animal. He managed to rip another chunk out of her arm before her creature slapped him away. Lola bound the wound with gossamer at once, but the blood she'd spilled remained on the ground, human and red.

"Now do you see why you can't win?" the fairy king taunted, rising back to his feet. "Anything I lose can be regenerated off your fear, but you've only got so much blood to spill. Add in the fact that there's nothing more important to me than my head, and even you have to see this is a losing battle. You think I was fighting dirty before? You have no idea of the hell I'm going to put you through if you don't give back what is mine."

Lola was about to tell him to put up or shut up when something tackled her from behind. It knocked her to the ground, sending Alberich's head spinning off into the darkness.

"Ha!" Alberich crowed, running after his head while his monster snapped its gold-dripping teeth at Lola's throat. "You're not the only one who can split themselves! I keep telling you, changeling, you have to learn to pay attention to more than one—"

He cut off with a grunt as Lola's bandaged creature slammed into him like a linebacker, kicking his head out of his reach. Alberich's monster stopped chomping at Lola to dive after it, but she grabbed its ankle and tossed it away.

It flew surprisingly far. The monster had felt enormous when it was trying to bite off her head, but once she tossed it into the air, Lola saw that it was actually no bigger than a medium dog. A horrifying, murderous, nightmare dog, but nothing close to the building-sized terror it had been.

It wasn't even faster than her as she snatched Alberich's head back into her hands, though Lola was less sure about keeping it. She'd successfully reasserted control over her magic, but she was still hurt. Alberich's power might have been an illusion, but the injuries he'd dealt to Lola and her creature were very, very real. Both of her forms were ragged and exhausted, while Alberich was more single-minded than ever. He attacked relentlessly, lunging at Lola with both his faces while she struggled to keep his head away.

She could see why he wanted it so badly. The fairy's head felt like a neutron star in her hands. There was more magic crammed into that gossamer lump than there was in Fenrir's entire pit, so much that Lola wasn't sure how she was going to break it.

That was the part of her crazy plan she hadn't gotten to yet. Victor had made cutting through fairy heads look so easy, she'd assumed that all she had to do was stomp on Alberich's and that would be that. As always, though, nothing was as simple as it looked on television. Even when Lola slammed the stupid thing into the ground, it just clanged like a hammer, not even chipping the thin, knife-like teeth.

It was infuriating. Getting Alberich's head was supposed to be Lola's *I Win* button, but all she'd done was back herself even harder into the corner. Now that his head was in play, Alberich was driven by a desperate fear of his own. He didn't even have to worry about his safety since, unlike Lola and her creature, he didn't bleed. He could slice his gossamer to ribbons trying to reach his head, which made him very hard to keep away, and she *had* to keep him away. If Lola dropped the ball now, then all she'd accomplished was to hand Alberich's head back to him on a platter. If she was going to survive this, she needed to move his head to somewhere he couldn't reach, somewhere safe, so Lola stuck it into the only place the king couldn't follow.

Down her own throat.

It happened in the blink of an eye. Lola knew how fairies grew their power, but she'd never had the urge to eat one herself until just now. Even inside her human death, though, Lola was still half gossamer. The moment she'd realized what needed to be done, her magic had moved on its own, transforming her face into a mass of teeth as she devoured the fairy king's head in one swift bite.

"*No!*"

Alberich's cry was over almost before it began. By the time Lola realized what was happening, both his shapes—the boy and the monster—had exploded into dust, which would have been incredibly satisfying if she hadn't been working so hard not to explode herself.

The moment she ate the king's head, all the condensed power she'd felt inside burst into her like a lake through a busted dam. Too late, she remembered what Alberich had said to Alva about how eating a monarch's head meant consuming all that they were. That definitely seemed to be true, except all of Alberich was turning out to be more than Lola could stomach.

There was so much arrogance, so much death. It tore through her gossamer like she was back in the Sea of Magic, only this time there was no DFZ streetlight to shield her. She was on the verge of being blown to pieces when something warm and furry pushed her back together.

She cracked her eyes to see her creature. It had curled its body around hers, using its bulk as a buffer against the raging magic. Her double was there as well, clinging to Lola with her eyes squeezed shut and her arms wrapped protectively over both of their heads.

Lola didn't know what good that would do, but she accepted their help with all her heart, wrapping her arms around the other just as hard as the exploding magic carried them all away.

Chapter 17

When Lola opened her eyes again, she was back in her own bed at her apartment.

This was, of course, impossible. Her townhouse had been destroyed along with the rest of her neighborhood during Fenrir's rampage. It also hadn't been anywhere near this big. The ceiling in her actual bedroom had barely cleared eight feet. This one was tall enough to fit her twelve-foot-tall creature with room to spare, something Lola knew for a fact since her fairy half was waiting at the foot of her bed, watching her with eager, beady eyes.

"Welcome back," said a familiar voice.

Lola turned her head on the pillow to see her doppelganger lounging on a cushioned window seat overlooking a park of green trees that *definitely* hadn't been in her old bedroom.

"The sleeping princess awakes!" she cried with her usual inappropriate cheerfulness. "How do you feel?"

"That depends," Lola said, pushing up on her elbows. "Where are we?"

Her other selves glanced at each other with matching worried frowns. "We're not sure, exactly. Things have been changing a lot since you went all Hungry Hungry Hippo on the fairy king, but our best guess is that we're inside your barrow."

That made sense. All real fairies had barrows, and Lola had eaten a pretty big one. There was just one problem.

"We're still inside my death, though," she said, pointing at the dark hole she could see winking at her from the top of her new room's towering ceiling. "I thought barrows couldn't reach down here."

"They reached well enough when Alberich stuck his in to make that golden bed for your body," her double reminded her. "He was the Underground King. Going deep seems to be one of his specialties. Makes sense you'd be able to do the same after eating him, especially since you're already half-human."

Lola frowned. "So you're saying this is my death barrow?"

"What? No! That's a horrible name!" her copy cried, aghast. "I mean, it's probably technically accurate, but this place deserves a way better title. Just look what it can do!"

She hopped off the window seat and ran over to the door that normally led to Lola's bathroom. When she yanked it open this time, though, the door led out onto a huge balcony that looked straight out of a travel magazine. It must have been in the DFZ since Lola recognized the lake, but the beautiful white-cloth tables set with gleaming silver and fancy wine glasses was definitely not a part of the city she got to see often.

"Where is that?"

"According to the signs on the buffet I raided earlier, it's the private deck at the New Regency Hotel," her double announced proudly. "You know, the big fancy one that's practically falling into the lake."

Lola did know it, but that just stirred up even more questions. "Why do I have a door that goes to a fancy hotel's private deck?"

"It goes to a lot of places," her double said with a face-splitting grin. "Toothy and I have been taking turns opening it ever since it showed up, and it seems to change locations every—"

"Wait, wait, wait," Lola interrupted, holding up her hands. "Toothy?"

"I had to call her something," her copy insisted, beaming at the furry lump, who snuffled bashfully. "Fairies always have elegant names. Surely yours deserves better than 'creature.'"

Lola wasn't sure if "Toothy" counted as elegant, but she couldn't argue with the logic, especially since her other half looked so happy to finally have a name.

"As I was saying," her doppelganger continued. "The door seems to change locations every half hour or so. We haven't gotten anywhere outside the DFZ yet, but I think it's pretty obvious what's happening." She lowered her voice to a conspiratorial whisper. "You're a sleep low road maker!"

That sounded ridiculous, but again, Lola found it hard to argue. "Huh," she said, leaning back against the pillows. "Guess I really am a fairy now."

"You're *way* more than that," her copy said as she shut the door on the fancy deck. "But there'll be time to sort through all of that stuff later. Right now, you should probably get back to your body. You've been asleep for a loooooong time, and your thread's been jerking like crazy."

Lola looked down at her wrist in alarm. Sure enough, the silver thread was dancing over her skin like a fishing line with a first-prize whopper on the end. It was odd to see now that she knew there was no one on the other side. Odd and frightening, because that string was connected to her physical body. What if she was having a heart attack?

"I think it'd be jerking a lot harder for that," her double said when Lola mentioned it, opening her mouth in a giant yawn as she plopped back onto the window seat. "You go see what's up. We're going to stay here and relax."

"Relax, huh?" Lola said as she climbed out of bed. "Guess you're my lazy side."

"Hey, Toothy and I did our time," the doppelganger said, reaching out to pet Lola's creature with her bare foot. "We've been protecting your gossamer butt for three days straight. We're tired and you're awake. That makes it your turn."

Toothy yawned in agreement and put her giant head down on the bed Lola had just vacated, but Lola herself could only gape. "I've been sleeping in here for *three days*?"

"Technically, you've been sleeping all over," her double said with a shrug. "We went through a lot of crazy stuff before we landed in the nice bedroom. This *is* a fairy barrow, though, so take all time estimations with a boulder-sized grain of salt. For all we know, you've been asleep for thirty years."

Lola *really* hoped not. She was already spinning herself a new outfit that wasn't bitten up and bloodstained. She was in a hurry, so she didn't put much thought into it, but the simple jeans and sweatshirt she'd been aiming for came together surprisingly quickly, and surprisingly *nice*.

"Whoa," Lola said, looking down at the beautiful stitching and the heavy, expensive-feeling cotton. "Guess we're feeling luxe today."

She rolled back her sleeve to check her arms, but Alberich's bite marks were gone. There weren't even divots left in her skin. All of her injuries seemed to have been healed without a trace, and Lola breathed a sigh of relief. She'd just conjured up some comfy sneakers for the walk back to Tristan's when she paused.

"Do you know what state the city is in?"

Her copy shook her head sleepily. Toothy was already snoring on the bed, a stream of drool leaking through her sharp teeth to soak the blankets. It was obvious Lola would be getting no more help from them, but when she turned to sneak out the door, her hand stopped on the knob.

She couldn't have explained it if someone had asked, but for some reason, going out into the city felt like a *really* bad idea. The hotel balcony had looked peaceful enough, but it was in a nice part of town, and it was facing the water. She hadn't been able to see any other buildings or people. For all she knew, the rest of the DFZ was burned to the ground.

Lola dismissed that thought with a grim shake of her head. Victor was the Hero for real now. Assuming the Spirit of the DFZ hadn't found someone else willing to help her break free, her old master was still in charge, and he'd never let a city he owned do anything so gauche as burn down. He'd probably already ordered the DFZ to remake herself in his image, which would be an even more depressing sight than smoking ruins. Lola was wondering if she could get her new door to connect straight to Tristan's when the thread on her wrist gave its biggest jerk yet.

She looked down with a jump. The silver line had been pulling nonstop since the moment she woke up, but this was different. The pressure was so intense now, it was actually lifting her arm into the air. But while that was definitely alarming, it also gave Lola an idea.

Carefully, she wrapped her hand around the length of thread closest to her wrist. She'd been hoping she could move it now like Alberich used to, but the silver line remained steadfast as a steel cable set into a bathtub full of cement. That was a bit of a letdown, but Lola didn't actually need to move the thread for what she was planning. She only had to move herself.

Just like she'd done before, Lola reached into the thread with her gossamer. Instead of pulling something down, though, Lola sent herself *up*, pushing all her magic straight toward the—

She'd barely begun the process when the giant version of her old bedroom fell out from underneath her like a trapdoor. Her double and her snoring creature went with it, leaving Lola tumbling through blackness like she always did whenever she passed through the Sea of Magic, except in extreme fast-forward. The wild spinning couldn't have lasted more than two seconds before her eyes popped open for the second time.

She was lying on her back in a bed again, but not the one in her apartment. The ceiling she was staring at now belonged to Tristan's guest room. Buster was even curled up on the pillow next to her, snoring his little cat snores into her ear. It was a peaceful, familiar setting, but Lola was certain she was dying.

She'd never felt this terrible in her life. All around her insides, things were *moving* and *squelching*. Her stomach hurt like fire, her hair pulled at her scalp like a greasy weight, and her mouth and throat were all wet and slimy. Her chest felt both constricted and too open at the same time, and her limbs were as stiff as rusty hinges. Her nose was clogged with something stiff that was also somehow drippy, and her eyes itched. How did *eyes* itch?

It was all more horrible than she could ever imagine. Lola was trying to figure out how to scratch her eyeballs without blinding herself when she heard something move.

She sat up with a jerk. The sudden motion sent Buster scrambling for cover, but Lola was in too much pain to care. Moving all at once like that had been a terrible idea. Even the parts she hadn't moved were complaining. She was struggling to breathe through the pain when a wonderfully deep, familiar voice rolled over her.

"Lola?"

She turned her head toward the sound, and her itchy eyes went wide. The Black Rider was looming over her bed. His leather suit was slashed all over and his cracked helmet was being held together by a strip of medical tape, but he was standing and… and *alive.* She was still marveling at the impossibility of that when he dropped to his knees, his gloved hands hovering just above where hers were fisted in the sheets.

"Are you in there?"

Lola didn't understand the question. It wasn't until her discomfort-distracted brain caught up with the fact that he was kneeling beside the bed in Tristan's guest room—the same bed her "sister's" body had been lying motionless on for a month—that she finally realized what was happening.

Her hands shot up to touch her face, mouth falling open in wonder as she felt the tiny ridges of her fingertips sliding over the even tinier pores and delicate peach fuzz of her cheeks. No gossamer body she'd made had ever achieved that level of fine detail, which made sense, because this wasn't gossamer. It was her body. Her real, *physical* body.

"I'm human," she whispered, wincing as the words—the first she'd ever spoken—grated across her tight vocal cords. She'd never realized vocal cords were actual *cords* until she'd felt them move. Like everything else, it was weird and uncomfortable and she hated it, but it was also magic, because it was *her*.

"I'm human," she said again, reaching down in wonder to touch the fancy bandage that was still wrapped around her stomach exactly where she'd seen Tristan putting it during her brief trip up to grab Alberich's head. "Like, for-real human!"

She looked back at Valente to ask if he was seeing this, and the smile fell off her face. "Oh my God, how are you *alive?*" she cried, reaching out to grab his arm. "I saw you die!"

"I did die," Valente said, pressing his gloved hand over hers. "Simon brought me back."

"Simon?" Lola repeated, barely daring to hope. "You mean he's not…"

"He's alive too," Valente assured her, extracting his arm from her death grip to wrap himself around her shaking body. "We're all alive, Lola."

She grabbed onto him with a sob, clinging to the ripped-up leather of his shoulders with all the strength her never-used muscles could muster. She couldn't smell Valente's wintry gossamer in this body. She actually couldn't smell anything but cat hair and herself. Unsurprisingly for someone who'd been in a bed forever, she *really* needed a bath. Mercifully for her ego, Valente didn't comment. He just hugged her tighter, letting go only to take off his helmet so he could look at her face-to-face.

"Wait!" Lola cried, covering her eyes before he'd lifted the black motorcycle helmet past his chin. "I want to see you, but this body is legit human. I don't know how it will react to your head. Just let me…"

She moved her gossamer, which felt super weird in this form. She wasn't sure how she was even doing it, but Lola had been making things out of fairy magic her entire life. The process was way more familiar to her than the constant breathing she had to remember to do now. All it took was a bit of smooshing, and there she was, standing beside the bed in her usual body with the nice jeans and fancy sweatshirt she'd conjured earlier.

"Oh, that is *so* much better," she groaned, rubbing her hands all over her unnaturally smooth, beautifully squishy gossamer face. "How do people stand being so biological?"

"You get used to it," Valente said, pulling off his helmet at last to give her a smile.

Lola smiled back. He looked just like she remembered. Same dark hair, same beautifully glowing eyes. He looked very tired, but otherwise no worse for wear. He didn't even have a scar from the… from the thing she didn't want to think about. She was about to go in for another hug when Valente turned away, setting his cracked helmet on the floor as he bent over the human body that had fallen back to the bed the moment she'd vacated it.

"Lola," he said quietly, examining her sleeping face like he'd never seen it before. "What happened? Where did you go? And how did you end up in your sister's body?"

"Actually, it's my body," Lola said, nudging him aside so she could pull the blankets back over her sleeping self. "Turns out, I never had a sister. *I'm* the baby the fairies stole, but I'm also the changeling. Twenty years ago, Alberich and Victor used blood magic to mash a human soul into fairy gossamer. I'm just what came out the other end." She brushed the dark hair away from her sleeping face with a smile. "Explains a lot in hindsight. Tristan always said my magic made no sense."

"I think you're perfect," Valente said, his eyes glowing brighter as he looked her up and down. "Though you are a lot bigger than you used to be."

Lola went still. There'd been so much going on, she'd temporarily forgotten that she'd eaten a fairy king, which sounded a lot grosser now than it had at the time.

"Um…" she said nervously, twisting her fingers. "What exactly do I look like? Other than big?"

"Like yourself," Valente said, tilting his head as he studied her. "Just *more*. Also toothier, if that makes sense."

It didn't, but Lola was happy to take it. "I'm just glad I'm not an evil little kid," she said, rubbing her face again just for the joy of feeling her magic. "But what about you? How did Simon bring you back? I saw Victor…"

"Cut my head in two?" Valente finished, giving her a smile that showed his fangs. "He tried his best, but Simon was better."

"How, though?" Lola insisted. "Other than the new bane, blood magic only works on people, and that's a fairy head."

"On a human body," Valente reminded her, giving her a warm look. "You of all people should be familiar with that."

Even though she no longer had a circulatory system, Lola felt her cheeks heat to roughly the surface of the sun.

"I don't know how Simon did it," Valente went on when he'd embarrassed her enough. "I just woke up and there he was. He's the one who got me out of the square and into the shelter of the lobby, which turned out to be a lucky stroke since whatever Victor did before his fight with the Wild Hunt took Simon right back down. I had to sneak his body out of the building when the reporters swarmed in, and it took him two days to wake up after I got us to safety."

"But he *is* safe?" Lola confirmed nervously, looking around. "Is he here too?"

Valente nodded and pointed at the door. Lola burst through it a second later, leaving the Rider scrambling to put his helmet back on as she raced across Tristan's reconstructed living room toward the man sleeping on the sofa.

The sight of him stopped Lola in her tracks. Not because he was scarred or injured or anything horrific, but because he looked so *normal*. The Simon napping on Tristan's leather sectional could have been the same one from before all of this happened. There was no sign of the emaciation from his coma, no wounds or horrible magical scars. He was even back in his usual black turtleneck. She was really starting to believe they'd gotten out of this unscathed when Simon opened his eyes.

"Whoa."

Simon's eyes were blue. That would have been weird enough seeing as they'd been brown his entire life, but the new color wasn't just any blue. Those were Victor's eyes in Simon's head. It was so unnerving that Lola actually took a step back. It wasn't a conscious reaction, but she still felt like a giant jerk when Simon winced.

"Sorry," she said, running to sit beside him. "But how did—"

"It's not important," Simon said in a voice that told Lola it was actually *very* important, but it was impossible to press the issue when he looked so genuinely happy.

"You're alive!" he cried, sounding more excited than she'd ever heard him as he threw his arms around her. "You scared us to death, Tinker Bell!"

"You're one to talk," Lola said, hugging him back. "I watched the whole thing on TV. I thought you were all dead!"

"We very nearly were," he said, burying his face in her hair for a moment before letting go to give her the classic fretful-Simon look that even Victor's eyes couldn't pollute. "But Lola, seriously, how are you here? The fairies said you blew up your gossamer to take out Alberich. The only reason we had any hope left was because your sister was still breathing."

"It's kind of complicated," Lola said sheepishly.

"Try me," said a new voice behind her.

Lola cringed. Unlike Valente and Simon, whose appearances were legitimately miraculous, she'd been waiting for Morgan to walk in since she woke up. Sure enough, the queen was sweeping into the room when she peeked over the back of the couch. Tristan was hot on her heels, his handsome face lighting up the moment he saw who was sitting on his sectional.

"I knew it!" he cried, bounding toward Lola. "I *knew* you weren't dead! Lola-cat's nine lives always come through!"

His queen didn't look so pleased. "Where is he?" she demanded, towering over Lola with her new daunting height. "Where is my husband?"

"About that," Lola said, twisting her fingers guiltily. "Things got a little crazy during the fight, and… um…"

"Save it," the queen snapped, narrowing her green eyes. "I can already see what's happened. You *ate* him!"

"Lola didn't eat anyone," Simon said, looking at her. "Right?"

Lola's fingers twisted faster. "Well…"

"I can't believe this!" Morgan wailed, throwing herself down on the sofa. "I knew I should have ripped him right out of that stupid human's torso! But Tristan convinced me to wait until we could do it without killing her, and by the time we were ready, it was *gone*. Eons of marriage, and I don't even get to eat his head!" She whirled on Lola with a look of pure fury. *"You stole my husband!"*

"I'm sorry!" Lola cried, even though she wasn't. At least, not about killing Alberich. She was very sorry about stealing anything from Morgan, but it seemed like that was the wrong thing to say.

"Don't be *sorry*," the queen snarled. "You defeated and devoured the last great fairy monarch other than myself. It is an insult to treat that as anything less than a triumph. I'm only angry because it was supposed to be *me*."

Lola winced. Morgan's yelling had brought back strong and uncomfortable memories that didn't belong to her. In them, she saw the queen as she'd been untold ages ago, beautiful and sharp as a thorn. Once they started, the images came in a flood. Some were intimate and embarrassing, but mostly, Lola saw plots and betrayals, along with a whole lot of severed body parts.

"Wow. You guys tried to kill each other a lot."

"Of course," the queen said haughtily. "What do you think marriage is? We swore a binding oath that we would be the only ones allowed to defeat the other, and then *you* came and stole that from me." She crossed her arms over her chest. "I demand recompense."

"Sure," Lola said, desperate to make this right. "So long as that doesn't mean you're going to eat me instead."

Morgan snorted. "You're not worth the effort. From the look of things, you only managed to capture a portion of his magic, probably because you're not a true fairy. You have no head to serve as a chalice, just that stupid mortal fleshy… *thing*." She waved dismissively at the guest room where Lola's body was still sleeping, and then her face grew thoughtful. "But gossamer is the essence of potential. We might still be able to grow you back up to strength given enough time, and it will be a nice change of pace to have an Underground King who isn't an ego-drunk lunatic."

Lola was still sighing in relief that Morgan didn't want to eat her when that last part registered. "Wait, Underground King?"

"What else would you be?" the queen asked haughtily. "I know you were raised by humans, but surely you've been around enough of our kind to understand that we are what we eat. Alberich was a nightmare because he ate nightmares. You ate Alberich, so here you are."

Lola pressed her hands over her mouth. She hadn't even thought about that. "Do I have to eat nightmares, too?"

The memory of the horrible hunger she'd felt in the hospital was already gnawing through her mind when Morgan shrugged.

"You're a king. Eat whatever you want. I don't care how you grow your power so long as I get my share." The queen lifted her chin imperiously. "The theft of my husband will cost you dearly. You don't get to make me a widow and just walk away."

"I fed you my dreams for three weeks," Lola reminded her hopefully.

The queen's nose went up even higher. "Hardly a royal sum. I suppose it will serve as a down payment, but don't think for a minute that you're off the hook. As soon as I've seen enough of what kind of king you'll become to know what I should demand, you will pay for the injury you've done me in full."

Lola supposed that was fair. From the intrusive memories she was still trying to clear out of her mind, Alberich had been a big part of Morgan's life. Usually a horrible one, but it seemed like they'd been sincerely attached to one another in their own weird way.

"Are you mad at me?"

The queen's dazzling eyes dropped as she heaved a long sigh. "I'm mad at him. He was supposed to be the strongest of us all, the monster king. I had to rally every remaining monarch to seal him away the first time. While his Hunt was riding, I was legitimately worried I might end up kneeling at his feet. Then he goes and loses to a human, followed by a *changeling*." She shook her head in disgust. "I still can't understand how he sank so low."

"If it makes a difference, I'm only half changeling," Lola told her honestly. "The other half is human."

That was supposed to be a bomb drop, but the fairies just nodded.

"I knew it had to be something like that," Tristan told her casually, handing his queen a glass of wine that he'd conjured out of thin air. "I was never able to figure out how Victor did it—if it was all his magic or if you had a human soul of your own somewhere—but your dreams were always too delicious to be one of us."

"Well, it was news to me," Lola said huffily, crossing her arms over her chest. "So, what do we do from here? Don't get me wrong, I'm thrilled we're all alive, but Victor won, didn't he?"

"Undeniably," Simon said, his new blue eyes locked in a thousand-yard stare. "By the time I got out of... what he'd done to me, the whole world had changed. He's conquered the DFZ entirely, banned all non-blood mages, kicked out the dragons, even declared martial law."

That was way worse than Lola had imagined. "And people just let him do it?"

"They welcomed him with open arms," Simon spat. "He's the Hero who saved the world. I'm surprised they haven't made him king yet."

"It's only a matter of time," Valente said from where he was standing behind Lola. "Victor will not stop until he's slaughtered every non-human and made himself master of the people who remain. The longer we wait to kill him, the harder it's going to get."

"Hold up, did you say 'kill him'?" Lola said, spinning around. "Not that I don't think that's a fantastic idea, but I didn't know knights could use that sort of language." Her brows furrowed into a knot. "And speaking of knights, I know this is waaaaaay late to the game, but how are you here? Surely Victor's not so busy he's letting you run around unsupervised."

"Victor doesn't 'let' me do anything anymore," Valente replied with a smile Lola could hear through his helmet. "He is no longer my master."

Of all the shocking things she'd heard in the last few minutes, that one hit Lola the hardest. "*How?*" she demanded, shooting off the couch to grab the Rider's shoulders. "He had you hooked harder than any of us. How did you get away?"

"By his own hand," Valente said smugly. "The knighthood oaths bound me to serve him unto death, and Victor killed me."

"He was the only one who could have done it," Simon added as Lola sank back to the couch in shock. "I'm certain he never thought I was capable of putting his weapon back together, or he would have killed me first."

"He must think we're both dead," Valente went on. "Otherwise, he'd still be trying to kill us."

"Or he doesn't care anymore," Simon said bitterly. "He's got bigger fish than us to worry about. His takeover of the DFZ put him at the center of the world's attention. Everyone who isn't in love with him hates his guts, especially the other nations and big magical powers like the dragons. They know he's coming for them next."

"So how do we take him out before that happens?" Lola asked.

"We don't," Morgan said, taking a huge swallow of her wine. "We tried our hardest, but the blood mage bested us. He's working at a scale above ours now, and frankly, we don't have the resources to catch up."

"Surely you can handle his mages," Lola said. "I know the blood magic bane sucks, but they're all garbage without their pills. I don't think they even can use blood magic on their own."

"His mages aren't the problem," Simon said in a flat voice. "The Hero's Army is dead. Victor shattered their souls pushing his own into godhood. If I hadn't been an actual blood mage, he would have done the same to me."

Lola had thought there was nothing she could hear about Victor that would surprise her anymore, but that made her gasp. "He killed his *entire* army? Weren't there thousands of them?"

Simon nodded, but she still couldn't believe it.

"And, again, people are *okay* with this?"

"They don't know about that part," Simon said. "Officially, Victor's blood mages died defending the city from the Wild Hunt's rear assault, which conveniently didn't get caught on camera. He's been holding public funerals every day since it happened, milking people's outrage to build his Hero image even bigger."

"Of course he is," Lola said, rubbing her temples. "But that should make things easier for us. Losing his army of faithful followers has to be a blow, right?"

Simon shook his head. "I don't think it matters anymore. Victor is the Hero for real now. He doesn't need an army. He *is* an army."

"All the more reason for us to take him out quickly," Valente insisted. "Before he gets any stronger."

"That's not our choice to make," said the fairy queen, draining her wine glass and holding it out for Tristan to refill. "I told you, Victor's passed beyond our reach. He's not even human anymore. He's a spirit rooted in a megalomaniac's soul." She took another glug off her refilled wine. "I say we let the dragons deal with him."

"She's right," Simon said, dropping his new blue eyes in defeat. "There's nothing we can do. I don't even know if my magic will work against the thing he's become."

"That doesn't mean it's hopeless," Valente argued. "Heroes can still die."

"But more often they kill," Tristan said, taking a long sip from his own glass of conjured whiskey. "Slaughtering Victor is something we've all dreamed about, but the tides have never been more against us. He's riding the highest high he's ever achieved, while we're all dead in the water. The Black Knight has no more monarch to empower him, the apprentice has a ghost in his brain he's still dealing with, and our court has only three fairies with their heads still attached."

Lola looked at Simon in alarm. "You have a ghost in your brain?"

Simon shrugged noncommittally as Tristan leaned forward.

"I don't often say this, but we have to face reality, Lola-lion. You might be reborn in Alberich's power, but the rest of us are done. It's time to step aside and let someone else deal with the blood mage. There should be no shortage of volunteers. The more power you accumulate, the more enemies you acquire, and

Victor's conquest of the DFZ has stepped on some very big toes."

"Someone will take him down eventually," Morgan agreed. "No one can make the world their enemy and walk away unscathed. We just have to be patient and wait for his reign to end."

Both fairies nodded as if this were only common sense, but Lola clenched her fists.

"No."

Tristan sighed. "I know it feels wrong, but—"

"Feelings have nothing to do with it," she snapped. "Victor's not a can we can kick down the road. Every day we wait, he's working to make himself stronger. That's why we have to attack him now, while Victor still thinks he's won and we're dead."

"But he *has* won," Simon said angrily. "You think I'm hiding in a barrow because I want to? I've been trying to kill that bastard for practically my whole life! But he nearly obliterated my soul this time. I can't go through that again."

"You won't have to," Lola promised. "Because we're not going to fight him the way he wants us to anymore."

Simon's desperate look fell into a confused scowl. "What?"

"I understand what you're all feeling," she said, looking around the circle of depressed faces. "I felt exactly the same way a few days ago, but a very smart girl helped me have a realization. All my life, Victor's been stronger than me. No matter what I did or how hard I tried to get free, he always smacked me down like I was nothing. I thought that was because I *was* nothing compared to him, but then I realized the only thing Victor's actually good at is lying. He gets you to buy into this fantasy world where he's unbeatable, and then he tricks you into fighting on his terms. He lies and connives and manipulates everyone to make sure he never steps onto a battlefield where the odds aren't grossly in his favor. That's the only reason he keeps winning."

The queen looked unconvinced. "That may be true for his human puppets, but Alberich—"

"Alberich was the worst offender," Lola insisted. "You said there was no way Victor could beat the Nightmare King in a straight-up fight, and you were right. Victor knew that, too, so he manipulated Alberich's pride and got him to charge straight into a trap. The Wild Hunt would have mopped the floor with him if Victor hadn't spent three weeks setting up every inch of that battle. It's the same trick he used on Fenrir and the one he's used on me for twenty years. He knew he'd made something powerful, so he did everything in his power to make me so afraid of him—so afraid of *myself*—that I never even tried. I didn't lose because he was so strong. I lost because I let him make me believe I was weak."

Simon had already opened his mouth to argue, but Valente got there first. "You have a plan."

Lola nodded grimly. "We need to stop letting Victor dictate how we fight him. All this time, we've been chasing his plots, rats in *his* maze. But if we flip that script back on him, force him into a corner he isn't expecting, then we get the advantage."

"You say that like it's simple," Simon said with a frustrated sigh. "What do you think I've been trying to do for the last two decades?"

"It's going to work this time," Lola promised. "Because it won't be just you. Victor might not actually be unbeatable, but he is incredibly strong. He's organized, he's experienced, he's ruthless, and now that he's made himself the Hero, he's got millions of other people's magic backing him up. He is a *horrible* opponent to face, but he's still just one person, while we are many. We're also the last people he's expecting to attack right now. That puts him at the disadvantage for once."

"I don't think those odds amount to as much as you assume," Morgan said after she drained her second glass of wine. "But I do hate him beyond reason, so consider me provisionally intrigued."

"I was in from the start," Valente said, his cracked visor reflecting Lola's face in two halves as he looked at her. "What did you have in mind?"

Lola smiled and pulled him down, gathering everyone into a huddle as she whispered her strategy for how they were going to kill the most powerful man in the world.

Thank you for reading!

Thank you for reading *With a Golden Sword*! If you enjoyed the story, I hope you'll consider leaving a review. Reviews, good and bad, are vital to any author's career, and I would be extremely appreciative if you'd consider writing one for me.

If you want to be the first to know when I put out new books, sign up for my New Release Mailing List. List members are always the first to know about everything I do *and* they get exclusive bonus content like the list-only Heartstriker short story, *Mother of the Year*. Signing up is free, and I promise never to spam you, so come join us!

If you need more books *right now*, you can always check out one of other my completed series, including eight more novels set in the DFZ! Just keep paging forward or select "Want More Books?" in your e-reader's table of contents. You can also visit www.rachelaaron.net for a full list of all my books, high-rez covers, and free sample chapters. If you want to know more about me IRL, follow me on Twitter @Rachel_Aaron!

Thank you so, *so* much for reading! I couldn't do any of this without you!

Yours always and sincerely,
Rachel Aaron

Want More Books?

With a Golden Sword is only the latest addition to my library.
I have plenty more titles for you to enjoy! Keep paging forward to
see my top picks for new readers or visit www.rachelaaron.net for
the full list. Thank you for reading!

Minimum Wage Magic

The DFZ, the metropolis formerly known as Detroit, is the world's most magical city with a population of nine million and zero public safety laws. That's a lot of mages, cybernetically enhanced chrome heads, and mythical beasties who die, get into debt, and otherwise fail to pay their rent. When they can't pay their bills, their stuff gets sold to the highest bidder to cover the tab.

That's when they call me. My name is Opal Yong-ae, and I'm a Cleaner: a freelance mage with an art history degree who's employed by the DFZ to sort through the mountains of magical junk people leave behind. It's not a pretty job, or a safe one-- there's a reason I wear bite-proof gloves--but when you're deep in debt in a lawless city where gods are real, dragons are traffic hazards, and buildings move around on their own, you don't get to be picky about where your money comes from. You just have to make it work, even when the only thing of value in your latest repossessed apartment is the dead body of the mage who used to live there.

"A catchy title, a plucky protagonist and a maximum effort by the author, honestly readers can't ask for more in the urban fantasy genre."- **Fantasy Book Critic**

"I love what Rachel Aaron has done with this novel to expand her stories within this unique world of her creation. I have developed a trust in her ability to write engaging stories of great characters which I feel most comfortable and eager to spend time with, and this book is no exception." - **TS Chan**

Nice Dragons Finish Last

As the smallest dragon in the Heartstriker clan, Julius survives by a simple code: stay quiet, don't cause trouble, and keep out of the way of bigger dragons. But this meek behavior doesn't cut it in a family of ambitious predators, and his mother, Bethesda the Heartstriker, has finally reached the end of her patience.

Now, sealed in human form and banished to the DFZ--a vertical metropolis built on the ruins of Old Detroit--Julius has one month to prove to his mother that he can be a ruthless dragon or lose his true shape forever. But in a city of modern mages and vengeful spirits where dragons are seen as monsters to be exterminated, he's going to need some serious help to survive this test.

He just hopes humans are more trustworthy than dragons.

*"Super fun, fast paced, urban fantasy full of heart, and plenty of magic, charm and humor to spare, this self published gem was one of my favorite discoveries this year!" - **The Midnight Garden***

*"A deliriously smart and funny beginning to a new urban fantasy series about dragons in the ruins of Detroit...inventive, uproariously clever, and completely un-put-down-able!" - **SF Signal***

The first and most popular DFZ series, complete at 5 books.

The Last Stand of Mary Good Crow

A gaslamp epic fantasy featuring a sprawling cast of colorful Western characters, crystal-mad bandits, ambitious necromancers, and cursed gunmen. Welcome to the Crystal Calamity!

The Montana Territory, 1876, and the discovery of magical crystal has sparked a rush that makes gold a thing of the past. The US Cavalry, the Sioux tribes, and the criminal underworld will stop at nothing to control the mines that produce the new miracle stone, but the beautiful crystals bring a darkness, a madness, and a horror that threatens to consume all who seek their power.

Mary Good Crow, a half-Lakota guide, can hear the crystal's song. She makes her living leading miners to fortune, but there's trouble brewing in the depths of the crystal caves that even she can't navigate. Bandits with crystal-augmented strength, ghosts that roam the living darkness, and madmen driven by the crystals' power to destroy all who seek their prize.

With Josephine Price, a mining heiress with secrets to hide, and Tyrel Reiner, a gunslinger haunted by a necromancer's legacy, Mary must navigate the dangerous world of the new Magical West. The beautiful song of the crystal has never led her false so far, but with war brewing on the plains and enemies in every shadow, embracing the power that's driven so many mad before her might just be Mary's only shot at survival.

What people are saying about Mary

"Possibly the best alternate historical fantasy that you will read." - **Fantasy Book Critic**

"Brimming with imagination, wonderful characters and captivating magic." - **Novel Notions**

"I very much enjoyed the twists and turns throughout this book and strongly recommend it. No one's allegiances are entirely set and the only genuinely good person in the story is Mary Good Crow. Even she has a dark side that she struggles to keep suppressed as a matter of sheer survival. I think fans of the Weird West and urban fantasy both will enjoy this novel." - **Grimdark Magazine**

Forever Fantasy Online

Forever Fantasy Online is the gritty, battle-filled tale of a raiding guild vs the world featuring rules-driven combat, incredible tanking, and the good side of guild drama!

In the real world, twenty-one-year-old library sciences student Tina is invisible and under-appreciated, but in the VR-game Forever Fantasy Online, she's Roxxy--fearsome warrior, respected leader, and main tank of a top-tier raiding guild.

In the real world, James is a college drop-out drowning in debt, but in FFO he's famous--an explorer who's collected every item, gotten every achievement, and done every quest.

Both Tina and James need the game more than they care to admit, but their favorite escape turns into a trap when FFO becomes a living world. Wounds are no longer virtual, stupid monsters become cunning, NPCs start acting like actual people, and death might be forever.

In the real world, everyone said being good at video games was a waste of time. Now, stranded and separated across thousands of miles of new, deadly terrain, Tina and James's skill at FFO is the only thing keeping them alive. It's going to take every bit of their expertise--and hoarded loot--to find each other and get back home, but as the stakes get higher and the damage adds up, being the best in the game may no longer be enough.

*"Rachel Aaron and Travis Bach have written an amazing story and a realistic LitRPG." - **The Fantasy Inn***

"Forever Fantasy Online is definitely a book for the gamers among us." - **Fantasy Book Critic**

*"Excellent characters, an engaging story and geek humour. What more can one ask for?" - **TS Chan***

About the Author

Rachel Aaron is the author of over twenty novels both self-published and through Orbit Books. When she's not holed up in her writing cave, Rachel lives a nerdy, bookish life in Broomfield, CO, with her perpetual-motion son, long-suffering husband, and far too many plants. To learn more about Rachel and read samples of all her books, visit rachelaaron.net!

Cover Illustration by Luisa Preissler
Cover Design by Rachel Aaron
Editing provided by Red Adept Editing

As always, this book would not have been nearly as good without my amazing beta readers.

Thank you so much Linda Hall, Julia, K Stoker, LJ Andrews, Sally Jenkins, Javier Rentas, Nancy Wise, Sarah Braun, Judith Smith, and Christina Vlinder.

Y'all are the BEST!

www.ingramcontent.com/pod-product-compliance
Lightning Source LLC
Chambersburg PA
CBHW060904210726
48293CB00006B/1951